Anna Jacobs grew up in Lancashire and emigrated to Australia, but still visits the UK regularly to see her family and do research, something she loves. She is addicted to writing and she figures she'll have to live to be 120 at least to tell all the stories that keep popping up in her imagination and nagging her to write them down. She's also addicted to her own hero, to whom she's been happily married for many years.

To contact Anna or to find out more about her books, do look at her website: www.annajacobs.com

BEYOND THE SUNSET

In the untamed outback of Western Australia, the Blake sisters are together again despite seemingly insurmountable odds. For Cassandra — reunited with the man she loves — the Swan River Colony seems like a miraculous refuge after her ordeals. And two of her sisters are in love with their new way of life. But when a messenger arrives from England, the fourth sister, Pandora, is eager to return to the Lancashire moors. However, the way home will be challenging for Pandora and her new protector. Reaching the ship to England involves travelling for many days; a journey across country which would daunt even a hardened explorer. And when she reaches Outham, a devious, dangerous enemy will do anything to prevent her taking charge of her family's inheritance . . .

Books by Anna Jacobs
Published by The House of Ulverscroft:

OUR LIZZIE
OUR POLLY
OUR EVA
CALICO ROAD
PRIDE OF LANCASHIRE
STAR OF THE NORTH
BRIGHT DAY DAWNING
HEART OF THE TOWN
FAMILY CONNECTIONS
TOMORROW'S PROMISES
KIRSTY'S VINEYARD
YESTERDAY'S GIRL
CHESTNUT LANE
SAVING WILLOWBROOK
FREEDOM'S LAND
FAREWELL TO LANCASHIRE
IN FOCUS

ANNA JACOBS

BEYOND THE SUNSET

Complete and Unabridged

CHARNWOOD
Leicester

First published in Great Britain in 2010 by
Hodder & Stoughton
London

First Charnwood Edition
published 2011
by arrangement with
Hodder & Stoughton
An Hachette UK company
London

British Library CIP Data

Jacobs, Anna.
  Beyond the sunset.
  1. Sisters- -Fiction. 2. English- -Australia- -Western
  Australia- -Fiction. 3. Australia- -History- -
  1788 – 1900- -Fiction. 4. Lancashire (England)- -
  History- -19th century- -Fiction. 5. Large type books.
  I. Title
  823.9′2–dc22

  ISBN 978–1–4448–0723–3

X000 000 040 5593
Published by
F. A. Thorpe (Publishing)
Anstey, Leicestershire

Set by Words & Graphics Ltd.
Anstey, Leicestershire
Printed and bound in Great Britain by
T. J. International Ltd., Padstow, Cornwall

This book is printed on acid-free paper

This book is dedicated to librarians everywhere for the wonderful service they provide, not only the books but the research help, which has been invaluable to me over the years I've been writing historical stories.

For this book, I'd particularly like to thank Tom Reynolds of the State Records Office of Western Australia, Gillian Simpson of the Australian National Maritime Museum, the Document Supply Service of the National Library of Australia, the Ask Us service of the State Library of Western Australia, the national Australian Ask A Librarian service, Sue Smith of the Albany Public Library, and the wonderful staff of my local Mandurah Library. Their input into my research was invaluable.

And finally, this time I had a new and interesting problem: how to describe a horse and cart crash. For this I had help on line from the USA — so thanks, David Yauch, Liz Goldman, Tracy Meisenbach, Ashley McConnell, Jennifer Smith and Jeane Westin, who really know about horses and carts. They were gentle and kind and informative as they corrected my mistakes. I still don't know how to drive a horse and cart, but I do know how to crash one!

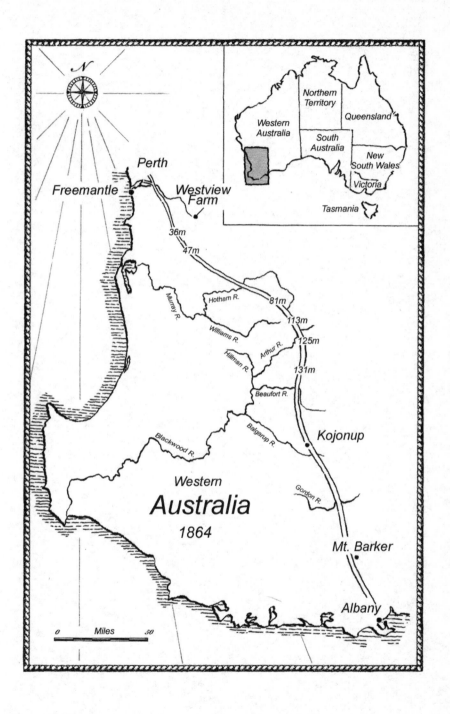

Prologue

Swan River Colony (Western Australia)
December 1863

Pandora Blake heard footsteps and tried to brush away the tears as she saw her eldest sister coming across the garden of the Migrants' Home towards her.

'Breakfast is ready.' Cassandra put an arm round her shoulders. 'Oh, dear! I don't like to see you so upset. You know we can't return to Lancashire. If we did, I'm quite sure our lives would be in danger.'

She nodded and tried to summon up a smile.

'Don't,' Cassandra said softly.

'Don't what?'

'Don't pretend with me. Isn't the homesickness getting any better at all?'

Pandora could only shake her head blindly and try to swallow the lump of grief that seemed permanently lodged in her throat. 'It was cruel of our aunt to force us to leave England. Why does she hate us so much?

'Father always thought it was because *she* couldn't have children.'

'That's not our fault.'

Cassandra gave her a quick hug. 'I know.'

'You should have seen her that last time she came to visit us. She was terrifying, and strange too. She had that piece of your hair that they'd

1

cut off, still tied with your ribbon, and we were certain if we didn't do as she asked and leave the country, she'd have you killed. We thought we'd never see you again. It was a miracle you escaped to join us on the ship.'

A bell rang from inside the building. 'Breakfast is ready,' Cassandra said again.

'I'll join you in a few minutes. I need to calm down.'

'All right.'

Pandora sighed as she looked round the garden, relishing a few moments on her own. The ship had been crowded with other single women brought out to the Swan River Colony as maids, some of them quarrelsome and noisy. All the Lancashire lasses had been thin at first after the long months without work because of the lack of raw cotton, but no one else seemed so badly affected by homesickness as she was. What was wrong with her?

She stared round. She'd thought she'd feel differently once they got here, but she didn't. It was so unlike the soft cool colours of her native Lancashire. Even at this early hour, the sun blazed down from a cloudless blue sky and she felt uncomfortably hot. Wiping her brow, she went to sit on a bench in the shade of a gum tree. It had pretty red flowers, but the leaves were sickle-shaped and leathery, of a dull green. Even the stray clumps of grass in the garden were more beige than green, burnt by the searing sun, while the ground was sandy, shifting beneath your feet as you walked. How anything grew in it, she couldn't think.

A pair of galahs flew across to perch in the tree, squawking harshly at one another. She'd called them 'parrots' when she first arrived but Matron had laughed and told her they were cockatoos, not parrots. Their calls were ugly, but they were pretty to look at, with pink throats and chests, pale grey wings, heads and crests.

One began to nip the flowers off the gum tree with its strong beak, not eating them but simply letting each one drop to the ground while it sought another blossom to pinch out. Was it doing this for sheer devilment or was there some purpose?

Even if she wanted to take the risk, how could she return to Lancashire? She didn't have the money for the fare and she didn't want to leave her sisters. No, somehow she'd have to come to terms with this terrible longing for home. She stood up, took a deep breath and went inside.

As usual the twins were sitting with their heads close together, talking animatedly. Pandora got herself a plate of food and didn't comment on the way Cassandra was staring at her plate, eating very little. Her eldest sister had her own problems, was now carrying the child of a man who'd raped her just before she left England.

Afterwards Pandora helped with the clearing up, trying to speak cheerfully to the other women.

She *would* get over this homesickness, she told herself firmly — or learn to hide it better. She'd never been a whiner, wasn't going to start now.

1

Mr Featherworth leaned back in his chair and studied the young man sitting on the other side of his desk. Not good-looking, Zachary Carr, too tall and bony for that, but still, he had a reputation for honesty and common sense, and a steady gaze. The late Mr Blake had thought a lot of him, had said several times that you'd go a long way to find a more decent fellow. That was much more important to the lawyer than how a man looked.

The more he talked to the young man, the more he warmed to him. Carr had been the breadwinner for his mother and sister for several years, so was clearly a responsible person, and he seemed intelligent too. He might never have travelled overseas before, but he was young and strong, and at twenty-five, he'd grown beyond a young man's rashness. He even knew how to ride a horse, because his uncle had a farm. That was a big advantage, because Mr Featherworth had been told there were no railways in the Swan River Colony.

Most important of all, though: Zachary knew the four Blake sisters by sight.

Yes, Mr Featherworth was sure he'd chosen the right person to send on this mission.

'It's not taken as long as I expected to find a

5

ship going to the Swan River Colony — or Western Australia as some call it now. I've booked you a passage on the *Clara*, which is due to leave London on January the 11th.'

Zachary's face lit up, then the date sank in and he looked startled. 'But that's only just over a week away! How will I ever get ready in time?'

Mr Featherworth held up one hand. 'Please let me finish.'

The younger man gave him an embarrassed smile. 'Sorry. I'm a bit excited about it all.'

The lawyer smiled back at him. 'It's not surprising. Few young men of your station in life are given an opportunity to travel to the other side of the world. But as you know, the Blake sisters had already left England when their uncle's will was read, so someone has to tell them they're the new owners of his grocery emporium, and escort them back from Australia.'

Zachary nodded. 'It was a sad business, that. I thought a lot of Mr Blake. He was a good employer and a kind man.'

'Yes indeed.'

They were both silent for a few minutes. Who would have thought the late Mrs Blake would go insane, murder her husband and force her nieces to leave the country in fear of their lives? The idea of all that still gave the lawyer nightmares.

'Now, as to the details of your voyage, I had at first intended to send you steerage, because one has to be careful when spending a client's money. But this is a vessel taking convicts to Western Australia, not a normal passenger vessel, and I've decided you'll be far safer as a cabin

6

passenger. Not that the steerage passengers mingle with the convicts, certainly not, but still . . . I was fortunate enough to secure the last vacant bunk for you — though you'll have to share the cabin with another gentleman.'

'What exactly does 'cabin passenger' mean?'

'It means you'll be travelling with the gentry, away from the convicts and in more comfort than the steerage passengers, both going out to Australia and when you bring the young women back. However, you'll not be in the first-class cabins, whose occupants eat at the Captain's table, but rather in the deck cabins, which have their own dining area and less generous accommodation. Your travelling companions will still be a better class of person than you would find in steerage, though.' He studied Zachary. 'You look worried.'

'I shan't know how to behave in such company. I've served the gentry in the store, but they live differently from us. I don't want to let you down — or embarrass myself.'

'I'm sure you'll do nothing to upset people, but if you're doubtful how to behave, watch others whom you respect and imitate them. You can also ask advice of the ship's doctor or one of the ship's officers, if need be. The main thing is not to pretend to know something you don't or be something you aren't. It'd not look good to be caught out in a lie.'

'Yes, sir. I'll try my best.'

'I'm sure you will or I'd not be sending you. Now, you'll need better clothing than you have at present — no, don't be embarrassed. In your

7

present position, your clothing is perfectly suitable. But for this journey you'll need other garments if you're to gain people's respect and assistance, not to mention extra changes of clothing for the three-month voyage. I've asked my tailor to make you some new clothes. He's prepared to work day and night to supply you with what you need. I shall myself escort you to London and we'll purchase anything else necessary from a ship's chandler near the docks.'

He paused and frowned, because this was a delicate matter, something his wife had pointed out. 'It might be a good idea for you to eat your evening meals at my house from now on, so that we can make sure your table manners are correct. There are niceties of eating, ways of using various pieces of cutlery . . . well, you understand, I'm sure.'

Zachary flushed but nodded.

'You'd better stop work in the shop immediately. Go and inform Prebble. Tell him we'll find a replacement till you return. Then come back and my clerk will take you to see the tailor. You'll also need to go to Hawsworth's to purchase underclothing and whatever else you're in need of. The clothing will, of course, be yours to keep afterwards.'

'Thank you, sir.'

'We'll discuss the arrangements you'll need to make for the journey home to Lancashire after our evening meal tonight. How surprised those young women will be to hear about their inheritance! They'll be so happy to be able to come home again.'

8

'And if they ask for details of their legacy, what am I to tell them?'

Mr Featherworth hesitated.

'I'm not asking out of curiosity, sir, but they're bound to want to know.'

'Broadly speaking, they own the shop, the building in which it's located, including comfortable living accommodation above it, as you know, plus several cottages and houses which are rented out and bring in extra income. There is also a tidy sum of money in the bank. This was to have been used to provide for Mrs Blake during her lifetime, but was not needed in view of her death so soon after her husband's — though that was a mercy, given her state of mind.'

He raised one finger in a cautioning gesture. 'Mind, you are not to tell anyone else, *anyone at all*, these details.'

Zachary nodded. No need to say that. He wasn't one to tattle about other people's affairs, let alone betray confidential information.

Excitement swelled within him. He was going to Australia, travelling the world! What wonders would he see on his journey?

★　★　★

Pandora walked back across the yard of the Migrants' Home to join the twins after speaking to a lady seeking a housemaid. It had been an effort to answer the questions. What did she care about finding a job when Cassandra was in such trouble? Before she left the ship, her sister had been accused of stealing money by her employers and was now confined to the Home. As if any of them would steal!

'The lady you were talking to looks very annoyed,' Maia said.

Pandora shrugged. 'I told her I couldn't take the job. She lives a long way from Perth, somewhere to the north. It takes five days to get there by cart. I don't care what Matron says, I'm not going that far away from you all.'

'I hadn't thought it'd be so hard to find work near one another.' Maia linked arms with her twin, Xanthe, and the three of them moved to a quiet corner.

But people pursued them there, all seeking maids.

'Why did you come to Australia if you don't want a job?' one demanded.

'I shall complain to Matron about your attitude,' another said huffily.

Pandora didn't try to respond to that. Bad enough to be so far away from her home. Unthinkable to be separated from her sisters as well.

★ ★ ★

A little later that day a well-dressed lady came into the Migrants' Home, accompanied by a man who moved through the crowd ahead of her. With a shriek, Pandora ran across, so happy to see someone from home that she flung herself into his arms, laughing and crying at once. 'Reece! I can't believe it's you!'

10

He stared at her in blank astonishment. 'What the — Pandora, what on earth are you doing here?' He looked round. 'Is Cassandra with you?'

'Yes, but it's a long story. Not for public telling and — ' she began, stopping as she realised who he was with. 'Mrs Southerham! Oh, I can't believe our luck! You're just the person we need to see.'

Livia smiled at her and the twins, who had come across to join them. 'Isn't Cassandra with you?'

'They told her she can't get a job yet. They think she stole some money. She says *you* gave it to her.'

'I did give her some.'

They all tried to talk at once, explaining what had happened.

Reece beamed at them. 'I can't believe it. Cassandra's here in Australia. I was going to send her a letter asking her to join me here.' To marry him.

Matron came over to see what was happening and speak to Mrs Southerham.

Reece listened for a moment or two, then asked who this Mrs Lawson was. Matron looked at him in puzzlement. 'Mrs Lawson is the sister of these young ladies.'

'Cassandra? Then she's the woman I want to marry.'

Silence, then, 'Is it a while since you saw her?'

'Yes.'

Pandora poked him in the ribs. 'We'll explain later.'

Matron finished talking to Mrs Southerham,

who confirmed that she had indeed given Cassandra the money, then went to write a note to the Governor. She took Reece with her, because he was insisting on seeing Cassandra. 'You can speak to her at the other end of the garden. I'll send her out to you.'

Pandora waited anxiously. She found it hard to talk to Mrs Southerham about a job because she was hoping desperately that Reece would still love Cassandra and, in spite of what had happened, still want to marry her.

When she saw him stride round the corner of the Home with an agonised expression on his face and walk out into the street without even stopping to explain, her heart sank. She said a hasty farewell to Mrs Southerham and hurried back to their quarters to find her sister.

Cassandra was weeping.

'Oh, love, what's the matter?'

'He walked away when I told him about the baby.'

Pandora had expected better of Reece, who had been a friend of the whole family back in Outham, who had courted Cassandra, but hadn't been able to marry her because he was out of work since the mills had stopped for lack of cotton from America. 'Then he's not worth loving. You were raped. It wasn't your fault.'

'How do you stop loving someone? I told myself it wouldn't be right to expect him to marry me, not now, but I hoped. I couldn't help hoping.'

It was a while before Cassandra calmed down and took up her sewing again, but Pandora hated to see the bleak unhappiness on her face.

Things seemed to be getting worse since their arrival in Australia, not better.

★ ★ ★

Zachary walked slowly through the streets of Outham, his head spinning with information and excitement. As he entered Blake's Emporium, Harry Prebble, who made everyone all too aware that he was now the temporary manager, looked up with a sour expression on his face and gestured to him to come into the back.

'You've been away long enough, Carr.'

The two young men stared at one another, antagonism fairly humming between them. Harry might have been chosen to run the shop until the new owners could be brought back to Lancashire, but Zachary knew he was still jealous of the other being sent to Australia to fetch them home. And he'd always been resentful of Zachary's extra inches. He was over six foot tall while Harry stood a bare five foot six.

The doorbell tinkled and Harry took a quick peep into the shop. 'There's Mrs Warrish. You'd better start serving now, Carr, and — '

'Mr Featherworth says I'm to stop work immediately because I sail next week and there's a lot to be done. He says you can take on other help while I'm gone. I'll get my things and leave you to it.'

'I need help now. I must say it's very selfish of you. Didn't you remind him it's Friday, our busiest day?'

13

'He and I were talking about the journey, not the shop.'

'It's all right for some!'

'*You* have nothing to complain about. You've been appointed temporary manager, haven't you?' Zachary bit back further hot words, annoyed at himself for giving his feelings away. He'd have loved to run the shop, and after working there since the age of twelve, he was sure he'd do it just as well as Harry. Better, because Harry always fussed about details and ordered the same old goods, never looking at what was happening in the world, how people were changing and wanting to buy different things.

Railways had changed everything in the past twenty years and it was now possible to get foodstuffs from all over the world as easily as they'd got them from Manchester in the old days. Mr Blake had often talked about this and Harry had listened with an intent expression on his face, but the implications never seemed to sink in.

'Well, don't forget that you'll be coming back to work under *me*.'

'*If* you get the appointment as permanent shop manager. That'll be up to the new owners.'

'Who else could they appoint? I know everything about how this shop is run. Haven't I worked here since I was twelve?'

'We both have!' And Zachary had been there for a year longer, actually.

'Well, I'll be able to *prove* my worth to Mr Featherworth while you're gallivanting round the

14

world, so the job's as good as mine. Those nieces of Mr Blake's are only mill girls, however intelligent they're supposed to be. They'll know nothing about running a shop, so they're bound to turn to me for advice. I'll make sure the profits rise while I'm in charge. That's what will matter to them.' He jutted his chin challengingly.

It wasn't worth arguing, so Zachary went into the rear of the shop and took down his apron from the hook on the wall, retrieving his lunch box. You couldn't afford to waste good food in troubled times like these. So many people in the cotton towns were going hungry for lack of work, thanks to the war in America stopping raw cotton getting through to the mills.

A year and a half ago, in 1862, Mr Blake had started providing food for his staff at midday and broken biscuits with their cups of tea at other breaks, knowing those still in employment were going short to help their hungry relatives and friends. But Harry had discontinued that practice as soon as he took over, not even providing cups of tea on the pretext that he didn't dare be extravagant with someone else's money. You'd think what he saved was going into his own pocket.

When he got back from Australia, if Harry was put in charge, Zachary intended to seek employment elsewhere, even if he had to move to another town to find it.

He left the shop and looked back at it thoughtfully. A huge plate glass window that had caused a sensation in the town twenty years previously when first installed, because it was so

15

different from the small panes that all the other shops had. Tins and boxes were displayed there in carefully arranged piles. The words BLAKE'S EMPORIUM stood out in foot-high golden letters on a maroon ground above the shop window.

It must be wonderful to own such a business.

He felt sad as he passed a group of men loitering on a street corner, their clothes ragged and their faces gaunt with the years of hunger. He'd be eating well at the Featherworths' that evening so on an impulse he shared the contents of his lunch box with them. Not much for each one, but something, and it broke his heart to see how carefully they divided the food, so that each would have the same amount.

Men like these were such a contrast to the more affluent customers who came into the shop. If only the war in America would end! People said the South was getting the worst of it now, but Zachary didn't care who won. He just wanted the Americans to start sending cotton again. Without it, the mills of Lancashire stood silent, no smoke pouring from their chimneys, or only a trickle when they fired up the steam engines to keep them working properly. The clear sky still looked strange to him, because on fine days he was used to seeing smoke trails criss-crossing it.

Even the relief schemes that had been set up in the town couldn't feed so many families adequately and that showed in people's faces.

Zachary realised he'd stopped moving and clicked his tongue in exasperation at himself. Why was he loitering around daydreaming when he had a thousand things to organise for his adventure?

★   ★   ★

Although Reece came back to the Migrants' Home the following day to apologise to Cassandra for walking out on her, she steadfastly refused to marry him.

Pandora watched them both from the shade of the tree where she had again taken refuge from the heat. They loved one another, she could tell. But although her sister had wept when Reece walked away from her, she said it only proved she was right to decide not to marry him. She didn't want the child to be treated badly. Strange how protective Cassandra was to her unborn baby.

Maybe if I met someone I loved, I'd be able to settle down here more easily, Pandora thought. But she knew with a sick certainty that she wouldn't. This place was . . . wrong for her. It wasn't *home*. She found the heat particularly trying and her face felt raw with sweat. Even the nights were hot, though occasionally an afternoon sea breeze that locals called the 'Fremantle Doctor' brought a little relief for an hour or two.

She was getting better at hiding her misery, though, and was rather proud of that.

At the moment her best hope was to find a job near enough to her sisters to see them regularly. Reece's employers, the Southerhams, had offered her a position as a maid of all work, and they were kind enough to say Cassandra could

17

go too. But they couldn't afford to pay two maids, so her sister would get only her keep.

It was a fair offer, probably as good as they were likely to get, given the circumstances, but Cassandra refused to accept it because Reece also worked for them.

Well, Pandora wasn't leaving her sister on her own, not in that condition, not if she had to defy the Governor of the colony himself.

Later that day a man called Conn Largan turned up at the Migrants' Home, offering jobs to the twins, caring for his invalid mother. They lived an hour's drive away from the Southerhams, which was quite close, it seemed, in Australian terms.

In the end Pandora confronted Cassandra. 'Working for the Southerhams is the only way we can all four stay together. You *have* to accept the job, whether Reece works there or not.'

And at last, because there truly was no other way to keep the family together, Cassandra gave in.

Pandora felt for her, they all did, but it was a relief to have their immediate future settled and to get away from the restrictions of the Migrants' Home.

* * *

The week following the interview with Mr Featherworth passed in a blur of activity for Zachary. The tailor finished his new clothes with amazing speed, finer garments than he'd ever worn in his whole life.

18

He was also supplied with an incredible number of other clothes. There were a dozen beautiful shirts, some in lightweight materials like gauze cotton, because the weather was much hotter in Australia. Each one had three matching collars and there was a whole box of studs for attaching them to the shirts. There were also a dozen travelling shirts of flannel, a dozen cravats of various colours, several sets of braces, cotton drawers at half a crown a pair, under-vests at four shillings and sixpence each, and nightshirts at ten shillings each.

He was speechless at how much this must add up to and tried to protest to the clerk that he could manage with less.

'Mr Featherworth has taken advice from those who've travelled overseas and this is the minimum number of garments you'll need on such a long voyage, young man.' Mr Dawson patted his shoulder. 'There are those who take twice as many clothes with them.'

Zachary could only shake his head in wonderment. He didn't tell anyone, but he was delighted to be so well turned out, for once. It was a struggle for him and his family to stay decently dressed on his wages alone. Normally his sister Hallie would have had a job too, at least until she got married, and her money would have been a big help in supporting their widowed mother. Because of the cotton famine, however, jobs were scarce and few families in Outham had more than one breadwinner.

But he remained concerned at how much this was costing the heirs. When Mr Dawson mentioned buying a trunk, Zachary felt comfortable enough with the lawyer's clerk to make a suggestion of his own. 'Why don't we check the attics above the shop and see if there are any trunks or other items of luggage? There are all sorts of bits and pieces stored there. I've seen them when I've carried things up for Mr Blake.'

'Very sensible idea, young man. We'll go there at once.'

Harry came out of the rear of the shop to see what they were doing when they entered the living quarters. 'Oh, it's you!'

He'd known perfectly well who they were, was just being nosey, Zachary thought, saying nothing.

'Carry on with your work, Prebble,' Mr Dawson said, in a sharp tone that said he didn't like Harry either. 'This is none of your business.'

When the clerk turned away, Harry glared at him, then saw Zachary looking and went back into the shop. But his expression had been so inimical that Zachary couldn't help worrying. Harry had a reputation for getting his own back on those who had upset him. He'd not be able to do much to a man like Mr Dawson, though, surely?

The attics were very dark and there was no gas lighting up here, so Zachary ran down to ask the maid for a lamp. 'How are things going, Dot?'

She smiled at him. 'It's been really peaceful. I'm so glad Mr Featherworth has let me stay on. There. This is a good bright lamp.'

'I'll see to lighting it.'

She lingered to chat. 'Mrs Rainey's cousin is

coming to live here soon. Miss Blair's been ill but she's a lot better now. She's been to visit and seems a really nice lady. I'll feel better to have some company.' She lowered her voice and glanced over her shoulder. 'Apart from *him*.'

'Harry?'

She nodded. 'He keeps coming in, saying he has to check that I'm doing my work properly. And he sits up in the sitting room sometimes after work. No one told me I'd have to answer to *him*.'

Amazed by what she'd told him, Zachary took the lamp up to the attic and with its help they soon found what they were seeking. 'There!' He pushed some boxes aside. 'A trunk. It's a little battered but I don't mind that.' He opened and shut it, finding all the hinges and locks in good working order. 'I shall be happy to use this one and save some money.'

The clerk nodded his approval and went back to searching, finding a large portmanteau of scuffed leather under an old rug.

Zachary hesitated, wondering whether to interfere, then decided the poor little maid needed protection. 'Dot was saying that Harry keeps coming in to check up on what she's doing, and . . . he sits in the owner's quarters after work sometimes.'

The clerk looked at him in surprise. 'What happens with the maid or in the living quarters is no concern of his, none whatsoever. I'll mention it to Mr Featherworth. No one need know you told me. You and Prebble will have to work together after you get back, so we don't want to

21

stir up bad blood between you. The Methodist Minister's cousin is to move into the flat soon, partly because I don't trust Prebble. He's taken a few liberties since Mr Featherworth made him manager. Miss Blair will make sure everything is looked after properly and will do a complete inventory of the contents for us. It's asking for trouble to leave a place with so many valuable things in it empty, especially in hard times like these.'

Harry came out again to watch sourly as Zachary and the shop lad carried the trunk and portmanteau down the stairs and out to a handcart.

'Have you no work to get on with, young man?' Mr Dawson asked sharply. 'This is the second time I've seen you neglecting your duties today.'

'I thought you might need some help.'

'Well, we don't.'

Scowling, Harry went back into the shop.

'Sitting in the flat, indeed!' the clerk muttered as they walked back down the street. 'Well, that's going to stop.'

Zachary had wondered why they felt the need for someone to occupy the flat. Mr Featherworth was a kindly man, but his clerk seemed more astute. Zachary didn't think they'd have any worries about the financial side of things, though. Harry Prebble had never been anything but honest and industrious during the years they'd worked together.

But Zachary still didn't like him, he admitted to himself — hadn't when they were boys, and trusted him even less as a man. He'd never understood why.

*   *   *

The next day Zachary's mother was advised on how to pack his new possessions for a long journey by no less a person than Mrs Featherworth. Two extra sets of clothing and underclothing you needed, because it was not only hard to wash clothes in sea water, to do it for so many people was impossible. Trunks were brought up from the hold each month so that people could change their garments during the voyage, which would last approximately a hundred days. Just imagine that! What a great distance he'd be travelling.

Every evening he went to dinner at the lawyer's house, the first time so nervous he doubted he'd be able to eat a mouthful. But his hostess was a motherly woman, whom he'd sometimes served in the shop, and it was impossible to stay afraid of anyone with such a warm smile.

'You won't mind if I help you improve your table manners, Zachary dear?' she said gently, taking his arm as she led him into the dining room, with Mr Featherworth and his two daughters following.

'I'd appreciate any help you can give me, Mrs Featherworth.' He tried not to stare round but was awed that they had a big room like this purely for eating in.

As everyone took their places, she pointed to

the cutlery in front of her and said in a low voice, 'The trick is to start from the outside pieces at each side of your plate.'

While Mr Featherworth said grace, Zachary stared down at the daunting array of cutlery. So many pieces for one meal alone. How much were they going to eat?

The minute grace ended, a maid carried in a soup tureen which she set in front of her mistress. Mrs Featherworth ladled its contents into bowls and the maid passed them round, then left. Everyone seemed to be waiting to eat and no one started until the mistress did.

Zachary took up the big round spoon on the right when the others did and watched how they used it before starting on his own soup, a brown meaty concoction served with crusty rolls.

The food was delicious and for once he had more than enough to eat. He only wished he could take some of his share home for his mother and sister to try.

After the four courses were over, they went to sit in the drawing room. Mrs Featherworth patted the sofa next to her and Zachary sat down, already trusting her.

'There are other things my daughters and I can teach you, for instance, what subjects to discuss with ladies, how to offer your arm.'

The two young women sitting nearby nodded their heads and smiled at him. Nice lasses, they seemed, about the same age as his sister. He wished Hallie had a fine dress like those they were wearing, because she was just as pretty.

'Do you enjoy reading?' Mrs Featherworth asked.

'I love it. When I have time, that is.'

'Good. We've found some books for you to read on the journey to help pass the time. I do hope you'll enjoy them.'

The elder daughter got up and from behind her chair produced a pile of about a dozen books fastened together by a leather strap that even had a carrying handle on the top.

He stared at them in delight: *A Tale of Two Cities* by Dickens, *Westward Ho!* by Kingsley, a book of poetry. He'd had little time for reading in his busy life, because the shop stayed open until late. 'Thank you so much.'

'We got you a diary too,' the younger daughter said. 'Mama thought you'd want to remember your big adventure. You can write down what happens every day. I wish *I* were going to Australia. It sounds *so* exciting.'

Mr Featherworth said little, but let his womenfolk do most of the talking, sitting watching them with a fond smile.

The older daughter carried a fancy wooden box across from a side table and set it on the sofa between Zachary and his hostess.

'This is an old travelling writing desk, which used to belong to my uncle,' Mrs Featherworth said. 'It was lying around in the attic, not being used, so we thought you might like it. We've furnished it with letter paper and envelopes, plenty of nibs, and ink powder so that you can make up more ink as you need it.'

He opened the lid and the box became a writing slope, the interior covered in dark red leather with a pattern embossed in gold round the edges. There were compartments at the front for pens, ink and sand bottles, though of course people used blotting paper these days not sand to dry the ink. 'Thank you. I'll take great care of it for you.'

'Please keep it afterwards as a memento of your adventure.'

He swallowed hard and tried not to betray that this extra unnecessary generosity had moved him almost to tears. From being a man struggling to dress decently as well as provide for his mother and sister, he was suddenly being loaded with possessions. He would, he vowed mentally, not let the lawyer down whatever happened.

His hostess patted his hand in a motherly gesture. 'If you have anything else to occupy yourself with, be sure to take it with you. The journey will go on for many weeks.'

Drawing materials, he thought. *I used to love drawing as a lad. I can afford some plain paper and pencils, surely? And a rubber, too.* He smiled at the memory of an elderly uncle, also fond of drawing, who'd always called rubbers 'lead eaters'.

Zachary walked home carrying the books and the writing desk, his mind humming with all the information. He was amazed at how pleasantly the evening had passed, considering how nervous he'd been. But the lawyer's daughters were nice lasses, for all their fine clothes, and you couldn't find a kinder lady than Mrs Featherworth, so he'd soon lost his fear of upsetting them.

It was cold and rainy and he couldn't help

26

shivering after being in such a well-heated house. It was hard to believe that he was going to a country where in summer the weather was hotter than it ever became in Lancashire, and where it never snowed in winter. It was hard even to imagine how that would feel.

When he got back, he found his mother and sister waiting up for him, eager to hear how the evening had gone.

Hallie pounced on the books while his mother marvelled at the travelling writing desk, running her fingers over the gleaming wood and examining each bottle and compartment.

'Oh, you're so lucky!' Hallie sighed. 'What wouldn't I give to have all those books to read! I've read everything I want to from the public library.'

'Choose one and read it while I'm away. It'll remind you of me.'

'Are you sure?

'Yes, of course.' He gave her a hug, surprised at how tall his little sister had grown lately.

She picked out *Mary Barton*, her fingers caressing the tooled leather binding of the novel. 'I'll take this one, then. Thank you so much, Zachary.'

He smiled indulgently. 'I know how you love your stories of romance and adventure.'

'It's nice to dream sometimes.' She gave him a quick kiss on the cheek. 'I'll dream for you now. Perhaps you'll fall in love while you're away, meet a wonderful girl on the ship or . . . No, better still, fall in love with one of the Blake sisters and then the shop will be partly yours.

That'll solve all our problems.'

He didn't like this and drew back from her. 'Don't be silly! Mr Featherworth is trusting me to bring them back safely, not to prey on them.'

'Falling in love isn't preying, Zachary.'

'It would be in this case.'

She flounced one shoulder at him. 'Oh, you! Sometimes you're too noble for words! And once you get an idea fixed in your mind, there's no changing it. Why can you not dream and let things happen as they will?'

Because he'd never been free to dream, he thought bitterly, biting back an angry response. He'd had the responsibility for supporting them from a very early age. Not that he minded, of course he didn't. And though they disagreed sometimes, as brothers and sisters always do, he loved Hallie dearly and didn't want to quarrel with her just before he left.

'Now, calm down, you two,' his mother said, giving her daughter a quick kiss, then her son. She lingered next to Zachary to beg, 'Don't let all this go to your head, son. It's a great adventure, to be sure, but you'll still have to come back and work at Blake's.'

'If Harry Prebble stays in charge, I'll be looking for work elsewhere.' He wished he hadn't told her that when he saw the anxiety in her face. 'Don't worry. I shan't do anything rashly.'

'No. You never do. I wish you did sometimes. We've stopped you being a young man, haven't we?' She began to light their candles ready to go up to bed, shaking her head sadly. 'As for Harry, you two didn't get on at school, were always

28

fighting one another till you grew so much bigger than him, and it doesn't seem to have got much better. It's not good to make enemies, Zachary love.'

'Sometimes enemies make themselves, Mum, whether we want it or not.'

'Well, see that *you* don't behave ungenerously, whatever *he* does. A man should do nothing he's not proud of, whether he's poor or rich. And the same when you're out in the world. Always make me proud of you, son.'

'I will.' He went to check that the front and back doors were locked, extinguished the paraffin lamp in the kitchen and made his way up to bed by the wavering light of his candle.

Zachary knew that whatever he said or did, Harry Prebble would always be suspicious of his motives and would continue to act in a mean-spirited way if left in charge. You had to stand up to a bully, or he'd get worse. Zachary had learned that lesson as a lad and it held true for grown men, too. But sometimes it was an unfair world and bullies had more power than you, so you couldn't challenge them, could only walk away.

No, he'd definitely look for other work. And surely, if he performed this task well, Mr Featherworth would give him a good reference?

2

Pandora woke to the screeching of parrots in the bush near the house and it took her a minute to remember that she was on the Southerhams' farm, a place they'd called Westview, because it looked down a slope towards the west. The sky was filled with beautiful sunsets most evenings, which everyone enjoyed looking at. But Pandora's main thought was always that England lay in that direction, far to the north-west, beyond the sunset.

The farm was very isolated, a long day's travel by cart to the south of Perth, in the foothills of the Darling Range. There were no other dwellings in sight and even her employers had only a tiny wooden hut to live in. The two maids slept in a corner of a big tent in which furniture was stored. Reece now slept at their neighbour's house. Kevin lived just a few minutes' walk away if you went through the bush.

Cassandra was still sleeping, though how she could do that through the parrots' din was a wonder to her sister.

It was warm already and though they'd slept with only a sheet to cover them, Pandora had tossed even that off during the night. Christmas was only a few days past, and a strange, sunny celebration that had been. The heat had continued through early January, day after day of it. Most people had sun-tanned faces, but her skin didn't turn brown, only reddened in the heat, which continued to trouble her.

She smiled at the best Christmas memory: her sister sitting holding Reece's hand. She'd hoped that being near to one another would bring them together and it had.

She'd played her part in this, helping him catch Cassandra on her own so that he could explain how he'd felt on hearing her news and exactly why he'd walked away. Then he'd proposed once again and whatever he'd said must have changed her sister's mind, because this time Cassandra had accepted him. She said she was now convinced that he'd care for the baby she was carrying, even though it wasn't his.

Once they were married, however, Pandora would be on her own here, working for the Southerhams, and she didn't know how she'd cope without her favourite sister's companionship and support. Seeing Cassandra regularly just wouldn't be the same. They'd lived closely and happily together all their lives until they left England. If Pandora's fiancé hadn't died of pneumonia, she and Bill would have rented a house close to her family. Now, who knew where they'd all end up?

She slipped out of bed and went into the main part of the big storage tent where they had a bowl to wash in. Feeling fresher afterwards, she put on her clothes and went out to use the primitive latrine then refill the washing bucket with fresh water from the well for Cassandra.

There was still some life in the embers inside the new iron stove they'd brought back from

31

Perth. Reece had installed it a short distance away from the hut, under a wooden awning to protect it from the rain and the prevailing winds. They burned wood in it, not coal, gathering the wood from fallen branches and trees in the bush nearby.

It seemed strange to do the cooking out of doors. Mr Southerham had wanted to build a kitchen on to one end of their shack, but Reece insisted people didn't do that here, because it made the place too hot during the summer and because of the fire risk.

Mr Southerham had given in, as he usually did. He took more care of his horses than he did of his wife's comfort and wasn't at all practical about everyday living. The two of them seemed to have no plans to provide proper accommodation for their maid. Did they expect Pandora to spend the winter sleeping in a tent? It might not snow or freeze here, but their neighbour said it rained heavily in the cooler months and was sometimes very windy. What if the tent leaked or blew away?

Lost in her thoughts, she got the stove going again, feeding it dried gum leaves which burned well because the leaves contained eucalyptus oil, then twigs and solid pieces of wood. Putting on the big kettle of water she went to draw yet another bucket from the well. Not her favourite chore, this. Oh, for a tap out of which came clean water, as they'd had back home! You had to filter the drinking water through muslin here.

Just before she got to the well she stopped to watch a kangaroo. It was sitting at the edge of the bush behind the house, scratching its chest with its short front legs while its baby hopped round it. It looked as if it was taking a well-earned rest. And that was the smallest joey Pandora had yet seen. She smiled as she watched it.

Then something startled the little creature and it dived head first into its mother's pouch, disappearing in a tangle of legs. Not until the big kangaroo had hopped away did Pandora start moving again. Such strange animals. She enjoyed watching them, and the other birds and animals that were new to her.

If this was only a visit and she was going back to Lancashire afterwards, she'd be enjoying her stay. There was so little here. It was just a big, empty land. Perth, the capital city of the colony, had roughly the same population as Outham: about three thousand people.

Sun beat down on her, hot already. She missed the softer, moister air of Lancashire, the vivid colours of autumn foliage, the neat little birds, the sound of Outham voices, everything. Dashing away a tear with the back of one hand, she told herself not to dwell on things that couldn't be changed, to keep her feelings to herself and not upset her sisters.

★ ★ ★

In Outham, Alice Blair finished packing her trunk and smiled at her cousin, who was helping her. 'I can't believe I'll be able to continue taking it easy, Phoebe. I can't thank you enough for arranging for me to look after the flat until the heirs return.'

'Will you be all right on your own?'

'I shan't be on my own. The maid will be there too. Dot seems a nice lass.'

'She is. And you and I will be able to see each other often.'

'You're not to disrupt your life because of me. You have your duties as a Minister's wife to attend to.' Alice clasped her cousin's hand briefly. 'I'm sure I shall soon make friends in Outham.' They'd be spinsters like herself, but she was used to that. A governess who was nearly forty didn't get much chance to make friends with married ladies, who had their own secrets to chat about.

'We'll see.'

'I mean it, Phoebe. I'm so much better now, you can stop worrying about me.'

'I wish there was some way of you earning a living in Outham, or that you'd accept Gerald's offer to come and live with us permanently.'

'We've discussed that before. I won't be a burden to you while I'm able to work.'

'But you don't even like being a governess.'

'I didn't say that!'

Phoebe smiled. 'Of course you didn't. You're not one to complain. But if you think I hadn't guessed . . . '

Alice sighed. 'I never could fool you. I like the teaching side of things, but I don't like the way my employers treat me. I don't fit in with them and I don't fit in with the servants. It's a lonely life.' She closed the lid and locked the trunk.

'Well, bring up those lads who're waiting so patiently and let's get my things taken across to the shop. I shall come and help out with the soup kitchen and the reading classes once I'm settled in. It's very sad how many people are out of work. Will the war in America never end?'

'We'll be glad of your help, but not until you've gone through everything in the flat and made the inventory for Mr Featherworth. That must come first.'

'Of course.'

When they got to the shop, Dot was waiting for them in the kitchen on the ground floor, hands clasped over a spotless apron. She took them up to the generous living quarters above the shop. The place looked clean and well cared for, which spoke well for her as a worker.

At last Phoebe went away and Alice allowed herself a small sigh of relief. So ungrateful of her to feel like this, but her slightly older cousin did have a way of taking over every detail of your life, given half a chance. 'Now, Dot, go and make a pot of tea and I'll join you in the kitchen in a few minutes to drink it.'

'You don't want me to bring it up to you, miss?'

'No. I'll come down to the kitchen and you can have a cup with me. And is there some cake to go with it? Or biscuits perhaps?'

'No, miss. Mr Prebble sends stuff in from the shop for me, but he doesn't send any biscuits.'

'Surely there was enough money provided for that?'

Dot wriggled uncomfortably. 'Mr Prebble

35

looks after the money, miss. He says to tell you he'll take care of the bills and accounts, like he's been doing for me, and you're to let him know what you want each week. He's sent me in plenty of food. I've not gone hungry, not once.'

Alice frowned. Mr Featherworth had told her how much housekeeping money she was to receive every week and it was a reasonable sum, but she had no intention of allowing the young man in the shop to take it over and dictate what she ate. 'What a good thing I've not taken my hat off. I'll nip across the street and buy a cake from the baker's until we can start making our own. Afterwards we'll go through what there is in the pantry and decide what else we need to buy.'

Dot looked at her in alarm. 'But Mr Prebble sells tins of — '

'He isn't in charge now, Dot. I am.'

When the new occupant had gone out, Harry popped into the kitchen. 'Where's she off to?'

'The baker's.'

'Didn't you tell her I'd see to the food?'

'Yes, but she said she'd rather do that herself.'

'Oh, did she?'

He looked so angry Dot was relieved when the shop doorbell sounded and he hurried back to check on the customers. He didn't like to miss a thing, that one, and always had to be telling people what to do. She hoped her new mistress would be able to deal with him, but she didn't have much hope of that, because he was a cunning devil. Dot saw a lot, working so close to him, but wouldn't dare say anything about it.

Miss Blair returned in a few minutes, just as

36

Dot was worrying that the tea she'd brewed might get cold and too strong.

'Here we are. I do love a good fruitcake. Put the teapot on the table and sit down.'

'It's not right, miss, me sitting down with you.'

'It is if I tell you to. I want to talk to you and I'm sure you're ready for a rest.'

'I don't usually sit down till I have my dinner at one o'clock, miss. Mr Prebble says there's no need for it.' He'd had her packing stuff for the shop a couple of times when she'd finished her work early. She didn't mind, really, because she liked to keep busy, but she didn't like the way he stood so close to her while she worked.

'Well, today you're sitting with me because we need to work out how we shall go on together. And from today, it's me you answer to, not Prebble. Please remember that.'

Dot looked at her companion's plain face, warm smile and thin body, and suddenly felt at ease. 'Thank you, miss. A cup of tea will be very welcome, I must admit, and a short sit-down too.'

She just hoped Harry didn't see them. There wasn't any door in the passage that connected the shop and the living quarters.

★   ★   ★

As the week leading up to his departure flew past, Zachary's mother tried not to show how upset she was at him going so far away. He knew she wept in private and was worried about the dangers of a long sea voyage, but this was such a

37

big chance for him she tried to hide that from him.

'You deserve this,' his sister Hallie said on the last evening. 'You're the best of brothers.' She came to plonk a careless kiss on his cheek and finger the travelling writing desk, which might be old but was still a handsome piece. He'd had it out on the kitchen table several times, fingering the inlay work on the outside of the lid and enjoying the luxury of such a well-fitted interior.

He shook her arm gently to get her full attention. 'You'll look after our mother, Hallie love?'

She turned towards him. 'You know I will. And we'll be fine, I'm sure. They'll send your wages round each week. We shall think ourselves rich without you eating us out of house and home.'

He gave the usual response to this teasing about his appetite. 'There's a lot of me to sustain.' But actually, he rarely allowed himself to eat freely at home, as he did at the Featherworths', because he and his family had to watch every penny. The tailor had said at his first fitting that he'd probably put on weight if he started eating better, so he'd made allowances for that in the clothes. Harry had been a bit embarrassed but he knew the man had meant it kindly. There were a lot of very thin people in Outham these days. He realised his sister was still talking and tried to pay better attention.

'If I can save any money while you're away, I'll put it in the Yorkshire Penny Bank, like you showed me.'

'Don't stint yourselves.'

Tears suddenly filled Hallie's eyes and she flung her arms round his neck. 'I'm going to miss you so much, Zachary love.'

He gave her a hug. 'I'll miss you, too. I wish you could come with me. Wouldn't we enjoy the adventure if we were together?'

She hugged him back convulsively then dried her eyes. 'Lasses don't get the chance to travel like men do.'

'One day I'll take you to see the sea at Blackpool.' It was an old promise, but maybe he'd be able to keep it after he got back. 'And don't forget, Uncle Richard has invited you two to go and see him sometimes. It's lovely out at the farm.'

She pulled a face. 'I don't like going there. He keeps trying to get me to ride one of his horses and I've always been afraid of them.'

'There's nothing to be afraid of. Uncle Richard's horses are gentle and well-fed. I like riding them, only wish I could get out there to do it more often.'

'Well, we will go and visit him, because Mum enjoys seeing her brother, but I'm still not going near those horses. Give me a good brisk walk any day, if I want to spend time out of doors.'

★   ★   ★

On his final visit to the Featherworths', Zachary overheard his hostess say to her husband, 'That young man will do. He has an innate courtesy which will carry him through situations where he

39

doesn't know the accepted way to behave.'

Her praise stayed with him and helped give him courage to face the unknown, not to mention the huge responsibility that was his alone: to find the four heirs somewhere in a distant foreign land.

He and Mr Featherworth were travelling First Class on the train, something Zachary hadn't thought he'd ever do. As he took a seat, he was even more thankful for his new clothes because the other passengers were well dressed. They spoke to one another quietly, their accents very different from his.

He made a solemn vow as the train drew away from Outham station that he would bring the Blake sisters safely back here and prove himself worthy of the trust being placed in him.

Mr Featherworth got into conversation with the gentleman next to him and Zachary, sitting by the window, listened to them chatting about the poor widowed Queen, wondering if she'd ever take up her public duties properly again.

Excitement humming through him, he stared out of the window at an England he'd never seen before.

★ ★ ★

Alice went to see Mr Featherworth the day after she moved in to ask that the housekeeping money be given directly to her from now on. Since the lawyer was away, his clerk received her.

Mr Dawson stared at her in surprise when she explained the purpose of her visit. 'The money's

40

always delivered to the house each week, not to the shop. I send the office boy with it. Prebble pays the wages out of the takings, but we keep the shop and house expenses separate.'

'Dot never receives any money. She says Harry Prebble takes care of everything.'

Mr Dawson rang a handbell and when a lad tapped on the door and came in, asked, 'What have you been doing with the money I've been sending to Dot at Blake's, Sidney?'

'Harry said to give it to him, Mr Dawson. He's been providing the food for her from the shop.'

'Has he, indeed. And did he make an accounting to you of how the money had been spent?'

'Yes, sir. Every week, sir.'

'Fetch the account books, if you please, and say nothing of this to anyone, least of all Prebble.'

The lad was back in less than a minute, looking worried. He set the account book in front of his employer and opened it at the most recent weekly page. 'I check the lists he gives me carefully before entering them, exactly as you've shown me.'

'I'm sure you do. I just want to check something.' Mr Dawson beckoned to Miss Blair and opened the book sideways on the desk so that they could both see it. 'This is an account of what has been spent each week. Would you know whether these items have been given to Dot?'

She studied it. 'Unless she's lying, and I don't think that girl has a bad bone in her body, there's one regular item here that she's never received

41

— biscuits. I'd have to ask her about the rest to be certain, but she and I checked the pantry together and it isn't all that well stocked. I had to spend some of my own money to buy a cake yesterday.'

He frowned down at the account book as she sat back in her seat. 'I'd be grateful if you'd not say anything about this until Mr Featherworth returns from London. In the meantime, I'll give you five pounds and you can stock up on what you need. It's your own business whether you buy from Blake's or elsewhere.'

'I'll keep careful accounts.'

'That would be best. And I'll make certain the lad gives the weekly housekeeping money to you from now on. If the amount we've agreed on isn't adequate, please let us know.'

'I'm sure it will be. I'm not a big eater.'

'In the meantime, you and Dot can start making the inventory, as agreed, even the items in the attic, if you'd be so kind. Everything will have to be shared equally between the four sisters, so we must do that as fairly as we can.'

When he rose to escort her to the outer door, he said with a smile, 'I hope you'll be happy in Outham, Miss Blair. And please don't think I'm being impudent, but my sister was wondering if you'd care to take tea with us one Saturday. She doesn't like to think of you knowing no one in town apart from your cousin, and I know Mrs Rainey is a very busy woman.'

'How very kind of your sister! I'd love to come to tea.'

She walked back, tired now, because she still

hadn't fully recovered from her long tussle with influenza, but much heartened by that interview.

She didn't want to deal with Prebble more than she had to. For all his politeness, there was something about him that made her feel uneasy. And he'd looked at her clothes with a scornful curl to his lip this morning, as if judging the price of every garment.

If he wanted a fight, though, she'd give him one. An uppity young fellow definitely wasn't going to dictate how she spent her food allowance or know where every penny went. She wasn't being paid wages, just bed and board, but she had some savings and this would give her time to recover fully before she sought another job.

She sighed. She didn't want to leave Outham again, but needs must. She wasn't going to be a burden to her cousins.

★ ★ ★

London was so big, Zachary was grateful to have Mr Featherworth there to show him how to get about such a big, bustling place.

They stayed in a hotel, another new experience, and ate their evening meal there. He'd have called it 'tea' but people here called it dinner. To him, dinner was the midday meal. He watched the lawyer closely and followed his example, breathing a sigh of relief after getting through the meal without making a fool of himself. When he thought about it later, he couldn't even remember what he'd eaten.

43

He had trouble getting to sleep, not only through excitement but because the streets outside seemed full of people and vehicles until a late hour. He couldn't help worrying that tomorrow or the day after he'd be going on board the ship and after that, he'd have no one to show him how to behave. He grew angry with himself then. He had a tongue in his head, didn't he?

The next morning after breakfast Mr Featherworth clapped him on the shoulder. 'Let's go and buy the final few items now.'

The area near the docks was even busier than the streets round the hotel, and the ship's chandler's was a vast echoing place, which made Blake's Emporium seem very small in contrast, though the latter was the largest shop in Outham.

In the chandler's they inspected ship's kits, which contained all sorts of bits and pieces, like blankets, a bucket or cooking pots. But Mr Featherworth said Zachary's food would be provided and he'd already sent bedding to the ship. 'Kits like these are for steerage passengers. Have you no kits suitable for cabin passengers?'

The man looked at him in puzzlement, then at Zachary. 'They usually take everything they need with them, sir. Is it you who's going on the ship?'

'No. It's my young friend, who has had to make this journey suddenly to help one of my clients and therefore hasn't had time to sort out all the equipment needed. We were told you'd help. Perhaps you could advise us?'

'I'd be happy to, sir.'

44

Zachary was disgusted to see a coin exchange hands. He'd think shame to need bribing to do his job in the shop, and what was this place but a glorified shop?

'I'd suggest taking along some treats, because the food can get monotonous, even for cabin class travellers — nuts, pickles, jam, dried fruit, that sort of thing. All food should be kept in tins or jars to prevent pests eating it.'

He studied Zachary again, not an approving glance, in spite of the bribe he'd received. 'Do you have a straw hat, sir. No? Well, you'll need one because of the heat near the Equator. I'd recommend buying two, as they sometimes blow overboard. And have you enough pairs of socks? I'd say you need three dozen at least. And marine soap, for use with salt water.'

Mr Featherworth was looking surprised, so Zachary said hastily, 'Surely I'll not need any more clothes? Are there no facilities for washing those I have?'

'The stewards will do that for you, but you'll need to pay them for doing it.'

The lawyer hummed and hawed, but they came away with yet more goods and clothes.

'I'll try to be very economical with my travelling money,' Zachary said as they walked away with a lad following them pushing the new possessions in a handcart.

'Not too economical,' Mr Featherworth said firmly, 'or you'll not fit in, nor will the young ladies on the way back.'

The following morning they went to the shipping agent to find out when the cabin

45

passengers were boarding and found it was that very day.

Zachary was thoughtful as they took a cab back to the hotel.

'You're very quiet. Is something wrong?'

He looked at the lawyer. 'No. Well, not exactly. But you've spent a lot of money on me, and you're trusting me with more. I'm praying that I'll not let you down.'

The older man laid one hand on his shoulder and gave it a quick, friendly squeeze. 'I've learned that people can only do their best, Zachary. No one can ever do more than that.'

'You know I'll try my hardest.'

'I'd not be sending you if I didn't have confidence in you.'

That thought heartened him greatly as they went to fetch his luggage. As he boarded the ship, he turned at the top of the gangplank and saw the lawyer watching him. A final wave and Mr Featherworth was gone.

Zachary squared his shoulders and followed the steward across the deck, twisting his way between crates and boxes, busy sailors and people who looked even more apprehensive than he felt.

Where were the convicts? he wondered. Would they be dreadful, ruffianly types? And would the cabin passengers look down on him because of the way he spoke? Once they got under way, would he be seasick?

He grinned suddenly. In spite of all his worries, he had never felt so free since his father died. This was an adventure and he meant to enjoy every minute of it.

★ ★ ★

Zachary was dismayed when he saw how small the cabin was. It had two bunks, one above the other, with a small washstand attached to the wall at the far end, leaving a narrow space beside it, partly behind the bunks, where they could presumably put their cabin luggage. There were two drawers underneath the lower bunk and a bucket and chamber pot inside the wash stand, both with covers and set securely into holes in the shelves.

There was barely enough room for a man as tall as him to get into and out of the lower bunk. The cabin door opened straight on to the deck, where a few well-dressed people (presumably the first class cabin passengers) were standing or sitting. Crew members worked or moved around them, hurrying about their duties, and down on the main deck there were piles of boxes, crates and more crew members.

The steward who had shown him to the cabin was very attentive and offered him a great deal of information about how the ship would function once it was under way. 'I'm Portis, sir, and I'll be in charge of the deck cabins, so if you need anything, you have only to ask.'

Primed by Mr Featherworth, Zachary gave him half a crown and thanked him for his help, though it went against the grain to give away money for nothing after so many years of frugality.

The coin vanished quickly into a pocket. 'Thank you, sir. I'll just show you the dining room, which is also the day area, though passengers mostly sit on deck unless the weather is inclement. After that, I must get back to work.'

Portis led the way into a room which had a large table in the centre, a table that was fixed to the floor, and chairs attached to the walls when not in use by hooks and sturdy leather straps.

He saw Zachary staring at them. 'You won't want chairs flying around when it's rough, will you, sir?'

'Er — no.'

'I'd advise you to make sure everything in your cabin is either in a drawer or in your portmanteau. If you leave things lying around, they're likely to get broken or damaged, even in moderately rough weather.

A man standing at the other end of the room stared at them as if he didn't like what he saw.

'Ah, Mr Gleesome. May I introduce you to Mr Carr, one of your fellow passengers. How is Mrs Gleesome feeling now?'

'Still not so well. I hope she'll get used to the motion of the ship.'

'I'm sure she will, sir.'

Gleesome nodded to them and wandered out, looking harassed and worried.

The steward winked at Zachary. 'A delicate lady, Mrs Gleesome, as you'll find. She'll have no choice but to get used to it once we leave, though. The ship turns back for no one.'

'Are many people seasick?'

'Some are. I always say you have to set your mind to it that you're not going to give in, then even if you feel a trifle nauseous, you soon recover. Let's hope you're one of the lucky ones who don't get seasick.' He gave a wry smile. 'It makes my job easier.'

Zachary went to stand by the rail and watch the busy scene on the dock. When he returned to the cabin, he found a young man standing there looking upset. The stranger appeared to be about twenty, was dressed as a gentleman but had a broad face with a childish expression that sat ill with the fine clothes. He was as tall as Zachary but much more muscular, looking physically strong. But his face — well, if Zachary hadn't known better, he'd have said the man was one of those who never really grew up, who had a childish mind in a man's body. Surely not? If he was like that, what was he doing on board a ship on his own? Or perhaps he had family in another cabin?

They studied one another for a moment and when the newcomer didn't speak, he held out one hand. 'I'm Zachary Carr. Are you sharing this cabin with me?'

'Yes. I'm Leopold Hutton, but people usually call me Leo. I don't like being called Leopold. My mother always calls me Leo, whatever *he* says.' He blinked as if close to tears at the mention of his mother and looked round. 'It's a very small bedroom.'

'Yes.' Zachary glanced down ruefully at himself. 'And we're both a bit tall for squashing into small places. Which bunk do you want?'

'The top one.'

'So do I. Tell you what, we'll toss a coin for it.'

The other nodded but made no move to take a

coin out of his pocket, just waited for Zachary to take the lead.

He lost the toss, so had to make do with the bottom bunk and studied it grimly, sitting on it and bouncing up and down on the hard mattress. He couldn't imagine how he'd sleep in such a cramped space.

'I've never been on a ship before,' Leo volunteered.

'Neither have I.'

'What did you do before you came here?'

'Worked in a grocery store.' He didn't intend to pretend to be what he wasn't, so added, 'I got a job there when I was a lad. I was one of the lucky ones and didn't have to go into the mill. Have you ever seen a cotton mill?'

'No. You started work when you were a boy?'

'Yes, twelve. What do you do with yourself?'

Now the tears did flow. 'I used to live with my mother. We were happy. Then she married my stepfather and he doesn't like me to be with them.'

'Oh. Is that why you're going to Australia?'

Silence then, '*He* said it'd make a man of me.'

'What did your mother say?'

'She cried a lot, but she always does as *he* tells her.' Leo began to sniffle, pulling out a handkerchief and mopping his face. But the tears kept flowing.

Dear heaven! Zachary thought. He *is* like a child. What's going on here? He patted the other on the shoulder and it seemed to help because Leo managed to stop crying.

'Men shouldn't cry. *He* gets angry if I cry. But

50

I want my mother. When I don't know what to do, she always tells me.' He stuffed the handkerchief in his pocket any old how, making a bulge in the beautifully tailored coat. 'Why are you going to Australia? Do you know what to do on a ship?'

'I've been sent by a lawyer to find the new owners of the store where I work. Their uncle died and the store belongs to them now, but they don't know about it. They'll have to come back to England.'

He had to explain this a couple more time before Leo seemed to understand. 'Shall we take it in turns to unpack? I'll go first, if you like and you can sit on your bunk out of the way.'

'All right.' Docile as a pet puppy, Leo climbed up on to the bunk and lay propped on one elbow, watching his companion with staring, pale blue eyes.

Zachary went to work. After placing his precious writing desk cabin on the floor he put his portmanteau on the lower bunk and unpacked his shirts, laying them carefully in the drawer, trying not to crease them. They nearly filled it. It wouldn't matter if his underclothing got crumpled, he felt, but the shirts would be on view to everyone. He worked awkwardly because when he knelt down, his feet touched the wall of the cabin behind him. He wished he had his mother's ability to make clothes lie tidily with a few pats of the hand.

All the time Leo watched him, sitting up now with one leg dangling over the edge of the bunk.

After a while Zachary decided he'd done as

much as he could. 'I think I'll take a walk round the deck. That'll leave you more space to unpack.'

Leo frowned. 'I've never unpacked anything before.'

'You can't leave your clothes in your portmanteau or they'll get crumpled.'

Still the other didn't move. Sighing, Zachary took charge. 'I'll show you how to do it.'

The relief on Leo's face was marked, then it was replaced by a frown. 'I can learn how to do things if you show me a few times. I can. I don't forget once I *really* know how to do something. My mother says I learn slowly, but I learn well if people will just have patience.'

There must have been some mistake, Zachary decided. How could anyone have sent this lad — and Leo wasn't really more than a lad, for all his man's body — out to Australia on his own?

'Get down and I'll show you what to do.' It took a while and Leo made no suggestions of his own, but he tried hard to learn how to fold his shirts, tongue sticking out at one corner of his mouth. As he'd said, it took several times of showing to teach him, but Zachary patiently went over and over it. Such a simple act, folding a shirt, but it had taken all of half an hour to teach his companion how to do it.

After they'd finished, Leo stood waiting expectantly.

'I'm going up on deck for some fresh air.'

'Can I come with you?'

Zachary didn't really want company as he took his bearings, but it'd be like treading on a puppy to refuse. Somehow he had to speak to the

52

steward privately and ask to see the ship's doctor about Leo. There must have been some mistake. A person like that poor lad couldn't possibly cope on his own.

Leo thrust his hands deep into his pockets. 'I wish my mother was here.'

'Don't start crying again.'

Leo blinked furiously and managed to keep the tears back.

Up on deck they stood by the rail staring out at the water they were soon to cross. So much water, Zachary thought, and when they left England they'd be out of the sight of land for a long time. It'd be best to keep busy so that time didn't drag. Mr Featherworth had found out that classes were often held on long voyages and Zachary intended to go to as many as he could. He loved learning new things.

'My mother cried when she said goodbye,' Leo said suddenly. 'My stepfather pulled her away from me. When he brought me to the ship, he said good riddance and don't come back.' His thick lower lip stuck out mulishly. 'I *am* going back, though, to see my mother. *She* said I could one day.'

'What will you do in Australia?'

'I'm going to work for a man my stepfather knows.'

'What's his name?'

'I don't know.'

'Will this man be meeting you when we arrive?'

Leo still looked puzzled. 'I don't know.'

'Didn't anyone tell you what to do when you get there?'

'My stepfather said I'd soon find out how to stand on my own feet.' He looked down with a frown as if he took that literally. 'Do they stand differently in Australia? Where is Australia? I've never been there before.'

They talked for a little longer, then Leo lay back and was soon dozing. Zachary slipped out of the cabin and found the steward. 'I have to see the doctor. It's urgent.'

'Are you ill?'

'No. It's something else.'

'Dr Crawford can't see anyone till after the ship's sailed unless they're ill. He has a lot to do.'

'Can I see the Captain, then?'

The steward frowned. 'Could I ask why, sir?'

'It's about my cabin mate. I'm sure there's been some mistake. He's no more fit to go to Australia on his own than a baby is.'

'Oh, you don't need to worry about that. I'll be keeping an eye on him, sir. His stepfather put me in charge of him, paid me well too.'

'Is someone meeting him at the other end?'

'I believe so, but I don't know the details. Not my business, once we've arrived. Now, sir, once we've left London, we have to go to Portland to pick up the convicts. The Captain and crew are all busy, so I'd be grateful if you'd let us get on with our work.'

Zachary wasn't satisfied and debated going to look for the doctor or one of the ship's officers, but he was unused to the way things were run and didn't like to make a fuss. It wasn't really any of his business. After all, the stepfather had at least made arrangements to have Leo looked after on board ship and to be met when they arrived in Australia.

Surely the ship's doctor knew what Leo was like?

3

Mr Featherworth arrived back in Outham on the Tuesday evening, to be greeted by a hailstorm. Wishing he too could spend some time in a warmer climate, he sat shivering in the cab as the horse clopped past the gas lamps that lit the streets in the better parts of town.

He was glad to be home again, feeling satisfied he'd done the best he could for his clients. It was a matter of waiting now and looking after their inheritance, but he felt sure that young man would bring the Blake sisters back safely.

When he went to his rooms the following day, it was his clerk who brought in his morning tea tray, not the office lad, a sure sign that Ralph Dawson wanted to discuss something with him. Well, his clerk had been with him a long time and could be relied on not to make mountains out of molehills, so it usually paid to listen to him. 'Why don't you fetch a cup and join me?'

When they were seated on either side of the fire, Ralph said abruptly, 'Something's cropped up with Prebble.'

'Oh?'

'It looks like he's been taking the money you sent to Dot and supplying her with food from the shop.'

'Is there anything wrong with that? You told me he keeps meticulous accounts. Does what he lists seems unreasonable?'

'No, it doesn't, but there's at least one item showing weekly — and every week too — which Dot has never received: a pound of plain biscuits. Miss Blair drew that to my attention when I showed her the recent accounts. She's going to check them with Dot and will let us know later this morning which items really were given to the maid.'

Mr Featherworth's heart sank. The thought of dealing with a dishonest employee, perhaps having to dismiss him, made him shudder. If Harry Prebble turned out to be a thief, how was he to find someone to run the shop until Carr returned, which wouldn't be for seven months or more? What did a lawyer know about the grocery business? 'I'm sure there will be some reasonable explanation.'

Ralph gave him a disbelieving look.

'You don't think so?'

'I've never liked Prebble, sir, you know that, which is why I urged you to find someone reliable to occupy the living quarters.'

'We need him.'

'We need someone to run the shop. *He* isn't the only person who could do it. An older man would be more reliable. We could still advertise for a manager in the Manchester newspaper, as I suggested we do in the first place, if you remember.'

Mr Featherworth wriggled uncomfortably in his seat. 'A stranger wouldn't know how things are organised and it's not for us to make a permanent appointment. That's the owners' job. I'd — um — better speak to Prebble, I suppose.'

'May I be present when you do, sir?'

'Yes. Definitely. I shall welcome your support. Send a message asking him to call this afternoon at two o'clock. And bring me the information Miss Blair sends as soon as it arrives. Oh dear, dear, dear! What a thing to happen!'

He watched the clerk finish his cup of tea and leave the room. Ralph came from a good family which had fallen on hard times, so hadn't had an easy life. This had made him wary, a wariness that had paid off more than once in their dealings with clients. Mr Featherworth didn't know what he'd do without his clerk. But one had to be careful about accusing a man of stealing.

The trouble was . . . Mr Featherworth sighed and admitted to himself that he didn't really like Prebble, either, not now he'd got to know him better. He'd not have appointed him as temporary manager if Zachary hadn't been the best man to send to Australia to bring back the heirs.

But surely there would be some explanation for the anomalies?

★　★　★

The *Clara* sailed from London on 11th January, heading for Portland, where it would pick up the convicts who, with their guards and the guards' families, made up the largest group of passengers. The felons had their own space on the ship and wouldn't be allowed to mingle with the other passengers, of course.

58

Zachary stood by the rail, hatless, enjoying the sea breeze lifting his hair. Within minutes Leo came across to stand next to him.

Today the normally talkative lad was very quiet.

'Is something the matter?'

He shrugged and rubbed the toe of his shoe against the edge of the planking.

'Tell me,' Zachary insisted.

'Someone said it.'

'Said what?'

'That I'm a half-wit.'

Zachary didn't know how to answer that but could see Leo was upset.

'My stepfather used to call me a half-wit all the time. And it's true. I can't even read. My mother tried to teach me and I wanted to learn. I did! Only I couldn't do it. All I'm good at is looking after horses and animals.'

'Who said you were a half-wit?'

Leo shrugged. 'Doesn't matter. I have to walk away when people say it. That's what my mother told me to do. She doesn't like me getting into fights, because even if I win, I get in trouble afterwards. So I don't fight any more.'

What sort of life had this poor creature led? 'I don't like fights, either,' Zachary said carefully. 'They only decide who's strongest, not who's right.'

Leo nodded but it was clear this subtlety was beyond his comprehension. He was in low spirits for the rest of the day and it was noticeable that at meal times he avoided the Gleesomes, so it was likely one of them had insulted him.

59

Zachary felt a surge of anger. He waited till later, knowing Mr Gleesome always smoked a cigar on deck after the evening meal while his wife gossiped with the other ladies.

Telling Leo to stay in the saloon, he followed the older man on deck. 'Was it you who upset Leo today?'

Gleesome swung round. 'What's it to do with you?'

'He's a friend of mine and not able to defend himself.'

'Mind your own damned business or I'll report you to the Captain for threatening me.'

Zachary gaped at him. 'I'm not threatening you. But if you don't leave Leo alone, it'll be *me* who's reporting you to the Captain.'

'A half-wit shouldn't be allowed to travel with gentlefolk. What if he attacks my wife?'

'Why should he do that?'

'Who knows why half-wits do anything? Now leave me alone.' He stormed away to stand by the rail on the other side.

A man moved out of the shadows and came to stand beside Zachary. His stomach tightened in apprehension as he saw it was the doctor. Had speaking out landed him in trouble?

Dr Crawford held out his hand. 'Well done.'

Zachary shook it, not sure why he was being congratulated.

'I heard Gleesome taunting that poor fellow earlier and was going to speak to him myself.'

'Well, let's hope he'll leave Leo alone from now on.'

'We'll make sure he does. He's right about one

thing, however: that young man clearly hasn't got all his wits. I doubt he's a danger to anyone, though. I've seen others like him.'

'I've been trying to speak to you about him. Did you know what Leo was like before he came on board?'

'No. They slipped him past me or I'd have refused to let him travel on his own. I did speak to the Captain, but he knows the father and told me not to interfere. Has Leo said anything about his family?'

'He seems fond of his mother but he's terrified of his stepfather.'

'What that lad needs is a simple job in the country.'

'He says he's good with animals.'

'There you are, then. I daresay you could keep a bit of an eye on him while he's on board ship.'

'I'm not responsible for him.'

The doctor smiled. 'I've seen how patiently you deal with him. I'd stake good money that you don't get rid of him until we arrive in Australia. If you need help, if Gleesome or anyone else gives you any trouble, call on me. I'll back you up.'

He strolled off and Zachary watched him go with a sinking heart. How could he attend classes with Leo by his side every minute? Or get into conversation with people? He'd seen how they avoided Leo, especially the women.

This was not going to be an easy journey.

★ ★ ★

After breakfast Alice asked Dot to sit with her at the dining table. 'We need to go through the accounts for the food you've received.'

The young maid looked at her in surprise. 'But I don't deal with the money, miss. It's Mr Prebble you need to speak to.'

'I just want to check a few things, so that I can change the order from now on.'

Dot's face cleared. 'Oh. I see, miss.' She took the chair next to Alice.

She was soon frowning as she read painstakingly through the lists, one finger tracing each word as she sounded it out. 'I think these are someone else's accounts, miss. I've never had no biscuits, nor no ham neither. Not that I'm complaining. I've et well enough. And the weights are different. I don't get that much flour and sugar.'

'Tell me exactly which items are different.'

Dot went through it again, saying how much she received each week, and Alice noted the amounts down.

'Perhaps these aren't the right lists, miss?'

'I'll check with the lawyer. Don't mention it to Prebble in case you're right. We don't want to upset him over a simple mistake, do we?'

'No, we don't, miss. He can be a bit sharp-like sometimes.'

'Can he? Well, he'd better not get sharp with me. Now, please carry on with your work, Dot. I have to go out for a while. I'll bring back something for dinner.'

'Not from the shop?'

'There's a market in town today, isn't there?

Some things will be cheaper there, and certainly fresher.'

'Ye-es. But Mr Prebble won't be best pleased. He says the shop's paying my wages, so it's only fair for me to buy everything from them. He sends out to the greengrocer's if I want fruit and vegetables. I mostly don't bother.'

'Just tell him I've taken over dealing with food from now on, and I like to eat a lot of vegetables and fruit, the fresher the better.' She fixed Dot with a firm glance, the one she'd used to quell unruly pupils.

'Very well, miss.'

She sounded so relieved that Alice stared at her. 'Are you afraid of him?'

Dot wriggled. 'Not afraid, exactly. But I wouldn't like to upset him.'

'From now on, you should be more concerned about upsetting me than Prebble. But I hope you won't be afraid of me.'

'No, miss. I was afraid of Mrs Blake sometimes when she acted strange, but I like working for you, because you talk to me and tell me things and I know where I stand. It got a bit lonely when I was here on my own and I kept thinking I heard noises downstairs at night. It was just my imagination, though, because nothing was ever taken.' Dot beamed at her as she stood up. 'I'll do the living room while you're out, shall I?'

What a nice willing girl she was, Alice thought as she went to put on her bonnet. She walked slowly along the main street to the lawyer's rooms with the accounts in her shopping basket, glad the storm had blown over. There was no warmth in the January sun, but its cheerful brightness still made you feel better.

Mr Dawson showed her straight in to see Mr Featherworth and stayed with them. When Alice explained what she'd found out, the lawyer made little distressed sounds and didn't seem to know what to do.

The clerk bent over the lists. 'Not a lot taken each week, but it'll mount up. And if Miss Blair hadn't noticed anything, no one would be any the wiser.'

'Perhaps there's some explanation?'

Ralph fixed his employer with a stern gaze. 'If there is, sir, we need to hear it.'

★   ★   ★

As Alice walked along to the market, she hoped Prebble would be dismissed. She didn't like the thought that he had a key to the whole building, which meant he had easy access to where she was living. She'd have felt better if there was a door that locked between the living quarters and the rear of the shop.

She soon forgot him in the cheerful bustle of the market. Even during hard times like this, there was still fresh farm food available for those with money. Her basket was soon so full she had to buy a string bag as well. She was particularly looking forward to eating the crumbly white cheese and the jam made by farmers' wives. In the end she decided to find a lad to help her carry the things back.

It was a man whom the stallholder summoned, after a whispered, 'He's out of work, miss, hope you don't mind? He'll only expect the same money as a lad would.'

'I'm happy to have his help.'

The man looked gaunt and when they got back he was puffing a little. She gave him a shilling and he stared at it as if he'd never seen one before.

'It's too much, miss.'

'Do you have a family?'

He nodded.

'Then take it for their sake.'

He drew himself up. 'Only for their sake. I'm not strong enough to do the stone breaking, so I have to take what jobs I can.'

'If you've nothing better to do, I'll be going to the market at the same time next week, and would appreciate help with my baskets.'

He nodded, raised one hand and walked off, the tired, slouching gait of a man with no energy to spare.

That encounter decided her. She would definitely help her cousin with the relief work now she was feeling better. Well, she would do once the inventory was completed. It was going to take longer than she'd expected, because Mrs Blake had been a hoarder. She'd have to ask Mr Dawson whether she should clear out the dead woman's drawers ready for the new occupants. Not a pleasant task, but someone had to do it.

As she turned to go inside, she saw Prebble watching her through the shop window.

She wasn't surprised when Dot came up a

short time later to say he'd asked to see her. 'Show him up.'

She didn't ask him to sit down.

'I noticed you'd been to the market, Miss Blair.'

She inclined her head and waited.

'And I couldn't help noticing that some of the things you'd purchased are items we sell in the shop, jars of jam, for instance.'

How had he seen that? The jam had been at the bottom of her basket. Had he dared to go and poke around in her kitchen? He must have done. It was the only way he'd have been able to see some of the items. She held back her annoyance, hoping it didn't show in her face. 'I don't consider that to be any concern of yours, Prebble.'

'I beg to differ, Miss Blair. We're both employed by the shop, have a duty to be loyal to it, and — '

'I'm not answerable to you for what I do, Prebble, so if that's all you wanted to see me about, you can go back to your work. *I* certainly have things to do.'

His expression was stormy for a moment or two, then it became glassy, as if he was hiding his feelings.

But though he wasn't a large man, he radiated such menace she was glad to see him go. She could see why the young maid was afraid of him and was thankful the bedroom she slept in had a lock on the door, because the open access from the shop still worried her. Dot said it had been the bedroom the master slept in towards the end

66

and he'd always locked the door too 'because Mrs Blake did wander sometimes'.

The events that led to Mrs Blake being locked away were still so vivid in Dot's mind that every now and then she shared a memory with Alice. It didn't paint a picture of a happy household. And it was thought that the madwoman had had her own husband killed, though no one had been able to prove that or catch the person who did it for her.

★ ★ ★

It was another hot day, with the sort of heat none of them had ever experienced until they came to Australia. Pandora stopped work to wipe her sweaty brow with her forearm. She was glad of the awning Reece had built to shade the outdoor table that was used for both cooking preparations and eating. She was making damper and her sister Cassandra was chopping potatoes to put in a stew.

It was hard working in such heat, though her sister didn't seem upset by it. And as for Reece, he positively loved the warmth. The Southerhams stayed out of the sun during the middle of the day. Lucky them! She wished she could do the same.

The food they ate was fairly monotonous, though they'd now brought back quite a few much-needed ingredients from the shop on the highway, which was close to where their other two sisters lived. To call a dusty track a highway had surprised them both. The track was quite narrow, with an occasional wider part. Kevin next door said this was where the wheels of wagons made deep ruts in winter so that other drivers took their vehicles to one side to keep to firmer ground.

The track led all the way down to a port called Albany on the south coast, about three hundred miles from Perth. Mail to England was sent from there because of the sheltered anchorage, which seemed strange when most of the population of the colony lived in and around Perth.

'I'm looking forward to living with Kevin. He's so interesting to talk to.' Cassandra scooped the potato pieces off the chopping board into a bowl.

'Reece seems fond of him.'

'I am too. I don't care if he was once a convict. He's kind and helpful, and that's what matters. Reece is building an extra bedroom for us on the side of Kevin's wooden house. There was a spare bedroom, but it was tiny, so he's removing the inner wall to that, which will make the living area bigger.'

Pandora suppressed an envious sigh. She didn't think she'd ever get used to living under canvas, or to the horrible insects and creeping things that joined them there. She lived in terror of finding a snake in her bed. Kevin said Australian snakes were very poisonous and some could kill you with one bite. She checked her bedding every night before she lay down because her bed was only a straw mattresses on a piece of old canvas. Reece said he'd build her a wooden bed frame before winter. She didn't like to trouble him to ask for it earlier because he worked from dawn to dusk every day.

'Have you decided what you're going to wear for the wedding, Cassandra?'

'The dress I wore at Christmas. It hides this better than my others do.' She laid one hand briefly on her expanding belly.

'I've got a lace collar you can borrow.'

'The one on your blue dress? Won't you need it yourself?'

'I'm not the person getting married, am I?'

'Thank you. I will borrow it, then. I do want to look as nice as I can.' Her face briefly took on the blissful glow it got when she spoke of marrying Reece, then the smile faded and she looked at her sister in concern. 'I keep worrying about how you'll go on when you're alone here afterwards?'

'I'll be fine.'

'You could look for another job if you're unhappy. Something closer to the twins, perhaps.'

'I'd rather stay near you. Truly.' She patted the lump of dough into shape and thumped it down into the second of the pair of heavy bread tins they'd persuaded the Southerhams to buy. 'There. That's done. I'm sick of making soda bread every day. Do you remember how easy it was when we just popped round to the baker's for a loaf?'

'Yes. But it's different here, with the nearest shop an hour's cart ride away. If we want to eat bread we have to make it. And at least we have a proper stove to cook on now.'

'Mrs Southerham didn't provide very well

when it came to food supplies and cooking utensils, did she?'

Cassandra looked over her shoulder to make sure no one was near. 'They're the most impractical pair. Why on earth they wanted to become settlers, I can't think. If Mr Southerham didn't have Reece to help him, he'd be in serious trouble. Once Reece has served the agreed time to pay back his fare to Australia, we're going to set up on our own and I can't think what Mr Southerham will do then. We've arranged for my work to be taken off what Reece owes them, a day of my work cancels out half a day of his. Mr Southerham didn't like that, but he didn't have much choice. Reece told him straight out he wouldn't let his wife work for nothing.'

'Why they think women's work isn't worth as much as men's, I'll never know,' Pandora said. She checked the beans that had been soaking overnight. 'I'll put these on to cook now, shall I? Thank goodness for dried peas and beans.'

'And tins of jam. We eat a lot of bread and jam here, don't we? I just wish there was more fruit and vegetables. Kevin's got a lemon tree and he grows melons, too. But he only put in enough for himself this year. Reece says he'll bring us a slice or two. They're delicious. There are grape vines too, but they've not fruited yet.'

'At least we get plenty of fresh meat. It's so easy for Mr Southerham to go out and kill a kangaroo. He's a very good shot.'

She'd managed to speak quite cheerfully this morning, Pandora thought as they separated to continue their work. She was getting better at hiding her homesickness. Maybe one day it'd fade completely.

It hadn't done so far.

★　★　★

Cassandra watched her younger sister put the second tin of dough into the oven, then clear up the mess of flour from the table top. Pandora's homesickness was no better, she could tell that. But her sister was trying so hard to hide it and what good would it do to keep mentioning it?

They must just hope she'd settle down as time passed and lose those dark shadows under her eyes. Once they started attending the monthly church services at the shop, they'd meet some eligible young men, surely. Cassandra's dearest wish was for her three sisters to fall in love and get married, then all of them settle close to one another.

There were supposed to be ten men for every woman here in the Swan River Colony, so it wasn't an impossible dream, surely?

It was three years now since Pandora's fiancé had died. Her youngest sister seemed to have got over losing Bill. Time she found someone else.

At least here in Australia they were all safe from their aunt. That was what mattered. If the price of staying alive was a few months' unhappiness for Pandora till she settled down here, then it was well worth it.

4

Harry watched Mr Featherworth and decided the old fellow was nervous. Now, why? What did they want to see him for today, anyway?

The lawyer cleared his throat. 'We're concerned that there are some — um, anomalies in the accounts for groceries supplied to the maid.'

Damn! How had they found that out? Well, good thing he'd been ready for any eventuality. These two silly old fools would never catch him out. The clerk was looking at him as if expecting the worst. Harry deliberately kept them waiting for an answer.

'The biscuits, for instance, and the amounts of flour and sugar supplied,' Ralph prompted. 'They don't tally with what Dot received.'

Harry gave him a slow, confident smile and saw him blink in surprise. 'No, they don't.'

'You admit it?'

'Yes. I've been doing it to save money for the new owners. I can give you the real accounts, which will show how much I've saved. What you've been giving that maid was too generous.'

Both men were frowning at him. He didn't understand people like them. Were they so stupid they wanted to spend more of their clients' money than they needed? They must be. Why else would they have sent Zachary to Australia cabin class. Harry hated the thought of that lanky idiot living in luxury on the Blake sisters' money, because Harry had plans for that money himself. He intended to woo one of them, and get the rest to appoint him manager permanently. He'd do whatever it took to achieve that. He tried again to explain.

'Dot didn't need such a generous provision of food, Mr Featherworth. She's only a small woman. If she'd complained of being hungry, I'd have increased what I gave her, but she didn't, not once. I asked her if she was satisfied and she said yes. You can check that with her. So I've saved money for the owners already and would have saved more if you hadn't appointed Miss Blair to live over the shop. There really was no need for that. I'd been keeping an eye on Dot, making sure she did her work properly.'

He waited, but they said nothing.

He pushed it a bit further, getting in a shot at the governess, whom he was determined to get rid of. 'I'm disappointed to see that Miss Blair isn't loyal to those who're keeping her, very disappointed. Only this morning she went shopping at the market instead of with us and when I suggested she confine certain purchases to the shop, she refused even to consider it.'

Mr Dawson drew himself up. 'What Miss Blair does with her money is none of your concern, Prebble. Am I not right, Mr Featherworth?'

'You are indeed. A lady like her can be trusted to make her own choices and decisions.'

Lady! thought Harry. She wasn't what he called a lady, just a scraggy old spinster, the sort that poked her nose in where it wasn't wanted. He realised Dawson was still speaking and began to wonder if he was the one who really ran this business, not old Featherworth. How could that be? Dawson dressed neatly but modestly and deferred to his employer all the time. But two or three times today the lawyer had looked at his clerk as if for guidance.

'If what you claim is correct, can you show me the real accounts?' Dawson asked sharply.

'Yes, of course.'

'I'll come back with you now and check them. If you agree, of course, Mr Featherworth?'

The lawyer nodded, frowned at Harry then turned back to his clerk, his expression softening as if he was speaking to a friend. They all stuck together, those who hadn't had to struggle for a living. Stuck-up snobs! Harry enjoyed scoring off them. That was why he'd taken the money at first, to show them he could manage things better than they could. And if they'd not found out about it, he'd have kept it. He had a few little sidelines bringing him in extra money. These two old men would have a fit if they knew half of what he got up to.

He'd find another way to prove to the new owners how capable he was, though, so that they thought well of him. If he got what he wanted out of all this, he'd not keep Featherworth as *his* lawyer.

'I'll leave you to deal with this matter, then, Dawson.'

That old man is soft, doesn't like unpleasantness, Harry thought as he walked back to the shop with Mr Dawson. This one is the fellow to watch.

74

He tried to chat but stopped when the clerk showed no signs of responding with more than the occasional nod or shrug.

In the small office just off the packing room at the rear of the shop — a place where he loved to sit and contemplate his new kingdom — Harry took the special account book down from the top shelf and passed it to Mr Dawson with a flourish.

Pity to lose this money. He'd had a savings bank account for a while now and had been looking forward to increasing the amount in it. He'd find other ways of rewarding himself for his hard work, though, now that he'd seen how easy it was to fool people.

Well, he always had taken the odd packet of this and that, and no one had ever noticed. He sold them to his family cheaply, and they knew how to keep their mouths shut. Let alone Prebbles always stuck together, they got good food more cheaply from him. He wasn't greedy, only took the odd packet, but it all mounted up, as his savings book showed. He loved looking at the total.

When the clerk had finished studying the books, Harry got down the small cash box and held it out. 'You'll find the money I saved there. I was going to give it to the new owners to show how well I'd done as manager. I'm finding as many ways to improve the shop's profits as I can and — '

'We don't require you to do that, Prebble. What we asked for when we appointed you was that you continue running the shop *as Mr Blake*

75

would have done until a permanent manager is chosen. Have you made any more changes that we don't know about?'

Harry hesitated, but decided this wasn't the time to conceal anything, not till he'd won their trust. 'I've stopped supplying those working here with dinners. It's an extravagance the shop can't afford in times like this.'

'Mr Blake used to supply dinners to his staff?'

He nodded. 'Sandwiches and such.'

'Then you should continue to do so.'

'It really isn't necessary. They're well enough paid to buy their own.'

'Do everything as he did it. If you can't . . . ' He let the words trail away into an implied threat.

Harry breathed in slowly and deeply before he spoke again. 'About the new assistant we need to hire? You said to leave it to you and get someone temporary. I've got a lad who comes in now and then, but it's hard to manage without someone who knows the shop. We have to keep valued customers waiting sometimes at the moment. Mr Blake must be turning in his grave. I can find someone suitable and — '

'I have the matter in hand and shall appoint someone before the end of the week.'

'Surely I should be involved in selecting this person? After all, I know what is needed better than anyone.'

'How many times do I have to remind you that you are in charge here only until the new owners come back, Prebble. The responsibility for running the shop until then is Mr Featherworth's, and he has delegated it to me. Do not get above yourself. No decision has been made about the future, because that's the owners' responsibility.'

'I'm just trying to prove myself . . . sir. Surely that's a good thing?'

'Making changes only shows *me* that you can't do as we've asked.'

As Dawson said nothing else, just stared grimly at him, Harry spread his hands in a gesture of surrender. 'If there is a fault, it's — '

'I don't intend to revisit that subject, Prebble. And start providing dinners again for staff.'

Harry watched sourly as the clerk walked round the storage and packing area, stopping behind the lad who was weighing out sugar and putting it into the special blue paper bags. He moved on to the shop, walking slowly round it, pausing occasionally to study something.

You'll not find anything amiss here, you old sourpuss, Harry thought. *I keep everything perfectly clean and tidy.*

When one of the two remaining shopmen had shut the door behind the clerk, Harry fixed a smile to his face and hurried to serve an important customer who had just come in.

Before the two shopmen and the shop lad left that evening, he told them he had arranged with Mr Featherworth's clerk for a new man to be appointed to help in the shop. 'Oh, and we've decided to start providing you with dinners again, as a reward for your hard work recently.'

They smiled as they waited for him to dismiss them. They'd learned to treat him with respect since he'd taken over, and so would the new man, whoever he was.

Pity. He'd been going to hire his cousin. Jimmy would have known how to show his gratitude for being helped to a good job by giving Harry a shilling a week from his wages for the first six months. And would have been absolutely loyal.

Who knew what the new person would be like and who he'd really be answering to?

★   ★   ★

Harry continued to feel annoyed at having his little scheme found out.

When he was making up the wages, he put Zachary's money in an envelope. The lucky devil! Where would his former workmate be now? Living in luxury on the ocean, that's where. It wasn't right to pay his family full wages as well. Not that Harry dared interfere with that, not with Dawson peering over his shoulder all the time.

Still, he'd deliver this money personally on his way home, have a look at Zachary's sister, see if there was any way of getting at Zachary through her.

He smiled. He didn't like anyone getting the better of him and in the street where he lived no one would even try. Even the better-off people who shopped at Blake's had their weaknesses just as the poorer ones did. If you could find someone's weak spot, you could make them do as you wanted.

★   ★   ★

By getting up early each day, Cassandra managed to alter some clothes to suit her expanding waistline, and to tack the lace collar Pandora had lent her on to the blue dress, which she sponged down and ironed as best she could on the table which was their only working surface.

On board ship she'd been given the trunk of the maid whom she'd replaced and told to keep its contents. Susan Sutton had fled to her family in Yorkshire at the last minute rather than go to Australia with her employers. It still seemed wrong to Cassandra that they'd simply given away their former maid's personal possessions, but Mr Barrett said if the new maid didn't want the trunk, he'd simply throw it and its contents away, because he wasn't spending good money to send it back to someone so ungrateful.

Cassandra had been able to bring so little with her when she escaped from the men her aunt had paid to kidnap her that she'd been forced to use the other woman's things. But she'd kept Susan's photos and other mementoes and intended to return them one day, and to pay for taking the poor woman's clothes.

She looked up, thinking she heard voices, but there was no sign of her employers getting up yet. Francis Southerham never appeared until quite late, nine or ten o'clock, which was mid-morning as far as Cassandra was concerned. He did little work apart from tending his beloved horses, going for rides and shooting kangaroos for meat. Was he lazy or wasn't he well? She saw Livia look at him sometimes, with her brow furrowed, as if she was worried about something. And he had a persistent cough that he tried to hide from his wife.

She'd mentioned it to Reece, who thought it was something serious. Well, they'd all seen people they knew succumb to the coughing sickness. But Cassandra hoped Reece was wrong. What would Livia do without the husband she loved so much?

She looked back at her needlework. She'd just finish this seam then start her chores. She'd tried sewing after she'd finished her day's work, but it made your eyes tired to sew by lamplight and insects battered themselves against the lamp, fluttering in your face if you got too close to it. They had to sit outdoors; there was nowhere else. It amused her that she and her sister had to sit at the cooking table while the Southerhams occupied their tiny veranda, as if to emphasise the differences in their stations. Put those two out here alone, though, and they'd be lost. So who was superior to whom?

What would Pandora do when she was on her own here? It'd be very lonely. And when the rainy season started she'd not be able to sit outside. Would she have to lie in bed on her own in the tent? That worried Cassandra.

She held the blue dress against herself. 'What do you think?' she asked her sister. 'How does it look by daylight?'

'The colour suits you and you'll make a lovely bride. We'll trim up your bonnet, too. I've got some blue ribbon that's a good match.'

'You're a love. I'll still be a very badly dressed

bride, though. I wish I could have a brand new outfit. But we have to watch every penny.'

'Reece isn't marrying you for your clothes. He'd still love you if you were dressed in rags.'

Cassandra smiled. She knew that now. 'The days to our wedding seem to be crawling past.'

'The first Sunday in February will be here before you know it.' Pandora lowered her voice to add, 'Once you're married, you'll be free.'

'I'll still be working here for a while.'

'It won't be the same. Your time won't *belong* to them after work. They're always asking us to do things after we've stopped for the day. It'll be worse when there's only me.'

Cassandra laid one hand over her sister's for a moment or two and gave it a quick squeeze. 'It's annoying, I know, but you'll not be here for ever, I'm sure. It's just a way of earning your bread for the time being. And since Reece and I will be living with Kevin on the next block, you'll be able to come and visit us often. It's only a short walk if you take the track through the bush.'

'I'll come and visit you as often as I can, probably more than you want.'

'Not possible, love.'

★   ★   ★

When someone knocked on the door, Hallie said, 'I'll answer it, Mum.'

She found Harry Prebble standing there. He eyed her in a way that made her feel uncomfortable. She was taller than him, but he still seemed threatening, somehow.

81

'I brought Zachary's money,' he said, holding out an envelope.

She reached out for it and he seized her hand, holding it so tightly she couldn't pull away.

'Don't I get a thank you?'

'Thank you.'

'Most lasses would give me a kiss for bringing the money round.'

She stared at him in shock. 'Well, I'm not most lasses.'

'You're not acting very friendly.' He let go of her hand.

Shuddering, she was about to shut the door when he shot out one hand to hold it open.

'Next time I expect you to be more friendly.'

'Well, I shan't be.'

He shook his head, making a soft tsk-tsk sound. 'You may change your mind.'

'Why should I?'

'For the sake of your mother.'

She couldn't understand what he meant.

He stepped back, smiling. 'You'll see.'

She shut the door and leaned against it. What had he meant? Should she tell her mother? No, it'd only worry her. And anyway, he hadn't threatened anything really. Had he?

★   ★   ★

The evening before their sister's wedding, Maia and Xanthe sat together in the kitchen at Galway House enjoying a final cup of tea.

'Do you like working here?' Xanthe asked idly.

Maia looked at her in surprise, wondering

82

what had made her ask this. 'Yes. I love looking after Mrs Largan. Poor lady, she's in so much pain and never complains. She's really interesting to be with and is teaching me all sorts of things. Do you like being the housekeeper better now you're more used to it?'

'It's all right. I have a lot to learn, so that keeps me interested. It was Cassandra who organised everything like that back home. We just did as she told us. It's a good thing I've got Mrs Largan to guide me, or you'd all be in trouble.' She stirred her cup of tea slowly. 'I'd not like to stay here for ever, though. There's not a lot to do, apart from the job, no library or proper church, nowhere to go for walks even. I'm grateful Conn lets us read his books in our free time or I'd go mad.'

'We've been so lucky to get jobs together in Australia. I'd hate to be separated.'

'It's bound to happen one day, unless we both dwindle into old maids together.'

'Would that be so bad?'

Xanthe stared into the distance. 'I think you were made to get married and have children.'

'I've never met a man who's tempted me.'

'And you're not likely to meet anyone here. As for me — ' She broke off as their employer came into the kitchen, flapping his hand at the moth that had tried to follow him inside the house.

'Any chance of another cup of tea?' he asked, cutting their confidences short.

★　★　★

83

Maia stared at him dreamily as Xanthe rose to do as he'd asked. He was a very good-looking man. She'd been lying when she told Xanthe she'd not met a man who'd tempted her. Conn Largan did. But he was far above her in station, so it was a hopeless attraction. She knew that and still couldn't prevent her pulse racing when he was close.

For once he sat down to drink his tea with them. Usually this happened only at meal times. He often seemed lonely and she knew his mother worried about him.

He accepted the cup Xanthe gave him with a smile. 'Are you looking forward to seeing your sisters tomorrow?'

Maia beamed at him. 'Yes. We still aren't used to living so far apart.'

'It'll seem strange them getting married in a barn.' Xanthe topped up her own cup from the big teapot and joined them.

'I miss proper churches.' He stared down into his cup, not trying to hide his sadness, for once. 'I miss the beauty of stained glass windows and the sound of a choir's voices echoing up to the rafters.'

'We didn't have real stained glass windows in ours,' Maia said, 'just coloured edges to the windows. The Methodist church was quite new, a red brick building. But our minister was a very caring man.'

'It was a clergyman who betrayed me,' Conn said abruptly. 'Even Catholics were expected to go to the churches the English set up and listen quietly as they were told to rejoice that England had stolen our country. After they took me away, the minister of that church told my mother she should forget she'd ever had a son like me. She never went to his church again, even though my father tried to persuade her to conform.'

He took another sip of tea, then it seemed as if he had to let out more of his pain. 'My father believed what they told him about me, can you imagine that? He didn't even ask for my side of the story. He lives in their pockets, tugging his forelock — yes sir, no sir, whatever you say sir.'

'It must have been hard for you to be imprisoned.'

He shrugged. 'Others had it worse. I survived, did I not? I saw others give up and die.' He drained his cup and put it down. 'I'll drive you to the service tomorrow. I like to attend when I can. The visiting clergyman is a decent fellow.'

'That's kind of you.'

'You'd better sit apart from me if you want to meet people and make friends. They don't like to get too close to emancipists. A man may receive a pardon, but once a convict, always suspect. Why, even the poor look down on fellows like me.'

With a twist of his lips that didn't quite turn into a smile, he stood up, gave them another of his nods and left them to clear up the kitchen.

'I never saw anyone as lonely as that poor man, even with his mother here,' Maia said softly. 'I wish there was something we could do to make his life happier.'

She realised Xanthe was looking at her with a smile. 'What's the matter?'

'You've started again, trying to solve everyone's problems. You've got a kind heart, love, far kinder than mine, too kind for your own good. I think you'd be happy wherever you lived as long as you were among people who were friendly. I'm — different. I need more than just to be with people.'

Her departure from the kitchen was as abrupt as Conn's and Maia didn't try to follow her. There were times when Xanthe needed to be alone. She knew her twin would never settle permanently in a place as quiet as this, and that worried her. Was that why Xanthe had spoken of them not being together? Was she trying to prepare her for a parting one day?

If Maia had to choose between looking after a woman who depended on her for everything and being with her twin, what would she do? She shivered, hoping it would never be necessary, because for the first time in her life, her answer wasn't instantly, 'My sister'.

5

The following morning the twins tidied up the kitchen quickly, then got ready for the wedding, trying to look their best. Mrs Largan insisted on seeing them and nodded approval.

'You must be the four prettiest sisters I've ever met. Usually there's one who's not as pretty, but all four of you would turn heads as you passed. I'm surprised you're not married already.'

Xanthe laughed. 'Not many heads to turn here, Mrs Largan, unless you count the kangaroos.'

'There'll be plenty of young men at church to show interest.'

Conn came into the kitchen. 'Are you ready? We can — ' He stared at them and let out a long, low whistle. 'You both look beautiful today.'

Maia could feel herself blushing at this spontaneous compliment, but Xanthe merely laughed and said, 'You're quite a fine fellow yourself, Conn Largan.'

'He is, isn't he?' Mrs Largan looked at her son fondly.

'Are you sure you don't want to come with us, mother?'

She shook her head. 'I'd rather rest and anyway, that barn never seems like a real church to me.'

When they got there, Maia noticed that people nodded briefly to Conn then looked away, not trying to hide their wish to have nothing to do with him. Some men even stood between him and their families, as if on guard.

No wonder he was bitter, she thought sadly.

While he drove into the side lot to see to his horse and cart, the two sisters waited outside the barn for the bridal party. Once he'd left them, people paused at the door to chat to them.

It wasn't fair. Maia had heard that half the population of this colony was made up of convicts. Were such people never to be forgiven? Besides, to her mind political prisoners like Conn were not bad people, not really. They were different from ordinary convicts. He hadn't committed a crime like killing someone or stealing.

From what he'd let drop, things his mother had said, he might not even have committed a crime at all. How could a man who was innocent be convicted like that?

And why was his mother living here if his father was still alive back in Ireland?

It was all very puzzling.

She looked down the road impatiently, dying to see the cart bringing her sisters.

★ ★ ★

Pandora was both glad and sad when the wedding morning came. Mr Southerham drove his wife and their two servants to the store in his cart, an hour's journey under the hot sun, so she put up an old umbrella Mrs Southerham had lent her. Cassandra seemed to enjoy the sun on her face and didn't turn bright red under its influence as Pandora did.

Reece drove behind them in Kevin's cart, with Kevin sitting on the bench beside him, making sure he did nothing foolish. Driving a horse and cart was only one of the many new skills Reece had had to learn. Cassandra would be going back to her new home with them after the ceremony, which would leave Pandora on her own with the Southerhams.

At the barn next to the store, they found the congregation gathered for the monthly Sunday service, with carts in rows in a nearby field, some horses with nosebags on. Not many people lived close enough to walk to church here.

The twins were waiting for them outside the big barn and their employer, who had been standing to one side, came to wish the bride and groom well.

After the sisters had all hugged one another, and then hugged Reece for good measure, they went inside. Pandora saw with surprise that when Conn would have gone to sit on a bench at the rear, Maia clutched his sleeve and pulled him forward to the same bench as them.

The Southerhams went straight to the front of the barn, as if certain the best places were theirs by right. The people there smiled at them and made room.

Most of the congregation frowned at Conn Largan and no one sat in front of or behind him. They treated Kevin like a pariah too, but he had stayed at the rear of the barn, sitting on his own so had not upset the usual seating arrangements.

She watched, intrigued as Conn continued to argue with Maia in a low voice. But her sister still kept hold of his sleeve — which was most unlike shy Maia.

The service started with readings and a short sermon. Pandora didn't join in the hymn singing because she couldn't hold a tune, but listened with pleasure to her three sisters, who sang beautifully. They moved into harmonies without realising what they were doing. It reminded her of the time they'd gone to sing on the streets of Manchester to earn money to buy better food for their sick father when they were all out of work.

At one stage the rest of the congregation fell silent to listen and her three sisters faltered to a halt in embarrassment.

The minister gestured encouragingly with one hand. 'Don't stop, my dear young ladies. Your voices are such a pleasure to listen to. We can't have a choir here, with me only visiting once a month and no one to train it, but I do hope you'll continue to attend and give us the pleasure of your beautiful singing.'

So they sang the hymn again, followed by another, then ended the impromptu concert, not wanting to seem to be showing off.

After the service, two weddings took place. Cassandra and Reece's was the second to be performed.

Pandora knew Cassandra had chosen a good man and smiled as she watched her sister and heard her confident responses. She'd give herself a year with the Southerhams, she decided suddenly, then look round for something different, even if it meant moving away from her sisters.

That decision made her feel better.

★ ★ ★

Cassandra smiled up at her new husband as she drew back from his kiss.

'Time to face them.' Reece offered his arm.

She suddenly became aware of their audience and blushed, but the smiles were kind and some of the women looked misty-eyed. She glanced quickly at her sisters, who were beaming at her, then walked with her husband towards the door.

Outside they accepted everyone's congratulations, finding that even strangers wanted to kiss the two brides and wish them well.

Some of the women came up to them carrying little parcels.

As if by arrangement, the first gave each bride a basket. 'I make them myself. They're not as fancy as the ones you can buy in Perth but they do the job. You always need an extra basket or two when you only shop every few weeks.'

'Some good tealeaves for a little treat,' one said, handing over a package.

'A jar of my melon jam and I've written down the recipe and put in some melon seeds for you. They're easy to grow.'

'Just a bottle of my special chutney that I make every year from apples and sultanas. I've given you the recipe and if you want a cutting from our apple tree, let me know.'

'I can tell you now: I'd love one.'

91

She was overwhelmed by their generosity; could only stand there as the basket she'd been given was filled up with homemade offerings and recipes. It was clearly an established ritual here.

'How can they be so kind to me and treat Mr Largan like a leper?' she asked Reece as they started to drive back.

'They're the same with me,' Kevin said drily from the back of the cart, where he'd insisted on sitting so that the newly-weds could be together. 'Emancipists aren't accepted socially, not even if they make a fortune. It'd soon be noticed and commented on unfavourably if we didn't attend church, though.'

She blushed at how tactless she'd been.

Kevin chuckled. 'Don't get embarrassed, lass. I'm used to it by now.'

So she turned back to smile at him, concerned when she saw how tired he looked. 'Are you all right?'

'Just weary. I'll have a restful day or two after we get back. But I enjoyed seeing you two wed.'

They waved goodbye to Pandora and the Southerhams as the track divided into two and let the ugly but willing horse Kevin had called Delilah pull them slowly up the slope to his farm.

It felt as if she was going home, Cassandra thought, exchanging smiles with Reece.

★　★　★

Kevin's shack was a little bigger than the Southerhams' and in a much better state of

92

repair. Reece helped Cassandra down and offered her his arm. For a moment or two they stood looking at the new room he'd built on one side of the house for them. Its wood was bright and new, unlike the time-silvered planks of the rest of the shack.

She and Pandora had helped Reece the last two Sundays, leaving their employers to fend for themselves. Francis hadn't liked that, because he considered maids should have only one Sunday a month off, but Livia had won him round.

Kevin had guided the building efforts because he'd been good at carpentry until he grew too weak to do as much physical work. The new room was made of slabs of roughly sawn tree trunk with smaller planks covering the joins. Huge pieces of bark covered the roof frame, held in place by ropes attached to big stones.

The wooden slabs had been left over from Kevin's original building work and he had kindly given them to Reece as a wedding present. They were well seasoned and though they might not look pretty, they'd made solid walls.

Once the new bedroom was finished, Reece had opened up his old bedroom to form part of the living room, it being easy enough to remove the wooden interior wall. It'd be good to have more indoor space if winter was as wet as Kevin said. The two men were even talking about building a sheltered passageway for her to get to and from the primitive kitchen, which only had walls on the sides facing the prevailing winds and was about ten yards away from the house. She had an American contraption called a 'colonial

93

stove' for her cooking, rather like the one they'd had in Outham, and it worked well.

It was so good to have somewhere to call home. You could never feel that a tent was home.

Reece led the way inside the house and to her surprise, he turned and swung her into his arms so that he could carry her over the threshold of their bedroom.

She heard Kevin laughing softly behind them, then Reece pushed the door shut with one shoulder and set her down in front of him, giving her a kiss that set her whole body tingling. His touch didn't frighten her in the least, which had surprised her the first time he kissed her. Maybe that was because it bore no resemblance whatsoever to the rough treatment she'd received from the men who'd raped her.

She linked her arm in his, looking round. Their room was only twelve foot square and the bed took up a lot of that space. Their trunks were set on either side of it with candlesticks standing on them. 'Where did the patchwork quilt come from?'

'I bought it at the shop. One of the women makes them. She's good, isn't she?'

'I've never seen one as pretty. You must have worked so hard to finish this, Reece.'

'I wanted us to have some privacy. I can't offer you much, but I can at least offer you that.' He gestured to the hanging rail which had a shelf over it. 'I'll make doors for the wardrobe but I thought I'd save that job for the rainy weather. Things *will* get better, Cassandra.'

'It's you I want most, not money or

possessions. And I'll work alongside you to build a better life for us and our family.'

'I'm going to look after you very carefully while you're in this condition. I don't want you overdoing things.'

She saw the anxiety in his eyes and remembered he'd had a pregnant wife once before and had lost both her and the baby. 'I'll not act foolishly, Reece, but I can't sit here and wait for the baby to arrive, so I might as well earn some time off your service to the Southerhams by continuing to work for them for a while.'

'As long as you're careful.'

'I'm feeling very well now, not even sick in the mornings. Was your first wife — not well when she was expecting?'

'She wasn't well when I married her, but foolishly I thought good food and a decent home would improve her health. And it did for a while. But the baby was too much for her.' He shook his head to banish the sad memories. 'That's not something to discuss on our wedding day.'

'It's part of your life, though, and I want to know all about you.'

'What, today?' he teased. 'We'll never get to bed if I have to recite my whole life story first.'

'No, you fool. For the rest of today, I just want us to be happy. Tomorrow I'll set this place in order, then on Tuesday I'll go back to work. I've already arranged with Mrs Southerham to have tomorrow off.' She went across to run her fingers over the two wooden chairs and small table that now sat beneath the single window. They were pretty pieces, of a much better quality than any furniture she'd had before. 'Where did you get these?'

'From Kevin. He has some pieces stored in his shed, for lack of space.'

'People have been kind, but him particularly.'

'He needs us, will need us more as the months pass. Unfortunately, I don't think he'll last another year. I shall miss him a lot.'

Reece moved to put his arms round her from behind and she leaned against him. He was quite tall, but only slightly taller than she was, because all the Blake girls were tall. She realised suddenly that she was no longer a Blake. 'Mrs Gregory.' She hadn't realised she'd spoken aloud until Reece echoed her words.

He kissed her again, so sweetly it brought tears to her eyes. 'I'll not be troubling you in bed till after the baby is born, my love.'

'No, Reece, I want to become your wife properly and besides, I *need* to wipe out the bad memories.' She had to stop because her voice shook, as it always did when she remembered the days of being raped and then raped again. It was a wonder she hadn't lost her mind, but somehow she'd survived and she didn't intend to let what had happened spoil the rest of her life.

She looked up into his eyes and the mere sight of the love that shone from them made her want to touch him, kiss him, love him. 'I'm so lucky to have found you again.'

'We're both lucky to have found one another. Especially as I was stupid enough to leave England and you.'

He didn't say it, but if he'd brought her here, all the trouble would have been avoided. It was no use to cling to might-have-beens, though. Life went on and you had to go with it or fall by the wayside.

They stood there for a few more moments then she moved away from him. 'Would you fetch my portmanteau in, please? I'll bring in the new basket, then I'll start unpacking the gifts before I make us a meal. Weren't the women at church lovely to give things to a stranger?'

The thought of those small offerings warmed her heart. They seemed a tangible promise of good neighbours and help in adversity. Next time there was a wedding, she'd bring her own present for the bride.

Reece followed her outside to the kitchen. 'I'll chat to you while you cook, and help if I can. Do you know how to work this stove?'

She laughed. 'Of course I do. Who do you think did the cooking for my family in Outham?'

'Good. I'd better warn you, then, that I always have an excellent appetite. I banked the fire up before we left.' He opened the air vents and peered inside. 'Yes, there's a glow to one corner. Soon have it burning up.'

He looked up at the roof and then the wall. 'I'll see what I can do to improve this place before winter comes.'

'We need a store cupboard with mesh sides for the food, someone told me today. You hang a wet cloth over it during the hot weather and it keeps things cool.'

'And we need to stand the feet of anything like

97

that in saucers of water or the ants will crawl into everything. Kevin taught me that. Strange ways of housekeeping they have here.'

'So much to learn. But if other women can do it, and make jams, pickles and who knows what else, so can I. Though I might have to ask the women at church for help and advice. Livia is kind, but she doesn't know much about housekeeping.'

'She's not as arrogant as Francis.'

After the evening meal Kevin, who was looking exhausted, retired to bed early.

'He doesn't look at all well,' she said softly.

'He won't talk about himself and he won't let me fetch a doctor.'

'Is there one near here?'

'No. I was thinking we might take you up to Perth when the baby is due.'

'I'd rather have a woman helping me in my own home. There must be someone who delivers babies round here. We can ask next month at church.'

She cleared away the food. There weren't long twilit evenings in Australia, but an almost instant darkness after the sun sank below the horizon, so they went to bed soon afterwards.

She nestled against him, afraid now the moment had come to make love, but determined to overcome her fears. But Reece was so gentle, his love showing in every kiss and caress, that she needn't have worried. She responded to his caresses instinctively, willingly and let him carry her into a tide of pleasure that swept her away and left her gasping in his arms.

'It's going to be a big baby,' he said afterwards, lying with one hand on her belly.

'Is it?'

'Yes. There's no doubt about your dates, so it's well grown already.'

Briefly, the doubts she'd felt before assailed her. 'I hope we'll love it.'

'Of course we shall. It'll be a baby, not a criminal. And I'll be the only father it knows. That's the only condition I make: it's never to know it isn't mine.'

She fell asleep with a smile on her face, one hand still clasping his.

★ ★ ★

Zachary suppressed a groan as Leo came rushing into the cabin, where he'd taken refuge to read in peace.

'Those sailors aren't treating the poor animals properly,' Leo announced, tugging at his friend's sleeve. 'You have to stop them. They won't listen to me. Come on!'

Zachary put his book down carefully, knowing by now that once Leo had something fixed in his mind, he wouldn't let go of it easily. 'I told you before, there are men whose job it is to tend the ship's animals and you have to leave it to them.'

'But they're not doing it *properly*. The animals might *die*. Come and tell them. The men laughed at me, but they'll listen to you.'

'I don't know anything about animals. Anyway, most of these are going to be killed for meat. I don't know why you're getting upset.'

'Lots of animals get killed for meat. I know how to kill them gently. We don't have to be *unkind* to them.' Leo's face crumpled on those words. 'It's wrong to hurt creatures.'

Zachary sighed. He knew people were unkind to Leo and that this upset the poor fellow. Strangely, he never used his strength or lashed out, was such a gentle soul. It upset Zachary to see this taunting and scorn. As a consequence, he'd found himself acting as unofficial protector. But who would protect Leo after he left the ship? It was the stuff of nightmares for anyone with an ounce of compassion: a fellow like that, little more than a child mentally, being turned loose in a strange country.

'Come *on*!' Leo tugged again and nearly yanked Zachary off the bunk.

'We'll go and look at them. I'm not doing anything else.'

But when he got to the animals, even he could see they were in distress, the crates in which they were cruelly penned not cleaned out and their water buckets empty. 'We'll go and see the doctor,' he said as a compromise.

Dr Crawford, who was responsible for the welfare of the convicts as well as the paying passengers, was for once free and easily persuaded to come and look at the animals.

'Can I fetch them some water?' Leo asked, shifting from one foot to the other.

'You can't look after them on your own.' The doctor frowned. 'I'll see if there's a convict who'll take over the duties. The crew member who's supposed to be looking after them isn't well, and everyone thought someone else had taken over the duties. Or so they say. In reality most sailors don't like looking after animals.'

'They're thirsty now,' Leo said. 'It's hot. They need water.'

Once he got into this agitated frame of mind, he didn't let go. Zachary gave in, knowing he'd get no peace if he didn't help Leo. 'I'll keep an eye on him this time, doctor. But if you can find a convict who's used to caring about animals, I daresay he'll jump at the job and let Leo help him.'

He moved to one side and said in a lower voice, 'I think it'd help Leo to have something to do. He can't fill in time by reading or writing a diary like the rest of us.'

The doctor nodded. 'You're very kind to the poor fellow.'

'I don't have much choice, sharing a cabin with him. And besides, he's a gentle soul.'

'Until he's pushed too far,' the doctor said. 'I've seen it happen when people goad fellows like him. Just stay on your guard.'

Zachary nodded to show he'd been listening to this advice, but he couldn't imagine Leo ever attacking anyone.

★ ★ ★

Two days later there was a storm and the passengers were locked down. When it was over, Leo and the convict now in charge of the animals went to check that they were all right.

To their dismay, they found that one of the

101

cows had a broken front leg.

'She's the one they told me was most valuable,' the convict said. 'They brought her out for breeding, but she'll have to be slaughtered. The owner won't be pleased about that. Still, they can't blame us for a storm, can they?' He went off to find an officer.

Leo went to examine the poor creature which was making distressed noises.

When the ship's doctor came to look, he shook his head. 'You can't set a cow's leg. She'll have to be shot.'

'I can set her leg,' Leo said.

They looked at him in surprise.

'Have you done it before?' the doctor asked.

Leo nodded. 'But it was a sheep. The farrier said I should practise on a sheep.'

'Did it recover?'

'Yes. If it's the front leg, you can sometimes mend it, if it's only a simple break. If it's the back leg, you can't do much. I can straighten it if someone will hold her down for me. I'll need a splint and a bandage.'

'He doesn't understand,' the convict muttered, tapping his forehead.

'He sounds as if he does. Sometimes people like him have special skills, as if to make up for their other problems.' The doctor frowned then shrugged. 'It's worth giving it a try. This is a very valuable animal.' He turned back to Leo. 'All right, young man. Show me what you can do.'

'Can't you do it, doctor?' the convict begged. 'I don't want them blaming me.'

'I've never tried anything with animals. He

clearly has. I'll be interested to watch and of course I'll stop him making things worse, if I have to, and put it out of its misery.'

Leo dealt with the leg with a speed that surprised them all. Ignoring the animal's struggles and the noises it was making, he felt carefully along the bone and pushed quickly. 'We need to tie it to the wood now,' he said.

'Is that it?' the convict asked, sounding disappointed.

Leo looked at him in puzzlement. 'It was only a simple break.'

'Will she recover?' the doctor asked.

'Some do, some just die. But she's young. It'd be better if I stayed with her.' He stroked the animal's head and she quieted almost immediately.

Several passengers and members of the crew came to look at the invalid, walking away muttering.

Leo ignored them, spending most of his time for several days by the side of the sick animal, which always seemed calmer when he was with it.

'Damnedest thing I ever saw,' the doctor said to Zachary. 'He did it so quickly, and look how well the animal responds to him. The owner is going to be very pleased about this if it recovers.'

6

On the day after the wedding Pandora woke early, thankful to see daylight lightening the tent walls. She'd started awake several times during the night, wondering what some nearby noise was.

After washing herself all over, she stood for a moment or two naked, feeling guilty at acting immodestly, but the air on her skin was so blessedly cool. Reluctantly she reached for her working clothes: drawers, one petticoat only, a cotton skirt, a camisole and a bodice from which she'd removed the sleeves in a vain attempt to keep cool. Over it all she tied a coarse twill pinafore, then lingered for a moment or two longer to stare at herself in the broken mirror Mrs Southerham had given them.

Her skin was a light golden colour now, though still much paler than everyone else's. She didn't spend any more time than she had to in the sun because she still found the heat uncomfortable. Her hair was shiny again though — she put up one hand to touch it. It had been dull during the times they'd gone hungry after the cotton mills closed.

Were people still starving in Outham? Was the Civil War still going on in America? They were cut off from the latest news here, because without a railway system newspapers took a long time to reach the country settlements. Mr

Southerham grumbled about that quite often.

If you went anywhere, you went on foot or by horse. Her employer had said he'd teach her to ride, if she liked. She'd remind him of that. If she could ride, maybe he'd let her go to visit Xanthe and Maia on her own occasionally. Surely she'd be safe with so few people around? And learning to ride would give her something different to do. It got so boring doing the same chores every day, with no one to talk to now, even. She'd never have chosen to be a maid. When she'd worked in the mill, it had been hard work, not particularly interesting, but she and her workmates had had fun as well, and her time off had been her own.

She took the bowl of water outside and threw it on the small row of plants struggling to survive. It didn't do to waste water here. It hadn't rained once since they arrived in December.

As she went to draw another bucket of clean water, she saw a few kangaroos hopping among the trees behind the house — females. Kevin said the male kangaroos could be dangerous, but the females were gentler. They seemed to go round in groups. She'd seen this lot before. The biggest one had a ragged ear.

When the animals had moved away, she got the fire burning and made herself a pot of tea, drinking it from one of the half-pint enamel mugs everyone used, though the Southerhams always got out their china teacups in the afternoons — *you have to keep up standards* — which made extra work for their maid. She had to wash the tea service carefully afterwards, with a tea towel in the bottom of the tin washing-up bowl to prevent chipping the fine china.

She swirled the dark liquid round her mug, watching the hollow in the centre, seeing how deep she could make it. There was no milk for the tea because the Southerhams didn't want the trouble of keeping a cow, and there was no other way of getting milk here. Anyway, milk would sour too quickly in this heat. She didn't add sugar, either, because she'd grown to like the bitter taste of unsweetened tea during the years when sugar was too expensive, years when they'd struggled to find one decent meal a day and a few pieces of dry bread the rest of the time if they were lucky. They'd had to re-use their tealeaves several times in those days, till finally the water was barely coloured, which was perhaps why she enjoyed strong tea now.

Mrs Southerham came out on to the veranda of their tiny wooden dwelling, yawning and stretching, then walked across to join her at the table under its canvas awning. 'Is there any tea left in that pot?'

'Plenty.' She started to stand up.

'Sit down. I'll get my own. I think the wedding went well, don't you?'

'Yes. Cassandra made a beautiful bride.'

'Not as beautiful as you will be one day.'

'I doubt I'll find another man like Bill.' He'd been the kindest man she'd ever met, and fun to be with.

'Oh, I think you might find someone else. I was quite on the shelf myself and resigned to

106

living and dying a spinster, when I met Francis. You'll see. A girl as beautiful and intelligent as you is bound to attract interest.'

Pandora didn't argue. It wasn't worth it. She didn't want to marry someone from round here and spend the rest of her life stuck miles away from anywhere. She went to get out the flour and bicarbonate of soda and set to work to make the first batch of damper, pummelling it hard, wishing people wouldn't keep harping on about her getting married.

As she straightened up from putting the tins of dough into the oven, she stared down the track that led up to the farm. She often caught herself doing this and sometimes her imagination conjured up an image of a man striding up that track and taking her away from this place, away from Australia and back to Lancashire.

How foolish she was! You didn't get knights in shining armour coming to rescue you in these modern times. She was trapped here in Australia. But one day she'd escape, even if it was only to go and live in Perth.

★   ★   ★

The following week, when Hallie and her mother went to market, a lad with a cap pulled down over his face and a muffler round his neck came running round a corner and bumped right into her mother, knocking her over.

Someone called 'Hoy!' but the lad ran away.

Hallie bent over her mother, who was gasping for breath. A man from a nearby stall came to

107

help Mrs Carr stand up. But she couldn't seem to catch her breath for a few moments.

Someone else brought a stool and when Mrs Carr did manage to get up she was glad to sit down on it.

'He seemed to — jab me in my stomach and — I couldn't catch my breath.'

Hallie knew then that this was what Harry had meant. He'd done it. Hurt her mother but made people think it was an accident.

'Careless young devil!' the man who'd helped them said. 'If I knew who that lad was I'd be round to tell his parents.' He raised his voice. 'Anyone know who he was?'

Heads were shaken. Most people had already gone back to their shopping.

All the way home Hallie worried about what Harry was going to want from her next week. The thought of kissing him made her feel sick.

But if she didn't, he might hurt her mother again.

Should she tell someone?

She didn't dare. She knew about the Prebbles. Everyone did. If you upset them, they got their own back on you.

★ ★ ★

In early March it rained, heavy drops that dried before they could wet the ground properly. But even that was something so unusual that Pandora went to stand outside, her head tilted up to enjoy the feeling of cool moisture on her face.

108

Cassandra, sheltering under the awning over the table, laughed at her antics. Pandora laughed back, dancing round, arms spread out. The Southerhams had gone for a ride, so they were alone, for once, and could relax — though there were always jobs to be done.

Reece also stopped to smile at Pandora's antics. He was working on the Southerhams' hut, because Livia had at last persuaded her husband to enlarge their dwelling by enclosing part of the veranda before the winter rains really set in. He was using bits and pieces of packing cases, as well as the huge strips of bark you could get from some trees. They would get some glass for windows next time they were in Perth.

To her disappointment the spatter of rain soon stopped and the brassy sun took over again.

'I wonder what winter's really like,' she said as they all three stopped for a mid-morning snack. 'I don't call that pitter-patter *rain*.'

'In winter it beats down so hard, it bounces up again from the ground,' Reece said. 'And it'll come straight towards us from the sea.' He gestured across the sloping land to the horizon. 'We don't get much rain from an easterly direction.'

Cassandra got out the mugs. 'I'm worried about you alone in that tent. What if it blows away?'

Pandora shrugged. 'If it does, I'll seek refuge in the house, or with you, perhaps.'

'At the very least I'll build a bed frame and erect a bark and pole shelter over the tent before the rains really set in,' Reece promised. 'I can't build proper living quarters without money to buy sawn wood, though.'

'Will Mr Southerham let you take the time to do that?'

'I'll insist. He can't expect you to sleep in a soaked tent that may blow away any minute. Even the horses have better shelters than you do.'

★ ★ ★

Francis and Livia were riding along a track they'd found in the bush when the rain started to fall. They had no idea who had made this path or where it led, but it was clearly man-made, though not recently used. He'd got Reece to clear away the regrowth and then Francis had walked along it to make sure the track was safe for the horses.

After a while the path turned downhill towards the main Albany road, which they could follow to the entrance to their own property and then come back up the hill.

'Rain!' Livia held out one hand, palm upwards, enjoying the feel of the drops. 'Oh dear, it's stopping already. I'd have loved a proper shower.'

'Mmm.'

He was lost in thought today and she hesitated, then reined in her horse. 'Let's get off and walk along this part. The horses will follow us.'

As they tramped along, she said what she'd been holding back for a while now, 'What's

110

wrong, Francis? It's no use pretending you're well. I've noticed you slowing down, tiring more easily . . . coughing again. It isn't — ' She broke off hating even to say the word.

He stopped to stare down at the ground and kick away a small branch. 'I do feel — more tired lately. And — I'm coughing up blood again. Not a lot, but a smear or two occasionally.'

She stopped dead, one hand on his arm. 'I'd heard you coughing, but you said it was just the dust. And it *is* dusty here.'

'I'd been hoping I'd get better once we'd settled in.'

'That's what persuaded your father to let you come to Australia in the end, isn't it? The doctors told him you had consumption.'

He nodded.

'You made light of it then, said it wasn't bad, told me the doctor was sure things would get better in a warmer climate. Oh, Francis!' Her throat closed with anguish and the last word came out muffled.

He came to take her in his arms. 'I didn't want to worry you.'

'We must go to Perth, find a doctor.'

'I saw doctors in England. There's nothing they can do about consumption that I've not done already, not really. I've come to a warm climate, changed to an outdoor life, and that hasn't helped. Oh, my darling, don't cry!' He pulled her into his arms.

She fought against tears but couldn't hold them back, weeping on his shoulder. But she didn't let herself weep for long. She had to keep

111

her courage up, look after him, make his last years as happy as possible.

He spoke against her hair, holding her close. 'I shouldn't have bought this land. It's used up too much of our money. That's why I didn't want to make too many changes here, because everything I spend will mean less left for you ... afterwards.'

'Don't worry about me. If we look after you, see that you get lots of rest, maybe there's a chance that you'll get better.'

'Maybe.'

Anguish ran through her, sitting heavily in her chest because she understood then that he'd given up hope of recovering — which meant he must be feeling worse than he'd admitted.

'My main worry is what will happen to you,' he said.

'I'll be fine. I'll have some money because I can sell the land again. Reece has made a lot of improvements, so this place should be worth more. Don't waste time worrying about me, my darling. We have to think what can we do to make your life as happy as possible.'

'Well, I'm enjoying living here more than in Lancashire, on the whole. I do enjoy the warmer climate. I've got you, some good horses, a place to ride, a veranda where I can sit and watch the sunsets. It's not a bad way to go.'

'That's why you've been avoiding kissing me.'

'Yes. Some people think it can be passed from one person to another. I ought to sleep on my own as well.'

'No. I love sleeping together.'

'I wake in the night sweating and uncomfortable.' He put one finger on her lips. 'No arguing. I shall be more comfortable sleeping on my own in the enclosed veranda.'

It required a huge effort to smile at him and nod, but she managed it.

As they rode back up the final stretch to their own land, she said abruptly, 'We'd better tell Reece.'

'I don't want to tell anyone else.'

'I've seen him looking at you, thinking you're lazy. He needs to know what's wrong so that he won't ask too much of you.'

'If he knows, Cassandra will, and Pandora too. They'll watch me, stare.'

'Let them. If you don't tell Reece, I will.'

He gave her one of his wry smiles. 'You're bullying me.'

She nodded, finding the courage to return his smile steadily, when all she wanted to do was weep.

'You tell them, then.' He helped her to remount, pulled himself up on his own horse and let it walk along the track at its own speed. They didn't speak much for the rest of the ride.

★ ★ ★

That afternoon Livia said she didn't want afternoon tea serving in the fancy cups. 'Francis feels tired. He's going to lie down. I'll have a cup with you today.'

Reece and Cassandra exchanged surprised glances.

113

'Something's wrong,' he murmured to his wife as he emptied the dregs from the big teapot over the garden, then took it across to the stove for her to make another brew. 'I wonder what it is.'

'Maybe they've changed their minds about staying here. Mr Southerham still isn't looking well.'

When Livia joined the three of them at the table, she accepted her mug of tea and said abruptly, 'I have something to tell you. It's . . . important.'

After she'd finished explaining, Reece spoke for the other two. 'I'm sorry to hear that, Mrs Southerham. I must admit I've wondered. I can't help noticing how quickly Mr Southerham tires now and how much thinner he's become.'

'We'll help you in any way we can,' Cassandra said gently.

Livia nodded, her words coming out muffled with suppressed anguish. 'Thank you.' She got up, leaving her mug of tea untouched and went back into the shack.

Reece sighed. 'They should have told us sooner. I had a friend whose daughter died of consumption. The doctor was a forward-thinking man and told him a few precautions to take. From now on, we're not sharing the same dishes and cups they use.'

'We don't use the same things most of the time anyway,' Pandora said thoughtfully. 'They have their fancy china, while we use the cheaper things. It's just the tin mugs.'

'We'll mark theirs,' Reece said. 'It's Livia I'm sorry for. How will she manage after he dies? A woman can't do the heavy work on a farm, not that he does much of it but he does look after the horses.'

'She'll sell Westview. She'll have to.'

'And go where? She hasn't got any friends in the colony.'

'Maybe she'll go back to England,' Pandora said.

'Her father died. She has no other close family.' Cassandra sighed. 'Life is hard for a woman on her own.'

He stood up. 'We'll help them in any way we can, but it means I can't stop working for them, even if I want to, because he'll only grow weaker. I can't leave them in the lurch. That'll delay our own plans.'

'He and Kevin are both failing. Who'll be the third one?' Pandora wondered.

'It's a foolish superstition that deaths come in threes,' he said sternly. 'I don't like to hear people say it. It's as if they're wishing for someone to die. I'm going back to work now.'

No one had wondered what would happen to her if the Southerhams sold Westview, she thought as she rinsed out the mugs, then got angry with herself for being so selfish. Francis was dying. She wasn't. And she had her sisters. They'd never let her want.

⋆　⋆　⋆

Hallie dreaded Friday all the following week, because she'd have to deal with Harry Prebble somehow.

She couldn't eat her tea, felt so nauseous after forcing something down that she had to go out to the privy and be sick.

When she got back to the kitchen she saw an envelope on the table.

'Harry Prebble called with Zachary's wages. He's such a nice young man, isn't he? Asked after you particularly.'

Hallie didn't know whether to be glad or sorry that she'd missed him. It had been accidental, but he'd blame her, she was sure. She'd make certain her mother didn't get knocked over next week.

But he'd think of some other way of getting at her, she was sure. She couldn't get the memory of his expression out of her mind. He'd enjoyed taunting her, threatening her.

★ ★ ★

Zachary sat on deck chatting to one of the other cabin passengers. He was amused that the man had sought his company, because at first on the voyage, the first class passengers had looked down their noses at those in the second-class cabins. But there were so few ordinary travellers in the ship, which was carrying mainly convicts and their warders, that boredom had set in for most people now. This had led to conversations that crossed all boundaries except those set around the convicts, who were closely watched and kept separate most of the time.

He felt sorry for them, would hate to have his whole life ordered by someone else. And few of

116

the convicts looked really wicked, but rather as if they'd had hard lives and were struggling to survive. One or two looked so ill that the slightest breeze might carry them off.

'So you've already read that book?' the man commented, sounding surprised.

'Yes. I used to read a lot back home. The free libraries have been a boon to thinking folk. I could never have afforded to buy so many books. My sister's the same, can't get enough to read.'

Leo came bounding up, looking happy. 'The hens are laying better now,' he announced.

The man beside Zachary turned up his nose and stirred in his seat as if thinking of leaving. A spirit of mischief made Zachary say, 'You'll be very glad of Leo's work when we're eating fresh eggs again, Mr Howish. Without him, those birds would have died. He's very clever with animals of all sorts.'

The man smiled reluctantly. 'I take your point. We all need one another here on the ship, don't we?'

Later that day Zachary went to read to a group of young children, with Leo trailing behind him. The charitable lady who'd been reading to them had grown tired of it and he'd not liked to see them disappointed. He found to his surprise that he had a talent for reading aloud, could keep them enthralled for an hour without any trouble. They were mostly the children of the prison guards who were travelling out to Australia with the convicts, but two were the children of cabin passengers. At least children didn't set invisible barriers between people saying one was fit to chat to and another wasn't.

The only convicts who had some leeway were those involved in producing the ship's weekly newspaper, making copies of the handwritten articles by various passengers. Most of the articles were on rather boring topics, such as 'The Pursuit of Knowledge' or 'Ancient and Modern Navigation' written in flowery, stilted language. He'd chuckled aloud at one, which addressed the reader as 'gentle reader'. He couldn't be bothered reading such articles, but had persevered with the 'Weekly Record' of their journey and the 'West Australian Sketches' which gave information about the colony. He made note of anything which might help him find his way about.

He was filling the time on board ship well enough, though he'd rather have had something more engrossing to occupy his mind, but he always had a sense of waiting and marking time. He kept wondering what the Blake sisters were doing, hoping he'd carry out his task well and get them safely back to England. His other main consideration was what he would do afterwards. The more he was away from Harry and the shop, the more certain he was that he couldn't work under the other man again. He'd learned to fly free, didn't want to go back into a cage.

Surely Mr Featherworth would help him find another job?

Or perhaps . . . perhaps Harry wouldn't get the job as manager. No, Harry wasn't stupid.

He'd manage the shop very carefully, make people think he was the best person to do it, even though he wasn't.

Zachary didn't rate his own chances of becoming manager very highly.

7

Before Pandora could raise the question of riding lessons, to her surprise Francis did. 'Are you still interested in learning to ride?'

'I'd love to.'

'Then I'll start teaching you. When I'm too weak to ride, you'll be able to go out with Livia.'

'When can we start?'

'Tomorrow morning. It's better not to ride in the heat of the day, for the horses' sake.'

Always with him the horses came first, she thought. What about her comfort? But the idea of learning something new made her bite back the words.

So instead of preparing breakfast, she found herself being taught about saddles and tack, shown how to approach a horse and how to offer it a sugar lump on a flat palm. She wasn't at all afraid of Duke, because Francis's horses were well trained and selected for their good temperaments. She'd often heard him say that.

When she was up on the horse for the first time, she felt nervous, because it seemed much higher than she'd expected, but Francis led Duke up and down, speaking to Pandora as gently as he spoke to his animals when he corrected her posture.

She was disappointed when he told her to get down.

He smiled. 'You did well. We'll make a

120

horsewoman of you yet. But that's enough for one day. I'd like to go for a short ride myself now. Livia? Are you ready, my dear?'

His wife, who'd been watching from the veranda, came across and untied her horse, which had been waiting patiently in the shade of a tree.

As the two of them rode off along the track, Cassandra came up to her sister. 'Did you enjoy that?'

'Yes, I did. It's very exhilarating being up on a horse's back.'

'So not everything is bad here.'

Pandora gave her a mock shove. 'You know I like some things. It's just the thought of staying here for ever, never seeing Outham again that upsets me, and sometimes a longing for the moors and Lancashire rain sweeps over me. I can't help that.' It was getting a little better though. Most of the time.

'I know, love. But you know what our aunt is like. She might even have us killed if we went back. Never forget how she had me kidnapped, and without anyone finding out what she'd done. Now, let's go and give their house a quick sweep out and tidy while they're away.'

* * *

Alice woke with a start. The full moon was shining directly on her window and in spite of the curtains, which didn't quite fit at the edges, she could see everything clearly. Something must have woken her, because she normally slept soundly, rarely stirring till morning.

121

Then she heard a sound outside on the landing and to her horror she saw the door handle turn, its faceted glass surface reflecting the moonlight so that there was no doubt it really was moving.

Someone was out there!

The door rattled, as if the person was trying to open it, but she'd shot the bolt, as she did every night. Slipping out of bed, she padded silently to the door, her eyes searching for a weapon to defend herself with if the intruder broke down the door.

It rattled even more loudly and someone called in a throaty voice, 'Are you awake, Alice Blair? Are you nervous? You ought to be. You're not wanted here.'

She didn't answer.

'You'd better leave town if you want to be safe. Leave town. Leave soon.'

The person rattled the door again then the handle stopped moving.

She didn't hear footsteps going down the stairs, didn't hear the outside door opening, but she went to the bedroom window, watching carefully. A few minutes later, just as she was about to go back to bed, she saw a man dressed all in black with a hat pulled down low over his face come out from the side alley and run across the street. He disappeared down an alley between the shops opposite. In spite of the bright moonlight she saw only his clothes and hat, not his face. He could have been anyone.

And what had he been doing for those few minutes?

Her heart was pounding. Did she dare leave

the room, go and see what the intruder had stolen? At first she thought not, then she decided that was cowardly. She'd seen someone leaving the house, hadn't she? It wasn't likely that anyone else was waiting for her.

She slipped on her dressing-gown then lit her bedside candle, wishing they had gas lighting in the bedrooms, because a candle could so easily blow out. For lack of anything better she picked up the water ewer in her free hand to protect herself with and went back to the door.

Still she hesitated to open it, then told herself she must. No one was going to frighten her away from this house.

Taking a deep breath she put the candlestick down on the nearby chest of drawers and slid the bolt gently open. She opened the door a crack, ready to slam it shut again. To her relief there was enough moonlight for her to see that there was no intruder waiting for her outside.

Picking up the candle she went out on to the landing, still holding the ewer as well. After a moment or two she raised her voice. 'Dot! Dot! Are you awake? We've had an intruder.'

There was an immediate patter of footsteps and Dot came down the attic stairs, a shawl round her shoulders and a poker in her hand. 'I heard him pass my room and go down the attic stairs, miss.'

'Do you have a bolt on your bedroom door?'

'No, miss, but I put a chair under the handle. And I always take this to bed.' She held out the poker in a hand that trembled.

'Have you had intruders before?'

'Yes, miss. Well, I think so. Only nothing was taken and Mr Prebble said it must have been my imagination. But I know I heard someone and I definitely saw a light pass my door once.'

'Is it far to the police station? Will there be someone there at this hour?'

'There's a policeman walks round the town centre every night. Mr Blake had a rattle to call him if needed. All the shopkeepers do.'

'Where is it?'

'I don't know, miss. It's vanished. I think *she* hid it. I asked Mr Prebble about it and he said there was no need for one and the town centre was quite safe.'

'We'll have to wait till morning then, unless we see the policeman on duty coming along our street.'

'We could keep watch from the sitting room, miss. We might see him pass by from there. Only if we put the gas lights on, we'll not be able to see outside very well.'

'But he'd notice that the place was lit up. Let's put all the lights on. Go and light a spill from the kitchen fire.' She saw Dot hesitating and realised the girl was afraid to go down to the ground floor on her own. 'We'll both go and get it. And we'll make some cocoa afterwards.'

Sure enough, there was a knock on the front door an hour later, and Dot peered out of the window to see a policeman standing there.

'I'll go downstairs and let him in, shall I?' She ran out of the room.

'I saw the lights. Is everything all right, love?' he asked.

'No, we've had an intruder. Come up and speak to my mistress.'

He wasn't much use, Alice thought wryly, watching him look round the house and find nothing. They'd already checked each room themselves, just to be sure.

'Are you certain you heard something, miss?' he asked for the third time.

'Absolutely positive. We both heard the intruder.' She hesitated, wondering whether to tell him what the intruder had said, but decided to ask Mr Dawson about that first.

'There's no sign of anyone breaking in.'

'He must have had a key, then.'

'Who would have keys to the shop?'

'The man who manages it, Harry Prebble. The lawyer, Mr Featherworth. And I don't know who else the Blakes gave keys to.'

'I shall have to report this to my sergeant. It's very puzzling. I'll walk past every half-hour or so for the rest of the night. You'll be quite safe now, miss.'

She didn't feel safe. Half an hour was a long time to manage without help if someone was attacking you. She didn't go back to bed, couldn't. She and Dot stayed in the sitting room, each occupying a sofa. Dot was soon asleep again, snuffling softly beneath her quilt like a tired puppy. But Alice didn't dare sleep in case whoever had a key tried to get back in again.

Who had come and threatened her? And why did he want her to leave?

She could guess who it might be, but she had no proof, so had only included his name among

125

the people she'd mentioned to the police as having keys.

She'd keep an even more careful eye on him from now on, however. And she'd forbid Dot to discuss this incident with anyone, especially those working in the shop.

* * *

The next morning she went round to see Mr Featherworth, but he was busy so she found herself talking to his clerk as she waited to see the lawyer.

Ralph stared at her in shock. 'I can't believe what I'm hearing, Miss Blair!'

'I suspect the policeman thought I was imagining it all, but I wasn't, Mr Dawson. Both Dot and I heard the intruder quite clearly. I don't want to be driven away, but as things are, anyone can walk into the living quarters from the shop and we're not sure who has keys to the shop. Why, they might leave the back door unlocked any night by mistake. Neither Dot nor I feel safe there.'

He sat without saying a word, his brow furrowed in thought, then said abruptly, 'I shall make sure something is done this very day to render the living quarters more secure. Whoever it was who threatened you, was trying to drive you away. I can't imagine why.'

'We'll need to feel secure from those in the shop, too.' She looked at him, not saying aloud what she suspected.

The look he gave her in return said he knew

126

what she was thinking. 'I take your point. You didn't recognise the man's voice?'

'No.'

When Mr Featherworth joined them, he was horrified by her news. 'My dear lady, you must move back to your cousin's at once. We cannot have you in danger.'

'I don't want to move! Apart from the fact that I need the job which gives me time to recover my health, I'd feel ashamed to let whoever it is drive me away.'

'I can't understand why anyone would want to.'

She waited for Mr Dawson to say something about that but he didn't, so she kept her suspicions to herself.

The clerk cleared his throat. 'Shall I go and examine the premises, sir? There may be something we can do to render them more secure.'

'But the expense! This is our clients' money.'

'And our clients are four young women, who will also need to feel secure there when they return. I'm quite sure they won't begrudge any money being spent on their safety.'

Mr Featherworth drummed his fingers on his desk, then nodded. 'You're right. I shall leave it in your very capable hands, Dawson. But don't spend more than you need to.'

Walking back with Mr Dawson beside her, Alice felt relaxed enough to chat normally. He was such a sensible, intelligent man. She smiled at him. 'I'm looking forward to meeting your sister, but if the living quarters haven't been made secure, I can't leave Dot on her own.'

127

'It'll only mean postponing your visit. You can come to tea another time.' As they walked through the private entrance, they heard someone shouting.

Mr Dawson put his finger to his lips and they both listened intently.

'Tell me where she's gone or you'll be sorry!'

'Miss Blair said not to talk to anyone about it. Mr Prebble, stop! You're hurting me.'

'I'm not just *anyone*, am I? I'm the manager of the shop. If you want to keep this job, my girl, you'll stay on the right side of me and — '

Dot let out a cry of pain and Alice could bear it no longer. She pushed past Mr Dawson and flung open the kitchen door.

'What are you doing here, Prebble?'

'Keeping an eye on things, miss. Dot's behaving so strangely I was worried about you.'

She saw Dot rubbing her arm and moved forward, pushing up the maid's sleeve to show a bruise already forming, the sort of bruise formed by flesh being deliberately pinched, not by a casual bump. 'Is that why you hurt her?'

'I didn't do that. She must have banged herself on something. She always was clumsy. If I was too zealous — '

'Wait for me in the shop, Prebble,' Mr Dawson said curtly.

'But I — '

The older man didn't raise his voice, but it rang with authority. 'Do as I say!'

When Prebble had left them, Mr Dawson looked at Dot. 'You did right not telling him anything. Well done. I'm sorry he hurt you. He won't do it again.'

'He'll — ' She bit off what she'd been going to say.

'Tell us,' Alice said.

She opened her mouth, then shut it and shook her head, whispering in a hoarse voice, 'I dursn't, miss. I just — dursn't talk about him. Not if you dismiss me for it.'

And what did that say about Prebble? Alice wondered. 'We'll leave it for now, then. Could you make some tea, please, and bring it upstairs? Take a cup for yourself as well.' She turned to find Mr Dawson studying the passageway that led from the narrow owner's entrance hall into the shop via another area used partly for storage.

'I think we could quite easily put a door in here, with a lock *and* a bolt on your side. We'll have the lock changed on your outer door too. That should keep you safe.'

'Dot would appreciate a bolt inside her bedroom as well.'

He nodded. 'May I look round the rest of the premises?'

'Certainly.' She led the way upstairs and they walked round the bedrooms in silence before moving upstairs again.

'The attics must be made safe as well,' he said after they'd checked the bedrooms.

They went up the narrow stairs to the attics.

'There!' He pointed and wove his way through the discarded items to the left-hand side of the big space to reveal another door, half-hidden by a pile of boxes. He tried to open it and found it locked with no sign of a key on their side. 'This needs seeing to as well. It leads into the other attics, which are used for storage for the shop.'

'I'd not have thought of that way of getting in.' To her annoyance her voice wobbled a little.

He came back to say gently, 'We'll have it all made secure before the day is over, I promise you, Miss Blair. I'll not stay for a cup of tea now, because I need to get things started, but perhaps another time?'

He had a lovely smile, she thought. He was quite an ugly man till he smiled, but then his whole face lit up with warmth and kindness.

She walked slowly back down to the kitchen to tell Dot what was to be done. The maid burst into tears of relief, but Alice hadn't finished.

'What did you not dare tell us?'

Dot stiffened.

'Let me try to guess, then you won't have told me anything, will you?'

Dot looked at her warily.

'You're afraid Harry Prebble will take it out on you if you don't do as he asks. Am I right?'

Still the girl hesitated, so Alice asked, 'Or hurt your family?'

Dot bit her lip, then nodded without meeting her eyes.

'I thought so. What's the other shopman like, the one they sent to Australia?'

Dot's face immediately brightened. 'Mr Carr is ever so kind, miss. You'd not meet anyone in Outham who'd have a bad word to say about *him*.'

'I shall look forward to meeting him then — and the new owners. Now, I'll go and work on the inventory and you can cook us a nice hearty soup for our dinner. We'll eat it together down here. We'll both feel better for having company, I'm sure. I've eaten too many meals on my own. Governesses aren't treated as members of the family in most households, you know. They're neither servants nor gentry.'

Dot looked at her in surprise. 'That must have been very lonely.' Then she clapped one hand to her mouth. 'Sorry, miss. I didn't mean to be impertinent.'

'You weren't. You were just showing you understood.'

She didn't tell the maid, but the other reason she'd be eating downstairs was to make sure Harry didn't try to get at her maid again. Once the new door was fitted, Dot should be safe enough. Alice decided not to go for a walk this afternoon either, because Harry must be aware of her habits, the way he was forever watching her out of the shop window.

From the living-room window upstairs, she saw Mr Dawson coming back along the street a short time later, but he went into the shop this time. It was fully fifteen minutes before Dot announced him and the poor man looked like a bird with its feathers ruffled.

He didn't waste his time on greetings. 'Prebble claims not to have a key to the attic door, and it opens quite easily now. He could have got up there by the back stairs, though.'

'But he must have a key. Who else could have locked it?'

'He says it's never locked but it sticks sometimes.' Mr Dawson smiled. 'It'll stick very firmly once we have the lock changed and a bolt added.

The locksmith will be here shortly, by the way.'

The workmen arrived just then and Mr Dawson went down to show them exactly what was wanted. They made a great deal of noise but it had been agreed that they'd not leave that night until the door was in place and able to be secured. She told Dot to make them cups of tea at regular intervals and to give them ham sandwiches at teatime.

'Do I buy the ham from the shop?'

'No, I will.'

Mr Dawson came round after he finished for the day and found the men still hard at work.

'Beautiful woodwork,' he told the foreman.

'The young fellow next door doesn't seem to think so. He says it's shoddy workmanship. He's complained about the noise too, says it upsets his customers.'

'Let him complain. He's not the owner of this shop.'

Mr Dawson left to get his evening meal, but asked permission to come back afterwards. 'I want to be here when the men finish.'

'I'd be happy to have your company,' Alice said. And she found it was true in more ways than one. When he returned they chatted comfortably together as the noise continued below and she enjoyed the evening, in spite of the reason for his presence.

Not until ten o'clock did the foreman ask to see them.

'I've finished, Mr Dawson.'

'You've done well.'

'It'll look better when it's fully varnished. The

132

first coat will be dry by morning.'

The clerk frowned. 'Oh, dear! That'll mean leaving the door open to dry.'

'Yes.'

'We'll have to find someone to stay here while it's being varnished, then. I'm not leaving Miss Blair and Dot unprotected.'

The foreman looked at him in astonishment. 'But it's an inside door. They'll be quite safe.'

'Keep this between ourselves, if you please, but they've had intruders more than once. I'll get someone to stay here. I know a good man who's out of work and will welcome a few extra shillings.'

He went back to tell Alice she was safe for the night and gave her a set of keys. 'You're the only one with a key to the new door, except for us. My employer and I will keep ours very safe, I promise you. And since you've had the other locks in the house changed and a bolt fitted on the attic and maid's bedroom door, you should both feel secure.'

'I can't thank you enough.'

When he'd left, Dot came out of the kitchen to look at the new door that blocked the way into the shop. 'I feel better already, miss. I'm still taking a poker to bed, though.'

'Do whatever you like.' Alice yawned as she went up to her own room. But though she didn't take a poker with her, she did bolt the door from the inside and wedge a chair under the door handle.

It would be a while before she felt safe again at night, she knew.

8

Like all the passengers, Zachary felt very excited on April the 10th when the Captain announced that the ship was nearing the coast of Western Australia. People stayed up on deck all day, feeling disappointed when there was no sign of land by nightfall.

Even the remaining animals, those brought out as breeding stock, seemed to know that the voyage was ending. They were restless, the pig grunting in its crate and the sheep bleating and edging to and fro, as far as the poor things could in such small, crowded areas.

Zachary woke very early the next morning and managed to get out of the cabin without waking Leo, who was a sound sleeper. When he went to the ship's rail, he saw a low-lying mass ahead of them, looking like a dark smear on the horizon.

'That's Rottnest Island at last,' a voice said and he turned to see the doctor standing nearby.

'Oh, yes. It was mentioned in the *Clara's Weekly Journal* a few weeks ago.' He frowned, trying to remember what had been said.

'Rottnest is a penal station for the black-fellows,' the doctor went on. 'They will keep stealing sheep and spearing cattle.'

It looked a bleak place to Zachary, low-lying scrubby land, and he couldn't help feeling sorry for anyone imprisoned there. One of the more sympathetic passengers had told him the natives didn't have the same ideas about ownership of livestock and couldn't really understand the legal niceties which decreed they should be banished to Rottnest merely for taking food. If that was true, it seemed rather unfair, like asking him to obey orders given in a foreign language he didn't understand a word of.

They stood at the rail for a few more moments then he said, 'I can't believe the journey's over at last.'

'Not quite. We have to wait for a pilot to take us in. Even then, we'll have another wait before we can disembark by small boat, because the ship won't be tying up at a wharf. The water isn't deep enough. They really ought to do something about improving Fremantle harbour.'

'I shall just be glad to get back on dry land, however we reach it.'

'You'll feel strange at first, as if the ground is still moving beneath you like the deck does.' The doctor hesitated then said, 'The Captain has asked me to sound you out about doing us a favour.'

'Oh?'

'I know you have urgent business here, but could you stay behind till we see whether anyone comes to meet Leo? We're worried about what's going to happen to him. He may have been raised a gentleman, but he's slow-witted and not at all fit to fend for himself. If I'd realised what he was like, I'd never have allowed him on board unaccompanied.'

'And if no one does come to meet him?'

'We'll have no choice but to report his presence to the Governor, who may decide he'll be safer locked away for his own protection.'

'He'd hate that. He loves being out of doors.'

'He'd hate to be beaten and bullied too, not to mention having his money and possessions stolen and going hungry. You know as well as I do that there are some people who prey on those weaker than themselves.' He waited, head cocked on one side.

'Oh, very well. I'll stay behind — for a day or two only. I can't spare any more time than that.'

'Thank you. As a partial recompense, the Captain said he would help you find out about getting a passage back to England. He'll be able to discover that much more easily than you would. As he told you before, you may have to go to Albany, on the south coast, if no ships are due to call at Fremantle. Mail ships call there every month or two and even though they don't go to England, you could take passage on one to Point de Galle in Ceylon. You'd easily find a suitable ship there and go back to England via Suez and Gibraltar. Galle is a coaling station for the Bombay, Singapore and China trade, and is a very busy port.'

'It hadn't even occurred to me that it'd be so difficult to get back to England — nor to the lawyer who sent me.'

'Yes. People joke about the ends of the earth, but I think the Swan River Colony really is one of the most isolated outposts Britain has. The other Australian colonies are much busier places. I'd not want to settle here.'

Nothing happened for a week or two and Zachary's wages were delivered by one of the shopmen on his way home. Hallie was just beginning to hope that Harry had tired of tormenting her when she met him in the park one Sunday. She'd cut through it on her way to visit a friend, as she often did.

She looked round in fear but he'd chosen his moment well and there was no one else in sight.

He grasped her arm so that she couldn't get away, his fingers digging in so hard that it hurt.

'It wasn't very friendly of you to avoid me, Hallie.'

'I'd gone out to the back. You came earlier that week.'

'Does that mean you're going to be more friendly in future?'

She couldn't think what to answer.

'I want a kiss next time . . . and after that, we'll see what happens.'

She wanted to say no, but she didn't dare. He was hurting her and smiling at her and she felt like a rabbit in a trap.

With a laugh he let go of her and took his hat off, bowing slightly. 'Nice to have met you again, Miss Carr.'

As he walked away, she saw two women staring at them and could tell that they thought she'd been meeting him secretly. She wanted to shout that she hadn't, that she hated him, but she didn't dare do that, either. All she could do was hurry home, forgetting her errands, to her mother's surprise.

★ ★ ★

Zachary watched the other cabin passengers disembark in small groups, some of the women making a fuss about the difficulties of getting down into the boat that would take them to shore. He felt impatient to get started on his mission, but one look at Leo, standing beside him staring across the water to the town of Fremantle with that slightly vacant stare, and he knew he couldn't leave the poor lad on his own. He might look big and strong, but he was too gentle for his own good, and even cringed away from the children on the ship, some of whom had tried to torment him until the ship's doctor had put a stop to it.

By the following morning Zachary was feeling impatient. What would he do if no one came to collect Leo? Take him along in the hunt for the sisters? It wouldn't be right to use their money for that. If he did, he'd have to pay it back — and with what?

A short time later a small boat came out to the ship and a man yelled up, 'My name's Sayrson. I'm looking for Leopold Hutton.'

'He's here,' one of the officers called back.

'Is he ready to leave?'

'No. He needs to get his things together and the Captain wants to see anyone asking for him.'

'I'd better come on board, then.'

Zachary had been listening to this and studying

the burly man. For some reason, he took an instant dislike to the newcomer, who heaved himself on to the deck grumbling audibly. The man might be well dressed but he looked brutal. There was no other word to describe his expression.

Leo, who had moved to the rail at the sound of his own name, took one look at Sayrson and moved closer to Zachary.

'This is Leo,' the officer said.

'Ah.' Sayrson studied him, nodding. 'You look a strong young chap. Your father has asked me to look after you and find you a job.'

'My father's dead.'

'Your stepfather, then.' Sayrson ran his eyes up and down Leo, as if he were a horse he was thinking of buying, and his smile became positively gloating as he stepped forward. 'He says you're a good worker.'

Leo backed away from him. 'I don't like you. I'm not going with you.'

Sayrson's smile vanished and he said in a harsh voice, 'You'll do as you're told, young man. Now, jump to it. Go and fetch your bags.'

'Where will you be taking him?' Zachary asked.

'What's that to do with you?'

'I've grown fond of him on the voyage. I'm concerned for his welfare.'

'Well, you don't need to be. I feed my workers well.'

'What sort of work will he be doing?'

'Physical work. What else is he capable of?'

Zachary could find no answer to that. 'So you're a relative?'

'Not me. Do I look the sort who'd breed an idiot? But I know his stepfather and have agreed to take charge of the lad this end. Better he stays with me than goes in there.' He pointed to a large building constructed of limestone blocks that looked well on its way to being finished.

Zachary looked at it in puzzlement.

Sayrson laughed uproariously. 'It's the new Lunatic Asylum. Now, this is my authorisation.' He held out a letter.

The officer standing beside Zachary took it and read it quickly, then handed it back. 'Very well, sir. I'll inform the Captain and have Leo's trunk fetched.'

'I'm not going with him.' Leo tried to back away, but could move no further.

'You've no choice, lad,' the officer said. 'Ah, Captain. This is Mr Sayrson, who's come for Leo. Mr Carr is a bit concerned.'

The Captain read the letter and turned to Zachary. 'This gentleman has the authority.'

'Leo can come with me instead. I'll look after him.'

Sayrson laughed. 'Why should I let him go with you when I've work for him? Besides, his stepfather gave him into my care, not yours. I've given him my word and I intend to keep it. Now, I've put up with your interference for long enough. Mind your own business, young man.'

Zachary could only watch helplessly as a strong sailor was recruited to help force Leo down to the boat, which rocked so wildly because of his struggles that Sayrson cuffed him about the ears. Although Leo was just as big as

140

he was, he cringed back and sat hunched up, looking as if he was crying. He was like an overgrown child, really, and as helpless as a child when it came to managing his life. How could the mother Leo spoke of with such love have allowed this to be arranged?

Had she known exactly what was to happen? Zachary doubted it.

Another sailor carried Leo's portmanteau down, then the boat cast off.

'I don't like the looks of that man,' Zachary commented.

'Nor do I, but there was nothing I could do except let him go,' the Captain said. 'The Governor won't see the need to intervene if there's someone responsible for him, because he'd be a charge on the authorities otherwise.'

It'd be a long time before Zachary forgot Leo's pleading and unhappy face growing smaller and smaller as the boat was rowed to the shore.

'Could you come to my cabin in quarter of an hour, Mr Carr?'

'Yes, Captain.'

He stood by the rail, looking across at Fremantle, which had a population of just over two thousand souls, according to articles in the ship's newspaper. Perth wasn't much larger, apparently, at just over three thousand. Surely in such small towns it'd not be hard to find the Blake sisters?

How would they feel when they found they'd been left what seemed to Zachary a small fortune? Would they take an interest in the shop? Or would they leave everything to a manager?

141

They might even sell it. He didn't know them well enough to hazard a guess.

He knew Harry only too well, though. The longer Zachary was away from his former colleague, the more certain he became that he'd have difficulty settling down to work under him.

He'd grown more confident in this new life, felt more sure of himself, something he hadn't expected. People said travel broadened the mind, but it did more than that — much more. It taught you a lot about yourself in comparison to others.

★ ★ ★

The first time Alice went to tea with the Dawsons, she was slightly nervous. They were, after all, strangers. But they made her so welcome she really enjoyed the visit.

'Perhaps you could come to tea with me next time?' she suggested as she got ready to leave.

'We'd be delighted,' Judith Dawson said. 'As long as my health permits. It's up and down, so I never know from one day to the next whether I'll be wheezing and unable to talk without coughing and spluttering, or whether I'll be able to breathe more easily.'

Ralph walked home with Alice.

'I like your sister.'

'So do I. But her health isn't good and I fear for her sometimes when she can't breathe.'

'Has she always been like this?'

'She's always been delicate, but she never complains.'

They walked slowly, chatting comfortably. The better she got to know Ralph, the more Alice liked him.

Did he like her in that same way? It was hard to tell, hard to hope, too, for a woman like her.

★ ★ ★

Alice invited Ralph and his sister to tea the following Sunday, but when the door knocker went, Dot showed only Ralph up to the parlour.

'My sister sends her apologies. She's having a bad day.'

'I'm so sorry.'

'I am too. I was looking forward to continuing our discussion about books.'

Alice hesitated. Should she? Would it cause talk to entertain him on her own? Oh, let it! 'Would you like to join me for a while? It seems a pity to waste the scones and cake.'

He beamed at her. 'I'd love to. Judith is sleeping now and probably won't wake for an hour or two. Our maid will send a lad to fetch me if I'm needed. She's very reliable. You're sure I'll not be putting you to any trouble?'

'On the contrary. It gets a bit lonely at times here.'

Two hours had passed before either of them realised it.

'I shouldn't have stayed so long.' He stood up.

She walked down to the door with him. 'I'm glad you did. I feel much more cheerful for some company.'

'No more troubles during the night?'

'None at all.'

'And Prebble has been very quiet, doing what he was asked and not going beyond his remit. I still can't trust him, though.'

'Neither can I. Will he be given the manager's job when the new owners get back?'

'Not if I have any say about it. The trouble is, the shop is indeed making more money under his management and Mr Featherworth is pleased about that.'

'Perhaps Prebble has learned his lesson.'

Ralph sniffed scornfully. 'Leopards don't change their spots.'

★ ★ ★

Zachary was shown into the Captain's cabin.

'Do sit down, Carr. I'd like to thank you for your help with Leo on this voyage and the Governor has sent his thanks as well. I'm happy to tell you that his aide remembers the young women you're looking for. There was a bit of a fuss when the oldest sister was accused of stealing, but it was proved that it was an error and the money was indeed her own. Since her new employer has purchased some land, we have her address. Two of her sisters went to another employer nearby.' He held out a piece of paper. 'These are the details.'

Zachary scanned the piece of paper eagerly, then frowned. 'It's not in Perth, then?'

'Apparently not. It's a good day's ride south. You'll have to seek other help than mine to find it, but this is a start and if she's still working

144

there, she's bound to know where her sisters are. Apparently maidservants change employment rather frequently here, or leave to get married.'

'Thank you. I'm extremely grateful for your help. It'll be best to start with the eldest sister, I'm sure. What about a passage back? Did you manage to find out what ships are expected?'

'Bit difficult, that. The *Clara* is going on to Madras next, not back to England, as you know, and there aren't any other ships known to be coming to Fremantle until the end of the year.'

Zachary looked at him in dismay. '*But that's several months away!*'

'I'm afraid so. Your best bet for a speedy return would be the mail ship that's due to call at King George Sound next month, the SS *Bombay*. It's due to arrive around May 1st, give or take a day. Even that makes rather a tight schedule for you.'

'I thought the mail ships stopped at somewhere called Albany in the south of the colony.'

'Same place. The town is Albany, the harbour is King George Sound. It's deep water and well protected. The Governor says you can send a message under his patronage on the coastal steamer that plies between here and Albany to book cabins for yourself and the four sisters. Then you can all take the next steamer down to Albany.'

'If I've found all of them by then.'

'Yes. And no one can guarantee whether they'll have any free cabins on the SS *Bombay*. I think you should accept this offer of help, though, and do your best to get to Albany in time. If you write a letter booking passages, I'll see it gets to the Governor and he'll send it on the coastal steamer with the official mail.'

Zachary was feeling rather overwhelmed. 'It sounds as if I'll have my work cut out to find the sisters and get them to Albany in time.'

'What other choice do you have? But there will be another mail ship two months after that, at least.'

Realising from the Captain's expression that he'd given as much time as he could spare, Zachary thanked him for his help and left. He wrote the letter booking passages then got himself and his baggage off the ship. He had little trouble with the customs and health checks, thanks to the doctor's help, then paid two shillings and sixpence to go up the Swan River on a small steamer to the city of Perth.

What he found there shocked him to the core. He already knew it was quite a small city, considering it was the capital of a British colony, but he hadn't expected it to look so . . . *unfinished* was the word that came to mind. Most of the streets weren't even paved and the loose sand underfoot made for slow and uncomfortable walking. This gave him time to study the irregular assortment of buildings that lined the streets and note how many blocks of land were left empty between them.

He found a small hotel and as it was getting dark by then, decided to wait until the following morning to make inquiries about getting to the address the Governor had given him.

As he was being shown to a table for his

146

evening meal, he stiffened. Surely that was . . . It *was*! The man who'd taken Leo away was sitting in the far corner, fortunately with his back to the room. Leo wasn't with him. Sayrson didn't turn round, so Zachary hurried to his own table and sat with his back to the others, hoping not to be recognised.

Fortunately Sayrson had such a loud voice that his conversation carried clearly across the room.

'Got myself a new helper, an idiot but strong. I'll be sending him out to the country tomorrow. He's a bit reluctant to work, but he's as frightened of being beaten as the next person.'

His companion laughed.

Zachary froze. *Beaten?* He couldn't bear the thought of gentle Leo being ill-treated.

There was the sound of chairs being pushed back and the two men said their farewells. Zachary kept his head turned away but was able to watch their reflections in the window as they left the room. He then saw them walk past outside and go their separate ways, so beckoned to the waiter and slipped him a coin.

'The gentleman who was sitting in the corner, a Mr Sayrson, do you know where he lives?'

The waiter shook his head. 'Sorry, sir. He's a stranger to me, just came in for a meal with the other gentleman.'

'I'll see if I can catch up with him. I'll be back shortly. Keep my table.'

Zachary hurried outside but Sayrson had vanished from sight. He walked along the street a little way, but couldn't see him and there was

147

nothing he could do to find the man in a strange city after dark, so returned to his meal.

Before he went to bed he asked the obliging waiter how he could set about tracing Sayrson.

'If he doesn't live in Perth, you could try the livery stables, sir. He'd have left his horse at one of them.'

That night Zachary lay in bed staring into the darkness, unable to get the word 'beaten' out of his mind, feeling as if he'd let Leo down badly.

He didn't manage to get to sleep until he'd decided to take an extra day in Perth to look for the poor lad. What he'd do if he did find him, he didn't know, but he couldn't leave Leo to be beaten and ill-treated by such a brute.

That meant postponing the business which had brought him here and he felt guilty about that, given the time constraints. But sometimes you simply had to do what was right. His father had taught him that. *Be proud of what you do in life, however humble your station*, he'd always told Zachary.

★ ★ ★

Alice finished doing the inventory for Mr Featherworth and since she found time hanging heavily on her hands in the evenings, she decided to see if Dot would like to learn to read and write more fluently.

Dot stared at her when she made the offer. 'Teach me to read 'n' write proper, you mean?'

'Yes. Would you like that?'

'I s'pose so. I'm not very clever, though. Mr

148

Prebble says I'm stupid.'

'Well, he's wrong. You're not at all stupid.'

'What about my housework, miss?'

'It'll still be there the next day if you don't finish it one day.' Since the young maid was still frowning, she said gently, 'Times are changing and people need to be able to read properly nowadays. It'll stand you in good stead for the rest of your life.'

Dot shrugged. 'Well, if you say so, miss, I don't mind giving it a try.'

It was a different matter when Alice started reading a story aloud. Wide-eyed, the girl forgot her diffidence, leaned her elbows on the table and listened raptly.

When Alice came to the end of the story, Dot sighed happily. 'I used to like it when my gran told me stories. She knew dozens of them. Fair take you out of yourself, stories do. I'd forgot that.'

'Then we must make sure you can read them for yourself from now on. There's a free lending library in town, you know.'

From then on the young maid soaked up the new knowledge like a thirsty sponge and the lessons were a pleasure for both of them.

Since it'd be months before the new owners of the shop could return from Australia, Alice also volunteered to help with the reading classes being offered to those still without work. There were some for men who weren't strong enough to break stones, as well as for the young women.

She felt nervous at first because these were grown men, but soon forgot that because she felt

149

so sorry for them. They were gaunt, their clothes were ragged and hunger was written on their faces. They might not be actually starving, thanks to the various charities in the town, but they obviously weren't eating properly.

Some of them surprised her, displaying a hunger of a different sort — for knowledge. They soaked it up in a way that put the spoiled children of the rich whom she'd taught before to shame. These people wanted to understand their world, to learn what life was like in other places, to follow the path of the war in America that had taken so much away from the people of Lancashire. She helped them read the newspaper and they were all glad that the war seemed to be coming to an end, though if the Union forces from the North won, what would happen about supplies of cotton from the South, without slaves to produce it, was anyone's guess.

Those who weren't really interested in learning, who were at the classes merely to earn their food and relief money, gave her no trouble. They seemed content just to be in the warmth of the Methodist Chapel Hall and to sit quietly.

Alice had only one worry now, but it was a major one and kept her awake sometimes: what was she going to do when the Blake sisters returned? She had made friends in Outham, as well as having her closest remaining relative there. She desperately wanted to stay in the town, hated the thought of returning to the lonely life of a governess.

★ ★ ★

As Friday approached, Hallie couldn't sleep for worrying about Harry's visit. When the door-knocker went she had to answer it because her mother had nipped next door to see the neighbours about something.

She opened it and stared at him, telling herself he was smaller than she was and he couldn't force her to do anything she didn't want.

'Mother not answering the door tonight?' he mocked.

She nearly said her mother was next door, but stopped herself just in time. 'She's within earshot,' she said.

'Then you'd better kiss me quietly,' he said.

'I'm not kissing you.'

'Don't you care about your mother's safety?'

She stared at him, feeling sick.

'It could be a knife in the stomach next time.' He grabbed her arm. 'Now I'll have that kiss.'

And heaven help her, she didn't dare pull away when he yanked her head down and gave her a brutal kiss.

'Nice soft lips you've got,' he said in a throaty voice. 'I wonder if the rest of you is as soft.'

He thrust an envelope into her hand and walked away laughing.

She couldn't move for a moment or two, feeling sick, shuddering. When she looked up a man was staring at her from across the street. She felt her face burn with shame and whisked inside the house.

She didn't even dare let herself cry, because her mother would want to know why.

The following morning, Zachary walked round Perth, armed with a list of the main livery stables drawn up by the helpful waiter. He tried to explore the streets systematically, but lost his way several times. He kept an eye on the most imposing building, using it as a marker. It was a large church, which he was told was the Roman Catholic cathedral. The Governor's residence was small and shabby in comparison.

At midday, not feeling optimistic about his chances of finding Leo, because he'd drawn a blank so far, he went up to a small bluff to look down at the city and try to work out some other strategy for his search. Below him lay Perth Water, a wide expanse of river with one or two small boats moving slowly across. It had been peaceful when he arrived yesterday, but the wind was getting up and its surface was now grey and choppy.

As he began to make his way back into the town, it started to rain and he slowed down, turning up his overcoat collar and wishing he had an umbrella.

At the next livery stables he tried, he saw Sayrson coming out. He stopped moving in shock, because he had just about lost hope of finding the man. Then he gathered his wits together and stepped off the pavement to stand under a very large tree, waiting there until the fellow had moved in the opposite direction.

Sayrson didn't notice him because he was hurrying as if to get out of the rain.

Zachary left his hiding place, intending to follow Sayrson but as he passed the garden to one side of the livery stables he heard someone sobbing from a shed-like building made of wood. One side of this formed part of the garden wall, so he clearly heard a man sobbing, his voice low and desperate.

Something about it seemed familiar and he stopped to listen. Was it — could that possibly be Leo?

He hesitated. He might lose his main chance if he went to investigate and let Sayrson get away. After all, he wasn't sure it was Leo. But it was definitely someone in great distress and that decided him.

The gate was only latched so he lifted the little iron bar quietly and entered the ill-tended garden. There was no one around to stop him and no windows looked out on to this area from the main stable block. He went towards the shed and listened again at the door. The person was still sobbing, but more quietly now.

There was a small window in the shed wall, but it was dirty and too high up to look through. The door was fastened by a bolt on the outside but the padlock on this was hanging open. After a quick glance round, Zachary drew the bolt back quietly and opened the door.

The man sitting in one corner cringed backwards, putting up one arm as if to ward off a blow. His face was bruised and swollen, but he was still easily recognisable.

When Leo saw who it was, he opened his mouth to call out.

'Shh!'

Leo didn't speak but he mouthed the word 'Zachary' and his eyes lit up with hope.

He was shackled by his left leg to the wall. It was a contraption more suited to a slave master of old than a civilised man and it outraged Zachary that anyone would treat another person like this.

'Have you come to take me back to the ship?' Leo asked hopefully.

'We need to get that chain off you before I can take you anywhere.'

'I've tried and I can't. That bad man has the key on his watch chain.'

Zachary studied the shackle, which was attached to a wooden post by a giant staple of rusty iron. Looking round, he saw a spade in the other corner. 'Turn your head away.' He used the corner of the spade to chop at the rotting wood and lever out the staple. His heart was thumping with anxiety the whole time in case Sayrson returned or someone else heard the noise and came to investigate.

It took a minute or two's hard work to loosen the staple and lever it out. There was no way he could cut the chain off Leo's ankle, so he picked it up and pulled the lad to his feet, shoving the end of the chain into his hand. 'Come on. Keep hold of that and put my overcoat over your arm to hide it.'

He went to the doorway and sucked in his breath in dismay. 'Shhh!' A man was standing in the garden, puffing on a smelly pipe. Zachary put his mouth near Leo's ear and whispered,

'We'll have to wait until he finishes and goes inside before we can leave the shed.'

Leo whispered back, 'Mr Sayrson's coming back later. He said we're leaving tomorrow. I don't want to go with him.'

Zachary put one arm round the lad's shoulders. 'I won't let him take you and hurt you again, I promise.'

His promise seemed to reassure Leo.

Zachary just hoped he could keep it.

★ ★ ★

Pandora felt happy that she was to have another riding lesson this morning. She loved being up on Duke and even Francis admitted that she was doing quite well at learning to ride.

He insisted they have the lesson before the heat of the day, for the horses' sake, though the weather wasn't nearly as hot now that it was autumn.

Livia waved one hand dismissively when Pandora worried about making the bread.

'You can do that later.'

'If it's all right with you.' She looked towards the path that linked the two properties. 'Cassandra and Reece are late this morning.'

'Well, they're both hard workers, so if they're late occasionally, I'm not bothered. After all, your sister is expecting a child.'

It was well after the riding lesson had ended that Reece came along the track on his own. Pandora abandoned her dough to run forward and meet him. 'Is Cassandra all right?'

He nodded and walked across with her to Livia. 'Sorry I'm late, but we didn't sleep very well last night. Cassandra had bad indigestion. To make matters worse, the baby was kicking a lot and she found it hard to get comfortable. We both overslept, I'm afraid. I've left her resting.'

Instead of stopping for dinner at midday, Pandora got permission to go and visit her sister.

She found Cassandra sitting on the veranda in a rocking chair Kevin had found for her. 'How are you? You look pale. I was worried when you didn't come this morning.'

'I'm just a little tired. Reece fusses too much.'

'You'd think it was his baby.' She realised this wasn't a tactful thing to say and added, 'He seems to be looking forward to having it.'

Cassandra smiled fondly. 'I'm so glad he feels it's his, now. We've agreed never to say anything different.'

'Of course not.'

'Where's Kevin?'

'Looking after Delilah. He spends a lot of time with that horse, sitting on a stool and talking to her. You'd swear she understands every word.'

'Isn't it strange what life does to us? Who'd ever have thought we'd end up in Australia or be working as housemaids?' Pandora smiled and corrected, 'Outdoor maids, really. What those two would do without our help, I don't know.'

'Reece is nagging me to stop work completely soon. I may just work in the mornings from now on, because I do get tired more easily, but I'd go mad with nothing to do while he's working here. And besides, every full day I work is another half day off the time Reece owes Mr Southerham.'

'You'll still be busy. You've your own housework to do.'

'Kevin does quite a bit, the lighter jobs anyway, and you know we take our washing and do it with the Southerhams'.'

'How is Kevin?'

Cassandra's expression saddened and she said in a low voice, 'He's always cheerful, but you can't help noticing he has more difficulty doing some things and gets tired more easily.'

'Francis is the same. I've heard him coughing sometimes during the night, now he's sleeping on the veranda. Yet Livia always stays cheerful. She's a wonderful wife to him. It makes me ashamed that I've let my homesickness get me down.'

'You seem happier than you were.'

'Yes, but . . . well, the feeling of loss is still there. Something inside me yearns for England. I can't believe you don't feel the same.'

'I do miss some things, but I'm enjoying life here and I love the warmer climate.'

'I don't! It's such a relief that the weather's cooler now.'

'Kevin says the winter rains will start any time and it'll get quite chilly. How did the riding go today?'

Pandora's face lit up. 'Wonderful.'

She chatted to her sister for a while, then had to leave and hurry back to work. What would she do when she didn't have Cassandra working with her most days? Go mad, probably. Amiable as they were, the Southerhams were always disorganised and would change their minds without warning after Pandora had planned and sometimes started another task. So she was often prevented from working efficiently, which gave her no pride in what she was doing.

9

As the man in the garden finished his pipe and knocked out the embers against his boot sole, it began to rain. He hurried inside and Zachary shepherded Leo quickly out of the shed. The chain clanked at the slightest movement and he tried to wrap it more securely in the overcoat. But it was still attached to Leo's ankle and someone was bound to notice that once they were out in the streets. And what would they think of a man carrying an overcoat in such weather instead of wearing it?

The rain grew markedly heavier and he looked up to see charcoal-coloured clouds massed overhead. No sign of any breaks in the lowering mass. Perhaps the worsening weather might help them get away because who'd willingly be out on a day like this?

As they turned a corner a few streets on, however, Leo bumped into a man and let the overcoat slip to the ground.

The man stopped dead, looked down at the chain and then stared at Zachary. 'Helping him escape, are you?'

'Only from an employer who's treated the poor fellow badly. He's not a convict but is being treated like one because he's not — um, quick-thinking. You can see for yourself how badly he's been beaten.'

All hung in the balance for a moment or two

then the man looked at Leo's childlike expression and gave them a wry smile. 'Well, I was a convict once and one of the guards treated me badly, so I know what it feels like to be beaten. You need help if you're to get him away, though. They're sticklers about masters and servants here, only it's the masters' rights the law supports all the time, not the servants'. They put one fellow in jail a while back for trying to leave his employment against his master's wishes. And he wasn't a convict or ticket of leave man.'

Zachary drew in a long, shuddering breath of relief that this man wasn't going to try to stop them. 'I'd be grateful for any help you can give me.'

'We can't stand out here in the rain talking about it. Look, I live just along the road. Come to my house. I must be mad, but I'll see if I can help you. Only hide those damned chains and stop them clanking.'

He shook his head as they tried in vain to do this. 'No good. You two walk behind me. If anyone stops you, I'll hurry on and pretend you're not with me. I can't risk people thinking I'm involved in something against the law. I've got my ticket of leave now and I don't want to go back into jail.'

He led the way at a brisk pace and to Zachary's relief, the people they passed in the street were more concerned to get out of the rain than investigate the faint clanking sound, though one or two did stare in amazement at the coat hanging over Leo's arm on such a day instead of protecting him from the downpour.

After a few minutes their guide stopped at a

narrow weatherboard house crammed between others of similar size. He flung open the front door and hurried inside, beckoning to them to follow with one hand. 'It's not grand but it keeps the weather off.'

They were just in time. Outside thunder boomed overhead, lightning flashed and even heavier rain beat down on the tin roof, producing a drumming sound that made it necessary to raise their voices to talk.

'It's just coming into the rainy season, first real rain of the year,' their rescuer said. 'Give me the cooler weather any day.' He held out one hand. 'Fred Moore.'

Zachary shook the hand, introducing himself and Leo.

'I'll get the fire burning up and make us a cup of tea while you tell me your story.' Fred put more wood on the smouldering embers and swung the soot-blackened kettle over the flames on its chain.

He listened in silence as Zachary explained what had been happening then looked at Leo. 'Poor sod. I hate shackles. They shackled me when I was a convict and they do it to the blacks too. I've still got the scars on my ankles. I'd not chain an animal like that, let alone a human being.' He stood up. 'Well, Leo my lad, let's get that thing off you, then we'll bathe those cuts and bruises. That fellow must have laid into you good and hard.'

'He slapped me.' Leo cradled one hand against his bruised cheek. 'When I hit him back, he hit me with a stick till I fell down.'

Fred didn't take long to saw off the shackles. 'I'll throw this damned thing into the river after dark. More important, what are we going to do with you two?' He looked at Zachary as he added, 'You'll need to get him right away from Perth or they'll recapture him. Do you have anywhere to go outside the city?'

So Zachary explained his mission.

Fred let out a mirthless laugh. 'Good luck to these sisters, wherever they are. I wish someone would leave *me* a bloody fortune.' He stared into the fire for a moment or two, then said, 'I think I can find a fellow to guide you, but you'll need to hire horses. Have you enough money?'

'Yes. But will they hire them to a stranger who's going out of town?'

'It's a bit of a problem, but I know someone who might help us. Leave that to me. Can your friend ride?'

They looked at Leo, who was holding his hands out towards the warmth and seemed too weary to pay attention to what they were saying.

'Can you ride a horse, Leo?'

His face brightened. 'Yes. I like riding. I like horses.'

Zachary grimaced. 'It's me who's not got much skill at riding. I've ridden my cousin's horse around his farm, but I'd not call myself an experienced rider, not by any means.'

'You'll be sore and stiff the first few days, then. But the only way to get around the colony is by horse or cart, and horse is faster. You could pay for a place in the mail wagon that goes to Albany, if that's where you're heading, but it

162

only goes every month or so. Besides, you need to find this place where the girl's working first and there's no saying how far away from the main road that is. The mail wagon wouldn't wait around for you, not even for half a day.'

'No, I can see that. Well, I can face being sore from riding. If I pay you for your time will you help us hire horses and find us a guide?'

Fred brightened. 'Yes. If I was a good man, I'd do it out of kindness, but I'm in need of money, so I'll ask you for five pounds because I'm taking a bit of a risk helping you. But for that, I'll make sure you get a guide you can rely on and he'll help you get horses. Where exactly is this place you're looking for?'

'All I have is the address.'

'Tell it to me.'

'If you have pen and paper, I'll copy the address out for you.'

Fred let out another snort of laughter. 'I'm not so good with the reading, and I'm even worse at writing. Just tell me the address and I'll remember it.'

Later that day he brought back a taciturn man called Bert, who nodded when introduced then listened to Zachary's explanation in silence.

Fred nudged his friend to speak. 'You know where they want to go, don't you?'

Bert nodded. 'More or less. It'll be one of the new farms in the foothills, but someone round there will know where it is.'

'We need to hire horses and we'd like to set off as early as possible tomorrow to get Leo out of Perth before most people are up and about,'

Zachary said. 'Can you arrange that?'

Bert frowned. 'Can't get ready for tomorrow morning. Have to get supplies as well as horses. Day after would be better.'

Zachary sighed. More delays.

When Bert had gone, he looked at Fred. 'Can you let Leo sleep here until we leave?'

'If he doesn't mind a blanket on the floor.'

They looked at Leo.

'You'll be all right here with Fred, won't you?'

Leo looked anxious. 'I want to stay with you.'

'It'd not be safe at my hotel. Sayrson might find you. You stay with Fred. I'll come round to see you first thing tomorrow and we'll set off the morning after.'

'Promise.'

'I promise.' He slipped Fred some more money. 'Get him something to eat. Now, what do I do with my trunk?' he wondered aloud. 'We can't take that on horseback.'

'Pack what you can in the saddlebags and send the rest down to Albany on the coastal steamer,' Fred said. 'What about your things, Leo?'

He scowled. 'Mr Sayrson took my bag and trunk. He said I'd not need good clothes and he was going to sell them. I've only got these clothes.'

Zachary turned to Fred again. 'We'll have to buy him some more.'

Another grin said his host expected to make additional money from this. 'I happen to know a second-hand clothes dealer.'

Zachary walked back to the hotel, shoulders hunched against the rain, trying to avoid the puddles that lay everywhere, in spite of the sandy soil. By now his boots were so wet they squelched as he walked and he was shivering.

Was he doing the right thing? He could only hope so.

★ ★ ★

Ralph Dawson went out after dark, collar turned up and hat pulled down so that he wouldn't be easily recognised. He knocked on a door a few streets away. 'Could I speak to your husband, Mrs Worth?'

'Come in, do.'

'I'd rather have a quick word here.'

Marshall Worth came hurrying to the door. 'Mr Dawson! Is something wrong?'

'No. I wonder if you'd come round to my house. I may have some more work for you.'

The man's face lit up. Ralph felt sorry for him. Marshall had been an overlooker in a small spinning mill until the lack of cotton closed the town's mills. Now, he worked at breaking stones, or doing anything he could to earn an extra penny or two.

'I'll come with you now.'

'No. I don't want us to be seen together. It may sound strange, but wait a few minutes then come to our back door and don't let anyone see you. It's all right — it's nothing dishonest. I'll explain later.' He left at once, hurrying home by another route. He felt a bit foolish, acting like this, but he wanted his dealings with Marshall kept secret and the other man's house was too small and crowded with children to be sure of that.

165

There was a knock on his back door shortly after he arrived home. He gestured to a chair. 'Would you like a cup of tea and a scone as we talk?'

The other hesitated.

'This is no time to be proud,' Ralph said quietly.

'Thank you.'

When they were seated, Ralph explained about the shop, the missing heirs and the temporary manager.

'Never trust a Prebble,' Marshall said at once. 'If you lived on certain streets you'd find people afraid of all that family, and though Harry Prebble works in a respectable occupation, there are rumours about him, too.'

'What sort of rumours?'

'The maid who worked in the Blakes' house before Dot was sacked for immorality, was expecting a child. She refused to say who the father was and drowned herself in the mill reservoir — only I happen to know the man who pulled her body out and he said it looked as if she'd been beaten. I saw her myself with Harry Prebble, not just once but several times. She never said his name, mind, so we can't be sure. I was surprised when you put him in charge of the shop.'

'There was no one else suitable. He seemed to have a clean slate there and I can't deny that he knows his job. But just in case . . . We want to appoint someone to work in the shop and keep an eye on what Prebble's doing. Would you be willing to do that?'

166

'I'd jump at the chance.' Marshall laughed. 'I've enough friends to be sure *I* won't end up in the reservoir. But I know nothing about shop work.'

'You can learn.'

'Won't he guess I'm there to spy on him?'

'Probably. But I'll interview a few other men at the same time.' Ralph hesitated again. 'There's the question of clothes. Do you have anything smarter than that?'

Marshall shook his head, embarrassment flooding his cheeks with colour. 'We had to pawn my best things to feed the children. Even so, our youngest died. Too weak to fight an illness she was, the doctor said.'

Ralph patted his hand. He'd heard many stories like this one. 'Then I'll give you some money and you can get something suitable from the second-hand clothes dealer.'

'Are you sure?'

'Very sure.'

And suddenly his childhood friend was weeping, strangled sobs that shook the man's whole body.

Hard times indeed, Ralph thought as he patted Marshall's shoulder, when a strong man like this was driven to near desperation.

★ ★ ★

The following morning, Zachary was back at Fred's house by nine o'clock. He was relieved to see Leo looking a lot happier.

'Your friend certainly likes his food,' Fred said with a smile.

'I was hungry,' Leo said. 'That bad man only gave me bread and water. Said I had to earn more.'

The other men exchanged disgusted glances.

'Mean sod,' Fred muttered.

Bert arrived a few minutes later and took Zachary to a small livery stables whose owner he knew. They paid for the hire of three riding horses and two pack horses. The owner said he trusted Bert to bring the animals back to Perth afterwards and the two men shook hands on it.

'They're not such good nags, but they'll get us there,' Bert said once they were back at Fred's house. 'My friend wouldn't let his best horses go so far away, even with me to keep an eye on them.'

Zachary wasn't as sure about the staying power of such sorry-looking animals but beggars couldn't be choosers.

He arranged to send his trunk on the coastal steamer and went back to see Fred again.

It was wrong to spend the money Mr Featherworth had given him on rescuing Leo, he knew that but couldn't help it. To treat a man as a slave just because he was slow-thinking, made his gorge rise, as did the needless cruelty. It wasn't necessary anyway. If you were kind to Leo, he'd work his heart out for you. Look how he'd cared for the animals on the ship. 'Can we be ready to leave first thing in the morning?'

'It's a Sunday.'

'What does that matter? We need to get Leo out of town.'

'All right. Better fetch your things from the

hotel now. We'll set off just before dawn. Don't worry. I'll see your trunk and bag safely on the coastal steamer for you on Monday.' Bitterness rang in his voice. 'I only steal when I'm hungry and you're paying me enough to eat well for a few weeks. I won't cheat you.'

A more unlikely guardian angel it'd be hard to find, Zachary thought as he strode back to the hotel for his things. The rain had stopped for the moment and the sky was looking brighter, but there was a moist chill to the air that had him shivering.

He still had to find the Blake sisters and get them to Albany in time to catch the mail ship — and this in a colony without railways. He didn't want to wait until July for the next mail ship or the end of the year for a ship from Fremantle.

What he was going to do with Leo when he left, he didn't know, only that he couldn't leave him in Perth to be ill-treated, just could not. He'd have to pay back what he'd spent on Leo, however long it took him, even if it meant continuing to work at the shop under Harry Prebble.

Sometimes doing what was right wasn't the most comfortable thing.

* * *

They set off at first light, with Leo dressed in a motley collection of garments. There were the three mounts and two packhorses carrying their possessions, plus food for them and the horses.

'These poor animals are old and tired,' Leo said disapprovingly. 'Aren't there any better ones?'

'Only these,' Bert said.

'We'll have to be kind to the poor things.'

Bert rolled his eyes and shook his head slightly as if praying for patience.

'Will we be able to buy more food on the way?' Zachary asked.

'Yeah.'

Getting information from their guide was like chiselling words out of stone, Zachary decided after a while and stopped trying to chat.

Bert had given Leo the ugliest of the horses to ride, an animal which had bared its teeth at Zachary when he approached it. It had let Leo handle it happily enough, though, nudging him for further attention.

'You're right,' Bert admitted after a while. 'He does know horses.'

The animal Zachary was riding refused to do anything but amble along.

After an hour they stopped to let him get down and stretch his legs. His thighs in particular were already aching from the unaccustomed exercise.

'We'll take it easy today,' Bert said. 'Y've not been on a horse much, have you?'

'No, not much and not for months.'

'Shows. But y've not got a bad seat for a beginner.'

By mid-afternoon, Zachary was in great pain, wondering how to manage for much longer.

Bert reined his animal in and the others

followed suit. 'I reckon we'd better stop for the night. You've had enough, Zachary.'

'Is there an inn near here?'

Bert laughed. 'No. We'll see if we can find a farm to sell us feed for the horses and let us sleep in a barn.'

'Are they likely to do that?'

'Don't know what it's like in England, but people don't turn away travellers here, even if they've not got a bed to offer them.'

With that Zachary had to be content. He prayed they'd find somewhere soon. He couldn't face getting on that horse again.

And tomorrow, Bert said, they'd be close to where the Southerhams now lived, might even find the farm.

10

Zachary woke in the dim light of early dawn on Monday morning, feeling painfully stiff from riding. A night sleeping on a prickly, rustling pile of hay hadn't helped much, either. He stood up, stifling a groan, trying not to wake the others.

But when he looked round, they were both gone and their blankets too. He listened, heard a voice and followed the sound to where Bert and Leo were tending the horses. Bert was whistling softly and Leo was talking to the horse he'd been riding the day before.

'There you are,' Bert said. 'I was just coming to wake you.' He grinned. 'Stiff?'

Zachary nodded.

'It'll wear off.'

They ate a hasty breakfast, provided by their hostess and paid for with more of Mr Featherworth's money, then set off again.

Zachary sighed as he forced himself to mount the horse and subject his aching body to more jolting around.

He hoped they'd find this Westview Farm quite soon.

*　*　*

Ralph summoned Prebble to see him. 'Mr Featherworth and I have decided that the vacant position at the shop would be better filled by an

172

older man who's out of work than some youngster. Why you had to dismiss that other man, I can't think.'

'A mill worker! We need someone who's good at arithmetic and can write a legible hand.' Harry tried not to scowl. He'd dismissed the temporary shopman appointed soon after Zachary left so that his cousin could come and work there. He definitely didn't want someone chosen by Mr Dawson spying on him.

'I'm aware of that. We're not thinking about the operatives, though many of them can read and write as well as you or I.' He ignored the younger man's scornful expression. 'We're thinking of men who've been in positions of authority in the mills, over-lookers or charge hands. I've found four who will be coming here for an interview tomorrow.'

He let the silence drag on for a while, seeing the outrage on Prebble's face, before adding casually, 'I thought you might like to join me in questioning them.'

'I can't recommend someone unsuitable.'

'You don't know that until you've met them. One might be just what we need.'

'How did you find them?'

'Mr Featherworth asked some of the mill owners and they recommended men who had been overlookers before these troubles came upon us.' This wasn't quite true because it was Marshall Worth who had suggested the names. The other three men would be paid to irritate Harry at the interviews and Marshall had vouched for their ability to keep the true

173

situation to themselves. Like him, they'd jumped at a chance to earn a little extra money.

'When are they coming?'

'Tomorrow morning. I saw no reason to wait once I had the names. I know you're short-handed again.'

Still suspicious, Prebble agreed to join him the following day.

As had been planned the men acted in a surly uncooperative manner when speaking to Prebble.

'You need to do mental arithmetic,' he said in a condescending tone. 'See if you can do these sums in your heads?'

Two of the men made such big errors that Ralph looked warningly at them but Prebble didn't seem to realise that they were leading him on.

The other one tossed back an answer and turned to Ralph. 'Do I need to answer this snirpy little chap? He's treating me like a child. I could do sums like that when I were seven year old.'

'Just do what he asks you.'

The man proceeded to toss answers back immediately each question had been asked, and each time he was correct.

Prebble breathed deeply and asked some more difficult questions.

Marshall spoke more calmly, but he too answered even the hardest ones instantly.

It was clear that such skill did not please their young interviewer.

When they'd finished and the men were waiting outside, Ralph looked questioningly at his fellow interviewer. 'Well? What do you think?'

'None of them are suitable. They won't know how to treat the sort of people *we* serve.'

'Mr Featherworth is determined one of these men shall have the job.'

Prebble sighed. 'Then we'll have to give one a try. But I must reserve the right to dismiss the man if he's not suitable.'

'That right belongs to Mr Featherworth, I'm afraid.'

'But I'm the manager.'

'Temporary manager. And if you upset Mr Featherworth in his act of philanthropy, he won't look favourably on you gaining the job permanently, believe me.'

Prebble gave him a dirty look that said he suspected a spy was being planted.

'So which one shall we choose?' This was a gamble but Ralph hoped it would pay off.

'Worth is the least unsuitable.'

'Not Freeman?'

Prebble shuddered. 'Definitely not.'

'I had thought Freeman the most intelligent.'

'I cannot agree. And he was downright impertinent to me.'

Ralph had enjoyed that and had had great trouble in keeping his face straight. 'Well . . . you have to work with him so I shall let you have your way in this and appoint Worth. But we'll review the matter after a week or so because I'm not at all sure about him. I still incline to Freeman. Let's bring Worth in and tell him, then you can take him back to the shop with you.'

'Now?'

'Why not? He'll be eager to start work straight

175

away because he needs the money. And of course, you'll provide him with a dinner as you do the other workers.'

Prebble threw his hands up. 'On your head be it. If he upsets the customers . . . '

'I doubt any of those men would ever put a job at risk,' Ralph said quietly. 'You know what it's like for them. Have you no compassion?'

'My job is to manage the emporium and make money for the owners, not run a charity.'

Ralph got up to ask Marshall to come in, thinking that he disliked Prebble more each time he had to deal with him.

★　★　★

As the two men walked briskly back to the shop, Prebble said curtly, 'You're only on trial, Worth. See that you work hard.'

'Oh, I'll do that, sir, never fear.' Marshall disliked all Prebbles on principle and hated calling this runt 'sir' but was determined to keep this job, the first he'd had in over a year, not to mention helping out his friend Ralph Dawson.

Marshall's wife had wept for joy when he told her in strictest confidence what was happening. His children would eat much better from now on, because you got food more cheaply when you worked in a grocery store, Mr Dawson had explained. And if there was anything suspicious going on at the emporium, Marshall would find out. He'd not let Ralph down.

At the shop Prebble found him a long apron and gave him the lowliest job there was, weighing out sugar and tea. Marshall finished the task as quickly and carefully as he could.

The shop lad gaped as he passed. 'You've not finished already?'

'Yes. What do I do next?'

'Better ask Mr Prebble.'

Prebble too seemed surprised that he'd finished so quickly, but offered no praise. Indeed, he seemed angry when he weighed a couple of the packets and found them accurately measured.

That was the moment when Marshall decided Mr Dawson's suspicions must have some foundation. Why else would a manager be upset when a man worked extra hard and did exactly as he'd been instructed?

* * *

In the late morning Pandora hauled the dripping wooden bucket out of the well and rested it on the rough stone wall, panting with the effort. She often wished she had one of the modern galvanised metal buckets they'd used in Outham, which were so much lighter.

She wasn't in a hurry to lug the bucket back to the cooking area, so stayed where she was for a few moments. She'd been working hard since early that morning, first doing the washing for Mrs Southerham with her sister, then continuing alone because Reece said Cassandra had had enough and needed a rest.

Her sister had obeyed him so meekly, Pandora knew he was right. In the last few days

177

Cassandra had begun to look very uncomfortable and move more slowly.

The rain had held off, fortunately, but from the look of the clouds, it'd soon start again. She'd suggested waiting until another day to do the washing, but Mr Southerham's fancy shirts were all dirty and since he insisted on changing his clothes every evening, they had to be done. How she was to get everything dry today, she didn't know. The Southerhams didn't even have a mangle so the clothes remained sodden and dripping after washing, however much you tried to wring them out.

It annoyed her the way they insisted on the necessity to 'maintain standards' as if they still lived in England and had plenty of servants, not caring about the extra work that caused her.

With a sigh she reached out to unhook the bucket from the well rope but drew her hands back as she heard the sound of horses' hooves in the distance. Swinging round, she stared down the rough track that led to the farm and saw some distant figures coming up the slope. It was so unusual for someone to visit Westview that she left the bucket and ran to find her employers, calling, 'Someone's coming along the road. Someone's coming.'

Livia came out of the shack and shaded her eyes with her hands as she too stared down the hill. Francis stepped out from the bark-covered shelter that served as stables to his precious horses and Reece appeared from behind the house, where he was doing some repairs.

Three men on horseback leading two loaded

packhorses were moving slowly up the track. They all looked weary.

'No one I know,' Mr Southerham said. 'Do you recognise any of them, my dear?'

'No. Perhaps they're pedlars.'

As the men came closer one of the figures began to seem familiar. Pandora waited a moment to be sure, then called, 'I can't believe it. I'm sure it's him. Yes, it *is*! He's changed a lot, though, looks stronger and more . . . ' She hesitated. She had been going to say 'in charge of himself' but that might sound strange. Instead she took a few steps forward and waited as the visitors came up the slope.

The man she recognised rode forward to her, ignoring the Southerhams, and dismounted with a smile. 'Miss Pandora Blake. It is you, isn't it? I remember meeting you once or twice.'

'Yes. You brought us some food and I saw you in my uncle's shop. I can't remember your name, I'm afraid.'

'Zachary Carr. And I still work in the shop, though not for your uncle now, of course.'

Pandora froze as a horrible thought occurred to her. 'Our aunt hasn't sent you after us, has she? What does she want now? She's driven us away from Outham. Isn't that enough?' Her heart began to pound and a shiver of fear after what had been done to Cassandra ran down her spine.

'No, no. It's all right. Your aunt is dead.'

Pandora was so relieved she felt shaky and clutched his arm without thinking what she was doing. 'Thank goodness! Oh, thank goodness!'

She didn't care if it was wrong to wish someone dead. Her aunt had been a wicked woman and had deserved to die if anyone ever did.

She realised she was still holding on to Mr Carr and stepped back with a blush. 'Sorry.'

The second man dismounted and came forward. 'The horses need water, Zachary. They're thirsty. Where's the water, please, miss?'

She realised from his expression and the way he spoke that he was one of those simple souls who stay like children all their lives.

Francis had joined them by this time, but was sizing up the visitors' horses rather than the visitors themselves. 'These are tired old nags. They should be put out to pasture, not dragged round the country. Could you find no better to ride?'

Bert bristled. 'No, we damned well couldn't. They've got us here, haven't they?'

'Only just, by the looks of them.' Francis turned back to Leo. 'The well is down here and we have a horse trough nearby that your animals can use. I'll show you.'

Leo thrust the reins of his horse and of the packhorse he'd been leading into Francis's hand and came for Zachary's mount, leading it away without a backward glance, his whole attention focused on the animals' needs.

The third man touched his hat to the ladies then led his own horse and the second packhorse in the direction of water.

Pandora had been trying to make sense of it and failing. 'If our aunt is dead, then why are you here?'

'The lawyer sent me to find you and your

sisters.' Zachary looked round, as if expecting to see them.

'They don't live here.'

'Oh. I wanted to tell you all the news at the same time.'

'Cassandra, my oldest sister, lives on the next farm, but the twins are over an hour away. We couldn't find jobs any closer to one another.'

'Could we send for Miss Blake, do you think?'

Reece came forward. 'Cassandra's my wife now, so she's Mrs Gregory. What do you want with her?'

Zachary hesitated then looked back at Pandora as he explained. 'You and your sisters have inherited the shop. It was yours even before your aunt died because your uncle didn't leave it to her.'

She looked so shocked he thought she was going to faint, so put an arm round her.

As she leaned against him, she raised one trembling hand to her lips and murmured, '*Then we can go back to England.*'

'Is that what you want to do?'

'More than anything.' Tears welled in her eyes.

'Are you all right? Can I get you anything?'

It took her a moment or two to pull herself together. He held her till he could see her eyes begin to focus properly and colour return to her cheeks.

'I'm just — astonished. I never expected — Oh, we needn't have come to Australia at all!'

Frowning, Livia came forward and gestured to Zachary, who didn't step back until he'd guided Pandora to one of the rough benches next to an outdoor table.

When he took his arm away, she held on to the edge of the table as if she felt dizzy, but after taking a few deep breaths she looked up again and gave him a faint smile.

'If I can just sit quietly for a minute or two, I'll be all right. I can't seem to take it in.'

Livia took charge. 'I'm Mrs Southerham. My husband and I own this farm. Shall we all sit down? I'm sure you gentlemen would like a cup of tea.'

'That'd be most welcome, Mrs Southerham.'

'I'll go and fetch Cassandra,' Reece said. 'She should be here when you explain more fully, Mr Carr.'

He didn't wait for an answer but strode off along the bush path.

Bert called from the water trough. 'Are we staying long? Should we unsaddle the horses?'

Zachary looked at his host and hostess. 'Could we spend the night here, do you think? We can sleep in the stables.'

'You can stay but I'm not sure where we'll put you,' Francis said.

'If necessary they can sleep on our veranda,' Livia said. 'There's no inn nearby and it may rain again, so they'll need shelter, Francis.'

'Thank you.' Zachary raised his voice to tell Leo and Bert to unsaddle, then sat down opposite Pandora, who still looked dumbfounded.

He'd forgotten how beautiful the youngest Blake sister was and found it hard to take his eyes off her. Such lustrous dark hair, such beautiful eyes. Like a princess in a child's story book, she was. But she had an air of sadness as well, which he didn't remember from the other times he'd seen her. He wondered why she was unhappy.

'I'll get the kettle boiling.' Livia walked across to the stove and slid the kettle on to the hottest part of the hob, then got some enamel mugs from the shelves that Reece had built next to it.

Pandora made no effort to help her mistress. 'I can't believe it,' she confessed to Zachary. 'We've all been so afraid of having any contact with people back in Outham because of our aunt. We didn't dare even write to our friends. When did she die? How?'

'She died about three months after you left. She was rather strange already but she went quite mad when she heard you'd been left the shop. She had to be locked away, for her own and others' protection, and after a while she simply refused to eat. They think she had her own husband killed, but since she's dead, there's no point pursuing that now.'

'*She* killed our uncle? Oh, no! How terrible.'

'I think so too. Mr Blake was a lovely man to work for and we missed him greatly at the shop.'

After a few moments of silence Pandora said in a tone of wonderment, 'We can go home then. We really can. I've been so homesick.'

His eyes were steady and his gaze was direct. 'For Lancashire?'

She nodded. 'Yes. I ache to walk down the main streets of Outham, stroll in the park, hear Lancashire voices. It's foolish, I know.'

'Not foolish. Home means more to some people. I'm starting to miss Outham myself.' He looked round. 'It's very different here.'

'Then you'll understand. My sisters love living here, but I just can't settle.' She gestured down the slope towards the horizon in the west. 'Lancashire is somewhere over there, travel beyond the sunset and then turn north, Reece says. I look in that direction every night, wondering what my old friends are doing, whether the mills are still closed for lack of cotton, if there's a mist drifting over the moors.' Her voice broke on the final word and she shut her eyes for a moment, taking some deep breaths.

He said gently, 'Times are still hard in Outham and the war hadn't ended when I left England, so the mills hadn't reopened. The North seems to be winning, though, so the war may end quite soon, which will be a relief to the cotton workers. But mists were still rising over the moors and I loved to watch them.'

'Do the men who're out of work still wait for those with newspapers to ask them if there's any news from America?'

'Yes. It's hard to be without work, without enough to eat, to see your family suffering. Charitable ladies are still running soup kitchens and those men who're strong enough break stones to earn a crust or two. The ones who aren't strong have to attend reading classes to get their relief money. If truth be told, I think most people will be too weary to celebrate when they hear the war's over. Times have been hard for years now.'

He waited for more questions, but she was staring into the distance so he didn't interrupt her thoughts. An unwary movement reminded him of how sore he was and he tried to ease himself into a more comfortable position.

After a while she asked, 'Who are your companions?'

Guilt shot through him as he explained about Leo. 'I've spent some of your money on rescuing him but I'll pay it back, I promise you. I couldn't leave him to be ill-treated. I just — couldn't.'

'You don't need to pay it back as far as I'm concerned. It's our money and I'm sure my sisters won't mind helping him. I certainly don't. Is that why his face is bruised?'

'Yes. He'd been badly beaten when I found him again.'

Livia interrupted to ask, 'I wonder if you'd lift the kettle off the hob for me, Mr Carr and pour the water into our big teapot?'

Pandora jumped to her feet. 'No need. I'm used to handling it.'

But he insisted on doing it, smiling at her as their hands met before she stepped back.

By the time the tea was brewed, Reece and Cassandra had appeared on the bush track, so Pandora got out more of the big tin mugs.

When invited to join them at table, Bert shook his head. 'I'll take mine over near the horses, missus, if you don't mind, and leave you folk to talk. Leo lad, you bring your tea and help me look after the animals.'

Smiling happily, Leo took a gulp of hot tea and walked away from the table.

Francis came to sit down with them. 'That young man may be lacking some of his wits, but he's very good with horses.'

'He's good with injuries, too,' Zachary said. 'Seems to have an instinct for caring.'

'It's a good thing. He'll always find a job looking after animals.' Francis put two spoonfuls of sugar into his tea, stirred it vigorously and raised the mug to his lips. 'Ah, that's good, my dear. I was ready for a rest.'

Once Cassandra and Reece had had their cups filled, Francis took charge. 'Now, Mr Carr, let's hear the full tale of what you're doing here, if you please.'

★ ★ ★

It was Pandora whom Zachary studied as he explained what had happened and why he'd been sent to Australia. It was her eyes mostly that drew his own back to her face as he spoke, so deep a blue, those beautiful eyes, gazing at the world with such intensity he wanted to know what she was thinking.

'So,' he wound up, 'Mr Featherworth sent me to bring you all back home to take up your inheritance, Mrs Gregory, Miss Blake.'

Silence greeted his final words and he allowed them time to consider the news.

'I don't know what to say,' Cassandra commented at last. 'Or what to do.'

Pandora stared at her in astonishment. 'What do you mean? It's obvious what to do, surely? We'll go home, and the sooner the better as far as I'm concerned.'

Zachary watched the oldest sister exchange

glances with her husband, saw Reece raise one eyebrow and Cassandra give a tiny shake of her head. Now what did that mean?

'Cassandra?' Pandora said in a voice which quavered.

'I'm not sure I want to go back to England,' her sister said at last. 'Reece and I have made so many plans for building a life here and . . . '

Mrs Southerham broke the silence. 'You'd be foolish to turn down such an inheritance and Blake's Emporium is very well thought of in Outham. Reece could run the shop, I'm sure. I'm glad for you, very glad, but we're going to miss you both greatly. And how Francis will manage without Reece's help, I can't think.'

'We need to consider it carefully.' Reece put his arm round his wife. 'Surely we could get some of our money sent to us here? It'd be welcome, I must admit.'

Pandora scowled at them. 'I don't need any time at all to think. I can't wait to leave Australia. Cassandra, surely you don't intend to stay here now that we have some money?'

Reece's voice was firm, the sort of tone others obeyed. 'Leave us to make up our own minds, Pandora. Apart from anything else, your sister is in no state to go on a long sea voyage at the moment.' His glance flicked briefly to his wife's stomach.

Cassandra spoke more gently. 'I know you've been unhappy here, Pandora love, but Reece and I love it. The sunshine in summer, the outdoor life. I don't think I can bear to go back to a cooler climate — I always did hate ice and snow

187

— and I definitely don't want to work indoors again, even in my own shop.'

'Nor do I,' Reece said.

As he listened and watched, Zachary kept his thoughts to himself. It wasn't for him to interfere. But he was on Pandora's side, couldn't imagine living anywhere except in England, and he absolutely loved working in the shop, finding the best goods for sale, making customers happy. Food was such an important part of people's lives.

'I'd go back to live in Perth if I hadn't invested all my money here.' Francis didn't try to hide the bitterness he felt.

In answer to Zachary's puzzled look, he added, 'I was tricked into coming to the Swan River Colony by my cousin, who painted glowing pictures of the opportunities — and by the doctor, who said my health would be better in a warm climate.'

Zachary suddenly realised why his host's cheeks were flushed, his eyes over bright: consumption. He'd seen it many times before. Poor man.

He gave them a few minutes but when no one spoke, he said, 'You can't delay making a decision for too long, I'm afraid. We have to get to Albany before the end of April or we'll miss the mail ship. And it's the 18th of April now. I'm told Albany is about three hundred miles south of Perth and — '

Reece's deep, calm voice interrupted him and drew everyone's attention instantly. 'Well, we can't decide or do anything until we've seen

Maia and Xanthe.' He looked at Zachary. 'I'd suggest we visit them tomorrow. We can set off first thing in the morning to tell them the news. Is that all right with you, Mr Southerham?'

Francis shrugged.

Reece turned back to Zachary. 'In the meantime, there's room at our house for you, Mr Carr, as long as you don't mind sleeping on the floor in the living room. And the other two could sleep in our stables with the horses. They're mainly empty now, but they're bigger than Mr Southerham's and they're waterproof. There's plenty of clean straw.' He looked up at the sky. 'I reckon it'll rain again later.'

'We've enough meat for everyone's evening meal,' Francis offered. 'I shot a kangaroo yesterday.'

Zachary thanked them for their offer of hospitality, but his eyes kept going back to Pandora, whose disappointment was obvious. She kept looking at her sister pleadingly and once asked her something in a low voice. He could see Cassandra's lips form the words 'Not now'.

The last thing he'd expected was to find that some of them didn't want to return. What would Mr Featherworth say to that? Would he think Zachary hadn't done his job properly?

Was he doing his job well? He still felt guilty about taking the time to rescue Leo.

★　★　★

'I'll do the cooking.' Cassandra knew to her cost how impatient Livia was and how often she burnt the food. Pandora was much better at putting together a tasty meal, but tonight she looked so upset, it would be better not to rely on her. 'And my sister will help me.'

'Are you all right?' Reece asked her as he went to build up the fire in the stove for her and get out the heavy, long-handled frying pan.

'I'm fine.' She smiled at him and for a moment it was as if there were only the two of them in the world.

'I'll fetch some meat.'

'I'll come with you.' As they walked over to the pit that kept fresh food cool in the warmer weather, she said in a quiet voice, 'I'm not sure I want to go back.'

'We can go later if you change your mind. We have enough money left to pay our fares.'

'I don't think I shall change my mind. But whatever I decide, I know Pandora will go.' She felt tears well in her eyes. 'She'll never be happy here. Oh, Reece, I can't bear to think of me staying and her leaving. The two of us have never been parted in our whole lives before, and I was as much a mother to her as a sister.'

He pulled her close for a moment. 'I know. There's no solution which will please everyone.'

'What do *you* want to do, Reece? Stop thinking about me and tell the truth.'

He answered without hesitation. 'Stay here in Australia. There's a good future for a man like me. I'd be working for other men if we went back, or indoors in a shop.' He wrinkled his nose to show what he thought of that. 'But if we could get some money from your inheritance, well, that'd make such a difference here. We could do so much with it, buy our own land or set up a business.' He looked back towards the group at the table. 'Now, we'd better get what we came for. They're waiting for their meal.'

She watched him use the short ladder to climb down into the pit and fetch some of the meat stored in a box whose sides were covered in muslin and whose feet stood in tins of water to deter ants and other creeping insects.

Cassandra let Pandora answer Zachary's questions about life here and got on with preparing the meal. Boiled potatoes, onions and kangaroo steaks fried in ham fat because kangaroo meat was very lean. Mr Southerham spoke slightingly of it and hankered for English beef, but she enjoyed the strong flavour and loved having fresh meat every day. She'd not eaten so well for years and surely that must be good for her baby.

After a while Zachary sat down again at the table and soon he and Pandora were chatting like old friends as she moved to and fro to fetch knives and forks, set a pile of plates ready and rinse out the tin mugs. Cassandra got on with the cooking and left them to it, surprised at how comfortable Pandora looked with Zachary. She hadn't seen her sister look so animated for a long time.

This legacy would part them, Cassandra was quite sure of that. A lump came into her throat. Given the great distance between Australia and England, they might never see one another again. But her own marriage had started the process of emotional separation, and already she and her sister weren't as close. She wished Pandora had someone to turn to, though, a husband as wonderfully reliable and kind as her own Reece.

What she didn't know was whether the twins would want to go back or stay — and whether she would still want to stay here herself if all three of her sisters went back to England. But as Reece had said, she couldn't travel anywhere till after she'd had the baby.

Life was like that. Just as you thought things were going well, something happened to change your plans, *will you, nill you*. Now where did those words come from? A Shakespeare play, she thought, but which one? She wished they'd been able to keep all their father's books and bring them here. She was always grateful that he'd brought them up to love reading and that the free library in Outham had improved on their simple education. Once her inheritance came through, she'd be able to buy books, since there were no libraries near here to supply food for her mind. She smiled. It'd be wonderful not to have to watch every farthing.

As they ate, she listened to Pandora asking Zachary question after question about Outham and the shop, the depth of her sister's longing for their old home showing all too plainly in her face and words. They'd known she was homesick but had felt she was getting over it. But even they hadn't realised how badly she'd still been hurting.

Zachary responded patiently, letting his food go cold as he answered Pandora's questions, smiling at her, gesticulating and drawing pictures in the air. From the look of him, he was quite taken by Pandora. In other circumstances, Cassandra would be happy about that. But now, he was an employee and her sister was part-owner of the shop where he worked. That made a big difference. Cassandra didn't want anyone courting her sister for the money. Not that he looked the sort.

Her big consolation was that if her youngest sister did go back, she felt she could trust him to look after her on the journey, because there was a quiet strength to him and a kindness, too. Actions spoke for themselves. How many men would have bothered to rescue Leo? The poor fellow was sitting at the end of the table, smiling happily from that bruised face. It must have been a very bad beating.

She could see that Reece had taken to Zachary as well. She couldn't bring herself to join in the conversation because the thought of losing Pandora made her want to weep. Her emotions were very near the surface these days. She was looking forward to having the baby, getting back to normal, being of more use to her husband. She wasn't one to sit back and let others work for her.

Reece put his hand over hers once, as if sensing her pain, and when she turned to him, he raised the hand to his lips briefly. He didn't offer her glib words of comfort, but the brief warmth of his mouth against her skin made her feel a little better.

She wouldn't know where she stood until they found out what the twins wanted to do.

11

It rained during the night, but only lightly and by the following morning, the sky was clear and the sun shining. Reece woke their visitors at dawn and after a hasty breakfast of bread and jam they walked through the bush to the Southerhams' farm to get the cart ready for the visit to Galway House. Kevin was lending them Delilah to draw it because she was a placid animal, suitable for an inexperienced driver like Reece.

Bert and Leo were to stay behind with the horses today, giving the elderly animals a good rest.

'This is the first time I've been in charge of a cart on my own,' Reece commented as he drove away from the farm.

'You know more about it than I do, that's for sure,' Zachary said. He was beside him on the driving bench, asking about the birds and plants he didn't recognise.

The two sisters sat together in the rear of the vehicle. Neither said much.

Once Pandora faltered, 'I can't bear to think of leaving you.'

'You've been very unhappy here, love. I do understand. You'll never settle.'

A sob was the only answer she received.

A few minutes later Cassandra said, 'I shall miss you dreadfully, though,' as if accepting a fait accompli.

The two men exchanged glances, but didn't comment.

When they drew up outside Galway House, the twins rushed out to find out what had brought them to visit so unexpectedly. Normally the four sisters only met at the monthly church service held in the barn of the one shop in the district.

'Is something wrong?' Xanthe let Reece help Cassandra down from the cart then gave her sister a hug.

'No. But we have some exciting news for you.'

Conn Largan came to the front door to welcome them and invite them inside. Although he was the twins' employer and a gentleman born, he was also an emancipist, and never stood on his dignity, insisting on being called by his first name and eating meals with his servants.

They went to join Conn's invalid mother in the big kitchen that served also as a living room for the whole household. The Southerhams would never allow this familiarity, Cassandra thought with amusement.

After introductions, Reece waved one hand at Zachary. 'I think you'd better explain.'

So he went through it all again, pausing from time to time to answer their excited questions.

In the end, Maia said in tones of enormous relief. 'We're free, then. Safe. She can't hurt us any more.'

'And we're rich,' Xanthe said in an awed voice.

Zachary shook his head. 'No, not rich. The lawyer told me to say 'comfortably off'. Between

195

you, you own the shop and a few cottages, and there's some money in the bank, but it has to be split four ways.'

'That sounds rich to me.' She laughed. 'And to think I've been wondering if I could afford the material for a new winter dress now that the weather is getting cooler.'

It was Conn who brought them to the crucial decision. 'Will you all be going back to England now?'

There was silence, then Cassandra took a deep breath and said it. 'I don't want to. I like living here and so does Reece. But if there's some money that could be sent, it'd help us set up our farm. Reece is thinking of making cheese as a sideline. There's a shortage of it in the colony and we could dig a cellar into the hillside to store it for ripening.'

Zachary saw a tear roll down Pandora's face and his heart went out to her.

'I'm going back,' she said in a voice thickened by emotion. 'I can never be happy here. I've tried and tried, but it's no use.' She made a pleading gesture to the twins. 'I'm hoping you two can help me persuade Cassandra to change her mind.'

Everyone looked at them.

Maia bent her head, then cast a quick glance at her mistress.

'You must do what's best for yourself, child,' Mrs Largan said gently.

'I don't know what's best. I like living in Australia. And — you need me.'

'We can find someone else to help me.' Mrs

196

Largan patted her with one twisted, arthritic hand.

'You've been better since I came here.' Maia gave her a tearful smile and clutched that hand tightly. 'And . . . I don't want to leave Galway House, either. I like living here.'

'My dear girl, my days are numbered and your life is just beginning. You mustn't give up your life for me.'

Zachary watched emotions warring in Maia's gentle face, saw her shake her head as if in bafflement, and wondered whether he was the only one to notice the way Conn was staring at her. It was a very revealing look, but within seconds Conn's face took on a shuttered look again. If Zachary hadn't been watching at just the right time, he'd not have seen how the other man felt.

The poor fellow must have learned to assume that blank facial expression as a convict, because it gave nothing away. They'd told Zachary that Conn had been a political prisoner, one given his ticket of leave on arrival because he'd brought money with him. Nonetheless the imprisonment until then must have been very hard for an educated gentleman to bear. Zachary could remember the convicts on board his ship, how hopeless some of them had looked.

'Tell her, Conn,' Mrs Largan urged. 'Tell her to do what's best for herself. She has her whole life before her.'

'I agree with my mother, Maia. I only ask that you don't leave until I've found someone else to help her.'

Zachary had to intervene. 'We have to set off quite soon, I'm afraid. There's a mail steamer leaving Albany around May the first and I've sent ahead to book cabins for us — if they have space. If not, we'll have to travel steerage as far as Point de Galle in Ceylon. We can easily find another ship going to England from there, I'm told.'

The Largans stared at him in consternation. The twins looked at one another. No one spoke.

He continued to give them the necessary information while all the time feeling sorry for them. 'For some reason, there aren't many ships leaving Western Australia this year, just the P&O mail ships, which only call at King George Sound. They're steam ships so we'll travel more quickly on them. If we miss this one, we'll have to wait two months for the next.'

Pandora turned to Xanthe. 'You've not said anything. Do *you* want to go or stay?'

Her tone was decisive. 'I doubt I'll ever go back to Outham, and definitely not to stay.'

Everyone stared at her in shock.

'Why not?' Pandora asked.

'Because there's nothing for us to go back to, not really, with Dad dead. The shop means nothing to me and I don't want to work there and have to fuss over women like our aunt's friends. It can be sold and the money divided between us. Like Cassandra, I'm enjoying the better climate and spending more time out of doors.'

She turned to Conn. 'I don't want to stay here at Galway House for ever, though I won't leave

198

you in the lurch. I never thought I'd get the chance to live the sort of interesting life you read about in books, had resigned myself to that. But if I've got some money, I can do as I please. Dad always wanted to see the world, didn't he?' Her sisters nodded. 'Well I'd like to travel, too, and do it for him.'

She turned to her twin. 'We want different things from life, Maia love. I've known that for a while. You're a homebody. I'm not. You ought to marry, have a family. That's what would make you happiest. I'm not intending to marry, not ever.'

Maia's voice was thick with tears and desperation. 'Xanthe, don't talk like that! We've never been separated before, not even for a day. If you feel the need to travel, I'll come with you.'

'You'd hate it. And us being separated was bound to happen one day. I don't want babies or a husband, but I *hunger* for a more interesting life.'

Her sisters were all looking astonished.

'Why don't you want to marry?' Cassandra asked.

Xanthe shrugged. 'If you're married, you're at the beck and call of your husband, and your time's taken up with raising children. Even richer women must do as their husbands say. And with all respect, Mrs Largan, it was bad enough working in the mill, where at least I had company, but I find doing housework all day on my own quite tedious. Only I thought I had no choice. If I do . . . if I've got some money, I'm definitely going to do something different with my life.'

'Travel can be dangerous for a woman on her own,' Conn said.

'How many women die in childbirth? That's dangerous too. Pandora's fiancé was young and strong, but he died from a sudden fever. Life is never safe.'

Maia burst into tears and it was Mrs Largan who comforted her, acting as if the gentler twin was a daughter of the house not a maidservant.

'You only have a day at most to decide,' Zachary said as the silence dragged on. 'We have to get to Albany. Bert says the main road we came from Perth on is the same one the mail wagon uses, and we can go that way rather than trying to get back to Fremantle. We should get to Albany in about a week. It might take longer, though, if the weather's bad, so I'd thought to set off as soon as possible, to make sure we don't miss the SS *Bombay*.'

They all began talking at once, gesturing and pleading, refusing and explaining. He took no part in the sometimes heated debate but continued to watch Pandora. Poor lass, she was hurting badly. But there was nothing he could say or do, for her or for her sisters. It was their decision.

'Perhaps you all need to think about this quietly,' Conn suggested. 'I could bring Maia and Xanthe over to Westview tomorrow.'

'I shan't change my mind,' Cassandra said.

'Nor I,' Pandora said in a voice choked with tears.

Conn turned to the twins. 'Do you need more time to consider it?'

'I do. And whatever the others say, I think we all do,' Maia said. 'You two heard the news yesterday; we only heard it a short time ago. It's not a decision to make lightly.'

Xanthe shrugged.

Zachary could only repeat, 'I'm sorry, but we have to leave quite soon. If you do decide to return to England, you should come to Westview tomorrow with your things packed, ready to leave the next day.'

After another of those heavy silences, Conn said, 'Perhaps you four would like to talk in private now? You could go and sit on the front veranda. I'm quite capable of making a pot of tea and bringing it out to you.'

'I'll set a tray,' Maia said, and was up doing it before anyone could stop her.

Zachary watched the four young women. Maia finished setting the tray and they left the room. They looked alike, could be spotted instantly as sisters, but they had very different natures and that showed, even with the twins. Some twins you could hardly tell apart but these two were very different from each other, in looks and character.

Pandora was by far the most beautiful of them all. The sight of her took his breath away, made him think thoughts he had no right to. She was the owner of the store where he worked, not a lass he could court. He had to remember that.

'It's a difficult decision for them to make,' Mrs Largan said in her soft lilting voice.

Zachary nodded. 'Mr Featherworth will be surprised not to see them all returning. He

201

assumed they'd jump at the chance. After all, they didn't choose to come here, they were forced. And what's to happen to the inheritance if only one comes back?'

'Presumably they'll sell the shop,' Reece said quietly.

'It's a bad time to sell. It'll not fetch half as much money just now. People are still facing hard times in Lancashire.'

'They can wait to sell the shop till times are better, or if Pandora wants to keep it, she can pay us back gradually for our shares. There are cottages as well, you said. Those could be sold, may even cover our share of the inheritance. Cassandra and I won't go hungry in the meantime. I'm sure I can make a go of it here — especially with a wife like her by my side.'

Conn's voice was bitter. 'You're very fortunate in your wife. They aren't all as loyal and hard-working as she is.'

Mrs Largan cleared her throat and he changed the subject. 'We're behind the times here with news, but we do get the occasional newspaper and I've been thinking the war in America is drawing to a close. Once that ends, the cotton industry will start up again.'

Zachary sighed. 'From something Mr Blake said to me after he'd started seeing his nieces and brother again, I think he was hoping his nieces would keep his shop in the family. He was very proud of the success he'd made of it. His wife's father didn't do half as well, you know. The emporium is much bigger now than when Mr Blake inherited it and could do better still once times improve.'

'You sound as if you love working there.'

Zachary smiled. 'I did when Mr Blake was in charge. He was a good employer, a good man too.'

'Who's in charge now?'

'Harry Prebble.'

Reece frowned. 'Is he related to Martin Prebble?'

'He's a nephew of Martin.'

'Bad blood there, then.'

* * *

As arranged, Marshall slipped round to Ralph's one evening after he'd been working at the shop for a week. He made sure he wasn't seen and went to the back door, not the front.

The door was slightly ajar and he took this as a sign to go straight inside. Only then did he tap on the inner scullery door.

'Come in.'

He found Ralph sitting in the kitchen, with the blinds drawn. No sign of Ralph's sister.

'Sit down, lad. I've just brewed a pot of tea.'

Only when each had finished drinking the first cup of tea in an appreciative silence did Marshall start to talk about Prebble.

'He thinks himself something, that little sod does. I'm used to telling people what to do, but if I took that tone with the mill lasses, they'd soon let me know what they thought of me.'

'What tone?'

'Like we're nowt but dirt beneath his feet. The

203

other fellows working there don't say owt, just do as he tells them, but the looks they give him behind his back would curdle milk.'

'Is he providing you all with dinners now?'

'Of a sort. He buys in the stale loaves from the baker's, uses the gristly bits from the ham, the rind from the cheese, things I'd have given my dog afore the cotton stopped coming.'

'You'd think the money for it came out of his pocket.'

'Aye, you would.'

Ralph considered this for a moment. He hadn't forgotten that cash box full of money and he still wasn't convinced it'd been intended for the new owners. 'What about his own dinners?'

'He takes them in the office, but I've kept my eyes open. He doesn't go short and there's no gristle on his plate.'

The men looked at one another, shaking their heads.

'Has he tried to upset you?'

Marshall grinned. 'Aye. Won't manage it, though. Thinks I'm dumber than I am. Useful, that, I reckon. I'll give him his own one day, see if I don't.'

'Do you see anything of Miss Blair? She lives above the shop.'

'No. She keeps the door to the living quarters locked all the time. I've seen him try it now and then. The maid comes into the shop sometimes for food, but she comes through the front door. He treats that poor lass like she's an idiot as well, keeps her waiting and serves others first, but he's all over the better customers. Nothing's too much trouble for *them*.'

'You do have to keep customers happy.'

'I don't think all of them appreciate his compliments and fuss.'

'Hmm. So there's nothing obvious to report.'

'Not yet. But he wouldn't risk doing anything, would he? Not the first week I'm there.' He chuckled. 'I did say summat sharp about you to another of the lads when I knew *he* was listening. Mebbe he'll stop being so suspicious of me.'

'Do you feel there's something going on?' Ralph asked.

Marshall tapped his nose with one finger and nodded. 'I saw one fellow come in, not the usual sort to patronise our shop, and Prebble shook his head. The fellow bought a box of matches and left. I know him from somewhere, can't remember where. It'll come back to me, though. I never forget a face.'

'Another cup of tea before you leave?'

'No, thanks. I'll be getting home now.'

The two men shook hands and Ralph went with Marshall to the back door. 'I'll just check that the back alley's clear before I open the gate. Same time next week?'

'Aye.'

He went to stand on a pile of bricks and saw two men standing in the back alley, so got quietly down again. 'I think you were followed here.'

'Nay, that I wasn't. I got Bill to walk a bit behind me to make sure of that.'

'Then why are there two men in the alley, near my house?'

'You've upset a Prebble. I reckon it's you as

205

needs to watch your back from now on, lad.'

Ralph breathed deeply. 'Can you find me a strong fellow to keep watch at night? I'll pay him a shilling a night and he'll be cosy enough in my shed.'

'I could find you a dozen in times like these.'

'One will be enough. How are you going to get out without being seen?'

'It won't be the first time I've climbed over garden walls. I'll have someone round here within the half-hour. Lock up till then. I'll tell him to knock on the front door. Three times, then three more. Don't open to anyone else. That little sod's got the wrong fellows if he thinks to play dirty tricks on you and me. I've got a few friends who have nothing better to do, who'll keep an eye out for us both.'

'We may be wrong. It may be nothing. But I'm not taking risks. If they upset my sister, she'll have one of her breathless attacks. Asthma the doctor calls it. He can't do much to help her, though.'

★   ★   ★

Conn saw signs of tears on all four of the sisters' faces as he carried the tray out to the veranda, so hesitated in the doorway. 'How's it going?'

Cassandra shrugged. 'Pandora and I haven't changed our minds.'

He set the tea tray down carefully on the rickety outdoor table and looked at the twins.

'I keep trying to imagine myself living in Outham again,' Maia said, 'and I can't. Besides,

206

I don't want to leave your mother.'

His eyes softened as he looked at her. 'I can't help hoping you'll stay, for her sake. And I'll point out to you now that you can always go back later if you change your mind. I'll help you if you need to.'

She nodded.

He looked at the fourth sister.

'I'm not going anywhere yet,' Xanthe said. 'Certainly not back to Outham.'

He heard his own Irish accent become more pronounced, as it did when he was strongly moved about something. 'Argh, life's hard sometimes. Terrible hard. If there's anything I can do to help, you have only to ask.'

It was Cassandra who spoke for them. 'Could we ask one favour?'

'Of course.'

'Could you bring my sisters over to Westview tomorrow for the whole day? We'll all help Pandora with the packing and . . . be together.'

'I'll do that willingly.'

'How will your mother manage?'

'She can move about, though slowly. If we leave everything she needs, Sean will keep an eye on her. It's different when it's only for a few hours.'

'That's arranged then.'

A thought suddenly occurred to him as he rejoined his mother and Reece. 'They'll need to sign papers giving Pandora the legal power to act on their behalf. I can draw them up for you, if you like, though you'd better not use me as a witness, given my circumstances.'

Reece looked at him in surprise. 'Do you know how to do that?'

Conn's face twisted into another of those bitter smiles. 'Indeed I do. Wasn't I a lawyer in my other life?' He saw the surprise on their faces and shrugged. 'I'm a younger son. I had my living to earn.'

He hadn't meant to tell anyone that, was annoyed with himself, so added, 'I'd appreciate it if you'd keep that information to yourself.'

As the men finished eating, Conn asked abruptly, 'How are you going to get to Albany, Mr Carr?'

'I'd thought to continue on horseback, though it's not a comfortable way to travel, but we'll need to hire another horse for Pandora. Only where can we do that? I didn't realise when I left Perth how isolated this place is.'

'Horseback won't do,' Mrs Largan said decisively. 'What about Pandora's clothes and possessions? You can hardly expect her to travel so far with only a change of clothing in her saddlebags. There'll be three months of sea travel to England. No, you'll need to go by cart.'

'We don't have one,' Zachary said.

'Kevin does,' Reece said. 'We came here in it today. It's a bit old but it seems sound enough. I'm certain he'll lend it to you, Zachary. And his horse Delilah.'

'Is that the one who pulled the cart today?' Conn asked. 'She's a sturdy creature, even though she's not the prettiest horse I've ever seen.'

Zachary nodded. 'Kevin thinks the world of

her. Only, Mr Southerham says we'll be lucky if the horses we've hired get us that far. They're poor specimens, even I can see that, and they tire easily.'

'I'll look at them,' Conn offered. 'I've got a gelding who's very strong, bigger than that mare. I'll bring him tomorrow, in case you need to borrow him. You won't need packhorses with a cart, at least. But I'll only lend you my horse if I find your guide trust-worthy. I care a lot about my animals and I'll not have them neglected or pushed too hard.'

* * *

On the return journey Pandora and Zachary sat together in the rear of the cart.

'Penny for them,' he said to her.

'My thoughts aren't worth a halfpenny, even.' She lowered her voice. 'I'm trying to think how to change Cassandra's mind. She'll regret it if she stays here, I know she will.'

'No one can know the future, or make decisions for someone else.'

'What do you know about it? You're just the messenger!' She immediately wished she could take the words back, felt ashamed of taking out her unhappiness on him. He clamped his lips together and said nothing for the next mile or two.

Suddenly she could bear her guilt no longer and put a hand on his arm, forcing him to look at her. 'I'm sorry. I shouldn't have said that.'

'Why not? It was true.' He shook her arm off.

And continued to stare straight ahead.

But she knew she'd hurt him and couldn't think how to set it right. Couldn't set anything right in her life at the moment, it seemed.

How could she possibly go back to Outham on her own and leave her sisters behind? And yet . . . how could she not go home?

★ ★ ★

Back at Westview they found no sign of the owners.

Bert was sitting by the table. He grinned at them and uncovered two loaves that were burned at the edges. 'I took the liberty of putting another couple of loaves on to bake, with so many of us to be fed. I hope that was all right?' It was Reece he looked at for approval.

'Good idea. Where are Mr and Mrs Southerham?'

'They've gone for a ride, all dressed up like gentry.'

'They *are* gentry.'

'Yeah, but this is Australia. We get a lot like them coming out here, thinking they're still ruling the roost in England. But they're not. I reckon men like you an' me stand a far better chance of making good lives for ourselves here.'

'I hope so. Where's Leo?'

'Clearing out the stables and making a new muckheap. Mrs Southerham found him some old rags to wear for it. Got to give him his due, that lad doesn't need telling how to look after animals. Shall I unharness the mare?'

'No, we'll be going back to Kevin's place soon. Perhaps you could give her a drink of water, though.'

'All right.'

Cassandra looked at the table and clicked her tongue in exasperation as she brushed some ants off it. They'd been after the breadcrumbs that hadn't been wiped away. Livia had probably wanted to read a book or simply sit and chat to her husband. Her mistress did some of the housework, not grumbling because she wasn't too proud to dirty her hands, but often she forgot to finish a task properly. How would a woman like that cope here without Pandora's help?

She turned at a sound from the stables and saw Leo come out with a barrow full of dirty straw, smiling cheerfully across at them.

Zachary moved over to speak to him, probably praising the lad for his hard work, since Leo beamed at him.

When the Southerhams returned, Leo offered to unsaddle their horses and Francis, who was looking tired today, let him do it. 'He's really good with animals. Is he going back to England with you?'

Zachary shrugged. 'I don't know. I'm a bit at a loss as to what I should do. I can't leave him on his own, but how can I deliver him into his stepfather's clutches again, even if I had the money to pay his fare back to England, which I don't? And if I borrowed the money for that, how would he earn a living there? He'd be no use working in the shop. And anyway, Harry wouldn't give him a job. Harry has no patience with people who don't jump when he says jump — unless they're rich, that is. Besides, Leo's too slow-thinking to work there. He can't read or do the necessary mental arithmetic.'

'Leo could stay here and work for me. I'd treat him decently.'

'And if you're not around?' He didn't say *when* but it was fairly obvious that Francis's days were numbered. Few recovered from the coughing sickness when it got to this stage.

'In that case I'll employ him,' Reece said. 'Look at him. He's enjoying the work.' He grinned. 'We don't all enjoy mucking out stables.'

'That's settled, then,' Livia said.

Zachary stood up. 'Not quite. I have to ask him how he feels.'

'Is he capable of deciding?'

'I think so.' He walked across to Leo. 'You're doing a good job there.'

The lad nodded several times, beaming. 'I like horses.'

'Would you like to stay here and look after the horses for Mr and Mrs Southerham as a job?'

'Are *you* staying?'

'No. I'm going back to England. But I didn't think you'd want to go back to your stepfather.'

Leo's smile vanished abruptly and he shivered. 'No. I wish he wasn't there. I wish it was just my mother and me, like it used to be. I miss her.'

'She's married to him now, for better for worse. You can't change that.' He waited, then repeated his question. 'So, would you like to stay

212

here and look after the horses for Mr Southerham?'

'What do you think?' Leo asked.

'I think you should find something to do that makes you happy. Mr Southerham is ill. If anything happens to him, Reece has promised to give you a job, so you'd be safe here.'

'Safe here,' Leo repeated, then looked at him. 'Can't you stay too? Don't you want to be safe?'

'I can't stay. I have to take Pandora back to England.'

Leo reached out to pat the horse, brow furrowed in thought. 'I'd better stay here, then. With the horses. I'm not going back to *him*.'

'Good lad.'

Zachary rejoined the others and said Leo would be happy to take the job. 'You'll pay him wages?'

'I can't pay much,' Francis said, 'but we'll look after him.'

'Pay him something. It's only fair. Reece, will you look after his money for him?'

'Yes.'

One burden taken from him, Zachary thought in relief, watching the Southerhams nod and go to sit on their veranda. Always apart from the others, those two. Did it make them happy?

'We'd better go home now,' Reece said. 'Are you coming?'

'I'll come a bit later,' Bert said, 'Leo wants to see the horses bedded down for the night. There's a moon and the path's clear enough.'

Zachary hesitated. 'I'll join you later as well, if that's all right with Pandora?'

213

She nodded. 'I need to wash some clothes if we're setting off the day after tomorrow. I can put them to dry in the tent in case it rains and iron them tomorrow.'

When Zachary saw her fetching a heavy bucket of water from the well, he went to help. 'Let me carry that for you.' He took it out of her hands.

'Thank you.' She stopped walking to say in a rush, 'I'm sorry I spoke so sharply to you on the way back. I've been regretting my rudeness ever since and . . . I didn't mean it like it sounded.'

His heart lightened a little. 'It doesn't matter.'

'It does.'

'Then I forgive you.'

Her smile was for him alone and for a moment he couldn't move, she looked so beautiful. Then he picked up the bucket. 'Where do you want this?'

He hoped she wouldn't have to sell the shop. What he'd really like was the job of manager. He knew he could do it better than Harry. Was there any chance of that? Probably not. Harry would have done the job well enough that they'd have no reason to appoint anyone else.

If Zachary did continue to work there, though, he'd be near Pandora and . . . He looked across ruefully. Already he knew how he felt about her — love had hit him like a bolt of lightning when she ran across to greet him. But she definitely didn't feel the same way about him. 'Just the messenger,' she'd said and even if she hadn't meant it nastily, he must remember that it was indeed all he was. He had to be sensible, for his mother and sister's sake. It didn't do to upset those you depended on for your living.

Shaking his head at his own foolishness, he helped her with the washing, moving heavy buckets and kettles, lending his strength to the wringing of clothes, all by lantern light. He pretended not to see her whisk her underclothes out of his sight. As if he didn't know what women wore. He lived in a small house with his mother and sister, after all.

Later, as he was walking along the well-marked path through the moonlit bush to seek his makeshift bed in Kevin's house, he went over his conversation with Pandora in his mind, remembering every word she'd said, every look she'd given him. It wasn't sensible to let his thoughts dwell on her, but who was to know?

It occurred to him quite forcibly that he'd never had a chance to be anything but sensible, not since his father died. Sometimes he wished he could live as carelessly as other young men, court a lass, laugh with her.

Not any lass, Pandora.

12

The following day Conn drove the twins over to say farewell to Pandora. Neither had changed her mind about staying in Australia and he knew it would be an emotional day for them.

He took with him the gelding, which he tied to the rear of the cart, in case Pandora needed another horse for the journey. The twins elected to ride in the back and leave him in solitary splendour on the driving bench. They were both subdued and Maia had reddened, swollen eyes.

Xanthe was more difficult to fathom. She was scowling at everything and everyone today. Con had never guessed that she found housework so boring and even her twin hadn't known of her desire to travel. What else was she keeping to herself?

Maia's emotions were always written clearly on her face and that pleased him. He felt he could trust her — and he didn't trust many people these days except his mother, who had given up everything to join him in Australia: husband, home, family. She'd done that because she knew he'd been falsely accused.

The rest of the family had not questioned the accusation. Well, he and his brother had never got on and he'd even wondered if his brother had helped manufacture the evidence. But Kathleen in particular should have known he was innocent. He pushed the thought of

Kathleen away, tried never to think of her. Didn't always succeed.

His father had found it easy to believe him guilty. Conn would never forgive him for that and he knew his mother felt the same. Theirs had not been the happiest of marriages, and he could guess how bitter their quarrels must have been before his mockery of a trial.

It had been Conn's friend Ronan, not his family, who had wound up his affairs and sent his money out to Australia after him. He'd repay Ronan for that one day, if he could. Indeed, his friend had talked of coming out for a visit one day. He hoped that would happen.

Conn's mother had left her home secretly to follow her son to Australia. She'd told him some of the estate workers had helped her, but refused to elaborate further. She had always been a much-loved woman and had sympathised with Conn's efforts to help the peasant tenants, who lived a hand to mouth existence on their estate. She'd never forgotten the failure of the potato crop and the famine that had followed in the late 1840s when the millions had died.

He'd found out when he was fifteen how grudging his father's attempts to help feed his tenants had been during that terrible time, and they'd argued about that, as they had about so many things. His father had been furious with Conn for taking the tenants' side. To his father, such people were barely human.

After a brief explanation of why she'd come to Australia, his mother had refused to talk about her husband again. But he knew she grieved in secret about her torn-apart family, and missed her other children.

To his surprise, he rather enjoyed the drive over to Westview. It was good to get away from Galway House occasionally. Not having to maintain a conversation with the twins freed him to enjoy the countryside, which had lost its beige, bleached summer look after several rainy spells and was turning green again.

He found life much more pleasant here during the cooler months. He didn't mind the heavy winter storms, well used to rain after Ireland, but he doubted he'd ever grow accustomed to temperatures over a hundred degrees that set in for a few days at a time during the hot dry summers. The hot spells seemed to sap his energy and willpower.

His mother liked the heat, though, and said her arthritis was always much better when the weather was warm. It was for her sake he stayed in such a lonely place, otherwise he might have moved on. He'd come to Galway House to lick his wounds, buying in a hurry, wanting to get away from the humiliation of being a convict. But he was regretting the isolation now. If he'd stayed in Perth, he might have made friends with other emancipists.

'We're almost there!' he called a short time later.

'I'm sorry we've been poor company,' Xanthe said.

'I've enjoyed the quiet. I've never seen the need to fill every minute with chatter.'

At Westview he greeted his host, unharnessed

his horse and untied the gelding. He handed the latter over to Bert and watched him care for it, since the man would have the job of bringing the horses and Kevin's cart back from Albany. Although Bert seemed capable enough, he seemed to show no affection for the animals.

Maybe Conn spoiled them, treating them like the children he could never have now. But they repaid him richly, with both affection and income. One of the good things to come out of this move to Galway House was that he was getting a name in the district and even beyond it for breeding or finding good horses. Indeed, he'd just had to take on another stable lad. People were prepared to do business with a man who had something they needed, whether he was an emancipist or not.

Getting Pandora to Albany was important or he'd not even have considered lending any horses to them. He saw to Nellie and the gelding himself. He'd bought the latter at a knock-down price the previous year, a good young workhorse which had been treated roughly.

He'd have offered to go to Albany with them, because he'd have enjoyed exploring the colony a little, but he couldn't leave his mother, even with good people to look after her. He was always afraid his father would turn up and try to take her back by force. So was she.

When he examined the hired horses, he shook his head in dismay. The poor creatures had been worked nearly to death and that made him angry.

'What shall we do with them until Bert comes back?' Francis asked. 'I can't care for them, I'm

219

afraid. I'm not in good enough health and Reece has enough to do with the other work.'

'I'll take them,' Conn offered. 'I can give them an easier time for a while. I hate to see poor creatures that have been treated like that. Is Kevin's cart in good condition? I didn't really look at it yesterday.'

They went to study the vehicle, which Reece had washed down that morning. It was small, four-wheeled and unpainted, of no particular type, looking as if it had been cobbled together anyhow. However, it was big enough for their purpose and would easily accommodate Pandora, her trunk and portmanteau, plus provisions and necessities for the journey.

'It's quite old,' Conn said doubtfully. 'And I don't know what sort of vehicle you'd call it.'

'A cart crossed with a market wagon.' Francis's lip curled scornfully as he studied it again. 'Not built by a regular coach-builder, that's for sure.'

'It isn't in too bad condition, though. I think it'll get them there. There's a made road to Albany, after all.'

'What does that mean?'

'It's been cleared and is not a bush track that winds around obstacles.'

'They don't have much choice about the cart. I can't lend them mine because we need it ourselves. I've offered to lend it to Kevin when he needs to fetch any supplies.'

Clearly he considered this a big concession so Conn murmured a few words about generosity. But he was still worried. 'What am I going to do about making sure my horses are well looked after on the journey?'

Francis looked up. 'What do you mean? There's nothing much you can do.'

'Nellie is quite a valuable mare, not a thoroughbred but sturdy, the sort of working horse people need. I'm hoping to breed from her. I'm not sure that fellow,' he jerked his head in Bert's direction, 'will treat her in the way I'd want. The gelding is a good horse, too, though badly treated in the past. It still needs a bit of cosseting.'

They watched Leo fetch a bucket of water for the women, then wander back to draw another for Nellie. He stood beside her, murmuring softly, and she butted her head against him, wanting attention.

'You know ... ' Francis broke off. 'No, perhaps not.'

'What were you going to say?'

'We could send Leo with them. He looks after animals better than he's able to look after himself.'

'Leo?'

'Why not? Zachary is still learning to ride and doesn't know how to drive a cart. Pandora's the same. Bert's going to have his hands full on the journey. Why not send Leo as well? He'll be a big help.'

Conn nodded slowly as the benefits of this sank in. 'Good idea. But we'll have to ask Zachary before we decide anything. He's the one paying the expenses.' He stood up. 'You're looking tired and I need to stretch my legs. I

221

think I'll walk across to Kevin's and put my suggestion to Zachary.'

Francis grimaced. 'I'm afraid I do need to rest.'

Conn looked at him uncertainly, not sure whether his companion admitted publicly what was wrong with him.

The other man's voice was sharp suddenly. 'It's obvious now, isn't it? I've got consumption. Since it's come up, I wonder, when I'm dead — though I hope I have a year or two left yet — could you keep an eye on Livia? Between you and Reece, she should be safe enough.'

'Will she be going back to England?'

'She says not. She has no close family left there.'

Conn was surprised. 'Then what will she do?'

'If she can sell this place, she'll open a small school. I think she'd do well at that. She's a good teacher.' He smiled ruefully. 'Not so good at housework.' The smile vanished. 'Which reminds me. Somehow Livia and I will have to get to Perth to find another maid.'

'Just put an advertisement in the *Inquirer*.'

'And appoint someone sight unseen from a newspaper advertisement? It's too risky.'

'You don't have much choice. No female convicts have been sent to this colony and female servants are hard to find. That's why they brought the group of Lancashire lasses out here in the first place.'

'The colony is not at all what I was led to expect.' There was a bitter twist to Francis's lips as he walked away.

222

Conn didn't say what he was thinking: at least *you* had a choice about coming here.

★ ★ ★

As much as they could, the men left the sisters alone together that day. The four young women were packing Pandora's trunk and bag for travelling, not only for the journey south, but for the sea voyage. They spent a lot of time discussing clothes, walking to and fro from the tent to the washing lines, where some garments were still drying. They did their best to iron them in almost impossible circumstances, wanting their sister to look the best she could on the ship.

When everyone had finished their midday meal, Conn produced the papers he'd drawn up, which the other sisters needed to sign to give Pandora authority to act on their behalf. 'I thought you'd be the best person to witness their signatures, Mr Southerham, together with Zachary.'

And so it was done.

After the meal Reece waited till the others had moved away before looking at Zachary with a very serious expression. 'You'll take great care of Pandora, won't you? She'll be upset about leaving her sisters.'

'I know. And you don't need to worry. I'll guard her with my life, if necessary.'

'I doubt it'll come to that, but we both feel we can trust you.'

'In return, I'll ask you to look after Leo when he returns from Albany. He's a gentle soul.'

'Of course I will. He's actually a very useful sort of fellow to have here.'

Reece went back to work and Zachary sat on, taking in everything he saw. When he got back, Hallie would want to know every detail. His eyes kept going back to the shack: another of these primitive houses and so isolated from other dwellings. How could anyone want to live like this? His own home, humble by most English standards, was a palace in comparison.

He'd write about this visit in his diary, which was quite a long document by now. He was looking forward to getting home again, missed modern amenities like running water, gas lighting in the shop, railways and newspapers.

But it had been a wonderful chance to see something of the world, and he'd see even more on the way back, since they would probably be returning via Suez and Gibraltar.

★ ★ ★

The day seemed to pass all too quickly. As the sun sank lower in the sky and the piles of neatly folded clothes vanished into the trunk and portmanteau, Conn, who was sitting on the veranda with the Southerhams, glanced surreptitiously at his pocket watch.

Francis noticed and looked at the sky. 'It's getting late.'

'Yes. I've been dreading this.' Conn went across to the group of women. 'I'm sorry, but it's time we were leaving. With such poor roads, we need to travel by daylight.'

'Time for a cup of tea first?' Livia asked.

He hesitated, then shrugged. 'Just a quick one.'

'I'll make it,' she said. 'Sit down with your sisters, Pandora.'

The four young women sat down on the rough wooden benches on either side of the table. They didn't talk, just sat together, perhaps for the last time ever. Once Pandora took hold of Cassandra's hand, looked down at it and gave it a quick squeeze, then let go and wiped her eyes. A little later, Maia leaned across to give Pandora a hug.

They all looked up as Livia said, 'Tea's ready.'

The men went across to join them, but it was a silent group who sipped their drinks.

In the end Conn decided this was only prolonging the agony. 'We'll be leaving now. I'll come back for the other horses tomorrow, Southerham.' He went to tie two of the hired horses to the back of his cart then helped the twins up into it.

Pandora walked along beside the cart to the bottom of the slope. As she stopped there to watch them drive off, she burst into tears, hearing Maia begin sobbing, seeing Xanthe hold her twin.

Who would there be to hold her from now on? Pandora wondered. Was she doing the right thing, going back? How did you know?

★ ★ ★

It seemed a long time before Pandora got to sleep that night. She'd hated sleeping in this

225

tent, but now, perversely, she didn't want to leave it. Who knew what would happen to her on such a long journey?

She wanted to weep, but couldn't. She'd shed so many tears today she seemed to have none left. Lying in the darkness, she listened to the night sounds outside, worrying about how she'd cope on her sisters' behalf, having to deal with so much money and run a grocery store. What did she know of such things?

When someone shook her, she jerked awake to see a man kneeling beside her bed, holding up a candle lantern. 'Reece? Is something wrong?'

'No, love. It's nearly dawn, time for you to get up.'

'Oh.' She heard her voice wobble and fought for self-control. 'I'll — not be long.'

'I'll make you a cup of tea. Cassandra sends her dearest love. She thought it best not to come, said it'd only start her weeping again. And I didn't want her falling as we walked through the bush in the dark, not in her condition.'

Pandora rolled out of her makeshift bed, washed and dressed quickly, then packed the final few things in her portmanteau, before taking it outside as she joined the men gathered round the table by the light of a lamp.

The cart had been loaded the night before with everything except Pandora's portmanteau. In the end it had been decided that Leo was to ride Conn's mare Nellie, something which pleased him greatly. The strongest of the hired horses was tied behind the cart, ready to spell Conn's raw-boned gelding who was to pull it

226

over the first stretch.

'I've poured you a cup of tea, love,' Reece called.

Pandora went to the table and drank thirstily but couldn't force down even one mouthful of the bread and jam. She pushed it away untouched. 'I'm not hungry.'

'I'll wrap it in a cloth for you to eat on the way,' Reece said. 'You need to keep up your strength.'

She nodded, grateful no one was trying to make conversation in an attempt to cheer her up.

She hugged Reece, clinging to him for a moment, then forcing herself to step back. He picked up the lamp and walked with her to the cart, his arm round her shoulders.

Zachary helped her up on to the back, where a blanket had been laid next to her trunk. 'You look tired. Maybe you can get some more sleep?'

She nodded, too unhappy to think what she was doing.

As they set off even the light seemed strange, for it was still only that false dawn that comes before the true sunrise, a time when everything appears grey or black.

Neither of the Southerhams came out to say goodbye to her. They'd done that the night before when Francis had paid her the wages owing to her. She felt better for having some money of her own.

Bert was driving over the first stretch with Zachary sitting up beside him. Leo rode ahead of them, looking absolutely at home on a horse.

After they'd been travelling for a while and

she'd calmed down, she couldn't bear to sit in silence any longer, so asked, 'Do you think we'll get there in time?'

Bert replied. 'It'll be tight, missy. It's only the 21st today. We ought to get there by the 28th to be certain. But the mail cart takes only a week to get all the way from Perth to Albany, and we're over a day's travel ahead of them, so I dare say we'll do it.' He spoilt this optimistic pronouncement by adding, 'Mind you, they have changes of horses on the way and we'll have to manage with these, so we won't be able to go as fast.'

'We can't push the horses too hard,' Leo said. 'Mr Largan told me to look after his two very carefully.'

'What do you think I'm going to do, whip them?' Bert snapped.

A little later he asked, 'Can you drive, Leo?'

'Yes. I like driving.'

'Good. For now, you ride behind and keep an eye on that spare horse, make sure it's all right. You can drive part of the way to spell me.' Bert began to whistle, a thin, monotonous sound.

At first Pandora sat on her own in the back of the cart, hugging her knees and trying not to let the jolting throw her around too much. After a while, she grew tired of that, because the boards of the cart weren't much cushioned by the blanket and folded tarpaulin she was sitting on. She looked at the two men and it seemed to her that they had the best place. 'Is there room for me on the driving bench, do you think?'

'If you don't mind a bit of a squash,' Zachary said. 'Let me help you up.'

228

The cart wasn't going fast, so she had no trouble clambering up to sit between him and Bert.

As they continued to bump along the rough road, Zachary braced himself on the armrest to his left and offered her his right arm. 'Here. You'd better link arms with me or you'll bounce right off this seat.'

She took his arm, grateful more for the warmth and human contact than for his strength.

She had never felt so alone in her whole life.

★   ★   ★

The following Friday Hallie's mother noticed how tense and upset she was.

'I don't know what's got into you lately, love. You're forgetful and you jump if anyone so much as knocks on the door.'

'I've not been feeling the best.'

'Have you got a fever?'

'No. I'm just — a bit down. I'd be better if I could get a job.'

That set her mother off worrying about the hard times and how many people were out of work and what was to become of the poor things if this went on for ever.

But Hallie hardly heard a word because the clock kept ticking and as soon as it turned nine, the time the shop shut on Fridays, she kept listening for the door knocker.

When it went, she jerked to her feet, her only thought to protect her mother.

She opened the door a crack and thought her heart would leap out of her chest as she saw Prebble standing there.

He thrust the door further open and stepped into the hall before she could stop him. 'I hope you're feeling friendlier tonight, Hallie.'

'I'm not. You've no right to treat me like this.'

'Might is right. How are you going to stop me?'

'I'll tell Mr Dawson.'

'And I'll tell him it's just a lovers' tiff. Who can prove it isn't?' He grabbed her breast before she could stop him and gave it a hard squeeze, hurting her so much she couldn't hold back a moan as she tried to push him away.

But he was stronger than he looked and trapped her against the wall, continuing to fondle her in that loathsome way.

Then a man's voice said, 'Are you all right, Hallie?'

Prebble moved away, smiling. 'Just having a bit of a kiss and cuddle. Aren't we, Hallie?'

She looked at his face and shuddered, but couldn't say a word.

Her tormentor felt in his pocket and shoved an envelope into her hand. 'Here's your Zachary's money.' He pushed past the man standing in the doorway and walked off whistling cheerfully.

It was the way he whistled so cheerfully that upset her. As if what he'd done to her was nothing. Hallie burst into tears, trying to muffle the noise with her hands, ashamed that Cousin John should catch her in this position.

'Nay, lass,' he said gently. 'I won't let him do it again.'

'How can you stop him? He'll hurt my mother if I don't do as he says.'

John's expression grew grim. 'Is that what he's been threatening?'

She nodded. 'Someone knocked Mum over at the market a few weeks ago, jabbed her in the stomach so hard she couldn't breathe. I know *he* arranged it.'

'Well, he won't arrange it any more.' He bent to pick up the envelope.

Her mother called, 'Are you all right, our Hallie?'

She realised her mother had opened the door of the other room so kept her back to it. 'Yes, I'm fine. I just got something in my eye.'

John moved to stand between them. 'Hello, Cousin. I'm back in Outham so thought I'd call in.'

'Eh, your mother must be glad to have you back.'

'She is. Sends her regards. I was just passing the time of day with your daughter. Fine lass she's grown into.'

'Yes, she has.' Mrs Carr turned and exclaimed, 'The tea's burning!' She vanished from sight.

'I *will* sort this out for you, Hallie,' he said in a low voice. 'He'll not trouble you again.'

'How can you?'

'I know one of his uncles. He's not as bad as the rest of them and owes me a favour.'

She looked at him, not daring to believe him.

'It'll be all right from now on,' he repeated.

She managed to eat enough tea to stop her mother questioning her about how she felt, and listened to a complicated explanation of exactly how John was related to them — some sort of distant cousin — and what he'd been doing in Manchester for the past few years.

When Hallie got undressed in Zachary's room, where she was sleeping while he was away, she was shocked at how bruised her breasts were. Prebble had hurt her so quickly!

He was a beast, a beast who pretended to be polite and hard-working.

Could Cousin John really make him leave her alone?

She couldn't go on like this, living in fear. And she wasn't going to give Prebble what he wanted.

★ ★ ★

They travelled slowly but steadily all through that day, resting the horses at regular intervals and alternating the one pulling the cart. Occasionally they'd meet another rider or vehicle and stop to exchange greetings, always asking about the condition of the road ahead.

Mid-afternoon they stopped briefly at Bannister, where the mail changed horses. The place seemed to consist of little but the way station, stables and stores.

Bert chatted to the people there, then came striding back to the cart carrying a loaf. 'You owe them five shillings for this,' he told Zachary.

'That's robbery!' Pandora said indignantly. 'How can one four-pound loaf possibly cost that much?'

'It's better to pay high prices than spend hours

waiting for a loaf to bake in a camp oven at night. They tell me there's a small stream a few miles down the road that's starting to flow, so I reckon we should push on and stop there overnight.'

Leo didn't join in the conversations very often, but Zachary noticed how he stared at everything, shutting his eyes regularly and muttering to himself.

'Are you all right?' he asked at one of the rest stops.

Leo nodded vigorously. 'Yes. I'm learning the road so I can find my way back to Mrs Southerham's house.'

'Bert will bring you back after Pandora and I've sailed.'

'I like to know my own way. I can always remember a road once I've been along it.'

Bert looked sceptical but caught Zachary's warning glance and shut his mouth on what he'd been going to say. Later, Zachary took him aside to make matters plain.

'Don't treat Leo as if he's completely stupid. He isn't. If he says he can find his way once he's travelled a road, I believe him. I've seen for myself how good he is with sick animals. On board the ship there was an accident in rough weather with several people injured. Leo set a valuable cow's leg so skilfully it healed straight and good as new.'

'*Leo did?*'

'Yes. He can't read or write and he doesn't think as you and I do, but he has his own skills.'

Bert shrugged. 'Well, he's good with horses,

233

I'll give him that. Never seen animals take to anyone like they do to him.'

As they set off again, Pandora asked, 'How far do we travel each day?'

'About forty or fifty miles, barring accidents,' Bert said. 'More if we can.'

'A train can take you hundreds of miles in one day.'

'And it frightens the animals in the fields.'

She laughed. 'Dad told me they used to say that in England when the first railways were built, but they were wrong. The animals don't seem to mind the trains at all.'

He shrugged. 'Well, trains will never replace horses, not in a big country like this.'

'No, I don't suppose they will. But I think they'll have trains between the main towns eventually and *I* still prefer travelling that way.' Travelling by cart was uncomfortable and already her body felt bruised all over from the jolting.

There was little to see, compared to England. No pretty villages like those near Outham, or the ones she'd seen through the train window on the trip to London. In fact, no villages at all, not what she'd call villages anyway. No farms either, most of the time, just every now and then a roof in the distance or a sign indicating a nearby property. Oh, and the occasional group of kangaroos or flock of parrots, but such creatures had lost their novelty for her now.

In fact, to her this land felt empty.

★ ★ ★

234

By the end of the first day's travel, Pandora was stiff and sore. They went on till it was nearly dusk and just as she was wondering if they'd ever stop, Bert reined in the horse and thrust the reins into Zachary's hands.

'I reckon this is the place they said would be good for overnighting. I'll take a quick look round.'

She stared at the flattened sandy space next to the road. It had a thread of greenery to one side, but there seemed nothing special about it. She watched Bert walk off between the trees and move down a small slope beyond it until only his hat showed.

He vanished completely from sight, but was soon back again. 'It'll do. The stream's flowing, which it doesn't do in summer. It's only a trickle at the beginning of winter, but someone's made two or three deeper pools where we can get water for the horses.'

She looked round and shivered at the darkness creeping in on them, couldn't help saying, 'I thought we were going to sleep at farms.'

He shrugged. 'We can look for shelter if it starts to rain, but that'll mostly take us off the road so it'll cost us extra time. You'll be all right sleeping on the cart tonight, missy. Probably sleep like a log after a long day's travel. Folk usually do.'

'Where will you three sleep?'

Bert grinned. 'On the ground. Under the cart, if it starts raining. That's why we brought the tarpaulins. Your Mr Largan thought of everything. Good bloke, he is, even if he is Irish.'

She looked at Zachary. 'Will you be all right on the ground?'

'I'm tired enough to sleep standing up. I didn't sleep very well last night.'

'Neither did I.'

He got down from the cart and turned to help her, his hands warm on her waist as he lifted her down. She could have managed on her own, but didn't say so, because it was nice the way he always watched out for her. Comforting.

Bert gave a wheezy chuckle as she winced and moved to and fro stiffly. 'You'll be sorer still by the time we arrive in Albany, missy. This road doesn't get any better.'

She was so exhausted all she wanted was to spread out her bed roll and lie down in it. But Zachary coaxed her into eating, toasting her a piece of bread and managing to do that without burning it.

'You're very kind,' she said, forcing a few mouthfuls down as they sat round the fire. His answering smile lit up his whole face. Strange, she thought, how plain he looked till he smiled, then suddenly he became attractive. She felt herself flushing on that thought and admitted to herself, not for the first time, that her reactions to Zachary were similar to those she'd experienced when she first met Bill.

It felt strange to lie on the cart and look up at the stars. Patches of cloud were drifting across the sky but in between them the stars seemed brighter than any she'd ever seen before. As another cloud started to obscure the moon, she yawned, wondering if it was going to rain. She hoped not. She was so very tired . . .

* ★ *

Pandora was woken by rain pattering lightly on her face. She couldn't for a moment think where she was, then realised she was lying on the cart. It wasn't yet daylight but the sky looked lighter in the east. More drops hit her cheek and she sat up.

Zachary came to the side of the cart. 'Oh good, you're awake. It's nearly dawn, so Bert says we may as well get ready to leave. Can you manage to get dressed under the tarpaulin?'

If she'd had one of her sisters there, they'd have giggled and helped one another, she thought as she wriggled around in the darkness, fumbling for her outer clothes. When she emerged from the tarpaulin, the rain was coming down in earnest and Zachary was waiting to offer her the umbrella as protection. The men, she noticed, had their hats on and sacks over their shoulders. She was using a shawl to cover her head during the journey. It was no time for hats or bonnets.

She felt guilty at taking the umbrella away from him, it being the only one they had, lent to them by Livia. Sheltering under it, she made her way along the stream to attend to nature's call out of sight of the men. When she came back, she found a pannikin of tea waiting for her.

'Good thing the embers were still alight,' Zachary said, 'or we'd have had trouble lighting a fire in this downpour.'

Bert chuckled. 'That wasn't luck. I know how to make a good camp fire and luckily it's not been raining for long. Here.' He held out an enamel plate to her with some bread and ham on it. He went to join Leo, who was fussing over the horses, as usual.

'Why don't you bring your food over here and eat it under the umbrella with me?' she suggested to Zachary. 'It makes no sense for you to stand out in the rain.'

When he joined her, they stood close together under the umbrella, using the back of the cart as a table. They didn't chat, just ate steadily, but as before she felt better for his closeness. There was something wonderfully comforting about Zachary, who never seemed to get angry or impatient with anyone.

'It's only this leg of the journey that will be so rough,' he said apologetically. 'You'll be much more comfortable on the ship.'

'I don't mind. I haven't exactly been living in luxury in that tent at the farm. I wonder how they all are?'

'They'll be wondering the same about us.'

'The Southerhams won't find it easy to manage without a maid but I shan't miss looking after them, I can tell you. It's hard work, you're on your own most of the time and as soon as you get the place straight, one of them messes it up again.'

Bert called for them to get up on the cart and that interrupted their conversation. She was sorry for it.

Once they were travelling again, Zachary asked, 'What will you do with yourself once you're back in Outham?'

'Work in the shop, I suppose.'

'Women don't usually work in shops like Blake's.'

'Why ever not?'

He looked at her in surprise. 'I don't know. I never thought about it. They just — don't.'

'Not even if they own the shop?'

'It's usually the husbands who own the bigger shops and the wives still don't work in them. I suppose they don't need the money. They keep busy with their children and home.'

She pulled a face. 'Well, I don't have children and I'd get bored sitting around on my own all day.'

'Since your sisters aren't coming back to England, I'd wondered if you were going to sell the shop so that you can send their share of the money back here.'

'They're leaving it to me to decide what to do. If I think it's worth keeping the shop and I enjoy running it, there are other things of my uncle's we can sell, cottages like the one we lived in near the park. We were only in it for a week, but it was a lovely house. After our uncle died, our aunt forced us to go to Australia.' She paused, then went on, thinking aloud, 'You said there was money in the bank as well, so depending on how much there is, I can send them that. I'm not rushing into selling anything. A good business will keep you for life. Money can be frittered away or banks can fail.'

'It seems strange hearing a woman talk about such things.'

'Who do you think manages the housekeeping

239

money in most families? Women, that's who. Besides, Dad taught us to use our brains and I was always the best at ciphering. I can add up figures more quickly than most men.'

'I believe you. You could do the accounts for the shop, perhaps.'

She lifted her chin. 'I'll do more than the accounts. If it's my shop, I'll serve customers too.'

He smiled. 'I can see you're going to turn everything upside down. And maybe that won't hurt. Harry just goes on in the same old way. He never thinks of trying anything new, not even when customers are asking for it.'

'What's he like?' There was enough light now for her to see Zachary's face suddenly go tight.

'He — er, works hard.'

'But you don't like him.'

He stared at her in dismay. 'I never said that. It'd not be fair for me to comment on him.'

She didn't press the point, but she couldn't help wondering why he didn't like Harry Prebble. There had been a Betty Prebble working at the mill, but on another floor and she'd not had much to do with her. A rather sulky woman, if she remembered correctly, but she did her work, which was what mattered.

She tried to remember this Harry from the few occasions she'd visited her uncle's shop, but couldn't remember anyone except Zachary and her uncle. In the hungry times, Zachary had once brought them round a sack of provisions, sent by their uncle, and she'd seen him occasionally in the street, though they'd not been acquainted. She always noticed taller men because at five foot ten inches, she towered over most men.

Well, she'd find out what Harry Prebble was like when she got to Outham. She wished her Dad could have lived long enough to benefit from their inheritance. She'd have bought him a whole boxful of books and paid for more Greek lessons, too. He'd had such a hunger for learning and so little opportunity to do it.

She blinked her eyes rapidly to drive away the tears that thinking of him brought to her eyes.

'Are you all right?' Zachary asked.

They were sitting so close together under the umbrella that when he turned his head, his breath was warm in her hair. 'I was remembering my father.'

'I think about mine sometimes. He died so young.'

She studied Zachary's face. He had clear, steady eyes, a nose that was perhaps too long, but nice lips, well-defined. His chin had faint bristles on it today because there had been no chance of shaving this morning. It'd be rough to the touch, rough on your lips if you kissed him, as Bill's chin had been sometimes. No, what was she thinking about! Kisses indeed!

But she did find Zachary attractive. She'd been so lost in the pain of parting from her sisters, she hadn't really thought about how she would get on with him on such a long journey, but she always felt comfortable with him. All three of her sisters had said they liked and trusted him, too, as had Reece.

She peeped at Zachary again, caught him smiling at her and smiled back, then felt herself flushing as she wondered what he thought of her, if he felt attracted too — not to her pretty face, which brought annoying attention sometimes from young men, but to herself, the Pandora her family and friends knew.

She hoped he did find her attractive. The idea of it made her feel warm inside.

★ ★ ★

Cassandra went across to help the Southerhams later in the morning but Reece insisted she work only for half days now and because she did tire easily, she'd agreed.

'What am I going to do?' Livia asked towards the end of the morning, not speaking as a mistress to a maid today but as one woman to another. 'I've little experience of housekeeping and Francis isn't strong. Will you make me a list each day of what else needs doing and show me how to do it?'

'Yes, of course. I'd suggest you make some changes in the way you live until you get a new maid, preferably two maids, because I shan't be available after I've had the baby.'

'What sort of changes?'

'Well, Mr Southerham doesn't really need to change his shirts every afternoon. It makes such a lot of extra work, especially now that the rainy season has started. How are you to dry and iron them?'

'I don't know, but he won't like that. He's says

242

it's important to maintain proper standards.'

'Then let him wash them.'

Livia chuckled.

Whose standards though? Cassandra wondered, but it wasn't her place to comment. If Mr Southerham had really thought about what he was doing and wanted to continue living like gentry, he'd not have come to a place like this, where neither of them seemed able to cope. Livia had been a kind and capable lady back in Outham, helping the poor, teaching girls to sew, but here she was helpless in so many ways when it came to doing the work involved in running a home.

'I'll see what Francis says. We definitely have to make some changes if we're to manage until we get another maid.'

And would they then go back to 'maintaining standards', Cassandra wondered. Would they go on pretending life here was like that in England?

Reece came across to them, nodding to Mrs Southerham then turning to his wife. 'Time you were going home now, love. You're looking tired.'

They walked back along the bush path together, because he wouldn't let her go anywhere on her own now she was so big.

As the path widened a little, she took his arm, more for the pleasure of holding him close than because she needed help. 'I wonder how Pandora is.'

'She'll be all right. Zachary will look after her. It's you I'm worried about. You're looking exhausted.'

'I am feeling a bit tired,' she admitted.

'Maybe you should stop work completely.'

'How can I? Those two can't manage without my help.'

'They'll have to once the baby's born. Will you be all right on your own this afternoon?'

'I'm not on my own. I have Kevin with me. He's good company.'

'I'm glad he's there. He likes having us around, too.'

After Reece had gone back, Kevin got her some food then insisted on her having a rest.

'I'll just lie down for half an hour. Oh dear, I feel so useless.'

'It's the Southerhams who're useless, lass. And it's not your job to look after their lives for them. Now, try to have a sleep.'

To her surprise she did manage to doze off, but she felt no better afterwards and it was an effort to get up and potter around. In the end she sat down to some sewing for the baby. There were still a lot of clothes needed for him. Somehow she was sure it'd be a him, she didn't know why.

13

The second day of travel was miserable. They were soon soaked to the skin, in spite of the umbrella and sacks. Only Leo stayed cheerful, not seeming bothered by the rain, more concerned with how it was affecting the horses.

As the afternoon wore on, Bert started looking round for somewhere to stay. Just when it began to seem as if they'd have to camp again, he pointed to a track to one side. 'That looks well used. I can't see any buildings from here, but there may be a farm at the other end. It'll be quicker if I ride along and find out before we turn off the road. Leo, lend me that nag of yours and come and hold the reins.'

It seemed a long time till he came back. Pandora couldn't help shivering and in the end Zachary put one arm round her shoulders and held her close while she kept the umbrella over them.

'Sorry.'

'It's not your fault, it's mine. We should have stopped and found shelter earlier. But I'd rather get to Albany early and be sure of our passage.'

She managed a shaky laugh. 'I'm beginning to think this Albany place doesn't exist.'

There was the sound of horses' hooves clopping wetly nearby and Bert reappeared. 'There is a farm, but the house is tiny, so though we're welcome there, we'll have to sleep on the

245

verandas. There isn't even room in their barn. Still, the verandas are sheltered from the rain and that'll be much better than camping in the open, eh? It's nearly dark, so we'd be foolish to push on. The owners have offered to make us some damper for tomorrow and give us something to eat tonight. They've got plenty of eggs.'

'How much will it cost?' Zachary asked, wondering if everyone in the countryside overcharged for things.

'They're not asking for payment but you ought to give them a few shillings anyway.' He looked severely at Zachary. 'This isn't England. I've told you before that most people are happy to give shelter and food to travellers. It's just that this family hasn't got much money, from the looks of the place.'

'How kind of them!' Pandora exclaimed. She couldn't stop shivering. Had she ever been so cold before? Her outer clothes were sodden and heavy.

The house was even smaller than the Southerhams'. As the couple had five children, there was certainly no way anyone else could sleep inside the one room. Fortunately, the place was much more soundly built than Westview, with a small veranda on either side, each of which had an end panel to protect it from the prevailing westerly winds and weather.

'We sleep out here ourselves in summer and we always put travellers here in winter,' the woman said cheerfully. 'Hardly get any rain blowing into those verandas because of the way my man built the house.'

Pandora looked at the place where she was supposed to sleep, because the men had said they'd cram into the other veranda. She didn't like the idea of sleeping at this side on her own, not at all.

'I'll get your bed roll, missy,' Bert said.

When he'd gone to the cart, she clutched Zachary's arm. 'Could you — sleep on my veranda, do you think?'

'It wouldn't be right.'

'Would it be right for me to be afraid all night long?'

He looked at her solemnly. 'No, that wouldn't be good. Are you sure?'

'Of course I am. Oh, Zachary, it's all so strange here.' She clutched his big warm hand. 'Please don't leave me alone in the darkness.'

He clasped her hand in both his. 'Of course I won't. Goodness, you're frozen.' He raised her hand to his lips and blew on it to warm it. 'You go inside for that cup of tea you were promised. I'll tell Bert and Leo I'm sleeping this side.'

When it came time to go to bed, Pandora put down the little girl who had clambered on her knee in the overcrowded room, stepped carefully round a toddler sleeping on a straw mattress with an older child on the floor near her feet, and let her hostess light her to the latrine.

'Zachary told me you two are going to be wed,' the woman said. 'You've a fine young man there. When's the happy day?'

She hoped she'd hidden her surprise at this announcement. 'Um — when we get back to England.'

Her hostess chuckled. 'I'd not leave it that

247

long, if I were you, or other women will be after a fine young fellow like him. Not to mention the chance of consequences from you being together. I only have to cuddle my man to fall for another baby. It's lovely to see how your fellow looks at you, though. Don't look so upset. I'm only teasing about other women. It's clear how much he loves you.'

Pandora swallowed hard. Did Zachary really look at her fondly? How could that be possible? It had taken her months to fall in love with Bill. She hadn't done so until she got to know him well and realised what a nice man he was. But she'd come to like Zachary much more quickly, couldn't deny that.

She'd been telling herself all day that this was just because she'd left her sisters and felt so alone. But she couldn't convince herself, because the attraction seemed all too real. She found herself turning to him, enjoying their chats, feeling safe against the warmth of his tall body. Zachary made her feel small and cherished, a delightful sensation.

'Don't forget to shake out your shoes for spiders before you put them on in the morning,' was her hostess's parting shot.

Pandora found Zachary was waiting for her on the veranda, with a battered candle lantern hanging on a nail in the sheltered corner, its flame flickering wildly. She was glad the light was too dim for him to see the furious blush that heated her cheeks at the sight of him. He'd spread out her bed roll, but his was still fastened up on the floor beside it.

'I'll just nip round the back for a minute or two,' he said. 'Now that you can see how little space there is, maybe you'll feel differently about me joining you here. I can always sleep with the other men if you've changed your mind. We're within earshot, you know. You'll be quite safe.'

She thought better of him for giving her a chance to change her mind but she still wanted him nearby, so she unfastened his bed roll and spread it out before she got into her own. It was perfectly respectable to lie like this, each sleeping in a separate nest of blankets. Why, they weren't even touching one another.

Other people might not see it as respectable, though, she admitted as she snuggled down, shivering, but *she* knew it was perfectly innocent, which was what mattered most.

She didn't try to get undressed, relieved that her clothes had more or less dried while they were eating their meal in the farmhouse, but she did take off her boots. Why did you always feel the cold more when it was damp? Shivering, she pulled the blankets up round her neck, trying to ignore the lack of a pillow and the hard planks beneath her.

Zachary came back, stared at his unrolled blankets then nodded, as if accepting her decision. He took off his boots, blew out the candle and slid into his blankets. 'Good night.'

'Sleep well.'

She was still shivering, tried to tell herself she was getting warmer, but knew she wasn't. She was so cold she couldn't get to sleep, but tried to keep still and quiet so as not to disturb him.

After a few minutes his voice reached out to her through the darkness.

'Your teeth are chattering, Pandora, and you're shivering so hard I can feel it.'

'I'm s-sorry if I kept you awake.'

'I'm sorry you're so cold. Look, if we combine our blankets, you can lie cuddled against me. I'll soon warm you up. I never seem to feel the cold and I'm quite cosy already. I'd not touch you in any way that's wrong, I promise.'

'Oh, please, yes.' She'd do anything to get warm again.

She got even colder as he rearranged the blankets, then he lay down again beside her and took her in his arms, pulling her close. Shivers still racked her, but as she nestled against him she sighed with relief as the blessed heat of his body began to warm her.

'That's better, eh?' he said a short time later. 'You've stopped shaking.'

'Much better.'

He chuckled, the air from his laughter blowing against her temple and sending a shimmer of awareness through her body.

She tried to dispel the feeling with a joke. 'You make a wonderful hot brick!'

'I've been called a lot of things, but never a hot brick before. There it goes, raining again.'

'It's not reaching us, though.'

'They built this house cleverly. But I still wouldn't like to have no neighbours nearby.'

'Neither would I.'

Silence fell, a companionable silence punctuated only by the sound of his soft breaths. 'I've missed having someone to chat to at night,' she confided. 'Until Cassandra got married, I'd always slept with one of my sisters.'

'I've never slept with anyone since I was a lad. There's just me and my sister, you see. After Dad died, Hallie started sleeping in the same bedroom as Mum, so I'm on my own in the other one.'

'It's lonely on your own. Dark thoughts creep into your mind in the middle of the night.'

'Is that what it's been like for you lately?'

She nodded, realised he couldn't see that in the dark and offered him words instead. 'Yes. It's nice to see Cassandra so happy, of course it is, but I miss her dreadfully. I'm going to miss all of them.' A sob escaped her.

'Shh now. No more crying. What can't be cured . . . '

' . . . must be endured.'

'My gran always used to say, 'Just be grateful you're alive and well'.'

'We never knew our grandparents. And my mother died when I was seven. But there was always Cassandra to look after me. She's been a wonderful older sister.'

'Well, now you've got me to look after you — until we get to England, anyway.'

'You'll still be there even after we get back. I mean, you'll be working in the shop, after all.' The silence that followed those words was so long, she prompted, 'Won't you?'

'I don't know. If Harry is made manager permanently, I shall need to look for another job.'

251

'You definitely don't like him.'

'Let's just say chalk and cheese.'

'Why won't you admit how you feel about him?'

He sighed. 'Because it's not fair when he isn't here to defend himself. After all, Mr Featherworth thought enough of him to make him manager.'

'And thought enough of you to send you to the other side of the world to find us. To me, that sounds as if the lawyer trusts you more than Harry.'

Another silence, then, 'I hadn't thought of it like that.'

It seemed obvious to her. 'Don't do anything in haste after we get back, Zachary. Promise you'll discuss it with me first if you feel the need to leave.' It suddenly occurred to her that it wouldn't be up to Mr Featherworth to appoint a manager. It'd be her responsibility. She was part-owner but had full power over running the shop, thanks to those papers signed by her sisters. That thought made her catch her breath, but she didn't speak it aloud, just hugged the idea close that she needn't lose Zachary after they got back. But she'd not say anything yet. He might not like the idea that she favoured him. He might not want her . . . affection.

She realised her attention had wandered. What was he saying?

' . . . so I'd never act hastily, Pandora, not with my mother and sister to think of. They depend on me for everything.' He hesitated, then added, 'That's why I can't think of marriage. All the lads I grew up with are wed, but I can't support

252

a wife, let alone children, much as I'd like to.'

She knew he was saying this as a warning — but was he warning her or himself? With a sigh of bliss for how much warmer she now felt, she snuggled against him. He was so comfortable to lie with, so . . .

When she woke in the morning it was to the shrill sounds of a flock of white-tailed black cockatoos shrieking and squabbling in the gum trees nearby. She'd seen them often enough now to recognise their calls. It was just getting light and . . . Zachary was gone.

She hadn't even noticed him getting out of bed. She touched the blanket where his head had lain, so close to hers, but it was cold now. Smiling she remembered how they'd chatted, how he'd got her warm when she felt as if she was never going to be warm again.

And all this without misbehaving in any way. But then she'd known he wouldn't do anything to upset her. She'd trust him with her life, *was* trusting him with her life.

★   ★   ★

Alice went down to the kitchen after breakfast to discuss the day's duties with Dot.

'Miss, did you hear anything last night?'

'No. What sort of thing?'

'Middle of the night, it was. Someone in the back yard of the shop. I'd have been fast asleep but that cat down the road was making such a noise.'

'I didn't even hear that.'

'Well, your bedroom's at the front. Anyway, I was lying there, trying to get to sleep again when I heard a sound. That back gate creaks a bit when you open it. I went to peep out of the window and that's when I saw a man in the back yard of the shop.'

'Could you see who it was?'

'No, miss. Let alone I didn't dare move the curtain more than a crack, there was no moon. I just saw a figure, a man.'

'What did he do?'

'I could only see him in the yard, couldn't see the back of the shop, but he went towards the shop and after that I didn't see him for a few minutes. Then he went away again, carrying something.'

'Was he a burglar, do you think?'

'I nipped out into the yard this morning but the back of the shop didn't look as if it'd been broken into.'

'Hmm. I'll mention it to Mr Dawson. Don't say a word to anyone else.'

'No, miss. I'd never dare. Only you've been that good to me, I don't like to keep anything back from you.'

'I'm glad you don't. You're a good worker, Dot. I've never had a maid as hard-working as you. And you don't need telling what to do, either, you just get on with it.'

The girl blushed bright red, trying in vain not to smile.

Alice was left very thoughtful. She would definitely mention it to Ralph Dawson when she next saw him.

It was strange, knowing something was going on next door but not being able to put your finger on what was wrong. She was glad of the new door between the two halves of the building, though. Very glad.

But she still locked her bedroom door at night and she knew Dot still took a poker up to bed with her.

Was Prebble stealing from the shop? Why? He had a good job there. Wasn't that enough? But who else could it be? Only he had a key to the side and back gates.

What would happen when the new owners returned?

Prebble seemed to think other people were fools and had a way of looking at her scornfully that made her want to give him a sharp set-down. But she didn't. Mr Dawson had matters in hand and wanted her to act as if nothing was the matter.

★   ★   ★

It was raining again when they set off that second morning. Pandora still felt shivery and huddled down on the seat, with her shawl wrapped tightly round her head and upper body.

Zachary looked at her in concern. 'Are you all right? You're very quiet this morning and you look a bit pale.'

She shrugged. 'I can't seem to get warm, whatever I do.'

'We could get a blanket and wrap it round you.'

It took her a minute or two to think this over. Even her mind seemed to be working slowly today. 'Yes. That's a good idea.'

He edged over into the back of the cart and opened his blanket roll, pulling out the thickest of the blankets.

'I think I might have caught a cold,' she said as he put it round her shoulders.

He looked at her in concern. 'I hope not. But you do look heavy-eyed.'

'I'll be all right. A cold's not much fun, but it won't make any difference to our travel.'

Each time they stopped that day, he fussed over her. They were all chilled and wet, so Bert lit a fire and brewed a pot of tea at midday.

By the time they started looking for somewhere to stop for the night, Pandora was feeling feverish and longing for nothing but to lie down.

They found a farm with a hay barn where they could stay, but when Zachary asked if Pandora could sleep inside, the woman stepped back a pace.

'I don't want to catch her cold. She'll be fine in the barn.'

'Can you bake us some damper?'

'I'd have to charge you for it,' she said grudgingly.

'We can pay.'

The barn was a draughty place, however, and even Bert grumbled about the area where they were told to sleep.

Leo shared his concern between Pandora and the horses. 'She needs a hot lemon and honey

256

drink,' he said. 'My mother always gives me hot lemon and honey when I'm not well.'

'We don't have any.'

'We could ask the people at the house.'

'They'd not give us any even if they had it. You don't often meet mean devils like them in the country.'

Bert and Leo put their sleeping rolls to one side of the sleeping area and left Zachary to bed down with Pandora.

'I shouldn't sleep close to you,' she said. 'I don't want to give you my cold.'

'I never catch colds. And you need to get warm.'

The trouble was, one minute she was shivering, the next she was too hot. She kept apologising for disturbing him, but he was much more disturbed by his worries about her. If she fell ill, it might make them late for the ship, so what should he do? Press on, or stop somewhere and risk letting her rest for a day or two?

★ ★ ★

In the morning Pandora was worse, and though she tried to make light of it, he could tell that it was a huge effort for her to get up.

'I'll go and ask them if we can stay here another night,' he said.

'No! I'll be all right. I can lie down on the back of the cart.'

'You're not all right. You need to be in a warm house, not out in the open air on a cold day with rain threatening. Even this barn's not good enough.'

But their host grew even more unfriendly when he saw that Pandora was ill and refused point-blank to let them stay longer.

'I can't have my wife getting ill. She gets a bad chest if she catches a cold. It was one of the reasons we came here. I'm sorry, but you'll have to move on.'

Furious, Zachary tried to make a warm place for Pandora on the back of the cart, and this time, she lay down in it with a sigh, murmuring that her head was aching. But when he turned to keep an eye on her, he could see that the jolting was making her wince sometimes and she looked so pale he was very anxious.

'We need to find somewhere to stop and look after her,' he said to Bert. 'She's not at all well.'

'I'll ask at the next mail post. They may know someone who'll take us in. But it'll make us late.'

'Then we'll have to be late! We don't want her cold to turn into pneumonia.'

Before they got to the next mail post, it began to rain heavily, so they covered Pandora with a tarpaulin and Zachary went to crouch in the back of the cart to hold an umbrella over her face.

It was a miserable, sodden party who arrived at the next mail stop, and to Zachary's relief, it was suggested that they try the wife of a nearby settler, who had a reputation for looking after anyone who was ill, because it was days' travel to the nearest doctor.

Granny Pithers took one look at Pandora and asked Zachary to carry her inside. 'Shame on you for taking that poor young woman out in weather like this! She'll be lucky if she doesn't get congestion of the lungs. What were you thinking of?'

'The people whose barn we stayed in wouldn't let us stop any longer when they saw she was ill.'

'Well, I don't call that Christian behaviour, I don't indeed. Good thing I have a spare bedroom. Your wife can sleep on the bed, but you'd be better on the floor.'

'She's — um, not my wife. We're engaged to be married, but were waiting till we got back to England.'

'You should have done it before you started. Still, I think she'll be better with you nearby, so you can bring your bedroll inside. Your friends can sleep in our barn. Will that young man be all right?'

'Leo will be fine. He's really good with horses.'

'Well, that's a blessing.'

Pandora snuggled down in the soft bed and fell instantly asleep. Granny came to check on her several times and Zachary slept very lightly, waking at intervals to make sure Pandora was all right.

'We still need to set off in the morning,' Bert insisted as they sat over an excellent evening meal of kangaroo stew.

'You'll leave when she's fit to travel and not before,' Granny said severely. 'There will always be another mail ship, but there might not be another Pandora if you don't allow her to recover properly. Such a pretty name. I must tell my niece. She's expecting a child next month. You're lucky you caught me at home. I'm going to stay with her for the birth. I do enjoy a birthing.'

Zachary kept counting off the days left to get to Albany. Would they get there in time? Would it be enough? Or should they abandon the attempt, return to Westview and try for the next mail ship?

It would all depend on how quickly Pandora got better. She must get better. He couldn't bear it if anything happened to her. Not only was Mr Featherworth trusting him to take her safely back to England, she was . . . Pandora.

He had no right to care about her as he did, and he'd never tell her how he felt, but he couldn't help loving her. It had been agony to lie beside her soft body, wanting to touch her, love her.

What a fool he was! He'd be trying to fly to the moon next.

14

To everyone's relief, Pandora was a lot better the following morning and insisted on travelling on. She lay in the back of the cart, well wrapped in blankets, claiming she was all right. Granny had given her a small chunk of smooth rock, which they'd heated before setting off and wrapped in some old rags. They reheated it in hastily lit fires whenever they stopped for a meal that first day. It became very sooty, but it made a huge difference to Pandora's comfort.

Again they travelled till nearly dark, which meant they couldn't overnight at the places where the mail cart changed horses. With time so short they didn't dare stop before dusk.

Pandora listened dreamily as Bert explained that mail stations were sited where you could find water all year round, which was important in the hotter seasons. It seemed strange to her to have some rivers which only flowed in the winter. Some of the stations were known only by their distance from Perth: 113 Mile or 131 Mile.

To her relief, it didn't rain and they were fortunate enough to find shelter in farms that night and the following night. And though they had to sleep in barns, these were better built and less draughty.

Each of those nights Leo and Bert made their beds together away from them without anyone asking them, and Zachary held her in his arms.

And if she was guilty of exaggerating how cold she felt, she didn't care. She loved sleeping close to him and was, she admitted to herself, in love with him. How quickly that had happened!

But he gave no sign he cared for her in that way and she was trying to work out whether this was because he didn't share her feelings or because he couldn't afford to care for any woman?

Surely the money she'd inherited wouldn't stand between her and an honest man? If that was what was making Zachary keep his distance mentally, she'd have to do something about it. She wasn't going to let foolish pride stop them.

But did he love her?

She wanted the same kind of companionable happiness that Cassandra had found with Reece, longed for it quite desperately. It would have been worth all the agony of coming to Australia if it brought her someone to love and make a life with.

If it was the money coming between them, could she ask him to marry her? She and her sisters prided themselves on thinking for themselves, but the thought of proposing to Zachary was still very daunting.

But if it was the only way, she'd find the courage to do it. She'd lost one good man, didn't intend to lose another.

★　★　★

Cassandra sat enjoying the leaping flames of a wood fire while chatting to Reece and Kevin, both of whom kept fussing over her. She was very tired of being so large and would be glad to have the baby and be done with it.

'I wonder where they are now?' she asked. No need to explain who 'they' were.

'They have been on the road for five days, so they must be nearing Albany,' Reece said.

'I keep worrying about her.'

'I'm sure we can trust Zachary.' He looked at her. 'You're not going to the Southerhams' tomorrow, if I have to tie you down.'

She grimaced but nodded agreement. 'The baby's dropped quite a bit now. I'm thinking it'll arrive early.'

He looked at her anxiously. 'I hope not. Mrs Moore can't come to help with the birthing for a couple of weeks yet. Are you sure?'

'I'm not sure about anything, but when I talked to her she told me what to watch out for. And the baby's definitely dropped. He's still kicking a lot, though.'

'What if he's a girl? What shall we call her?'

'It'll be a boy.'

'Just humour me. Think of a girl's name.'

She looked at him in surprise. 'I don't know.'

'How about another Greek name? I'm sure your father would like that.'

'You choose one, then.'

'Sofia,' he said at once. 'I read it in a book years ago and decided if I ever had a daughter, she'd be called Sofia.'

She smiled. 'It's going to be a boy, but I do like the name Sofia. We'll keep it for another child.'

They had to stop at the settlement of Kojonup, which was still three days' travel from Albany, because the hired horse had cast a shoe. Leo insisted the poor creature needed a whole new set and Bert agreed. It cost four shillings to have the old shoes removed, and seven shillings to have a set of new ones fitted.

Zachary paid for this with money he kept in a small coin purse. He only kept a pound or two in change in it, just enough to pay for their everyday expenses. The rest, a frighteningly large number of shiny golden sovereign and half sovereign coins still, was securely stowed in a canvas money belt he wore round his waist at all times. He'd been carrying the new, lighter weight copper coins when he set off, but once in the Swan River Colony, he'd found people using mostly the heavier, older coins.

He hadn't been separated from that money belt since he set off from Outham and of course, he'd kept an account of every single penny he'd spent, including the amount needed to rescue Leo, which he'd pay back if Mr Featherworth thought it necessary, whatever Pandora said.

Each night as the two of them slept next to one another he had to keep reminding himself that he shouldn't get close to her *in that or any other way*. He managed to control his body — just — but somehow, once they were together in the darkness, he found himself chatting to her, cuddling her closely and generally behaving as any young man in love would. He couldn't help his feelings. Not only was she beautiful but she smiled happily when she woke next to him in the mornings. They never seemed to run out of things to discuss or say to one another, while the feel of her sleeping head against his chest or shoulder filled him with hopeless longing and protectiveness.

Bert teased him once or twice about his sweetheart, but he ignored that.

He mustn't take advantage of the situation and her loneliness by telling her how he felt about her. She had so much money that nothing could come of his feelings. This friendship was just temporary, caused by them being together while travelling. Once they got back to Outham, she'd have other things on her mind, other people to look after her, and she'd soon forget about him.

Besides, he knew what people would say if he married her — fortune-hunter, they'd call him — and he had too much pride for that.

Why did he have to meet her now, when she was out of reach? Why hadn't he met and courted her when she was poor like him?

He kept an eye on Leo, but the lad was as happy caring for the horses as Bert was to leave that chore to him. Leo had such a trusting, happy nature if treated kindly. All the poor fellow seemed to ask of life was to be allowed to care for the animals and live quietly.

Worried about what would happen after he and Pandora left Australia, Zachary tried talking to Leo about it.

Leo listened carefully, then nodded. 'I'm going

265

back to Westview after you get on the ship — it's all right, I know my way. I'll wait for you there.'

'I shan't be coming back to Australia, Leo. That's what I'm telling you. But it won't matter because you'll be safe with Reece and the Southerhams. You'll be able to look after their horses for them. You'll enjoy that. And they'll pay you a wage, so you'll have your own money.'

Leo frowned. 'You will come back one day to bring Pandora to visit her sisters. I know you will.'

'I don't think it'll be me who brings her. By then she'll probably be married and come with her husband.'

Leo laughed aloud at that. 'She'll be married to you.'

'I can't marry her. I've no money and she has a lot.'

'She can share hers with you, then.'

'I'd not ask her to.'

Leo looked at him very solemnly. 'You will marry her. I know you will.'

And nothing Zachary said could change his mind about that.

★ ★ ★

Just before they got to Mount Barker, the last stopping place for the official mail cart, they had to drive to one side of the track to avoid some particularly deep ruts. Others had obviously done the same and the track fanned out to both sides, as it had a few times before. It was so unlike English roads, Zachary thought. Here in

266

Australia there was often unoccupied land between one settlement and the next, so vehicle drivers could leave the road and choose the easiest terrain.

Suddenly an even bigger jolt than usual jerked him out of his musings and had him clinging tightly to the handrail beside him. It felt as if one of their front wheels had hit a rock hidden by the mud.

Bert muttered in annoyance as the horse slowed down for a moment or two. Just as it started to speed up again, they hit another rock, not a big one, but enough to jar the cart badly.

With a cracking sound, the wheel broke off at the axle cap and went spinning to one side. The front corner of the cart on Bert's right side thumped to the ground. Everything happened so suddenly they were thrown violently sideways.

Bert let out a yell shrill with pain, then moaned as he struggled to keep his place. Only Zachary's strong grip saved Pandora from being pitched sideways off the now sloping driving bench. She clung to him tightly as the vehicle settled down a little further on the damaged side.

After that first yell, all Bert's attention was focused on the horse which was still trying to drag the cart forward. He began talking to it, 'Easy now, easy. Whoa. Back up now. Easy.' His face a mask of agony, he took both reins into his left hand, not using his right hand at all. He kept talking and pulling gently on the reins to signal to the horse to stop moving forward.

As soon as he saw the wheel come off, Leo urged his mare into a canter, moving quickly to the front of the cart. Once he was ahead of the gelding he vaulted down, leaving his mare slightly to one side.

The sight of Nellie standing there quietly seemed to calm the gelding down and he stopped trying to haul the damaged vehicle forward.

Leo began speaking gently to the horse as he moved round towards the driving seat. 'Give me the reins, Bert.'

With a sigh of relief he let them go.

When Leo had hold of them, he carefully unhooked the lynch pin and guided the horse forward and away from the cart, still harnessed to the now unattached shafts. The gelding didn't seem upset by the need to drag them.

'Good lad, good lad!' Bert exclaimed. He groaned and bent forward, clasping his right arm to his body with his left.

'Are you hurt?' Zachary asked.

There was no answer for a moment, then Bert said in a strained voice, 'I think I've broke me bloody arm.'

Zachary pulled away from Pandora. 'Let's get you off the wagon. I need to see to Bert.'

'I can clamber down on my own. Just swap places. Bert needs your help far more than I do.' Once she was on the ground, she hurried to the front of the cart to see if Leo needed her.

The gelding was standing there, still harnessed to the unattached shafts. Leo picked up Nellie's reins and thrust them into her hands. 'Hold these. Keep speaking to her. Horses run away sometimes if they're frightened.'

Without waiting for her answer, he ran round to the rear of the cart and released the third horse, which was standing shivering, its head pulled down by the rope still attaching it to the vehicle.

Making soothing noises, he led it with him to the front and gave its reins to Pandora as well, then began to unhitch the gelding from the shafts. 'The horses are all right,' he called to those still sitting on the cart. 'They're settling down now.'

'Bert thinks he's broken his arm.' Zachary was now supporting their driver, whose face was chalk white and who looked ready to faint any minute.

That drew Leo's attention briefly away from his beloved horses and he stared at Bert, then finished unhitching the gelding and gave its reins to Pandora. 'Lead them to the side of the road and stay with them. They're settling down again now. I have to look at Bert's arm.'

She felt nervous at being left in charge of three large animals, but stood her ground, trying not to show it. She talked to them softly, as Leo had, without caring what she said, but couldn't help wondering what she'd do if they tried to run off and dragged her along. But although the gelding tossed its head once or twice, none of them moved their feet. It was as if they were comforted by being next to one another.

Leo went to the side of the cart and looked up at Bert.

'Can you help me lift him down?' Zachary asked. 'He's hurt.'

'I can manage on my own.'

Zachary helped ease Bert to the edge of the cart seat, after which Leo took the smaller man's whole weight and laid him gently down by the side of the road.

Bert was obviously in great pain, alternately groaning and cursing, once apologising to Pandora for his language.

Leo knelt beside him. 'We have to get his coat and shirt off, Zachary. I have to see his arm before I set it.'

'He's not touching my arm!' Bert yelled, yelping as he moved involuntarily and hurt himself again.

Zachary laid a calming hand on Bert's shoulder. 'I've seen Leo set a broken bone before.' He didn't remind their guide that it had been a cow's leg, because he knew that wouldn't reassure the injured man. But what choice did they have, here in the middle of nowhere? 'He has a feel for that sort of thing. I'd let him help me, I swear to you.' He waited a minute, then added. 'Besides, there's no one else and we can't leave it like that or it'll not heal properly.'

After more muttered curses, Bert let his head drop back. 'All right then. But if this goes wrong . . .'

'It won't,' Zachary assured him, though he wasn't at all certain of that. But everyone knew broken limbs were best dealt with before the flesh around the break swelled up. 'Let's do it quickly. If I cut your coat and shirt off, it'll hurt less than undressing you and — '

'You're not ruining them. It'd be a waste of

good clothes because it'll hurt either way.' After another unwary movement, Bert roared, 'Just get it over with, damn you!'

Leo had been checking Bert's clothing and undoing his coat and shirt. He pulled back both collars, ready to slip both garments off at once. After a look at Zachary, who nodded and lifted Bert's body, Leo very quickly removed the garments.

Bert let out a smothered scream and fainted.

Leo began to feel the arm. 'It's not a bad break. I can push the bone together. We have to tie it to a flat piece of wood to keep it straight till it heals.'

'Are you sure of this?' Zachary asked, worried they were doing the right thing.

'The farrier at the big house taught me. He says I have a gift for healing. *He* doesn't call me stupid.'

And with that they had to be content, because they were miles from any habitations and there were few doctors in Western Australia anyway, certainly none in most country districts.

'There are some broken side rails on the cart,' Pandora offered. 'Would one of them do for a splint?'

Leo got up and without a word wrenched some strips of wood off the damaged side. He looked round, still frowning. 'I need some cloth to tie his arm to this.'

'I can find you something if you take the horses,' Pandora said.

Leo moved to tie them loosely to a tree while she opened her portmanteau and pulled out a pinafore. 'I need some scissors. I can't tear this into strips.'

'There's a knife in the cooking box,' Zachary called, from where he was still kneeling beside Bert.

She fumbled through it, her hands shaking as she heard Bert regain consciousness and start groaning again. She cut the strings off her apron and then sawed the hemmed edge off jaggedly with the knife, and made a couple more strips from the material above it. 'Is this enough?'

'Yes.' Leo knelt by Bert. 'It'll hurt,' he warned. 'Zachary, you and Pandora hold him down. He mustn't pull the arm away when I'm straightening it.'

'Can you do that, Pandora?' Zachary asked.

She swallowed hard and nodded. A sick, greasy feeling settled in her stomach, but this was no time to give in to faintness, so she forced herself to do as Leo directed.

He didn't tell Bert he was about to straighten the bone, just nodded to her and Zachary. As they tightened their grasp, Leo moved the arm, holding it tightly enough to feel the break move together. The injured man screamed and convulsed.

When Leo stopped moving the limb Bert sagged back, eyes closed, sweat trickling down his brow. Pandora used what was left of her pinafore to wipe his forehead.

Leo now had the arm supported by two pieces of wood and was binding it carefully in place against Bert's body, with Zachary's help. When he'd finished he turned to Zachary for directions, as did Pandora.

Zachary looked round. 'How on earth are we to get help?'

'I wish we had some laudanum,' Pandora said.

'I've got some rum on the cart,' Bert suggested. 'It'd help the pain if I got drunk. Should've had a good slug before you did it.' He shuddered at the memory.

'I don't think getting drunk would be good for you.' Zachary frowned, thinking aloud. 'There's nothing we can do to mend the cart, so we'll have to get help. A few minutes before the accident you said we weren't far from Mount Barker, Bert. There must be someone there who can come out with a cart and take us and our things to an inn — you did say there's a small inn there?'

'There is,' Bert said faintly. 'And Mount Barker's about an hour away.'

'Will you be all right if I go for help, Pandora?' Zachary asked.

'Yes, of course.'

'Leo, which horse should I ride?'

'Nellie.'

'Look after Pandora and Bert. I'll come back as soon as I can.'

Leo nodded, then looked up at the sky. 'It's going to rain.'

Zachary stared at the dark clouds massing above them. 'I can't leave you like this.'

'Just go for help,' Pandora urged. 'We'll be all right.'

He set off, not daring to urge the horse to gallop, because he wasn't confident enough of his skills as a rider to stay on a galloping animal, but he managed to urge it into a trot over the smoother ground.

After a few minutes rain began to fall and he hunched his shoulders against a heavy downpour, hoping the tarpaulins were keeping the others dry.

It seemed a long time before he saw a huddle of buildings ahead and breathed a sigh of relief. When he got closer, he saw that one of them had a sign saying 'The Bush Inn' and muttered, 'Thank goodness!'

A man standing in the doorway brightened up at the sight of a rider. 'Good afternoon, sir. You'll be needing a bed for the night in weather like this.'

'Yes. Four beds, actually. But first we need help getting the other people here. We've had an accident and our cart's been damaged. The axle cap broke on rough ground and we lost a wheel. Our poor driver has broken his arm. Is there someone who can help us?'

'There isn't a doctor hereabouts. Nearest is in Albany.'

'One of our party was able to set the arm. He says it's a simple break, so he straightened it and fastened it to a splint.'

'You were lucky to have him.'

'Yes. But they're sitting out in the open a few miles back and they'll be soaked. Can someone help me fetch them here?'

'I've a cart. I'll have to charge you for its use, though.'

'I can pay. One of the party is a lady.' He saw

the landlord raise an eyebrow and added hastily, 'She and I are betrothed. We have to get to Albany before the end of April to catch the mail steamer to England.'

'You're cutting it close. It's the thirtieth tomorrow.'

'I know.'

The landlord grinned. 'Well, I reckon we can help.' He yelled for someone called Martin to come quickly and within minutes a man had gone hurrying off to harness a horse to the inn's cart while a lad gave Nellie a feed and drink.

The landlord produced a big tin mug of strong black tea for Zachary while this was happening, and he cradled it gratefully in his cold hands between sips.

It was over an hour before they got back to the scene of the accident, to find Pandora sitting on her trunk on a small slope by the side of the road, holding the open umbrella over herself and Bert, who was slumped beside her. Their lower bodies were covered by a tarpaulin. Leo was standing with the two remaining horses. He smiled cheerfully at the sight of the rescue party in spite of the rain dripping from his hat brim and running down his face.

Zachary was off his horse in seconds, hurrying forward. 'Are you all right, Pandora?'

'Just c-cold again.' Her attempt to smile was unconvincing.

The injured man tried to move, groaning in pain, and all attention turned to him.

'We'll shift your baggage into our cart first,' Martin decided, 'then we'll use the trunks to stop him rolling around in the back. It's going to hurt to move him.'

Bert opened his eyes and glared at the newcomer. 'I'm not deaf. I've broke me arm not me ears. There's some rum in me bag, but they won't let me have any.'

'Surely it's not good for him?' Pandora whispered.

Their rescuer grinned. 'A swig or two of grog never hurt anyone. Wouldn't mind one myself. Keeps the cold out nicely, rum does.'

They passed the bottle round, even persuading Pandora to take a sip. But though the strong spirit burned down her throat, giving an illusion of warmth, she disliked the taste and refused to have any more.

By the time they got back to the inn, Bert had had enough 'little swigs' to make him tiddly and was considerably more cheerful. Their helpers carried him inside and laid him on a narrow bed in a room containing several other beds.

'Can't offer you a separate room to sleep in, miss,' the innkeeper said apologetically to Pandora, 'but we've put clean sheets on the bed in the corner for you. Your fellow can sleep in the next bed so you'll be all right. Not that I'd let anyone lay a finger on you in *my* inn.'

'Thank you.'

'Better get out of them wet clothes. You two can change in my back room, and we'll deal with this poor chap here. What about him?' He jerked his head towards Leo, who was looking rather vacant now his special skills weren't needed.

'He needs to change too. I'll sort him out

some clothes when I'm ready. He's good with animals and sick people, but he's not . . . ' Zachary hesitated.

'He's not all there,' the man said cheerfully, tapping his forehead. 'If he's good with animals, he'll not go short of work, though.'

'He's already got a job waiting for him, but he's helping us get to Albany before he starts it. Can we hire your cart to take us there tomorrow?'

'As long as you get it straight back to me. Be best if I send Martin with you to drive it and bring it back again, I reckon. I'll know it's safe then.'

'What about getting ours repaired in the meantime? It's not mine, it's a borrowed cart and they'll need to take it and the horses back to their owners.' He wondered if Leo would manage that, but Bert would be able to direct him, even with a broken arm.

'If you've got the money, the repairs can be done. Good thing it's not a big dray or we'd be in trouble. I'll get my neighbour in to speak to you before you leave. He's handy with repairs. Has to be, living so far from everywhere. Martin can bring a new wheel back from the wheelwright in Albany. Now, get out of them wet clothes, you two, before you catch your death.'

Pandora was too cold to let embarrassment stop her from changing and began to fumble in her portmanteau with fingers so stiff and numb they wouldn't bend properly.

'Shall I wait outside till you've put dry clothes on?' Zachary asked.

'No. You're as wet and cold as I am. Just turn your back.'

277

But she couldn't undo the small buttons on her chemise and in the end had to ask for his help.

'Just a minute,' he said. 'I'm not — '

It was too late. She had turned round and seen him standing there, bare-chested. For a moment she couldn't tear her eyes away, then she averted her gaze. But the image was still there in her mind. How strong and beautiful his body was! Like one of the Greek statues her father had shown her drawings of. Zachary's face might not be handsome, but his body was very pleasing to the eye.

He hastily pulled on a dry vest and thrust his arms into his shirt sleeves. 'Right. What did you want me to do?'

'I can't unfasten the buttons. My hands are still so cold and these are rather small and fiddly.'

He came to stand close, avoiding her eyes, touching the damp material gently as he undid one button after another. He took care not to let her chemise flap open.

She quivered involuntarily as his fingers brushed lightly against her skin. Each button seemed to take an age to unfasten. Suspended in the moment, she was aware only of him.

After he reached the final button and his hands dropped, she had to force herself to step back because what she really wanted was to walk into his arms and lay her head against his chest. 'Thank you. I can manage now.'

He turned and walked abruptly across to the other side of the room, but not before she'd seen

278

the longing in his eyes, not to mention the fact that his body had reacted to hers the same way Bill's had done sometimes. That was good — wasn't it?

When she was dressed again, she said, 'I'm ready,' in an unsteady voice.

He turned. 'We have to make sure you don't have a relapse.'

'I'll be all right. I'm feeling much warmer already, not like last time when I couldn't stop shivering.'

They went back into the main room without looking at one another, leaving their damp garments on a wooden clothes horse in front of the fire.

Leo was standing to one side of the fire, his wet garments steaming gently. Zachary sorted out some clothes for him and took him into the other room to change in privacy.

Food was provided in the public room, but Pandora didn't notice what she ate or whether anyone else spoke to her. She was conscious only of Zachary, squashed beside her at the common table, his thigh touching hers, his strong, capable hands cutting up his meat and passing bread to her. When they joined the ship they'd be separated, and she hated the thought of that.

After the meal, Zachary said, 'If we set off really early tomorrow, we may have a chance of making it in time. Are you up to that?'

'Yes, of course.'

'Better get to bed straight away then.'

Since the inn had only three rooms in all, the public room, the owner's living quarters and the guests' sleeping quarters, there were two other men sleeping in the room with them that night, as well as Bert and Leo. The strangers stared at Pandora in such a hungry, appraising way, she was glad Zachary was sleeping beside her.

It took a long time for her to get to sleep, tired as she was, but she watched him fall asleep almost at once. Firelight showed that if she stretched out her arm she could touch him. She almost did so.

Whatever happened from now on, she wanted to be with him. Whatever she could do to make that happen she would. If that made her a forward hussy, then so be it.

On that decision, she smiled and fell asleep at last.

* * *

The following Friday, Hallie woke feeling sick with fear, but when she went out to the market, leaving her mother at home because it was raining, she saw their cousin John Stoner again.

He came up to her, raising his cap politely. 'I've spoken to Tom and he's had a word with Harry, who claims he was only teasing you for a kiss.'

'He hurt me. He wanted me to — ' She couldn't finish it.

'Well, he'll leave you alone from now on.'

'Are you sure?'

'Yes, very sure.'

'Thank you.'

Even so as nine o'clock passed, Hallie began

to feel afraid, her skin going clammy. She pretended to read her book, but couldn't take in a word.

When the door knocker went, her mother looked up. 'That'll be Zachary's wages. It's kind of Harry to bring them round each week, isn't it?'

'Yes. I'll go.'

At the door Hallie found the shop lad. He held out an envelope and ran off.

She shut the door and leaned against the wall, feeling dizzy with relief.

★ ★ ★

Harry walked home that night feeling furious. Who the hell did his cousin Tom think he was to spoil a bit of fun? It'd have given Harry a great deal of satisfaction to use Zachary's sister like a whore. It'd have been even better if she'd fallen for a child. And she'd not have dared say a word to anyone.

He knew how to terrify lasses.

But Tom was much older than him and didn't always agree with what the rest of the family did and somehow, you didn't mess with Tom. He was a big man, took after the Stoner side of his family, and good with his fists. The Stoners hadn't the wit to take what they wanted from life. They were sickeningly honest. But so strong you didn't dare run up against them.

He shrugged. Ah, well, there were plenty of other fish in the sea. Who needed a tall scrawny thing like Hallie Carr?

15

In the morning Bert was much better and as the landlord agreed to keep an eye on him till the woman who was to care for him arrived, they were able to set off as soon as it started to get light.

Pandora could see how worried Zachary was about them missing the ship and set herself to distract him by asking questions about the shop and how her uncle had run things. She already knew that he loved the work and when she asked about the changes he'd like to make, he soon stopped being guarded about himself and talked for over an hour, encouraged by her prompting and questions.

Martin sat quietly beside them on the driving bench, not saying anything, but clearly listening.

'I've bored you,' Zachary said suddenly.

'No, you haven't. I hadn't understood how much there was to do that customers don't know about. I shall enjoy learning about it all. I'm definitely not going to sit upstairs like an idle lady and let someone else run it for me, though.'

'I'm not sure Harry will allow that.'

She stared at him. '*Harry allow?* He doesn't own the shop.'

'He *is* manager at the moment. He's very clever about getting his own way and will make it difficult for you to go against his wishes.'

'We'll see about that.' The more she heard

282

about this Harry, the less she liked the sound of him. *He* didn't own the shop; she and her sisters did. And she'd make that very plain.

Anyway, Zachary would be there to help her and back her up, not to mention the lawyer.

★ ★ ★

Marshall was finding the shop work more interesting than he'd expected, even though Prebble still gave him all the lowliest jobs and seemed to hate it when he had to serve in the shop at busy times. He'd not been pleased when Marshall showed that he could add up the prices in his head as well as the next man without making mistakes in the amounts he charged.

Several times Marshall came to work in the morning to find things not quite as he'd left them the night before in the packing area. The changes were always very slight, but he was quite sure things had been moved — or taken. He didn't say anything because it was such tiny changes, but he began marking levels before he left and memorising how many packets there were on a shelf.

It was cleverly done, he had to admit. A couple of times a week a few items were taken, just a little here and a little there. If you weren't looking, you'd never notice.

He didn't say anything to Prebble but he added it to the list of things he'd noticed and shared the information with Ralph at their weekly meetings.

Once Ralph had begun to employ a man to

keep watch on his house, there had been no more men seen standing in or near the back alley, but Marshall counselled him to keep the watchmen on for his sister's sake.

'It galls me, Marshall lad, to have to pay out good money just in case.'

'It'd gall you even more if your house was broken into, your sister upset or yourself hurt.'

'We could be wrong, you know. Maybe it isn't Prebble. Maybe it's just chance. Mr Featherworth insists that we have to be able to prove it beyond doubt before we accuse him.'

'It's not chance that food is being taken from the shop when he's the only one with a key to the gates. And I know that family better than you do. Prebbles are not to be trusted. You keep paying a watchman.'

Ralph sighed.

Marshall smiled. 'I never thought to say it, but I'm enjoying shop work. It's quiet in that back room and a man can think as he packs the sugar or flour or tea. And our dinners are a lot tastier since Mr Featherworth popped in that time. I can't thank you enough, lad, for giving me this chance to do some honest work.'

★ ★ ★

Alice had also noticed the new employee and seen how different he was from the others. When she mentioned it to Ralph, he hesitated, then explained why.

In return she told him what Dot had seen the night of the storm.

284

'Tell me again. Every single detail.'

'She saw a figure come into the back yard of the shop. We checked in the morning but there was no sign that anyone had broken in, so we decided it must have been someone looking for an open window, as thieves do. But all the back windows of the shop are barred and the door is very sturdy so we'd have seen if anyone had broken in.'

'I wish you'd told me about this sooner.'

'We didn't think much of it because neither of us has seen anyone loitering since then. And we'd have heard the back gate squeak if it had been opened. You can't mistake the sound.'

'Perhaps they climbed over the side gate instead. Would Dot have seen that?'

'No, she wouldn't. That gate is out of sight of her bedroom unlike the back gate.'

'It's very worrying. I must admit I shall be glad when the owners return and the responsibility for the shop is taken off my shoulders.'

'I shan't. I shall have to find myself a new job once that happens and I expect I'll have to leave Outham.'

'Leave? I thought you'd look for a job round here to be near your cousins.'

'I doubt I'd find one here, given the hard times, and governesses have little free time, even if I did.'

'I should miss you.'

'And I you. I've not had friends like you and Judith for a long time.'

He gave her a strange look then took his leave. She couldn't help hoping the look meant what she thought it did, though she told herself she was past the age of such foolish hopes.

★ ★ ★

Because of the muddy road conditions, the cart didn't reach Albany until the early evening. As they approached the town, the taciturn Martin stirred himself to say he knew a good place for them to stay the night.

'We need to find out first whether we've got cabins on the *Bombay*,' Zachary said.

'You won't find anything out about your passage till tomorrow. The ship isn't in yet, as you can see, and the agent will have shut the office hours ago. He won't thank you for disturbing him at home, so you might as well get a good night's sleep.'

Zachary had been concerned for Pandora, who was white with exhaustion, though she'd not complained. 'Very well. Where do you recommend we stay?'

'My mum will put you up for a night or two if the ship's late. She doesn't charge as much as some and she's a good cook. She won't let you two sleep together, though.'

'We don't sleep together in that sense,' Zachary said curtly.

Martin winked at him. 'A-course not.'

He opened his mouth to protest, but Pandora jabbed him in the ribs, so he said nothing more.

Princess Royal Harbour took Zachary's breath away. The inlet was big enough to contain several islands. No wonder the mail ships stopped here and not in Fremantle. They'd be well protected from storms. Small boats and a couple of larger ships were rocking gently to and fro on the water, as if someone had put them to sleep for the night.

The town itself reminded Zachary of Fremantle in some ways, though it was much hillier. There was the same patchy pattern of settlement across the townsite, with empty blocks of land between some houses, though there were more buildings along the seafront, set closer together as if jostling for a view so magnificent it took your breath away.

The town was overlooked by a small but steep hill at whose foot stood a large house with a windmill behind it. Martin obligingly pointed out the convict depot, which seemed to be the largest set of buildings.

'Got a lot done in Plantagenet Shire and Albany since the convicts arrived,' he said. 'They've built roads and them lighthouses on Breaksea Island and Point King. Some folk worry about the convicts causing trouble, but they haven't done. I reckon it's good to set them to useful work. Have to watch people don't stow away on board ships leaving for eastern Australia though. The police search all the ships before they're allowed to leave.'

In the town itself some of the streets were rolled and gravelled, which was an improvement on the rutted track they'd been following all week.

'Let's go and see my mum, then.' Martin clicked his tongue to signal to the horse to walk on.

Mrs Tyler brightened when her son told her he'd brought her some paying guests and within half an hour, Pandora was able to retire to a small but comfortable bedroom with a jug of hot water.

She sighed with pleasure as she closed the door. To wash herself all over was a wonderful treat after the days on the road. As she took her stained clothing off, she looked at it in disgust, choosing instead some of the clean clothes intended for wear on board the ship.

Martin said Leo could sleep with him on the back veranda. He'd been very kind to Leo, saying at one stage to Zachary, 'I reckon if you treat them decently, people like him are less trouble than a lot of so-called normal folk.'

'You're right. But not many would agree with you.'

'I don't pay no attention to what others think. I choose my own way in life.'

Here it was again, Zachary thought, this independence that so many ordinary Australians seemed to exhibit. He couldn't imagine Martin kow-towing to customers at the shop in Outham as Harry did. Do I fawn over them when I'm serving? he wondered. He didn't think so, though he tried to be courteous and help them find what they needed, whether the customers were rich or poor.

Pandora only stayed up for an hour, enough time to eat a meal and tell their inquisitive hostess something about their adventures, after which she gave in to her yawns and excused herself.

'The mail ship's due in tomorrow, unless they've had a stormy trip,' Mrs Tyler told Zachary as she got a makeshift bed ready in the small dining-room-cum-parlour. 'Comes from Sydney and Melbourne, it does. Doesn't stay long here, though. Just stops to deliver the mail and stock up with coal. Them steamships use a lot of coal, even though they use their sails as well as their engines. Still, Albany being a coaling station brings jobs to the town, doesn't it? They buy fresh fruit and vegetables here, too. It all helps.'

'I need to see the P&O agent first thing tomorrow, then. The Governor said he'd send instructions via the coastal steamer that we were to be given passage.'

'The steamer came in a couple of days ago, so the agent will know about you. His Excellency must think a lot of you to do that.'

'I was able to help the Captain with Leo on the voyage out here.'

'Poor soul.' She gave Zachary a stern look. 'You and your young lady should have got married before you set off on this journey, you know. It's clear she's a decent lass — I can always spot the other sort — but it doesn't look good, you travelling so far together. Not good at all.'

He didn't know what to say to that, so made a faint noise in his throat, which seemed to satisfy her.

Even a makeshift bed felt wonderfully soft after sleeping on the ground for the past week. He blew out the candle and snuggled down.

Pandora would be warm enough without him tonight, but he missed having her beside him, even though it had been a form of delicious torture not to make love to her as he ached to do.

He wished he really was going to marry her, wished he dare ask her.

Oh, he was a fool! She was not only beautiful but wealthy, compared to him. Once she settled in again in Outham, she'd forget her fondness for him and turn to men of her own sort. It was just because the journey had thrown them together that she was turning to him.

He'd not change though. He loved her deeply and always would.

★　★　★

In the morning, Mrs Tyler roused him even earlier than arranged. 'I'm sorry, Mr Carr. I couldn't let you sleep any longer because we need to use this room for breakfast. It's usually a married couple or a single man I take in, you see, so no one normally needs to sleep in here. But what with Martin and Leo on the back veranda, I had nowhere else to put you. I've woken your young lady as well. You did say you needed to find out about the mail ship. The ship's come in, Martin says and is just finishing docking. The P&O agent will be at his office already and my Martin will show you where to go as soon as you've eaten.'

She left the room, still trailing words.

Next time the door opened it was Pandora.

'Mrs Tyler said you were up.'

She looked so gorgeous in a blue skirt and top, with a short, darker blue jacket, that she took his breath away. 'Did you — sleep well?' he managed after a few seconds.

'I didn't stir till Mrs Tyler woke me. I missed having you near, though, when I went to bed. It seemed strange sleeping on my own. How was your bed?'

'It felt soft and warm after sleeping on the ground.' He couldn't resist adding, 'I missed you too.'

They both fell silent and it was a relief when Mrs Tyler bustled in with the food. They ate quickly then let Martin take them to see the shipping agent while Leo ate a more leisurely breakfast under Mrs Tyler's supervision, after seeing to the horses.

As they parted company outside the agent's office, Zachary asked Martin to see whether the wheel could be repaired, and if not, told him to buy a new one.

★　★　★

The agent was indeed in his office early but he didn't seem at all pleased to see them. 'So you're the young man the Governor wrote to me about. I wasn't sure whether you'd get here on time. The ship will be leaving again later today, you know.'

Zachary introduced his fiancée.

'No one said you two were engaged. I was expecting four sisters.'

'The others didn't want to go back to England. And . . . I wasn't sure Pandora would have me, so I couldn't tell the Governor about her and — ' He took her hand and forgot what he was saying as she smiled at him.

The agent tapped a ruler on his desk to gain their attention. 'There's a problem about the passage, I'm afraid.'

They both looked up.

'What?'

'There's only one cabin free, because the All England Eleven cricket team is returning home on the SS *Bombay*. This cabin wouldn't be available, either, but a gentleman who was going to England has fallen ill.'

'Oh.'

'I can't let an unmarried couple have the two berths in the same cabin, though. It wouldn't be right.'

'Could I travel steerage perhaps and leave the cabin for Miss Blake?' Zachary asked.

'The ship's crowded and every berth is taken, except for those in this cabin. If you travel steerage, it'll upset the arrangements.' He looked at them disapprovingly over his pince-nez. 'It's a good thing the other young women didn't come. We couldn't have found room for them all. There is a way round your problem, though. If you really are engaged, get yourselves married now and that will sort out the matter of the cabin. We don't condone immorality on the P&O line.'

Zachary stared at him in shock, swallowed hard and saw that Pandora was looking equally surprised. *Get married!* There was nothing he'd like better. But gaining a passage was a poor reason for marrying, he thought sadly.

'I'll give you ten minutes to decide,' the agent said. 'Go outside and talk about it, then let me know what you want to do. I know ladies like to have a lot of fuss at weddings, but see if you can persuade her to do without it. Ten minutes and not a second more!'

'But . . . how can we get married so quickly?' Pandora faltered.

Zachary turned sharply to stare at her. Surely she wasn't seriously thinking about doing this?

'Any of the clergymen in town will marry you,' the agent said in a bored voice.

'Without calling the banns?'

'They didn't call any banns for my sister's wedding,' Pandora said. 'The clergyman only came to hold a service once a month in the district, so it wasn't feasible.'

The agent nodded. 'Exactly! Here in the colonies you can't always stick to the details of the marriage process, which was, after all, set up for Britain. The important thing is to make sure that people are properly and *respectably* married.' He glanced at a clock on the wall and rustled some papers. 'Nine minutes to go. I'm an extremely busy man today.'

Zachary took her outside to speak privately and they both stood on the veranda watching a light shower silver the air and feeling faint drifts of moisture on their faces.

'We'll have to wait for the next ship,' Zachary said. 'What a thing to suggest!'

'There may not be a cabin free on that one,

either. And anyway, the agent is suspicious of us already.' Excitement began to stir in Pandora. Maybe this was the perfect excuse to get what she wanted, which was Zachary. He wouldn't ask her to marry him, she was sure, so she'd have to do the asking. Did she dare take the risk of him refusing her? Yes, she did. She'd lost one fiancé already. Life was too uncertain not to seize happiness when you could.

Taking a deep breath she said, 'Actually, I'd *like* to marry you, Zachary. Wouldn't you like to marry me?'

He stared at her as if she'd suddenly grown horns.

She waited, growing more and more anxious as the seconds ticked away and he said nothing. What would she do if he turned her down? She couldn't even bear to think of it.

'I can't take advantage of you like that.' He spoke stiffly, not even sounding like the Zachary she knew. 'It wouldn't be right.'

'I knew you'd say that. But it's *me* taking advantage of you,' she said recklessly. 'After all, you may not want to marry me. Perhaps I've mistaken what you feel?'

His voice was harsh. 'There's nothing I'd like better, Pandora — *nothing in the world!* I think we're both aware of the attraction between us. But how can I marry?'

'If it's money you're talking about, I've got enough for both of us.'

'You think I'd marry you for *that*?'

He swung round with his back to her and she thought for a minute he was going to walk away

294

so grabbed his arm. 'No. I don't think you'd marry me for my money, Zachary. But the money does make it possible.'

'Not for me, it doesn't.'

She spoke angrily. 'Are you going to let your stupid pride come between us?' When he didn't reply, just stiffened, she added more gently, 'If you really would like to marry me . . .'

His eyes lingered on her and his voice became softer. 'Of course I would. You're — the most wonderful woman I've ever met. I can't help loving you, even though I know I shouldn't. But your money — '

'Doesn't matter to me. I'll give it away if it stands between us. Zachary, *please* . . .'

'I've gone over and over it in my mind. You think you'd like to marry me because you've had to leave your family behind and I'm here, looking after you, being kind to you. But once we got to England, you'd regret it, I know you would. Why, you could marry well with money like that behind you, someone from one of the better families in town. No, you'd definitely regret marrying an ordinary chap like me.'

'Are you so terrible to live with? I find you easy to get on with and kind to everyone. Look at how you rescued Leo.'

'That's not the point. I keep telling you: I'm poor! It'd be *your* money keeping us and that matters. People would talk, say hurtful things, upset you. It wouldn't be *right*! And what would Mr Featherworth say? He *trusted* me to fetch you back safely.'

She was so angry at him she grabbed his

hands and pulled him towards her. 'You're a fool if you think I'd listen to such rubbish. Didn't you hear me? I *want* to marry you, Zachary, you and no one else.' She could feel the heat in her face and tears of humiliation were welling in her eyes. 'Why are you making me plead with you?'

But he still kept her at arm's length. 'Because I love you and want the best for you.'

'You're the best for me because I love you too.'

He stared into her eyes and the silence wrapped round them, a silence she didn't dare break as one emotion after another chased across his face, such a dear face now.

Words came jerkily. 'Give me a minute to think, Pandora. Don't . . . say anything.'

As she let go of his hands, he turned his back on her and she watched him. It was the longest minute of her life. She tried to count the seconds as they ticked slowly away but kept forgetting where she was up to. His back was so rigid. But he did love her, he'd said so. *Please!* she prayed silently. *Please!*

When he turned back, his face was set and determined, and her heart gave a skip of pure terror that he was about to refuse her.

He took a deep breath. 'If I did agree — if we did marry — it'd be on condition that we didn't consummate the marriage. I've read that you can have a marriage annulled if the couple haven't bedded one another.'

She felt devastated. 'Don't you — want me in that way?'

His voice became even harsher. 'Of course I do. But I'm *not* going to take advantage of you.

Once we get back to England, I'd want you to wait a month or two and then decide whether to make it a real marriage or not.'

'But I know now that I shan't change my mind. I *love* you.'

'You think you do. You're alone in the world, with only me to look after you. No, you *think* you love me, but we can't be sure. I want to give you the chance to change your mind.'

'I shan't do that, Zachary.'

'Then if you still want to be married to me — and it'll be your choice — we can make it a proper marriage.'

He cupped her face in his hands and bent his head, kissing her slowly and tenderly on the lips, as if she was the most precious thing in the world. She closed her eyes and gave herself up to the wonderful feelings he roused in her. For the first time in years she felt she could find happiness again — a husband, home, family.

When the kiss ended, she murmured a protest and flung her arms round his neck to keep him close.

He laced his hands behind her waist, looking at her solemnly.

'I don't like your conditions, Zachary. I don't think they're necessary.'

'They are to me.'

She was hoping he'd kiss her again, give her a chance to persuade him that the delay wasn't necessary, but someone cleared their throat behind them and they swung round to see the agent standing in the doorway watching them with a wry twist to his mouth.

'I suppose this means you've agreed to get married.'

'Yes,' she said quickly.

Zachary put one arm round her shoulders. 'Could you please tell us who to see?'

'There's St John's on York Street. First church ever built in the colony, that was.'

'I saw it. And afterwards, you'll let us have the ship's cabin?'

'It's yours as long you have the money to pay me. In fact, we might as well do that now, then afterwards you can just bring your marriage lines to show me.' He pointed to the harbour. 'There's your ship. It'll be leaving first thing in the morning, so you'd better go straight on board after you're married.'

They went inside the office and Zachary fumbled with his money belt, taking out the necessary amount. The money Mr Featherworth had given him had seemed like a small fortune in England, but since he'd arrived in Australia, he'd been spending it rapidly, more money than he'd ever spent in his whole life before.

Only as he was paying the agent did it occur to him that he'd better make sure he knew the details of their journey. 'Um — we're paying to go to England. How exactly do we get there?'

'This ship will take you to Point de Galle, in Ceylon. It'll need to coal there. Then it's going on to Bombay, so you'll have to transfer to another P&O ship. There are plenty that stop at Point de Galle, so you'll have no trouble finding one to Suez. Just go and see the agent. From Suez you have to travel overland by train to the port of Alexandria, which is on the Mediterranean Sea. There you'll take another ship to Southampton via Malta and Gibraltar. They're building a canal to link Suez to the Mediterranean, but those in my company who know about these things say it'll never amount to anything. Too narrow.'

They exchanged startled glances and he saw her mouth the legendary place names. *Suez. Mediterranean. Malta.*

'I'll give you a receipt for the fares, to show you've paid the company for the whole voyage to England. Don't lose it.' He opened a drawer and pulled out a piece of printed paper, picked up his pen and dipped it into the inkwell. 'You may as well sit down. This will take me a few minutes. I'll need some details from you.'

Zachary sat next to Pandora on a wooden bench and answered the agent's questions. In the pauses between, he avoided meeting her eyes, staring determinedly down at his hands, which were clasped so tightly his knuckles were white.

Were they really about to get married?

When they went outside again, he looked at her and for once, let his heart have its way. 'If you decide you want to make it a proper marriage, I promise you I'll always do my best to make you happy. Always. I love you very much, Pandora.'

16

Cassandra was feeling very low in spirits. Not only was she missing Pandora, but she was trying to guide Livia into doing a maid's work. With the best will in the world, Livia simply didn't know how to do the various tasks needed, and the job of teaching her was quite arduous. Although Reece had said his wife wasn't to carry on working, Cassandra did walk across to the Southerhams' with him a couple of times a week, out of sheer pity for the hapless pair.

In the end Reece said. 'This time you're not getting round me. This is definitely your last day at the Southerhams', Cassandra love. If Livia wants to find anything else out, she must come to Kevin's and ask you.' When she would have protested, he took her in his arms and said gently, 'Do you want to put the baby's life at risk?'

She sagged against him. 'No. But I feel so sorry for them.'

'I was going to drive over to the shop soon. I'll go on Sunday and ask if anyone has a daughter who'd like to work as a maid for them, even temporarily.'

'I doubt you'll find anyone.'

'I might. Some of the families we see at church are very short of money.'

Cassandra wasn't the sort of wife to let a husband dictate to her, but she knew he was right, knew too that he only spoke from love. And she did feel exhausted even after half a day's work. 'All right.'

As they finished their breakfast, she couldn't help saying, 'I shall feel better when we've heard from Pandora. Surely it won't be long now? They've had time to reach Albany and for Leo to be on his way back.'

'The ship leaves today, if it sticks to its schedule, so we should see him within a week or so, if everything goes well.'

'I keep wondering how Pandora's feeling, what she's doing.' Wanting to weep, but trying not to show how sad she felt at losing her sister.

Reece said nothing, but squeezed her shoulder with one hand then said, 'Come here!' He pulled her against his chest as she fought for self-control.

'Well,' she said after a while, 'let's get ready for work.'

He kissed her cheek. 'I'll walk you across to Westview. You can stay two hours then I'll walk you back.'

No one had ever made her feel so warmly cherished as Reece. She smiled at him mistily and took his hand. Never mind that it slowed you down to walk with hands linked. It was so much nicer like that, as if their hearts were connected by the warmth of their joined hands.

* * *

At Galway House the twins were thinking of both their sisters. Mrs Largan tried to reassure

301

them that Pandora would be all right and reminded them that Cassandra was still a month from having the baby, but they still kept worrying.

'I shan't feel right till I hear Pandora got away safely,' Maia said.

'Well, even if she does, it'll be a long time until we hear anything,' Xanthe said bitterly. 'The distances are too far for comfort here. No railways, no telegrams, no neighbours or villages even, so that news can spread. I can perfectly well understand why Pandora wanted to go back to civilisation.'

Maia stared at her in dismay. 'Are you regretting that you didn't go with her?' She saw her sister's fierce expression soften.

Xanthe reached across to give her arm a little pat, the way she occasionally did. 'Sometimes I regret it. But you still need me here, so it was right for me to stay.'

'I'll always need you nearby.'

'No, you won't. One day you'll marry and then it'll be your husband you turn to.' She saw Mrs Largan looking at them anxiously and smiled at the older woman. 'Sorry. We're not getting on with the work very well today, are we?'

'Bother the work. It's natural that you'll both be anxious about Pandora.'

'And Cassandra,' Maia added.

★　★　★

Zachary and Pandora left the agent's office and made their way to the church of St John the

302

Evangelist on York Street.

'Will this one do?' he asked when they stopped outside.

'It doesn't matter to me where we get married, as long as we do.'

'Let's go and find the minister, then.'

It took them nearly an hour to do that and the minister looked at them in disapproval when they explained what they wanted.

'I cannot approve of such a hasty marriage. What your family was thinking of, young woman, to let you set off on such a long journey without the protection of this man's name, I cannot imagine.'

Pandora held back her anger at his officiousness, afraid he'd refuse to marry them. 'We had to leave quickly after we received an urgent summons from England. The sister I was living with is about to have a child, so she couldn't come with me, and the minister only comes to the barn where we worship once a month.'

There was silence, then the minister let out a sniff that still sounded disapproving. 'Very well. Meet me at the church in an hour's time. You'll need two witnesses.'

'I don't like him. I wish it was a kinder man marrying us,' she said wistfully as they walked out of the clergyman's house.

'You can always change your mind.'

'Zachary, will you stop saying that!'

'I don't want you to do something you'll regret.'

She sighed and tugged at his hand. 'Come on. I shan't change my mind and I need to look my best for my one and only wedding.'

'You always look beautiful.'

'So do you.'

He chuckled. 'With this bony face?'

'Your kind nature shines through and makes it beautiful.'

He stopped walking to stare at her, unable to speak for shock.

Smiling, satisfied that she'd surprised him, she tugged him forward again.

★ ★ ★

Mrs Tyler gaped when they told her what was happening, gaped again when asked to be one of the two witnesses to the marriage, together with her son Martin.

'Well, I never!' She stood for a moment in thought, then turned to Zachary. 'You go and fetch our Martin from the stables at the end of the street while I help Pandora get ready. Good thing I've got some winter daisies blooming in my garden. Can't have a wedding without a bouquet, can we?'

But it was a wedding without anything very special, not even the shining brightness of new love, Pandora thought wistfully. She hadn't got new clothes and her oné straw hat was very plain with a narrow brim decorated only by a navy blue ribbon.

Mrs Tyler frowned at the sight of this and went to her bedroom, returning with a much prettier knot of ribbons attached to a white silk flower. 'Here, we can fasten this to your hat. It'll brighten it up a bit.'

'I can't take your — '

'It's my present to you. Can't have a wedding without presents, can we? Let me help you with your hair. Such lovely hair you have. It's a pity to hide it all under the hat. You'll make a beautiful bride, whatever you wear, though.'

Mrs Tyler proved surprisingly adept. 'There's not many suit a centre parting like you do,' she said through a mouthful of pins. 'I don't know why young women ever started wearing it like that.'

Pandora watched in the mirror as her older companion puffed the side hair out to hide all but the lobe of each ear and twisted two long strands into thin plaits, which she looped towards a loose chignon low on the neck. Pandora usually screwed her hair into the tightest knot she could and skewered it with hair pins to keep it in place, but this . . . well, it did look nicer. Would Zachary like it? She hoped so.

'There. What do you think?'

Pandora stared at herself in the mirror and nodded. 'It looks lovely. Thank you. Look, I need to write a letter to my sisters, but my writing things are at the bottom of my portmanteau.'

'I've got some writing paper and some ink ready made up. Won't take me a minute to find them.'

Pandora gave her a quick hug. 'Thank you. You're so kind.'

Face red at the unaccustomed compliment but with a smile softening her lips, the normally gruff Mrs Tyler bustled out of the room.

Pandora took one more look at herself in the mirror, then hurried to finish packing.

When she went into the small parlour where Zachary was waiting, she held her breath. His expression said all she could have hoped.

'You look even more beautiful than usual.'

They stared at one another for a moment or two and it felt as if they were alone in the world, then he nodded and offered her his arm.

Leo accompanied them to the church, smiling broadly. 'I said you'd be marrying Pandora,' he told Zachary.

'Yes.' It'd have been nice to have asked Leo to be a witness, but they needed someone able to sign his name. Zachary didn't want anyone to be able to question the legality of the marriage if . . . if Pandora didn't change her mind once they got back to England.

The ceremony itself was brief. The bride and groom made their responses without faltering while Mrs Tyler mopped away a sentimental tear or two. Leo continued to beam at everyone and Martin fidgeted with his collar, as if uncomfortable inside the church.

By the time they had signed the parish register and received their marriage lines, it was well after noon, so they had to get their luggage and board the ship.

Pandora gave Leo a parting hug. 'Don't forget to tell Cassandra all about the wedding. I've given you the letter for her. Don't lose it.'

'Won't lose it,' he repeated, nodding several times and patting his pocket.

Martin cleared his throat to get their attention.

'Time to go. I'll nip down to the house and fetch the handcart with your luggage, Mrs Carr.'

Mrs Carr! She was a married lady now, Pandora thought as they walked through the streets. She should feel different. But she didn't. Now it was done, she felt numb more than anything. So many things had changed in the past two weeks and she felt exhausted. She hadn't recovered completely from the cold and hardships of the trip to Albany. Indeed, she felt as if she'd been running non-stop for nearly a year and now all she wanted was to have a good long rest.

Beside her, Zachary was equally silent and a quick glance showed that his expression was thoughtful. She promised herself to make it a real marriage well before they arrived in England. Surely, living so closely together, sharing a cabin, he would want to love her?

'I've never seen a steamship before,' she said as they approached the ship after showing their marriage lines to the agent. 'It's much bigger than the *Tartar* was. And how strange it looks with the chimney in the middle and the big sails on either side of it.'

'They call it a funnel, not a chimney.'

She pulled a face at him. 'Well, it looks like a small mill chimney to me.'

'I should think it'll travel more quickly than a sailing ship, though it'll use the sails as well as the engine.' He paused, his voice taking on a hushed tone. 'I can't believe we're going to Suez, across Egypt by land — *Egypt!* — and then across the Mediterranean. Me, Zachary Carr,

307

going to all those places I've only read about!'

'How Dad would have loved to see them!' She heard her voice wobble on the words. 'Cassandra and Reece always used to read books about other countries when they could get them, and now they're settled on an isolated farm in Australia and I'm doing it instead of them. Yet *I* never wanted to travel. Strange, isn't it, where life leads you?'

'At least you're going home now. You must be happy about that.'

She nodded, but her feelings were all but overwhelming her. How far away from her sisters she'd be! Would she ever see them again? And yet, she was longing desperately to see Lancashire, to feel herself truly at home once more.

She realised Zachary was saying goodbye to Martin and thanking him for his help, so added her gratitude to his and gave Leo another hug for good measure. Then they were moving on to the ship, leaving the soil of Australia.

She let her new husband do the talking to the officer who greeted them. She tried not to pay attention to the way the other passengers were staring at them as they followed the officer across the deck to their cabin.

Now that it was all done, the tiredness had taken over.

★ ★ ★

Zachary stood back to let Pandora go inside their cabin first. It was a little larger than the one

308

he and Leo had occupied on the way to Australia, but still not all that big. He took care to slip the steward a tip while Pandora — *his wife!* — studied their bunks and the tiny space left for them to move around.

'It's not that much bigger than steerage was coming here,' she whispered when they were alone.

'No, but it's a lot more private. Besides, we'll be spending quite a lot of time on deck or in the day cabin if the weather isn't good. We have our meals there.'

'I see. Do you want the top or bottom bunk, Zachary?'

'I don't mind. I'll take whichever you don't want.'

'I think I'd prefer the bottom one, then. I'd be afraid of falling out of the top one. What a pity we shan't be able to sleep together. I love it when you hold me in your arms.'

He was trying not to think about that because not giving in to the temptation to make love to her when she cuddled up to him was the hardest thing he'd ever had to do. 'It's probably a good thing in the circumstances.'

'We could always sleep together on the floor. It's no harder than the beds we've shared during the journey.'

He put a stop to that quickly and sharply, because he was a man not a saint. 'It wouldn't be right.'

'That's your opinion, not mine.'

He was relieved when someone knocked on the door. It proved to be a sailor bringing their bags into the cabin.

'Your trunks have been taken down to the hold, Mr Carr,' he said.

'Thank you.'

The steward turned up again a few minutes later, to tell them about meal times and various other details of shipboard life.

Zachary listened carefully, not wanting to embarrass himself when dealing with the other cabin passengers, but it sounded very similar to his previous voyage.

'Let's unpack and go up on deck,' he said when they were alone. 'I'd like to have a breath of fresh air.'

★   ★   ★

When the *Bombay* set sail later that day, Zachary and Pandora went up on to the part of the deck reserved for cabin class passengers to catch a last glimpse of Albany. A movement of the deck made her stumble against another lady and apologies led to introductions.

No rowdy laughter and teasing here, and fewer restrictions on where they could go, Pandora thought. Polite conversation and pleasant smiles. So different from her voyage to Australia with the other mill lasses, where they'd been herded here and there like a flock of unruly sheep. She gazed up at the black smoke pouring from the funnel. It looked even more like a mill chimney at the moment to her, but the chimneys had stopped smoking in Outham when the mills closed for lack of cotton.

She really wanted to go to bed and sleep for a thousand years, but made the effort to attend the evening meal for cabin passengers. It was called dinner, not tea, and was much more elaborate than she'd expected. Zachary seemed quite at home with the array of cutlery so she followed his example on how to eat, while trying to respond to the people closest to them, who all chatted politely.

Inevitably someone asked, 'How long have you been married, Mrs Carr?'

As Pandora blushed, Zachary smiled and took out his pocket watch. 'Just over eight hours.'

There was silence then their companions began to congratulate them and someone called for wine to toast the newly-weds.

Pandora had never tasted wine before and although the deep red colour was beautiful, she found the taste disappointing, having expected it to be sweet. But she hid her feelings and took tiny sips now and then, refusing a second glass.

Everything still felt unreal, as if this was all a dream. And if it was, she didn't want to wake up. Zachary might make her wait to become his true wife but she knew she'd not change her mind, that they'd be together eventually.

Unless *he* changed his mind.

It had been such an eventful two weeks she was glad when they took an early leave of the others. She hadn't got her old energy back, she couldn't understand why, because she usually enjoyed excellent health.

'Would you like to take a turn round the deck?' Zachary asked.

'No, thank you. I'm so tired I'd like to go straight to bed.'

But when they got to the cabin she hesitated, realising she'd have to undress in front of him and feeling shy about doing that.

He gave her hand a squeeze as she hesitated in the doorway. 'I think I'd like a little fresh air before I seek my bed.'

When she was alone, she marvelled at how understanding he was, standing smiling foolishly for a moment or two. Then she yawned and stretched, her body aching with tiredness, and picked up her nightdress, a simple cotton garment, old and shabby like most of her clothes.

After she'd undressed, she got into bed and waited. Where was Zachary? It seemed to be taking him a long time to stroll round the deck. The whole ship couldn't be much more than sixty or seventy yards long.

The night wasn't warm and she snuggled down under her covers.

Eventually someone knocked on the door and he said, 'It's me,' before opening it. After closing it, he glanced at her by the light of the lamp hanging on its safety hook. 'You look to be nearly asleep.'

'I am. I'm not usually so tired.'

'Well, you've only just recovered from an illness and a tiring journey.' He found his nightshirt and blew out the lamp.

She let her eyes close and found it comforting to hear him moving nearby. The bunk frame moved as he climbed into the top bed and she smiled again.

He was here. She was safe. Sleep wrapped itself round her like a cosy blanket.

It took him a lot longer to get to sleep. Hearing her soft breaths below him, remembering the feel of her lying against him gave him a restless hour before he settled.

★ ★ ★

Leo and Martin arrived back in Mount Barker late that night after an uneventful journey. Bert was glad to see them.

'We're setting off back as soon as that damned cart is mended,' he announced.

Leo ignored this, his mind on one thing only. 'I have to see to the horses.'

When he rejoined Bert in the public room, supper was almost ready.

'Did you hear what I said? I want to set off tomorrow as soon as the damned cart is mended.'

'Let me look at your arm first.' Leo took off the cloth sling, his hands gentle. 'It's healing properly.'

'It's not hurting as much.' Bert hesitated then added, 'Thanks to you.' He knew how lucky he was to have had someone who knew how to set the arm properly.

Leo nodded absent-mindedly, concentrating on tying the sling, tongue out at one corner of his mouth.

Bert watched him, not interrupting until he'd finished. 'Can you manage the horses and driving without my help, lad? It's not going to be easy and it'll be at least a week's travel.'

'Oh, yes. They're good horses.'

'Fine. That's settled then.'

They sat and waited for the landlord to bring their food across. It was good, Bert thought, to have a companion who didn't talk at you all the time.

At last the food arrived. 'Mr Carr's already paid the bill,' the landlord said, 'even remembered to pay for the repairs. It was a pleasure to do business with someone like him.'

Martin came in to join them. 'I can attach the new wheel as soon as it's light. The rest of it's been repaired already. You were lucky there wasn't more damage done.'

'Good.' Bert tackled his food one-handedly, with renewed appetite.

'Did I tell you Zachary and Pandora had got married in Albany?'

Bert nearly choked on a mouthful of potato. 'They didn't!'

'Yes. They had to do it to get the last cabin. That P&O agent is a real stickler. Still, they were engaged, weren't they?'

'They love one another,' Leo said. 'I'm glad they're married.'

'Me and Mum acted as witnesses. Oh, I nearly forgot.' He pulled a letter out of his pocket. 'She wrote to her sister. Can you take it back?'

Leo reached out for it. 'I've got another letter to her sister. I'll keep them together.'

Martin put a forkful of meat into his mouth.

Without being asked, Leo reached across to cut up Bert's meat.

Bert was relieved. He was sick of trying to manage one-handedly, but Leo had already done one or two small tasks for him without being asked. He was a strange lad, but good-hearted. They'd have been lost without him on the journey. He'd even prevented the accident going from bad to worse.

It just went to show you shouldn't judge people by their appearance.

Bert cleared his plate without more conversation, though Martin yabbered on a bit. Luckily there was another traveller who was happy to chat to him. Bert liked to chew his food in peace.

* * *

The first morning on the ship Pandora woke with a start, uncertain where she was for a moment or two. Then it all came rushing back to her. She was *married*. On her way back to England.

'I'm awake,' Zachary said quietly from above her head. 'Do you want to get dressed first or shall I? If we ring the bell, the steward will bring us some hot water.'

'You'll need to shave while the water's hot. I'll wait to get up.'

She watched him shave then he hesitated and looked at her, so she turned her back to the room and waited for him to finish his ablutions. A tear trickled down her cheek. This wasn't what she'd expected of marriage, or what she wanted.

'I'm ready now, Pandora. I'll go and wait for you in the day cabin.'

315

She tried to speak cheerfully. 'I won't be long.' But she didn't feel cheerful. She felt disappointed. Bitterly disappointed. She didn't want him being all noble about their marriage. She wanted . . . him. Properly.

Not all the cabin passengers were there for breakfast, one or two being 'indisposed', though the sea wasn't really rough, just 'a bit lively' according to the steward.

After breakfast, Pandora went to stand by the rail, waiting for her husband to join her. She found herself surrounded by young men and didn't know how to tell them to go away. She didn't want to offend anyone, but she'd never learned how to flirt and wasn't going to start now. It turned out they were the All England Eleven and had been in Australia to play cricket.

She was relieved when Zachary joined her, summed up the situation at a glance and said cheerfully, 'Thank you for keeping my wife company, gentlemen, but I'll take over that pleasant task now, if you don't mind. After all, we are on our honeymoon.'

With murmurs of regret they moved away.

'I was so glad to see you,' she confessed in a whisper. 'I didn't know what to do. They were saying such silly things.'

'Just smile and let them do the talking. You must expect to attract attention, you know.'

She looked at him in puzzlement.

'You're a beautiful woman, Pandora.'

'Oh, that. I wish I wasn't. I don't like to attract that sort of attention. Anyway, don't let's talk about them any more. Did you fetch our books?'

'Yes. We'll find a sheltered place and read.'

'That'll be lovely.'

She couldn't remember the last time she'd had nothing pressing to do and could simply sit down to read a book. But she found it hard to settle today. When she looked up after reading the first couple of pages a second time because nothing seemed to be going into her mind, she saw him staring into the distance, making no attempt to read.

He turned to her. 'You don't have to stop reading just because I'm too lazy to concentrate.'

She laid her book down and leaned back, closing her eyes. 'I feel lazy too.'

After a few moments of silence, he asked abruptly, 'You're not regretting anything, are you?'

'Getting married, you mean?'

He nodded.

'How many times do I have to tell you that I wanted to marry you?'

'I have to be sure.' He reached across to clasp her hand for a moment, then they lay quietly on the deckchairs, resting.

She woke with a start, realising she'd drifted off. Zachary was still there, smiling at her. 'I can't believe I fell asleep,' she said in bewilderment. 'I've only just got up.'

'You're still pale. I'm sure a long rest will be good for you.'

'How long does it take to get to Point de Galle?'

'About a fortnight, I think.'

That evening, he asked about the whole

317

journey and several people chimed in with information.

'About fifteen days to Point de Galle. Nice place to stop, that.'

'About seventeen or eighteen days to get to Suez from there.'

'Six weeks in all to get to England, give or take a few days.'

Pandora knew her map of the world and frowned. 'How do we get from to the Mediterranean Sea from there? Is there a road?'

One man laughed. 'It's all very civilised these days, my dear young lady. We go by train to Alexandria and that takes only a couple of days, as long as the train doesn't break down. In Alexandria we take another steamship.'

An older man smiled reminiscently. 'The first time my wife and I went to Australia was by sailing ship. Later we went via Egypt, using the overland route. She was an intrepid traveller, my Mary. We went back to England several times. We had to go by horse and carriage from Suez to Cairo at first — about eighty miles but it felt more like five hundred. Dreadful roads, they were. We were black and blue from the jolting by the time we arrived. The next stage was down the Nile in a filthy old steamer. Mary suffered dreadfully from bug bites, poor thing, but she always laughed about that sort of thing. And finally, the last stage was in a stuffy canal boat to Alexandria.'

Some of the older passengers began to exchange anecdotes of the old days and Pandora was content to listen.

That night at bedtime Zachary again went out for a walk on deck and it was so long before he came back that she could feel herself falling asleep.

She woke in the night to hear his slow, steady breathing above her and sighed. She wished he was holding her in his arms again.

★ ★ ★

The old gentleman who'd travelled by the overland route in the old days asked if he could sit with them the following morning, clearly longing for a chat. Pandora put down her book in relief. She kept finding herself watching Zachary instead of reading, wondering what he was thinking.

'I'm going home to live permanently in England,' Mr Plumley confided. 'I have two sons in Australia and two in England, grand-children in both places. But since my wife died, I long for the old country. Foolish, isn't it?'

'If you're foolish, so am I,' Pandora said. 'I was so homesick I couldn't wait to leave Australia, even though my three sisters are still there.'

'It's tragic how families are torn apart by distance.' He shook his head sadly. 'When you're young, it's a big adventure to travel and settle in another country, but as you get older you long to see the old places, old friends too, those who are still alive, that is. I doubt I'll ever see my Australian children and grandchildren again, unless they come to visit me.' He brightened. 'My Paul may do that, though. He's done well for himself and he takes after his mother, loves seeing new places. But I doubt I'll see George again. He's a homebody. I don't know how we got a son like that.'

They sat with Mr Plumley quite often after that and accepted with great relief his offer to guide them through the process of finding a ship for Suez in Point de Galle. He didn't seem to mind when she fell asleep on him, just said if she'd been ill her body needed peace and quiet to repair itself.

It was a comfort to chat to him during the day, but nights were still fraught with sudden tensions and Pandora sometimes longed to shout at Zachary and ask him what was wrong with her that he didn't even want to touch her.

But pride stopped her doing that. Pride, and his gentle courtesy. It created a very effective wall between them, as if they were strangers somehow.

17

Zachary stared in delight across the pale turquoise water as a warm wind blew around them. How different it was here at Point de Galle from the English Channel, where the water had seemed dirty brown. Inland stood a range of mountains with one sitting proudly higher than the rest. Below that sat a huge fort overlooking the harbour and town of Galle.

Pandora echoed his thoughts. 'Isn't it beautiful?'

'Very.' He longed to put his arm round her shoulders or take her hand, but wouldn't allow himself to give in to temptation.

She fanned herself with a piece of folded paper, moving it languidly to and fro in front of her flushed face. 'I wish it wasn't so hot and humid, though. That makes me feel tired all the time.'

Indeed, she was still so lethargic he was worried about her health. He heard her sighing and mopping herself with a damp cloth during the night to get cooler. But when he asked if anything was wrong, she said she was all right. Only, he knew she wasn't. She was nothing like the vibrant, energetic young woman he remembered seeing in Outham.

As their ship was eased into the deep, sheltered water of the harbour, Mr Plumley came up to them. 'Ready to disembark? It'll take a while, so don't get impatient.'

'We're grateful for your help,' Zachary said.

'It's good to have some young company.' He gestured to the ramparts. 'We'll take a walk along those later, once it's cooler. They're a favourite promenade for travellers.'

In a confusion of shouting, what seemed like hundreds of dark-skinned men poured on to the ship and began moving luggage and cargo off it. When the passengers disembarked, Mr Plumley took the Carrs straight to the P&O agent and waited patiently with them for Mr Bailey's attention.

'We shouldn't take up your time like this,' Zachary said to their companion.

Mr Plumley smiled. 'What else should I do with it but help my fellow human beings? Besides, seeing things anew through your eyes adds to my own pleasure.'

To Zachary's relief, there was a ship leaving for Suez in two days' time and it had a cabin free, so all that remained was to find somewhere to stay until they could board it. Once again, this was easily accomplished with Mr Plumley's help. Then, as the sun began to slip below the horizon with tropical swiftness, they all took a gentle stroll along the ramparts.

'What do you want to do tomorrow?' the old man asked.

'See as much as possible,' Zachary said.

'As long as I can stay out of the direct sun,' Pandora added.

'We can hire a vehicle and keep you in the shade for most of the time,' Mr Plumley said. 'If you're too hot, we can easily bring you back. Well, we'll come back during the middle of the day anyway. It's too hot to stay outside then.'

So for the first time in his life, Zachary saw coconut palms and breadfruit trees, tasted strange spicy dishes which made Pandora fan her mouth and laughingly confess that she preferred plain food. It was fascinating to hear people speaking in a variety of different languages, for there were travellers from many countries wandering the streets while their ships took on coal.

And it did seem that Pandora perked up a little as they did the sightseeing.

But the main problem had not been solved for Zachary. Why he'd been foolish enough to agree to this sham of a marriage he couldn't now understand. A temporary attack of madness caused by intoxication with her, not so much her beauty, but her very self.

No, not intoxication, just plain, old-fashioned love.

But he loved her too much not to give her the chance to change her mind when she was in a more rational state, however many restless nights it cost him. He couldn't live with himself otherwise. His mother had often teased him for having such firm principles, but that was how he was made.

★　★　★

The journey was uneventful, and Leo and Bert arrived back at Westview at about two o'clock in the afternoon a week after leaving Mount Barker. They drove up the slope and were met by Reece and the Southerhams, all eager for news of Pandora. A young girl who hadn't been there last time stayed by the cooking area, watching them.

'I have to see to the horses,' Leo said at once.

Bert smiled to see the frustration on his companions' faces. He was used to Leo's single-minded attention to the animals now. 'Give them the letters first, lad.'

Leo stopped. 'Oh, yes.' He pulled out two crumpled letters from his pocket and passed them to Reece, then went to unharness the horse.

'They got on the ship safely,' Bert said. 'I didn't see them do it myself because of this.' He waggled the rapidly healing arm still in its sling. 'But a fellow from Mount Barker went with them for the last stage of the journey.' Another waggle of the arm drew their attention to the cart. 'We had a bit of an accident. Wheel came off.'

'Pandora wasn't injured?' Livia asked sharply.

'No. Just me.'

Francis was paying more attention to the livestock. 'The horses are not in bad condition, considering. Kevin and Conn will be pleased. And the cart's been well repaired.' He clapped Leo on the shoulder. 'I'm glad to see you back. We'll have to introduce you to Patty, who's come to help my wife.'

Leo ignored the reference to the new maid and repeated, 'I have to look after the horses now.'

'And you'll be helping Reece about the place from now on.'

More nodding. 'I like him.'

Reece looked at the letters, which were addressed to his wife. He was itching to find out what was in them, but they were addressed to her. 'You've got enough help for the next hour. I'll take these across to Cassandra and let Kevin know you're safely back. I'll drive his cart round there tonight by road after I finish work.'

'Can't you read the letters now?' Francis asked in surprise. 'You're her husband, after all, and we're dying to find out what happened.'

'No. They're addressed to her.' He knew most husbands wouldn't hesitate, but he would never open something addressed to her.

⋆ ⋆ ⋆

Cassandra looked up to see Reece hurrying along the bush path. 'Is everything all right?'

'Yes. Leo and Bert just got back and they brought two letters for you from Pandora.'

She tore open the first one, scanning its single page quickly. 'They had an accident with the cart, but she and Zachary weren't hurt and went on to Albany the next day. She thought they'd be in time for the ship.' She passed the letter to Reece and opened the second one, letting out an exclamation of shock.

'Is something wrong?' he asked.

'Pandora and Zachary have got married!'

They stared at one another for a moment open-mouthed, trying to take in the news.

325

'She says she loves him. See.' Cassandra passed the letter to Reece.

'It happened very quickly. I hope he's not after her money.'

They both had a think, then shook their heads at almost the same time.

'No, I can't imagine him marrying her for money,' she said. 'He has such an honest face.'

'I really liked him.'

'And she wouldn't lie to me. If she says she loves him, then she does. Oh, I'm so glad for her.' Cassandra went to link her arm in Reece's and lay her head against his shoulder. 'It's wonderful being married to the man you love.'

'And to the woman you love.' He kissed her very gently. 'You look tired.'

'I'm tired all the time now. I don't think it'll be long.'

'I'd better go across to the shop and see if anyone else can help you. Mrs Moore will be at her other birthing. Maybe I should bring one of your sisters back. The girl I brought to help the Southerhams is too young to know anything about childbirth.'

'I think we can wait a day or two yet. We'll see how I go.'

★ ★ ★

Eighteen days after leaving Point de Galle, Zachary and Pandora arrived in Suez. They'd had a pleasant voyage with a group of polite people, which included some of their former travelling companions. It seemed hotter here and

326

even Zachary, who tolerated the warmer weather far better than his wife did, felt as if he could hardly breathe. Pandora wilted even before they arrived at the port, lying exhausted on her deckchair, eating little, tossing in her bunk at night in the slightly larger cabin they were occupying on this leg of the journey.

He forgot his own discomfort in trying to help her, making sure she got plenty of water to drink, which Mr Plumley said was the most important thing.

'Some people,' the old man confided one night as they stood together by the ship's rail, 'just can't cope with heat. Your wife is one. I should keep her in England and the cooler countries from now on, if I were you.'

'I shall,' Zachary said.

'It does my heart good to see how much you two love one another. Brings back memories of me and my Mary. I miss her sadly.' He shook out a large crumpled handkerchief and blew his nose vigorously.

Zachary looked at him in surprise. *Love one another?* Why did Mr Plumley sound so certain of that?

Of course the thought of Pandora loving him, wanting to stay with him, coloured his dreams that night and he slept badly, dreaming of her and waking in a tangle of sweaty sheets.

She stared at him as they drank their early morning cups of tea, reaching out one hand to touch his cheek. 'You didn't sleep well, either.'

'Like you, I'm finding the heat very trying.'

She smiled sadly. 'It's not the heat that's the

327

problem so much as your conscience warring with . . . other needs.'

He took her hand and kissed it but as she raised her face involuntarily towards his, he had to step back or he'd have pulled her into his arms and kissed her as he'd dreamed of. Going to the washstand, he stood with his back to her dabbing his face with a damp cloth. He heard her sigh. He was so tempted to turn back to her, knew she'd welcome his loving.

But his conscience stood sentinel once again, his conscience and the thought of the trust Mr Featherworth had placed in him.

★ ★ ★

The train journey to Alexandria was the next stage in what was beginning to seem like a never-ending journey. Other travellers talked of going sightseeing, some were staying longer in Alexandria in order to do so. Zachary and Pandora were in agreement that all they wanted was to get home — and he couldn't decide which of them wanted it more, she out of homesickness, he out of frustration with their situation.

Every time the train stopped, sellers crowded round the windows trying to force goods and trinkets upon them. The men were dressed in baggy trousers, many wearing a type of hat like a flower pot. Mr Plumley called it a fez.

Zachary bought Pandora a painted fan from a seller who had a whole basket of them, and chose one for himself at the same time, thinking he'd give it to Hallie when he got back. He bought his mother a pretty shawl, so fine and light it'd be useless for keeping warm, but the blue would match her eyes and he knew she'd treasure it even if she never wore it.

When he showed the shawl to Pandora, who was waving her new fan languidly to and fro in front of her flushed face, she said he had very good taste.

'They were all pretty, but blue is my mother's favourite colour.'

'How do they make the material so fine and transparent?' she wondered. 'What count of thread must they be using? And the dyes — they're gorgeous.'

'Would you like a shawl?'

'Yes, please.'

'What colour?'

'You choose.'

So he found one in a deep rose pink, whose fabric glimmered as he held it up to show her.

She touched it with tears in her eyes. 'It's beautiful. Oh, Zachary, I'm so sorry.'

'Sorry for what?'

'That I'm exhausted and lethargic all the time. I can't understand why I don't get better.'

'Mr Plumley says some people are like that in the heat and I'm to keep you in England from now on.'

'Oh, yes. Even to see my family, I don't think I can face this journey again. How my father would scold me and tell me to pull myself together! But Zachary I'm trying and I just *can't*!'

'I know.' He took her hand, held it in his until

329

the train set off again, chatted until he got her to smile, and counted the sightseeing well lost for the pleasure of being with her.

At least in Alexandria it wasn't as hot and Pandora began to look a little better, didn't have to be coaxed to eat and agreed to go out to see something of the city.

There was a new tram system which their guide took them for a ride on. He was clearly more proud of this than of the antiquities.

'Very modern city,' he kept telling them. 'Very modern.'

★ ★ ★

Cassandra was woken during the night by a sharp pain. She waited, wondering if the baby was coming. Surely not? It'd been very quiet lately, not moving about nearly as much, and she'd begun to feel that she'd be able to last until Mrs Moore could come to help her with the birth, which would be a great relief.

Several pains later she shook Reece's shoulder. 'I think the baby's coming.'

He sat up abruptly. 'Hell! And Mrs Moore won't be able to come for another couple of days.' He swung his legs out of bed and went to light the candle from the embers of the fire.

Kevin came out of the other bedroom, blinking. 'Is everything all right?'

'Cassandra's having the baby. Can you sit with her while I go to fetch Livia.'

'She's a nice lady, but she won't be much use to you.'

'I know, but there should be another woman to help.'

'Why don't you bring that lad with you as well? Leo's used to delivering foals and such. Better than nothing.'

'Leo?'

'Can't hurt.'

Reece was back half an hour later with Livia and Leo. The latter seemed perfectly happy to be involved, though everyone else except Kevin was dubious as to what use he'd be.

But as the hours passed and the baby didn't appear, Reece began to feel frantic as he heard Cassandra stifling her cries of pain and saw how tired she was looking.

Leo listened and watched, then said, 'Can I look at her? I've seen a baby born and I know what to do. The groom's wife had hers in the stable. It arrived before they'd expected it.' He smiled at the memory, then added, 'Women need more help than animals do.'

'The lad's the only one who knows anything,' Kevin pointed out to Reece. 'You told me they wouldn't let you stay with your first wife.'

'They didn't let me into the bedroom till she was dying,' Reece said, the memories of that adding to his terror now. If he lost Cassandra he didn't know what he'd do! She was his friend as well as his love.

So Leo went into the bedroom and Cassandra, exhausted by the pain and far beyond such petty emotions as embarrassment, let him feel her stomach.

'I think it's the wrong way round,' he said.

'See. This is a leg. We turn foals when they're like that.'

Reece and Livia stared at him in dismay.

It was left to Cassandra to say, 'Turn it then, Leo. I don't want to lose my baby.'

'We need hot soapy water, plenty of soap,' Leo said. 'And the farrier always made everyone wash their hands when they were dealing with new foals.'

He began to work on Cassandra, a serene expression on his face, while Reece hovered anxiously nearby as the minutes ticked slowly past.

To everyone's amazement Leo suddenly smiled. 'That's better. It can be born now.'

And sure enough, within a few minutes, the head was out and almost immediately afterwards, the baby was lying there, crying lustily.

Again it was Leo who knew to tie and cut the cord.

When he'd done that, Livia wrapped the child in a cloth, tears in her eyes, and handed the baby to Cassandra. 'Here's your daughter.'

She'd been lying with her eyes closed, but she opened them abruptly. '*A girl!*'

Reece came to kneel beside her. 'Yes. Still happy to call her Sofia?'

She looked at the tiny crumpled face beside her and was unable to speak for emotion. Pressing a kiss on the child's forehead, she murmured, 'Sofia. Yes, it's a lovely name.'

He smiled down at them and admitted to himself that he was glad the baby was a girl. He knew he'd find it easier to love a girl than a boy.

* ★ *

A week after leaving Alexandria the ship had docked in Gibraltar, from where they moved out of the Mediterranean on their last leg to Southampton. Zachary was relieved not to meet rough weather in the Bay of Biscay and the last stage of the voyage passed without incident.

With the cooler weather Pandora improved quickly, regaining her old energy and looking even more beautiful than before.

At last they were told one morning that they were nearing England and like most people, they went up on deck straining to catch a first glimpse of the coastline. Pandora stood beside him, jigging about in excitement, her eye sparkling, her cheeks rosy.

When a smudge appeared on the horizon and one of the officers confirmed that this was indeed England, he saw tears well in her eyes and spill down her cheeks.

'I can't believe we're nearly there.' Her voice was husky with emotion.

As he put his arm round her shoulders, she turned in his embrace, sobbing against his chest without regard to who saw or heard her.

It was Mr Plumley who took charge. 'Come along, my dear young lady. Perhaps you should lie down and take time to compose yourself.'

But she gulped to a halt, wiped the tears from her eyes and smiled at them. 'I'll be all right in a minute or two. It was just — I've longed for home so much, so very much.'

She went to the day cabin for luncheon, but

333

was soon back up on deck, staring at the horizon, looking happy and vigorous once again.

When they docked in Southampton she was impatient with the formalities and ran the last few feet down to the dock, spinning round in a circle heedless of the rain that was falling on her upturned face. 'We're here,' she said to Zachary. 'We're really here in England.' She bent to lay her hand against the ground for a moment, then stood up, eyes sparkling with tears of joy.

'And with a fine summer's day to greet us!' he teased.

'I don't care if it rains every day. It's *English* rain, *English* air.'

'We could stand here all day getting nice and wet — or we could retrieve our luggage and find out how best to make our way to Lancashire.'

She grasped his hand and dragged him to the Customs shed. 'Let's not waste a minute.'

They said goodbye to Mr Plumley, who had been met by one of his sons. After booking places on the train to London the following morning, they found a hotel near the station.

Pandora felt so much better she decided the time had come to put an end to her husband's foolish heroism. 'You've got me here safely, Zachary. I can't thank you enough. I couldn't have managed without you to look after me when I was ill. And it seemed to take until Gibraltar before I felt to be myself again. I'm sure Mr Featherworth will be delighted with you.'

He nodded, but his expression remained stern and she could see that he didn't share her euphoria. 'What's the matter? Aren't you glad to be back?'

'Yes, but . . . I've been wondering how I'll ever fit into the life of a shopman again,' he admitted.

'You won't be a shopman. You'll be part-owner of the shop. You'll be running it. *You*, not that Harry person.'

'At best I'll be the owner's husband . . . if you still want me once you've settled down.'

'Surely I've proved by now that my feelings won't change?'

He gave her one of his determined looks. 'I haven't changed my mind. We're doing nothing about our marriage until *you* have had time to settle in.'

'But what are we going to *do* when we arrive in Outham? Live apart without telling anyone?'

'Yes.'

'I won't do it. You're my husband and I want you by my side. If you won't live with me, I'll come and live with you, if I have to camp on your doorstep to persuade you. I mean it, Zachary. I'm not going to change my mind and I'm *not* going to deny my marriage.'

'You make it impossible for me to do the right thing.'

'Who are you to decide what's right for me?'

'I'm your husband.'

'Then act like one!'

They argued intermittently until they fell asleep, but she couldn't make him change his mind.

When they arrived in London, he insisted on her taking off her wedding ring and staying

335

overnight in a hotel near the station in separate rooms, as Miss Blake and Mr Carr. He went out to send a telegram to Mr Featherworth saying they'd arrive the following day. 'I shan't tell him about us until we're face to face,' he said.

Alone in the hotel bedroom, she cried herself to sleep. Why did she have to love the most stubborn man in England?

They argued on and off all the way to Lancashire, by which time each was exhausted.

★　★　★

As they walked out of the station in Outham early that evening, a lad came hurrying towards them.

'I work for Mr Featherworth. He sent me to meet you, Miss Blake, Mr Carr. And if you please, you're not to talk to anyone about anything at all till you've seen him. It's *very* important, he says.'

They looked at one another in surprise then Zachary found a cab to take them and their luggage to the lawyer's rooms.

Before she got into it, Pandora stood for a moment staring round. 'Home,' she said softly. 'I thought I'd never be able to come back to Outham.' She raised her eyes to the green ridge above the town. 'I'm going for a walk up there on the moors as soon as I can. I've missed them so much.'

Zachary had missed them too and almost said they'd go together, then remembered the youth sitting opposite him and bit back the words.

336

They passed Blake's Emporium and as Pandora would have said something, he said, 'Shhh. Mr Featherworth said not to talk about anything.'

The youth nodded vigorously and she shrugged, clamping her mouth shut in an exaggerated way and throwing Zachary a mischievous glance as she did so.

They left the youth to keep an eye on the luggage and were shepherded straight through to Mr Featherworth's room. As he came forward to greet them, they heard someone hurrying along the corridor and Mr Dawson joined them.

He didn't waste time on civilities. 'Why have you only brought back one sister, Zachary? Surely you looked for the others too?'

It took them a while to explain why Pandora's sisters hadn't returned.

When she handed over the documents giving her the right to handle their business affairs, Mr Featherworth held up one hand to stop her talking for a moment then scanned them quickly.

'Drafted in a hurry,' he said, 'but not bad. They'll serve. It was a good idea to have Francis Southerham as one of the signatories. His signature is known in the town and he can't be accused of having an interest. We shall need a copy making of this, Dawson.' He passed it to his clerk then turned back to his visitors. 'Please continue.'

When Zachary faltered over the tale of their marriage, it was Pandora who took over.

'I wanted to marry him. I fell in love with him very quickly.'

Mr Featherworth cast a glance of disapproval at Zachary, and Mr Dawson's face expressed the same emotion. She couldn't bear them to think ill of him, so said hastily, 'I had to persuade him to do it. He said it wasn't right.'

'I'm in complete agreement with him on that matter,' Mr Featherworth said sharply. 'My dear young lady, you are in comfortable circumstances. This young man, worthy as he is, is not even in a position to support a wife. I cannot help feeling that you've betrayed our trust, Carr.'

Zachary opened his mouth and she knew what he was going to say. 'Don't!' she begged. 'Zachary, please don't tell them.'

'Tell us what?'

He looked steadily at the two older men. 'We've not consummated the marriage.'

They both looked at him in relief. She could have wept.

'I thought it only fair that she have a way to get out of it,' Zachary added. 'In case she changed her mind once she settled down here again. Getting married was the only way we could get a passage back to England for two months, and . . . I do love her. So I did it, married her. But she was alone, ill and unhappy, so it was only natural she'd turn to me, think she cared about me. So I wanted her to be sure.'

She leaned forward to refute this, even though she could feeling herself blushing. 'But I *am* sure! I always have been. *He*'s the one who won't — make our marriage real.'

There was silence, then Mr Featherworth looked at Zachary with a return of his old cordiality. 'That was well thought of.'

Mr Dawson added softly, 'And it can't have been easy.'

Zachary nodded, looking at Pandora again, sure that circumstances would take her away from him now they were back. 'It was very difficult. But I love her too much to trap her.'

'If you love me, then be my husband!' she pleaded again.

He shook his head. 'Not yet.'

'If I wasn't so tired, I'd go on arguing, but I can hardly sit upright. But be warned, all of you: I won't let anyone annul my marriage,' she declared. 'Not unless Zachary proves that he doesn't care for me.'

The two older men smiled at them and Mr Featherworth said quietly. 'No one will do anything you don't wish for, my dear Miss Blake. But for the moment, I think it'll serve our purpose better if we don't reveal the marriage and if Zachary goes back to work in the shop, where he'll be the best person to see what he can find out. Tell them what we suspect, Ralph.'

'We have reason to believe Harry Prebble is stealing goods from the shop. Not large amounts, but probably enough to double his income. That family dabbles in a few suspicious areas. I don't know why Mr Blake took on someone with that background.'

'Harry begged for a job, said he wanted to work honestly. Mr Blake believed in giving people a chance and I have to admit that Harry worked hard for him.'

'Hmm. Well, I think he's stealing from the

shop and thinks we don't know. That young man is overconfident and scornful of others. It will be his downfall in the end, I'm sure.' He explained about Miss Blair and the intruder, about placing Marshall Worth to work in the shop.

'I can't believe Harry would steal!' Zachary exclaimed. 'He doesn't need to. He's bound to get on, because he's a hard worker and good at his job . . . even if I don't always agree with his methods of running the shop.'

'We've not *proved* it's him yet, I must admit, but there's no one else who could be doing it. No one else has a key to the building or the gates.'

'It's a dreadful thing to do, rob people when they've trusted you,' Zachary said.

'Some people are greedy, want what other people have and have no scruples about taking it,' Mr Dawson said quietly.

Mr Featherworth shuddered. 'My clerk has been handling that side of things. I don't know how I'd have coped without his help, I really don't. I'm a lawyer, not a policeman.'

Zachary thought of the plump family man he'd seen in his home, happy in the bosom of his family, and found it hard not to smile at the thought of Mr Featherworth acting as a policeman, trapping criminals. He saw that Mr Dawson was watching his employer with an indulgent expression on his face, and when he turned to Zachary, he smiled, as if they were accomplices in helping the lawyer.

Mr Dawson looked up at the clock on the wall. 'You have another appointment in a few minutes, Mr Featherworth. Shall I take these young people into my room to discuss the practicalities, then escort them home? I didn't like to think of putting Miss Pandora into those living quarters alone, with only a young maid, even with the new locks in place, so I took the liberty of sending a message to Miss Blair, warning her of Miss Pandora's imminent arrival and asking her to stay on for a while.'

'Will she do that?' Mr Featherworth asked.

'Oh, yes. She doesn't wish to leave Outham. She's made some good friends here, as well as having her only close relatives living in the town.'

'That was very well thought of.'

* * *

Zachary sat in the heavily loaded cab opposite Pandora as the horse clopped through the streets. Most shops were still open and it wasn't dark yet, but few people were around. When they stopped outside the emporium, she looked across at him and said very emphatically, 'I shan't change my mind.'

He stared at her, not allowing himself to respond.

Mr Dawson filled the silence. 'Remember to say nothing about your real situation, my dear Miss Blake. And Zachary, please contain your impatience. We're relying on you to find some way of proving what's going on.'

'I'll keep my eyes open too,' Pandora said.

'Oh, my dear young lady, this is not work for a woman. Please leave that sort of thing to us.'

341

'It's *my* shop, mine and my sisters'.'

As Zachary helped her out of the cab, Harry came to the shop door, a smirk on his face.

'So you're back, Carr.' He stared at Zachary for a moment or two, frowning as if he hardly recognised him then turned to Pandora. 'May I be the first to welcome you to your new home, Miss Blake.' He looked back down the street. 'I presume your sisters are following?'

Pandora inclined her head. 'Thank you for your welcome, Mr Prebble. I shall look forward to working with you.'

Mr Dawson made shooing motions with one hand and Harry hesitated then went back into the shop.

It all seemed very dream-like to Zachary — or rather, like a nightmare. He wanted to tell Harry to stay away from her, but he no longer had the right. Already being back in Outham was putting a distance between him and Pandora. Whatever she said, the gap could only get wider.

When Dot answered the doorbell of the living quarters, she beamed at them and held the door wide, saying simply and with obvious sincerity, 'Welcome home, Miss Blake. Mr Dawson said you were coming today. This way, please.'

'I'll help the cab driver carry your trunk up,' Zachary said.

'Thank you. You've been very helpful.'

She followed the clerk upstairs. 'I've never been inside the living quarters before.'

'You'll find them very comfortable,' Mr Dawson said. 'Ah, there you are, Miss Blair. Allow me to introduce you to Miss Pandora

342

Blake, who is very tired indeed.'

'Welcome home,' Alice said. 'What a long journey you've had.'

Pandora returned her smile. 'Thank you. I'm very glad to be back but I'm exhausted. Could I just have something to eat and go straight to bed? I'll make more sense in the morning, I'm sure.'

Alice turned to the maid. 'Dot?'

'Ham sandwich and a piece of cake be all right, Miss Blake?'

'Just a piece of cake and a cup of tea.'

Zachary and the cab driver puffed upstairs with the trunk and Miss Blair showed them which room to put it in.

'I'll leave you ladies alone,' Mr Dawson said. 'I'll come round again tomorrow morning, Miss Blake. I hope you sleep well.'

'I'll show you out,' Alice said.

Left alone with Pandora, Zachary hesitated. 'Are you feeling better now?'

'I shall be once I've slept. I'm sure you're exhausted too.'

'Yes. It's been very . . . tiring.' He turned to follow the others down the stairs.

'Zachary . . . ' she called.

He swung round. 'Yes?'

She said it again and would go on saying it until he believed her. 'I shall *not* change my mind.'

'You think you won't. Wait till you've settled in again.'

'How long do I have to wait to prove that to you?'

'Two or three months.'

She drew herself up. 'No. That's too long. One month then I'm telling everyone. You can move in with me or not after that, but I'll still tell everyone.'

'Pandora, you mustn't — '

She went back into the parlour with a toss of her head and slammed the door on him.

★ ★ ★

The cab dropped Mr Dawson off at the lawyer's rooms first and he paid the driver for the whole journey. 'Don't forget,' he murmured to Zachary. 'Keep quiet about your changed circumstances.'

'Yes.'

The clerk hesitated. 'You love her, don't you?'

'Too much to spoil her life.'

'Oh, I don't think marrying you would spoil her life, but I do think we need to sort out the other business first. No need to go to work on Monday, or for a day or two. We have a lot of things to sort out first and you'll need to recover from the journey.'

Zachary stared as the clerk got out of the cab. Did Mr Dawson mean what he'd said about him and Pandora? Was there really hope that others would approve of the marriage? He couldn't even think about it clearly at the moment, just leaned his head back against the seat, weary beyond belief.

When the cab stopped at his home he got out, staring at the house in shock. It looked so small. And all the houses in the street were crammed

344

closely together. For a moment an image of the wide spaces of Australia floated before him, the sky that seemed higher and brighter blue, the magnificent sunsets.

The front door opened and with a shriek, Hallie flew out to hug him. 'How brown you are. And surely you've grown taller?'

His mother came to kiss his cheek and hold him close for a moment, then she stepped back and turned to her daughter. 'Calm down, Hallie, and let your brother get inside.'

By the time he'd hugged his mother again and got his luggage inside, he was walking like a man half asleep.

'Sorry. I'm too tired to talk tonight. Have you something to eat, Mum? Then I'd like to go to bed.'

'Of course we have. Mr Dawson let us know you were coming, so I made a nice lamb hotpot.'

He ate mechanically then went upstairs, wondering whether he'd find it difficult to sleep. He let his clothes fall anyhow on the familiar old chair in the corner, then crawled beneath the covers, letting the world fade away.

He'd done it, brought Pandora safely back. But at what cost to himself?

18

Pandora woke around nine o'clock and rushed to stare out of her new bedroom window at the town, and best of all the moors rising behind it. Sighing happily, she slipped her arms into her old dressing-gown and made her way down the stairs, finding Dot at work in the kitchen.

'Where's the privy?' She'd used a chamber pot the previous night, too tired to do more than fall into bed.

'There's an indoor bathroom, miss. At the end of your corridor. I showed you last night.'

Pandora laughed. 'I'd forgotten. Everything seemed to pass in a blur. Sorry.'

'Mr Blake had the bathroom installed just after I started work here. It's very modern. Hot water comes out of the right-hand tap if you run off the cold first. Miss Blair lets me have a bath in there every week, but Mrs Blake wouldn't let me go near it except to clean.' She sighed blissfully at the thought.

'Is there enough hot water for me to have a bath now?'

Dot nodded and smiled at the stove. 'Plenty, miss. I've only to get the fire burning up to heat more afterwards. This house has all the modern conveniences you can think of. It's a pleasure to work here . . . now. Oh, and miss!'

'Yes?'

'Miss Blair says I should call her Miss Alice

now, because your names are similar. Is that all right?'

'Of course it is.'

Pandora went back upstairs and enjoyed the wonderful luxury of an indoor bathroom with all the amenities, emptying her slops, then soaking in the hot water, and washing her hair.

When she came down, Alice was waiting for her.

'Did you sleep well?'

'Very soundly, thank you.'

'Are you going to chapel this morning? My cousin said you and your sisters used to attend.'

Pandora was about to say no, then it occurred to her that Zachary might come to see her there, so she nodded. Besides, she wanted to give the Minister and his wife her sisters' fond regards. The Raineys had helped Cassandra to escape from Outham and their aunt. 'If I can get my hair dry in time.'

'Go and sit by the stove in the kitchen.'

But she couldn't bear to sit still for long. When her hair was almost dry she hurried upstairs and dressed in her best, the dress she'd worn for the wedding. It was quite old and had faded a little. One of the first things she was going to do was order some new clothes, she decided. She wanted to look her best for Zachary and she could afford to have a few new outfits.

★ ★ ★

Zachary slept until nearly ten o'clock the morning following his arrival and woke to

347

the sound of church bells. He lay there for a moment or two, enjoying the morning sunshine pouring in through the curtains, which he hadn't drawn tightly the night before. Then hunger and his body's needs got him up.

He was surprised at how shabby his bedroom now seemed after the beautiful fitments on the ships. They might have been short of space, but they hadn't been short of polished brass and gleaming woodwork. Still, he was lucky to have a room of his own. Few people had that privilege. Only he missed Pandora dreadfully already, missed her smile, missed chatting to her.

Stop it! he told himself firmly and went downstairs.

Hallie beamed at him as he went out to the privy, calling, 'I'll have a cup of tea waiting for you, love.'

He came back inside, still in his nightshirt and the dressing-gown Mr Dawson had bought him for the journey.

She fingered the fine woollen material. 'You have some lovely clothes now. Are you going to wear the new ones to work?'

'I don't think so. I'll just take up some water for a quick wash, then get dressed.'

When he went down again, his mother and sister joined him at table. Once he'd taken the edge off his appetite, he started telling them something about his journey, interrupted regularly by Hallie who could never keep quiet for long.

'We saved some money out of your wages, Zachary. It was easy to save without you eating

348

us out of house and home.' Her smile said she was only teasing, but he knew his appetite had been a problem in the days when they'd been watching every penny. It might be a problem again now if he went back to a shopman's wages.

'You look well, son,' his mother said. 'I'd swear you've grown taller and broader. And you seem more — in charge of yourself.'

'It gives you confidence, travel does. Oh, I've so much to tell you. And that was a wonderful breakfast, just what I needed. Are you two going to church?'

'We go to the Methodist Chapel now. I can understand Mr Rainey's sermons. I never understood a word of what Mr Saunders said. Besides, we don't like the way the Vicar treats people who're out of work. You'd think it was their fault.'

'Are things still bad in the cotton industry?'

'Yes. Though the relief works are better organised, I think. At least they're keeping people alive.'

He looked down at the remains of his bread and ham, feeling suddenly guilty for eating so heartily.

'It won't do any good to others for you to miss a meal,' his mother chided. 'Eat up. Now, I'd better get my hat on for chapel. I'll clear up after I get back.'

He suddenly remembered that Pandora went to the Methodist chapel. 'I think I'll come with you, after all.'

★ ★ ★

349

As they walked along to the Methodist Chapel, Pandora said impulsively to Alice, 'Can you stay on here for a while? Or do you have a job waiting?'

'No job. And I'd be happy to stay on if I'm not in the way.'

'I'd welcome the company. I'd like to speak to your cousins after the service. They'll want to know what happened to my sisters.' Surely there would be no harm in telling the Raineys about that?

Her heart suddenly started beating faster as she saw Zachary. Hard to miss him when he was a head taller than most people. Their eyes met across the paved area in front of the chapel and he stopped walking to smile at her. Then he bent his head to say something to the two women he was with and they all moved in her direction.

Alice stopped walking. 'You'll want to say hello to Mr Carr. You two must be good friends by now after spending so much time together. Or irreconcilable enemies.'

Pandora could feel herself blushing. 'Friends,' she managed.

Zachary stopped in front of them. 'Miss Blake. You look well rested. And Miss Blair. How nice to see you again! I'd like you to meet my mother and sister.'

They exchanged greetings then Mrs Carr said, 'We'd better go inside, love. The service will be starting soon.'

'Let's sit together,' Pandora said.

Zachary hesitated, but she knew it'd be rude for him to refuse. She put up her chin and gave him a challenging look. She wasn't going to make it easy for him to get rid of her.

She managed to sit next to his sister and the two of them chatted in whispers while they waited for the service to start. Hallie was full of questions about Australia and the journey back, and her lively intelligence reminded Pandora of her brother. It'd be nice to have Hallie for a sister — though nothing could take the place of her own sisters. Tears came into her eyes at the thought.

'Are you all right?' Hallie whispered.

'I was just thinking about my sisters. I do miss them.'

Hallie squeezed her hand. 'I missed Zachary while he was away. He's the best of brothers.'

He'd be the best of husbands, too, if he let himself, Pandora thought. One month, she repeated to herself. That's all I'll give him.

After the service was over, she waited for Mr Rainey to speak to the parishioners who needed to see him. Some of them were wearing ragged clothes, but he treated them all with patient courtesy, flashing her a quick glance and smile to say he'd noticed her presence. There was no sign of Mrs Rainey, who must have slipped out after the service.

Eventually he turned to her, holding out both hands to clasp hers. 'Pandora, my dear, how wonderful to see you home again! Have you time to come and tell me about your journey?'

'Yes, of course.'

Alice touched her arm. 'I'll walk home alone.'

But Pandora saw Mr Dawson step out from under a sycamore tree near the gate and offer

Alice his arm. The two of them looked so comfortable together she stared for a moment and then smiled. You couldn't mistake love. Did her feelings for Zachary show as clearly?

Sighing, she turned back to Mr Rainey.

Sitting in their comfortable, untidy parlour, she told the Raineys about her sisters, how Cassandra had married Reece, thanks to their help in getting her to Australia.

Mrs Rainey beamed at that news. 'And you, Pandora, what do you want now? I saw you with Mrs Carr's son. You looked — as if you were good friends.'

How she felt about him must show, then. She blushed, hating to hide anything from them. 'We are. But he — says he can't support a wife.'

Mrs Rainey frowned. 'But you have money.'

'It's come between us.'

'He's right, really,' Mr Rainey said. 'The world would judge him badly if he married you.'

How she kept back the anger at that remark, Pandora didn't know. Perhaps she'd grown more used to hiding her thoughts. But if a Minister of religion felt that way, how would other less charitable people feel?

Catching sight of the clock, she took her leave of them and walked slowly home.

On the way back she met Harry Prebble and when he stopped to greet her, she felt obliged to do the same. He was well dressed, surprisingly well dressed for a young man who worked in a shop — and several inches shorter than her.

'I hope you've recovered from your travelling now, Miss Blake.'

352

'Yes, thank you.'

'I've done my best to keep the shop profitable, in spite of the hard times.' He smirked at her. 'I think you'll be pleased when you see the figures. I'll be happy to explain them to you.'

'I'm not even thinking of such things yet. But when I do, I shall be able to understand the accounts perfectly well without any help.' She turned to leave and to her dismay, he fell in beside her.

'I'm going the same way,' he said. 'Allow me to escort you.'

It was the last thing she wanted, but she couldn't see how to get out of it without appearing rude, so began to walk more briskly, relieved that it was only a couple of streets.

She was thoughtful as she took her leave of him and went up to the parlour. He was — obsequious. Yes, that was the only word for it. And yet there was a scorn behind it. As if she needed help with understanding figures! But there was something else about his manner that she didn't like, though she couldn't put a finger on exactly what it was. Whatever it was, he made her feel uncomfortable.

She definitely wouldn't have appointed him as manager, even if she hadn't had Zachary to do the job. She didn't even want Prebble working in the shop, but you couldn't just dismiss for no reason a man who'd worked hard for you. She could only hope Zachary would find out what had been going on and give them a good reason to get rid of Prebble.

She spent the rest of the day unpacking and

discussing with Alice the best way to replenish her wardrobe.

Alice also told her about the relief efforts in the town and that brought back memories of the callous way the ladies from the established church had treated her and her sisters when they attended sewing classes.

It suddenly occurred to Pandora that normally such ladies would be calling on the owner of the shop and asking her to join them in their relief work. Well, she'd help where she could, of course she would, but she wasn't going to Saunders' church. What she really wanted to do now was learn how the shop was run and make a place for herself in it.

And no one was going to stop her doing so — not Zachary and certainly not Mr Featherworth.

★ ★ ★

The following morning Zachary was woken by someone hammering on the front door. He stared round, surprised all over again to find himself in his old bed.

Footsteps ran lightly up the stairs. Hallie. He'd recognise her tread anywhere. She tapped on the bedroom door.

'The shop lad from Blake's is here.'

'What does he want?'

'He's brought a message from Harry Prebble.'

'Give it to me.'

'It's just a message. Harry says you're late and to get round to the shop quickly or he'll dock your pay.'

354

Zachary was suddenly wide awake. He sat up in bed. 'Is the boy still here?'

'No. He went back straight away.'

'I'd better get up.'

'But you said Mr Dawson told you not to go into work for a day or two.'

'He did. But maybe I will anyway.'

'That's not fair. You're still tired or you'd not have slept in. It's nine o'clock. You never normally sleep so long.'

He grinned at her. 'Well, now that I'm awake, I'm hungry.'

'Mum sent me out for some eggs.' She lowered her voice and added, 'I think she's trying to build you up before you go back to work for that horrible Harry Prebble.'

Zachary smiled at the vehemence in her voice. Somehow, Harry had lost the power to upset him now. He'd try to keep the peace at the emporium, at least until he'd found out what was going on there, but after all he'd seen and done, Harry Prebble seemed like small fry.

He went down and enjoyed a leisurely breakfast, chatting to them both. They were interrupted by another knock on the door before he'd finished. He stood up. 'I'll see to that.'

Opening the door, he found the shop lad there again and that annoyed him.

'Harry says you're late and he's definitely docking your pay.'

It was a deliberate insult to send a verbal message to this effect. Everyone in the shop would know about it. 'Tell Harry I'll be in tomorrow or the day after.'

355

'He'll be angry. Well, he *is* angry.'

'Let him be.'

'But he's the *manager*. He might sack you if you get on his wrong side.'

'Oh, I don't think he'll do that.' Zachary was about to close the door when he saw the office lad from Featherworth's approaching along the street, so waited to see if he too was coming to the house. The shop lad lingered, obviously hoping to hear something, which he'd no doubt pass on to Harry.

'Come in before you give me your message,' Zachary told the lawyer's lad and shut the door in the other one's face.

He showed the youth into the rarely used front parlour.

'Mr Dawson has sent you a note and asks for an answer now, if you don't mind.' He held out an envelope.

Zachary took it and read the brief note it contained.

Dear Zachary
If you could come into Mr Featherworth's rooms about eleven o'clock this morning, we could make a start on the accounts. No need to rush in earlier. You've more than earned a rest.
R. Dawson

Zachary smiled at the lad. 'Tell Mr Dawson I'll be there at eleven.'

He went back to pour himself another cup of tea and assure his mother that he could deal with Harry.

She looked at him, opened her mouth then shut it again.

'What were you going to say?'

She sighed. 'I was worried you'd got a bit above yourself, what with the travel and all. Harry Prebble *is* the manager now, so it won't do to upset him.'

He didn't dare tell her the truth, didn't want to tell her lies. 'He's only temporary. If he gets the job, I'll not be working there any longer. But I don't think he will get the job and from what Mr Featherworth said, I reckon my job is safe, Mum — as safe as I want it to be.'

She frowned at that, clearly not convinced. He knew she worried about being a burden, worked hard to make the money he earned go a long way. He wished he could tell her everything, hated deceiving her, but she might let something slip. She was terrible at keeping secrets, always had been.

He left the house early to stroll round the park before he went to Mr Featherworth's rooms. There were still people loitering at the street corners, gaunt-faced, wanting work not leisure. He stopped to chat to one or two men he knew, thinking how old and worn they looked. They questioned him eagerly about Australia, seeming to find great satisfaction in knowing someone so well-travelled.

He'd go to the library later and read the newspapers. He was so out of touch with what was happening here in Lancashire. The Civil War might be taking place in America but the lack of cotton was affecting folk over here very badly.

How long was it now since the mills of Outham had been working? Two years at least. And how many children and old folk had died for lack of proper nourishment? Far too many.

★ ★ ★

When Pandora woke on the Monday morning, she didn't linger in bed, but went down to get a cup of tea and a slice of bread and butter. The sun was shining and she decided to treat herself to a walk on the moors.

'Should you go up there on your own, miss?' Dot worried. 'There are rough men on the tramp these days, seeking work. The town's not as safe as it used to be. If you wait another hour Miss Alice will be up and she likes going for walks, too.'

'I can't bear to wait. I'm only going as far as the lower ridge. I have to see the moors properly again. I missed them so much while I was away.'

'Don't they have any moors in Australia, then?'

'No. Even the trees are different there. And in the summer it's so hot sometimes it's like standing in an oven. Give me a rainy day in Lancashire any time!'

She grabbed a shawl, not wanting to bother with a hat, and hurried off down the street, turning her face up to the gentle sunshine that didn't sear your skin.

She found the steep street that led up to the moors more tiring than she'd expected, because she was out of practice at walking, but at last she was rewarded by one of her favourite views. Below her, to the right lay the town, with its terraces of red-brick houses, showing as long lines of grey slate roofs. To the left lay the moors, stretching into the misty distance, with only the occasional farm breaking the slopes, not red brick like the terraces in town, but with whitewashed or grey stone walls. The farm fields were green, with dry stone walls making patchwork patterns, but the uncultivated wilder parts of the moors were a greenish brown.

Suddenly she felt uneasy, as if she was being watched. She swung round but could see no one. Still the feeling persisted.

In the stillness of the early morning she heard a rock go clattering down a slope to her left and knew there was indeed someone nearby, someone who was hiding. Giving in to her instincts, she ran headlong down the hill, not stopping till she came to the first of the houses.

She'd never, ever felt afraid like that before when she went walking on the moors. Had someone really been following her? Or was it just her imagination?

She walked quickly back to the house, not telling Alice or Dot about her sudden panic.

It must have been someone on the tramp. It was too early in the morning for most people to be out walking for pleasure.

Her first thought had been that she would tell Zachary and see what he thought about it. Tears came into her eyes, because she couldn't. Oh, she missed him so much!

Zachary was shown into Mr Dawson's office just before eleven o'clock. He handed over his carefully kept accounts and what was left of the money and they chatted in more detail about what he'd seen and done.

Mr Dawson frowned at the amount expended on Leo, but shrugged when he saw the note signed by the sisters to say they fully approved, and lost his frown altogether when he heard that Leo had more than repaid them by helping Zachary and Pandora get to Albany.

'Fate works in the strangest ways sometimes,' he mused.

He finished going through the accounts, then sat back, smiling at the younger man. 'You're good with figures.'

'I wasn't always able to be as neat as I'd have liked.'

'But unless I'm much mistaken, you were always accurate.'

'I hope so.'

'I kept an eye on your mother and sister, but they seemed to have no trouble.'

'No. They're good managers. It's just a pity Hallie can't get a job. She frets about being at home. It's a good thing she has the lending library to visit.'

Mr Dawson sat back. 'You didn't mention that the shop lad was at your house this morning. Why was he there?'

'Harry sent him twice to tell me I was late for work. He says he's going to dock my pay.'

Mr Dawson let out a little growl of anger. 'That young man oversteps his mark. Once we've got to the bottom of this pilfering, it will be natural for Pandora to make you manager in his place.'

Zachary couldn't stop himself beaming. 'Yes, she's said so. I'd love that.'

'Tell me your thoughts about how the shop should be run.'

Mr Dawson led him on for quite some time, nodding and prompting and asking questions.

When Zachary realised how long he'd been speaking he faltered to a stop.

'You'll make a good manager.' The older man hesitated then added, 'The other thing we have to consider is your hasty marriage.'

All Zachary's joy left him.

'Am I right in thinking you care for Pandora?'

'Very much.'

'And that she cares for you.'

'She thinks she does. But it can't be. I do understand that.'

'I don't see why not.'

Zachary couldn't speak for a moment or two. 'If you could bear with me while I sort out Prebble — and if Pandora is still of the same mind — we can announce your marriage as soon as he's gone. Can you cope with working in the shop for a while, put up with his arrogance?'

'Um — do I still have to answer absolutely to him? If so, he'll find an excuse to sack me, I'm sure.'

Mr Dawson steepled his fingers together. 'In some ways, I'm afraid we'll have to leave him in charge. But he'll have no right to sack you and I shall make that clear to him.'

'Thank you.'

'Could you start work tomorrow?'

'Yes, of course.'

'We've suggested to Marshall Worth that you and he act as though you dislike one another, so that Prebble doesn't grow suspicious.'

'I don't know Worth so that'll be easy enough.'

'Then enjoy the rest of today. And it would be perfectly normal for you to call on Miss Blake to ask how she's feeling.'

'I'll do that this afternoon, then.' He stood up to leave.

'Oh! I nearly forgot. Mr Featherworth is very pleased with how you carried out your task and there will be a bonus for you. In the meantime you'll need some money, so here is an advance payment.' He handed over an envelope that clinked.

Zachary set off to walk home, feeling very happy about his future, though the present would not be easy to endure.

19

Ralph stopped for a moment outside Blake's Emporium, approving the sparkling clean windows and the tidy piles of goods on display there. At least the place had been kept in good order.

He could see Prebble staring at him from the back of the shop, so pushed open the door and walked inside. That young man did altogether too much staring.

Prebble came across to him at once. 'How can I help you, Mr Dawson?'

'We'll speak in your office.' He let the other show him behind the counter but didn't hurry, stopping once or twice to study his surroundings. The packing area behind the shop was also immaculately clean and Marshall was sitting there, a faint smile on his face, weighing sugar from a big sack into pounds and putting it into bags, then carefully folding the tops. How ridiculous and demeaning to keep an intelligent man like that working on the sort of task usually left to the youngest member of staff!

He winked as he passed Marshall, but said nothing.

Inside the office Prebble gestured to a stool, but Ralph took the more comfortable chair behind the desk. He saw the young man press his lips together as if annoyed at that but ignored him.

'About Mr Carr . . . '

Prebble made a scornful noise in his throat. 'He's not come to work today, though I've sent two messages to his house. I shall have to dock his wages this week.'

'You'll do no such thing. I'm surprised you didn't check with me first to find out when he had been asked to return to work.'

'If he cares about his job, he should be doing it now. He's back from his holiday, isn't he?'

'Holiday? He's had a long and tiring journey, faced major problems on the way and acquitted himself well. He needs time to recuperate from such exertions. I'd offered to give him a few days off, but he said he'd come back to work tomorrow.'

'I see.'

'Zachary will still be answering to me. He's your equal in experience and as you're temporary manager only, you have no power to dismiss him, or to dock his wages.' Ralph paused to let that sink in.

'Who's in charge of the shop, then?'

'You are. For the moment. But I'm sure Zachary will be happy to work with you.'

'If I can't tell him what to do, how can I run things properly?'

'I shouldn't think he'll need much telling. He's an intelligent young man and knows his job. What's more, I don't wish to see him wasting his time packing sugar once he starts again. He's well thought of by the customers and they'll want to ask him about his journey.'

Prebble's expression was so sour, Ralph felt

suddenly sure he would do all he could to make Zachary's life miserable and damage his reputation with his new mistress. Well, he wouldn't succeed there. Ralph only hoped she would keep quiet about her marriage, as she'd agreed. He desperately needed an expert opinion on what was happening at the store. He'd better emphasise that when he went to see her.

'There's another thing Mr Featherworth wanted me to raise with you. The tea that you blend in the shop — Blake's Best — Mrs Featherworth doesn't think it tastes as good as it used to.'

'I changed the blend slightly. It's saved quite a lot of money. People will soon grow used to it.'

'*What?* Please change the blend back to exactly what Mr Blake used to produce. I've spoken to you before about petty cost-cutting. It doesn't do with customers of this class.'

Prebble breathed in deeply.

'I presume Marshall won't be doing such menial jobs for long?' Ralph asked. 'He's a very capable man.'

'I suppose you expect him to work in the shop.'

'That's what he was hired for.'

Prebble's expression was sour. 'If *you* want Marshall to serve customers, I'll need to employ someone else to do the general cleaning. I have an elderly relative who could come in for a couple of hours a day, if that's all right? She'll only ask sixpence an hour. I've employed her occasionally when we've been busy.'

Ralph decided to yield a little. 'If you consider

it necessary. I'm pleased that you keep things so clean. I'm sure Marshall will not let you down serving in the shop.'

Prebble hesitated, then burst out, 'I know he can handle the goods and the change, but the problem is, he's not *presentable!* He speaks too broadly and doesn't know how to deal with the better class of person. I know he's a hard worker, I can't fault him on that, but he isn't the sort we normally employ in this shop.'

'He is now. And I'll remind you that Mr Blake hired you when *you* weren't presentable. Have you no compassion?'

Prebble scowled. 'My job now is to run the shop efficiently, not dispense charity.'

★   ★   ★

Shaking his head at this attitude, Ralph left the shop and went to knock on the door of the living quarters. When Dot showed him up to the parlour, he was pleased to see that Pandora was looking much better, with colour in her cheeks and a sparkle in her eyes. He nodded to Alice, who smiled as she stood up.

'I'm sure you'll wish to speak to Miss Blake privately.' She left the room.

Such a quiet, restful woman! he thought. How she'd remained unmarried, he'd never understand. His sister thought he should ask Alice to marry him and he was tempted, but he found the prospect of proposing and making such changes to his life at his age rather daunting. Still, he would hate to see Alice move away from

Outham, would miss her greatly. Fortunately, there was time yet to give the matter more consideration, to work out how to do it.

He turned back to Pandora, who was sitting waiting expectantly, and took the seat she indicated. 'I've been going over the accounts from the journey with Zachary. He's an honest young fellow, though I expected nothing less from him, and he's good at figures.'

'He's kind, too. I warn you, I'm *not* letting anyone un-marry us.'

'No one's asking you to, but I do honour him for giving you the opportunity to change your mind. It's not always easy to do the right thing. If you can be patient, we desperately need him back in the shop for a while, to see if he can figure out what's happening and help us trap Prebble. We need proof or we can't act.'

'You don't like Prebble, either, do you?'

'No.'

'He was waiting for me when I walked back from the Raineys' yesterday and insisted on escorting me home. It can't have been by chance that he was there because he doesn't live in that part of town.' She grimaced. 'He's very polite, but . . .'

'Yes, there's always a but, isn't there? We'll get to the bottom of this, never fear.'

She put up her chin defiantly. 'Better do it quickly, then. I've given Zachary a month, after which I'm telling everyone about our marriage.'

Dot, who was carrying some sheets the laundry had just delivered up the stairs to put them away, nearly dropped them as Pandora's clear voice floated out to her through the half-open door. *Married! Her new mistress was already married to Zachary?* As the implications of this sank in, she shivered in delight. Oh, how she wished *she* could be the one to tell Harry. Then her smile faded. No, she didn't. He'd be furious that his rival had stolen a march on him and would hit out in any way he could. Though how he thought a snirpy little fellow like him would attract a lovely young woman like Miss Blake, Dot couldn't understand.

She carried on up the stairs, hugging the sheets to her chest. Eh, it couldn't happen to a nicer fellow than Zachary Carr and she wished the two of them well, 'deed she did.

In the parlour Pandora suddenly remembered Leo. 'About the money spent on rescuing Leo. My sisters and I fully approve of that. He was such a kind fellow and so good with horses. His face was badly bruised when he first came to us because he'd been shockingly beaten. And we couldn't have managed without him on the journey.'

Ralph nodded, smiling benignly. 'It's your money, my dear lady, I just thought you'd like to know that the accounts are in order. You can see them if you wish.'

'No, thank you. I trust Zachary absolutely.'

He trusted the young man, too, Ralph realised, and always had. 'Then if that's settled, we'll move on to the other thing I came to discuss with you, money. I shall, if you approve, provide you with a valuation of all the assets your uncle left to the four of you, then help you work out ways to give your sisters at least part of their share. I presume you're not intending to sell the shop? No, I thought not, given your husband's great experience in that area. So once we've sorted Prebble out, we'll discuss how to get the money to your sisters.'

'Good.'

'And finally, you'll need some money for your own daily use. In addition, if you'll tell me which shops you wish to patronise in Outham, I'll open accounts there for you.'

He paused, amused by her startled expression. Remembering what he'd heard about the intelligent Blake sisters, he prompted, 'The bookshop, perhaps? And a dressmaker? My sister suggested Miss Poulton's. You'll find her very polite and prompt, and I'm told she has an eye for what suits a client. As for groceries, just give Prebble lists of what you need from the shop or send Dot round and her purchases can be put on your account. Have you any idea how much money you'll require for your personal daily needs?'

She shook her head. 'I can't imagine having enough money to do what I want. But you're right. I shall be patronising the bookshop as well as the library. I think I'll go out and buy a book this very afternoon, to celebrate. And I badly need some new clothes.'

He pulled out a small leather pouch and handed it over to her. 'Mr Featherworth thought twenty pounds to begin with. Is that enough?'

He watched her eyes widen and saw her swallow hard before she clutched the pouch to her bosom. She didn't say anything, seemed too stunned by it all to speak. 'If it's all right with you, we'll continue to have Prebble pay the takings to us until things are settled, one way or the other.'

'Oh, yes. I don't want to deal with him. And whatever happens, whether you trap him or not, I won't have him as manager.'

'You won't need him with Zachary Carr by your side.' Ralph was amused by her blush. He took his leave, well satisfied with his day's work. If anyone could figure out how to trap Prebble, it was Zachary, who had worked in the shop since he was a lad.

What was there about Prebble that made him feel so suspicious? He was hard-working, went to church regularly, spoke politely, and yet . . . He shook his head, baffled.

★ ★ ★

Zachary was at the shop on time the following morning, amused to see that the other shopmen had got there earlier than they used to and were already at work. Prebble would no doubt enjoy keeping them on their toes, squeezing extra hours of work out of them, he was sure, because he'd always treated the younger shop lads in the same way. Mr Blake had had to speak to him once or twice about it.

Zachary went through into the packing area, hanging his spare apron up on its old peg. He didn't join the others in the shop to take the covers off, dust and set things out, but took the time to study the packing area. There were one or two small changes but he was pleased to see it had been kept as clean as ever. Harry's voice made him turn round.

'There you are! I'd like you to come in a bit earlier in future.'

'Why?'

'So that we can get the shop in perfect order before we open.'

'We always managed that before without adding extra hours to an already long day.'

'Well, I'm manager now and I do things a little differently.'

The shop's bell rang and Harry darted across to peer through the narrow pane of glass in the door that led into the public area. 'Mrs Butley's cook. Go and see what she wants.'

Zachary found the tone rude, but said nothing. He knew and liked the cook, so was happy to attend to her.

In the shop the rosy-faced older woman beamed at him. 'I heard you were back from foreign parts, Mr Carr.'

'I am indeed, Mrs Jarrod. And what can I get for you this morning?'

'My mistress has taken a fancy to a boiled egg for breakfast and I used the last one yesterday in a cake.'

He'd guess the general maid had seen him walking to work and the cook had been despatched to try to find out any gossip she could for her mistress.

He took her bowl and walked across to where the eggs were kept. 'Half a dozen?'

'Yes, please. What was Australia like?'

'Very different from Outham. I saw kangaroos hopping about and parrots flying in the gardens. It was winter there and it rained very hard, but it never gets cold enough for frost or snow. In the summer it's extremely hot, they tell me, and the air feels just as if you'd opened an oven door.'

'Just fancy! Kangaroos. I've seen pictures of them at a lantern show. Strange creatures, aren't they? But no use for meat or milk.'

He smiled. 'I ate kangaroo meat several times and it was delicious. Quite a strong flavour and not fatty.'

'I'd like to try it, I must admit. I — um, gather that only one of the sisters came back with you. Are the others coming later?' She looked at him expectantly.

He didn't intend to gossip about Pandora or her sisters, so all he said was, 'That's up to them.'

After she'd left there was a stream of customers for small purchases, many of them clearly there to talk to him. Word of his return had spread quickly, as news always did in Outham. He sometimes wondered if news wafted through the air.

'You say very little about the other sisters,' Harry said later as Zachary went to have his midday meal. 'Why didn't they come back?'

'It's not my business to discuss that.' He looked down at the plate of food provided for him and lifted the top piece of bread from his sandwich. 'That's mainly gristle. I'll go and get myself some ham scraps.'

372

Harry glared at him. 'It's up to me to decide what the staff eat. I'm not wasting the good stuff on them. That ham's here to make a profit for the owners.'

'Mr Blake believed his staff should be properly fed.' Zachary went into the shop with his plate, finding plenty of trimmings of the sort that they sold off more cheaply and taking enough to refill his sandwich.

'Did you hear what I said?' Harry snapped as he came back in.

'Yes. But you wouldn't want me to eat gristle, I'm sure.' He sat down and began on the sandwich, wishing the other would leave him in peace. This was ridiculously petty behaviour.

To Zachary's relief, after hovering for a moment or two longer, Prebble went into the office, muttering something about having his dinner while things were quiet. He shut the door, something old Mr Blake would never have done, except when his wife was on the prowl.

Why had Harry done that? Was he hiding something in the office?

During the afternoon Zachary was getting some new wrapping paper down from the hall cupboards when the new door at the far end opened and Pandora came out of the living quarters.

They both stopped to smile at one another.

'How are you?' she asked.

'I'm well. I must say *you* look a lot better.'

'I feel it.'

Harry opened the door at the far end of the hallway. 'Ah, Miss Blake! I thought I heard your voice.' He frowned at Zachary. 'They're waiting for that wrapping paper in the shop, Carr. I'll attend to Miss Blake.'

Zachary winked at Pandora and left them alone.

★ ★ ★

Immediately Pandora began to feel uneasy. Prebble came towards her and stopped right next to her, standing just a bit too close and eyeing her up and down in a way she detested.

'How can I help you?' he asked.

'I don't need any help. I've come to explore.'

'Let me show you round.'

'No, thank you. I can find my own way. I'll ask if I want to know anything.'

'I'm sure you'd find it more interesting if I was there to answer your questions straight away.'

She drew herself up. 'Mr Prebble, I neither need nor want your company. You're employed to run our shop, not fuss over me.'

She heard him suck in air, his mouth half-open in surprise, as if her sharp retort had taken him by surprise. He didn't move for a moment or two, then he turned away from her. But he'd forgotten about the glass fronts to the cupboards and they reflected his face quite clearly from where she was standing. The expression she saw once his back was turned to her was vicious, there was no other word for it: vicious.

She didn't move on after he'd gone back into the shop, but began to study her surroundings,

374

which were quite new to her. The glass-fronted cupboards in the corridor contained various sorts of wrapping paper, big rolls of it, brown, white, waxed, and boxes of paper packets of various sizes and colours. There were other necessities like balls of string, pencils, labels and boxes of what looked like smaller office items.

When she'd seen all she wanted, she went into the packing area. Here a youth was weighing out rice into packets, folding the tops carefully and stacking them in neat rows. He stood up at once when he saw her.

'Do sit down.'

'Thank you, Miss Blake.'

'Do you put these packets into the shop now?'

'No, we stack them on the shelves here ready for when they're needed. We do jobs like this in slack times.'

'Don't let me stop you working. I'm just having a look round.'

She began to move slowly along the shelves, studying their contents. Beyond the packing area was a big store room. She'd never seen flour and sugar in such huge sacks. There were wooden crates containing jars of jam, some of the modern tinned food, including even the novelty of tinned meat, though she'd heard it wasn't very nice. Still, any hungry family would welcome it, she was sure.

In fact, Blakes supplied almost every necessity for feeding a household, though people usually bought fresh fruit and vegetables from the market or from a greengrocer.

She found steps that led down into a cellar so

went carefully down these. Some daylight came in from a large barred window that led into a light well about two yards by one. A grating was set into the footpath above this. It was much cooler down here and she found butter, cheese and eggs, draped with dampened muslin to keep them fresh.

When she went upstairs, she tried another door and found herself in the office.

She distinctly heard the lad packing rice gasp in shock as she went inside. It was furnished with a roll-top desk, a comfortable chair, and shelves containing ledgers and boxes of papers. She sat down on the chair her uncle must have used, feeling sad all over again at his untimely end.

The door opened and Harry stopped in the doorway. 'Oh! I thought you'd gone back into the house.'

His expression of surprise looked false to her and she guessed that the lad had run to fetch him. 'No. I'm still familiarising myself with the shop and how it's run. I'm exploring the office now.'

'My dear Miss Blake, there's no need for a lovely young woman like yourself to bother with business matters. I can tell you anything you wish to know and you can trust me to keep the paperwork in order, so — '

'But how can I learn how our shop is run, and help with that, if I don't understand what you do here?'

He blinked at her in shock and moved closer to the desk. 'But surely *you* won't be involved in running the shop?'

'I certainly shall. When I'm more familiar with how things are done, I intend to serve in the shop sometimes, too.'

His shocked expression changed to utter horror. 'But women don't serve in shops like this one. Believe me, Miss Blake, the customers wouldn't expect it and some might dislike it. And there's no *need*! *I* can do all that's necessary.'

'As the owner, I should be foolish not to familiarise myself with every facet of running this shop. And the customers will soon grow used to me serving them, I'm sure.'

'But the other ladies in the town don't work in their husband's businesses. There's a lot of mental arithmetic involved, too, and — '

'I can add up as well as you, I'm sure.'

His sneering expression at that remark showed a disdain for women she'd met in other men and that further annoyed her.

'A woman as lovely as you will soon find a husband, I'm sure.'

She hated his compliments. He was standing very close to her now, and the way he was looking at her made her feel extremely uncomfortable.

'And he'll be a very lucky man,' he added, with a soulful look.

He couldn't mean . . . Ugh! She'd never marry a man like him. Never! Something about him made her shudder.

He laid one hand on her arm and only the memory of Mr Dawson's request not to upset him stopped her from throwing his arm off violently. She pulled hers back, though.

'If Carr told you that you needed to work in the shop, he was wrong!' Harry said earnestly.

'Zachary said the same as you and I gave him the same answer. It's *my* shop — mine and my sisters', I mean — and I want to be a part of what goes on here. I wasn't bred to be idle, Mr Prebble, and I don't intend to start now.'

She walked out of the office, hating the fact that he didn't move and she couldn't help touching him as she passed.

When Zachary touched her, she loved it.

Oh, she wished this charade weren't necessary, wished it more desperately with each day that passed.

★ ★ ★

From the other side of the glass pane in the connecting door, Zachary watched Pandora hurry out of the office, face flushed. She stopped to shudder, then squared her shoulders and came towards the shop. He swung the door open, smiling at her.

'I can't stand him,' she said in a low voice.

He was startled. 'What's he done?'

'I'll tell you when we're alone. At the moment there don't seem to be any customers in, so could you please show me how the shop is organised?'

'Of course.' He began the tour, explaining why the shelves were arranged in a certain way, showing her the tools kept under the counter, including a bowl of water for rinsing the hands

378

quickly, and the marble slab at one end of the counter for cutting pieces of butter and cheese, or slicing ham.

Partway through the tour Harry came out of the back and stopped in the doorway, scowling at them. After a moment he walked across. 'I'll see to Miss Blake now, Carr.'

Pandora swung round. 'I asked Zachary to show me round and I'm happy with how he's doing it. Don't let me keep you from your work, Mr Prebble.'

She was magnificent, but unfortunately her dislike for Harry was only too clear. She wasn't good at dissembling, as Zachary had already found out.

When she left the shop, he went into the back room to fetch some more packets of flour and stopped for a moment, puzzled. There had been one or two more packets of flour on this shelf, he was certain of it because he'd always had an excellent memory for details. Old Mr Blake had often complimented him on that.

Where had the flour gone? Not into the shop, that was certain.

Frowning, he put some more one-pound and two-pound bags into a basket and carried it into the shop to fill the shelves. When he took the basket back to the preparation area, he stood still, surveying the piles of goods on the shelves one by one, committing them to memory.

Then the shop doorbell rang and he went back to serve a customer and speak yet again about his journey to Australia.

* * *

After carefully locking the connecting door, Pandora went back up to the parlour, thoughtful now. She found Alice sitting with some embroidery.

'How did your visit to the shop go?'

'It was — interesting. Or it would have been.' Alice raised one eyebrow.

'Prebble would keep fussing over me, but he didn't want me to look inside the office. I wonder why. You'd think *he* owned the shop, not me.'

'I find him officious and patronising.'

'Yes. But there's something else about him. Something . . . repulsive. I can't bear him to touch me.'

'He touched you?'

'Patted my arm. And I had to brush past him to get out of the office.' She shuddered.

'I can't stand him either. Well, it's more than dislike. He frightens me.' Alice explained about the intruders. 'I've always thought it was him. Or else he was behind it. He didn't like me coming to live here, was bossing Dot about before and taking some of the money meant to go on her food. Just a bit here and there, but it mounts up. He said he was saving it for the new owners and produced a cash box containing the exact amount, so Ralph — Mr Dawson couldn't accuse him of wrongdoing.'

'Horrid little weasel. I can't understand why Mr Dawson appointed him as manager.'

'Would you have preferred Prebble to come

and find you in Australia?'

Pandora looked at her in horror. 'No! I suppose after my uncle was killed, there was no one else left to run the emporium. Zachary loves it. He'd make a good manager.'

'The customers certainly prefer him. While he was away I heard a lot of people say it was more pleasant shopping here when he was around, how they used to wait to be served by him.'

'Zachary's a lovely man.'

Alice smiled. 'And you're fond of him.'

Pandora couldn't deny it. 'Very. But he hasn't got any money and I have the shop.'

'Do you love him?'

'Yes.'

'Then fight for him. Don't let anything stop you. I didn't fight and I lost the man I loved when I was younger because of my father's interference.'

'Don't worry. I shan't let anything come between us.' She smiled fondly for a moment, picturing Zachary, then changed the subject. 'Would you like to come into town and help me choose some dress materials? I need to find a dressmaker who can make some up quite quickly. My clothes are all dreadfully shabby.'

Alice slipped her needle into the edge of the embroidery and put it down. 'I'd love to come.'

In perfect accord the two women went out shopping. They chose three lengths of dress material for Pandora, vivid colours that would go well with her dark hair. Afterwards they took them to a dressmaker of whom other ladies spoke well, and there they received a flattering degree of attention.

But Pandora had definite views on what she wanted. She stared at the fashion plates the dressmaker was showing her. Huge skirts like pyramids. Elaborate trimmings with loops and swirls of braid or little waterfalls of frills peeking out from beneath a scalloped hem. 'Oh, no! I don't want such full skirts. Or such fussy decoration. I think they look silly and how would you walk briskly in one, let alone run?'

The dressmaker blinked at her in surprise. 'Ladies don't usually need to walk briskly and certainly not run, Miss Blake.'

'Well, I'm not a lady and I love a good brisk walk. In fact I don't want a crinoline frame at all. A couple of petticoats, perhaps, with flounces round the hems. That's as far as I'll go.'

'But you'd look so good in a fashionable dress with your slender waist and elegant figure.'

'It'd drive me mad to have six yards of skirt hem bobbing around my legs.' Pandora smiled at her. 'Don't waste your time on trying to make me into a fashionable lady, Miss Poulton. I just want to look — reasonable. With nice materials and colours.'

'I can make you whatever you'd like.' The dressmaker took out a sheet of paper and pencil, staring down at it thoughtfully.

'Here, let me.' Pandora took the pencil out of her hand and sketched a matching skirt and bodice.

'You draw well.'

'When I have time. Can you do that with the dark green? And change the sleeves and skirts a bit for the other colours.'

'Easily.'

'Good. How quickly can you make one up?'

The dressmaker looked at her speculatively. 'Would you mind us doing the seams with a sewing machine? We're very modern here and I've had a sewing machine for a few years. Some ladies still prefer hand sewing, but the machine does very neat work, I promise you.'

'I'd not mind at all. I've never seen a sewing machine. Can I look at it?'

The dressmaker took her into the workshop and showed her the machine, which stood on its own little table.

'It was made by Sugden, Bradbury and Firth in Oldham and cost us seven pounds. My brother was the one who insisted I buy it. He loves anything mechanical. I was a bit nervous when I first used it, but now I love it, and so do my girls.'

The women in the sewing room smiled and nodded.

As they came out of the shop, Alice couldn't help chuckling. 'You shocked her with your disdain for fashion.'

'I know. But she agreed to do what I wanted in the end. And I think I redeemed myself in her eyes by my interest in her sewing machine.' Pandora gave a little skip of excitement. 'How wonderful to have some brand-new dresses! We always had to buy ours second-hand and a lot of mine were passed down by my sisters till we all stopped growing taller.'

'You'd better go and buy a new hat as well.

That one is rather battered.'

'I suppose so.'

Again Pandora received flattering attention, and again she had to convince the milliner that she didn't want anything fussy. She came out wearing one of the two new straw hats she'd purchased. Both had small brims and neat trimmings, though the one she intended for Sunday wear did have a soft, curly feather trailing along one side of the brim and hanging down a couple of inches at the back.

'Now, on to some shopping that I shall really enjoy.' She led the way to the bookshop, where she bought half a dozen books, wishing once again that her father had lived to see this day.

Back in her bedroom, tidying herself up and putting away her purchases, Pandora looked into the mirror. The face that stared back at her was rosy, the eyes sparkling. She was pretty, she admitted. She didn't usually care about that, but now she wanted to look as pretty as she could for Zachary. He said he loved her and he certainly looked at her admiringly. Why did he still insist on keeping his distance? Surely she'd proved that she wasn't going to change her mind about their marriage? What if out of pride he refused to remain her husband?

No. No, she wouldn't let him do that. Determination filled her. She'd claim that the marriage had been consummated, if necessary. Mr Featherworth and Mr Dawson might approve of him keeping his distance, but they were old. They didn't understand or perhaps they'd forgotten how much you could love someone, how much you could miss being with him. And they thought too much about money.

Well, she knew better. It was important to have enough money to live decently and feed your family, of course it was, but what counted most in the world was your family and those you loved. She'd lost her sisters. She wasn't going to lose Zachary as well.

And if she had her way, if fate was kind to her, she'd make a new family, have several children and love them all. Boys who looked like their father. Girls who weren't too tall and who were quite pretty. Being too pretty was a burden. It had often irritated her that men couldn't see beyond her face. And being tall could make things difficult, too. Most men wanted a woman shorter than they were.

If they didn't need to find out what was wrong at the shop, she'd stop this silly charade at once and insist Zachary move in with her.

If he'd agree to do that. Her thoughts always stopped short at his steely determination. No one would ever force Zachary Carr to do something he believed wrong.

20

That evening, Pandora went into the shop and asked Zachary to fill her a basket with a few staples for a family she knew who had fallen on hard times.

He began taking things off the shelves, seeming to understand without being told what they might need. 'Is that enough?'

'That's fine.' She felt someone close behind her and turned to find herself almost nose to nose with Prebble, so edged back towards Zachary.

'Doesn't Dot usually do your shopping, Miss Blake?' Prebble asked. 'It doesn't do to pamper a maidservant, you know.'

She'd had enough of him poking his nose into her affairs. 'Kindly mind your own business, Mr Prebble, and leave me to mind mine!'

Zachary let out a snort of laughter, which he tried but failed to disguise as a cough.

Colour high, Prebble took a couple of steps backwards, but remained close by and didn't stop watching her and what she was taking. She turned her back on him and examined the basket, nodding. 'That's enough. I don't want my friends to feel over-whelmed.'

Zachary noted down the items in the account book then carried the basket to the door for her. 'Where are you going?' he asked in a low voice.

'Just to Pelson Street. I want to visit Bill's

386

parents. They were on very short commons when I left Outham and I wasn't even able to say goodbye to them. Mr Dean may be working on one of the relief schemes, so I've left it till evening to visit them.'

'They'll welcome this food, then. Are you sure the basket isn't too heavy?'

She laughed. 'Men often say things like that. Have you felt how heavy a small child can be? No one worries about a woman carrying a child.'

He looked a bit surprised at that. 'You're right. I hope your visit goes well.'

She enjoyed the late sunshine, strolling along. After a few streets she began to feel uneasy and wonder if she was being followed. Then she stopped to chat to an old acquaintance and forgot about that. But the minute she started walking along on her own again, the strange sensation of someone staring at her came back.

She tried swinging round suddenly, in order to catch her pursuer, but could never pin anyone down as being the one following her. Something was making her feel uneasy, though, and she felt quite sure she wasn't mistaken.

Because of meeting old acquaintances, it took longer to get to Pelson Street than she'd expected and there were fewer people around by then. She was relieved when Bill's father opened the door.

He beamed at her and ushered her in with a wave of one hand. 'Come in, lass, come in. I said to the wife you'd be round to visit soon. We knew you'd not grow too proud to talk to your old friends.'

'We were happy to hear you'd done so well for yourself, love,' Mrs Dean said. 'You'll be set for life now.'

Pandora set the basket on the kitchen table, noting the absence of ornaments and some much-loved pieces of furniture. 'I've brought a few things for you.'

Both of them immediately stiffened.

'Please don't let pride come between us. I know you'd share what you had with me if I fell on hard times.'

All hung in the balance for a moment or two, then Mrs Dean sobbed and came to give her a big hug, burying her head against Pandora's shoulder for a moment before pulling herself upright and wiping away the tears. The two women began to unpack the food and Bill's mother was unable to speak for emotion by the time they'd finished.

'I'll see you home, lass,' Mr Dean said later. 'You left your visiting a bit late.'

'I've walked these streets many a time at dusk,' she protested.

'When times are hard, some people can be tempted into robbing others.'

But as they left the house, she saw Zachary waiting for her at the end of the street. Her heart lifted at the mere sight of his dear face and she beckoned to him and introduced the two men, then nipped into the kitchen to fetch Mrs Dean to the door.

'Your young man, is it?' she asked.

'Yes,' Pandora said. 'Only we're not telling anyone about it yet, so keep it to yourselves.' She led the way back to the front door. 'Zachary, this is Mrs Dean, Bill's mother.'

After they'd said goodbye, Zachary offered her his arm. 'You shouldn't be walking the streets on your own at this hour, love.'

'Don't you start. Mr Dean said the same thing. He was going to escort me home.'

'He's right. The war in America might be coming to an end, but people are still on short commons here in Outham.'

They walked along the next street, their steps matching well, not needing to talk for the sake of talking.

'It's lovely to be on my own with you.' She gave his arm a friendly squeeze. 'I've missed you so much.'

He stopped walking to cover the hand lying on his arm with his left hand. 'I've missed you, too, love.'

'I want to tell the world about us.'

'I do too, but I've found one or two details that don't look right in the shop, so we'd better not do it yet.'

'You have?'

'Yes.'

'Then maybe Mr Dawson's right about Prebble.'

'He's a clever man, Mr Featherworth's clerk. He'd not make a fuss for nothing.'

'You're clever too.' As they began walking again, she added, 'I'm beginning to suspect that Mr Dawson is rather fond of Alice — and she of him.'

'Then I wish them luck.'

Again, their eyes met and they smiled at one another. Her heart lifted. He'd not smile at her like that if he didn't care for her, not Zachary.

He escorted her back to the shop, refusing to come in for a cup of tea. Still smiling, she locked the door behind her, peeping in at Dot, who was reading a book by the light of the kitchen lamp.

'Sorry, miss, hope you don't mind me reading, only I've finished all the housework.'

'You can read as much as you like. I don't expect you to work every hour of the day. And when I've read them, you can borrow my new books too.' There had been no books in the house before, Alice said. How dreadful!

Dot sniffed and gave her a watery smile. 'You and Miss Alice are that kind to me. I've never had such a good position.'

'Well, you're a hard worker. But when you come to a good place to stop reading, could you make us a pot of tea, please?' She'd have done this herself, but had already found that Dot would rather do such tasks herself in 'her' kitchen.

Pandora ran lightly up the stairs. Things were looking up. Zachary had called her 'love' and had said he too wanted to make their marriage known. She couldn't wait!

★　★　★

Harry listened to the lads he paid to keep an eye on Pandora every time she left the house. He was still angry about her giving away good food, but the anger turned to red-hot fury when he

390

heard that Carr had met her and walked home with her.

'Did she look annoyed to see him?' he asked, remembering his own reception when he'd insisted on walking her home.

'No, she took his arm and hugged it close. They were laughing together as they walked. Looked a proper pair of love birds to me.'

He handed out sixpences grudgingly and told them to keep their eyes peeled from now on.

'You're not having her, Carr,' he muttered when he was on his own. 'And you're not managing this shop, either. Even if she doesn't let *me* court her, I'll make damned sure *you* don't get a sniff of that money. Nor shall anyone else.'

But how to do it? He had to put paid to Zachary's involvement with the shop once and for all. And it had to be planned carefully. Very carefully indeed. Nothing must go wrong. He hadn't put all this effort into the emporium to let someone else benefit from it.

★　★　★

One of the things that continued to worry Zachary was the atmosphere in the shop. Except for Marshall, the other assistants absolutely fawned on Harry. There was no other way to describe it, they *fawned*.

When he went out to the privy, Zachary met Marshall on the way back.

'Need to speak to you,' the older man said, not even stopping as he walked past.

He realised why Marshall hadn't stopped when he found Harry just inside the door as he came into the packing room again.

'You certainly take your time out there,' Harry said accusingly.

'One can't deny nature.'

'Well, now that nature's been dealt with, we need some tea blended. You'll need to use up the rest of the new stuff I was trying out, then Mr Featherworth wants us to go back to our old best blend.' He snorted in disgust. 'Just because his wife prefers it! We make far more money with the new mix.'

'A lot of people liked our old blend of Blake's Best.'

'Well, see what you can do.'

Zachary got out the various containers of tea and sniffed the new type, wrinkling his nose. It wasn't particularly good, didn't even smell fresh. It must be some job lot that hadn't been treated too well during its journey from India. Without being told, he went into the shop and took off the shelves all the packets of Best.

Harry hurried after him. 'What are you doing?'

'Getting rid of this muck. Mr Featherworth's right.'

'It's perfectly good tea, that.'

'It's not. I'd throw it in the bin, but I suppose we could let it go cheap to cover costs.'

'I forbid you to do that. Put those packets back this minute.'

'No. That tea will give the shop a bad name.'

'It'll make more money for us.'

'We can ask Mr Dawson, if you like.'

All hung in the balance for a moment or two, then Harry swung on his heels and marched off to the office.

Marshall winked at Zachary as he passed by and whispered, 'I'll come to your house after work.'

What was going on here? Zachary wondered as he started mixing the tea according to the formula Mr Blake had used. He sniffed the resultant blend and nodded his head approvingly. But to be sure, he boiled a kettle of water on the gas burner and made a pot of tea, letting it brew for the requisite time and trying it out, just as Mr Blake would have done.

'*What are you doing now?*'

Zachary ignored him and raised the cup to his lips, taking a mouthful and tasting it carefully. He shook his head. 'Even this is too dry. It's been kept too long.'

'You get a better price if you buy larger amounts,' Harry said.

'Mr Blake would never buy in too much at once.'

'Mr Blake is dead and I'm running the shop now.'

'Correct me if I'm wrong, but I believe Mr Featherworth wants the shop run exactly as it was before.'

'It can be run more efficiently, as I've proved.'

'It's not our shop, Harry. It belongs to the Blake sisters, and Pandora's in charge for them.'

'*Miss Blake* to you!'

'No. Pandora. At her request.'

'You used that journey to worm your way into her good books,' Harry said accusingly. 'But when she sees how efficiently I run the shop, when I explain how much more money I can make for her, she'll soon come to value me and change her methods. You'll see.'

Zachary knew from years of working with him that Harry only cared about money but the hatred on the other man's face disturbed him and he made a mental note to watch his back. If it were up to him, he'd bring everything into the open, sack Harry and reorganise the management of the shop.

It had been such a happy place to work when old Mr Blake was alive, and could be again.

He sighed. It wasn't up to him. And he was missing Pandora even more than he'd expected to, missing sharing their days, chatting about anything and everything. She was his wife and unless she asked for her freedom, which he didn't believe she would, he wanted to stay married to her. Mr Featherworth might think he'd done the right thing in not consummating the marriage, but he was beginning to consider he'd been stupid to let it continue till now. He loved her so much and she loved him too, kept saying she hadn't changed her mind. Who cared about the money?

He knew he'd changed greatly, grown stronger mentally. It wasn't only the travel, but being loved by a beautiful woman. That gave you extra confidence. He smiled reminiscently, thinking about their time together, then forced himself to stop that and concentrate on what he was doing.

He sipped the tea again, swilling it round his mouth slowly. It'd have to do, but he'd make sure they didn't order too much loose tea of any sort at one time from now on.

He looked down at the teapot and topped it up with more boiling water, then called to the lad sitting at the other end of the bench. 'You might as well have a cup. Be a shame to waste it.'

'I'm all right, thanks.'

When Marshall came in for something he made the same offer.

'Don't mind if I do.'

Harry at once popped into the packing area from his office. 'You're not paid to drink tea on duty, Marshall.'

Zachary looked at him. 'Are you going to waste it?'

'Yes, if it interferes with the work.' He came forward and picked up the teapot, moving to the sink.

Furious, Zachary took it out of his hands, heedless of how hot it was. There was a short struggle, but he was much stronger than the smaller man. 'I say it's stupid to waste anything.'

The door opened and Pandora came in, staring in surprise at the two men struggling over a teapot.

Harry turned to Marshall and the lad. 'Out!'

They both went into the shop, Marshall with his lips pressed together, his anger clear at being spoken to like that.

'What's going on here?' she demanded.

'Carr is wasting good tea, brewing up during working hours.'

'I'm blending the tea and your uncle always said the only way to tell if the blend was right was to have a cup. Would you like to try some, Miss Blake?'

'This is how my uncle did it?' She looked first at Zachary and then at Harry.

'Yes.'

'Your uncle was a wonderful man but he had old-fashioned ways,' Harry said. 'I'm arranging the work more *efficiently*, Miss Blake.'

'I think I should like to try a cup. And you ought to as well, Mr Prebble.'

Zachary poured cups for them. 'I'm not adding milk or sugar because we want to taste only the tea. This is our best blend. Harry had been experimenting with a new mixture, but it wasn't as good and Mr Dawson told us to go back to the old blend.'

She sipped the tea thoughtfully, saying nothing.

Harry took a big mouthful, swallowing it immediately, looking bored.

Pandora stared into the white teacup, studying the remaining liquid. 'It's a slightly different colour from the one we've been using, isn't it? Though our packet says it's Blake's Best.'

He nodded and watched her sip again, saw Harry gulp down the rest of his cup without trying to taste it properly.

'I like this one better,' she said at last.

'Your uncle was a connoisseur of good tea. He taught me a lot about blending it, but I'll never be as good at it as he was.'

'Well, I can't taste any difference whatsoever,'

Harry snapped, 'and the new blend makes much more profit.' He looked at Pandora. 'Surely you want to make as much money as you can?'

She cocked her head on one side, thinking, then shook it. 'No, I don't think I do. Oh, I want to make money for myself and my sisters, but I want to give people good service too. My uncle was well thought of in the town. If I can live up to his reputation, I'll be satisfied.'

Harry stared at her in open-mouthed amazement.

'I'll give the other lads a cup each,' Zachary said. 'They need to learn the difference between the various blends.'

'They've *work* to do!' Harry snapped.

'A few minutes won't hurt, especially if they're learning something,' Pandora said.

This time he didn't hide his anger, but stormed into his office, though he didn't close the door.

'I'll call the men in. Would you like to pour?' Zachary asked.

'Good idea. I've not had a chance to talk to them yet.'

Marshall sipped his tea as instructed, rolling it round his mouth and looking surprised. 'I've never had the money to drink this sort before. It's good, isn't it?'

The shopmen sipped in silence, eyeing the office door warily, saying nothing. As soon as they could they put their cups down and went back to work.

The shop lad seemed astonished to be offered a cup of the tea. He looked even more surprised when he sipped it. 'This one *is* better, isn't it?'

Zachary nodded. 'Definitely. You have to learn about tea as part of your job, Joe. Sip it slowly. Take the time to taste it properly.'

He did so, smiling. 'It's lovely. Nicest cup of tea I've ever had.'

Harry came out while he was speaking and walked past them without a word.

The lad looked anxious suddenly. 'He heard me, didn't he?'

Zachary looked at Pandora and rolled his eyes, then began to rinse out the teapot.

She took it out of his hands. 'I'll do this. You get on with your work.'

He could imagine them working together like this once everything was sorted out. He'd show her all the little jobs that were needed behind the scenes, make her understand about suppliers, keeping stocks at the right level and choosing the best products they could find. When times were better and some of the more expensive items came back into the shop, they'd taste them together.

Not grand dreams, his, but cosy ones.

★ ★ ★

That evening there was a knock on the back door and Zachary found Marshall there. 'Come in.'

The other man stayed in the scullery. 'I'll not be long. I just wanted to see if you've noticed the petty pilfering at the shop yet.'

Zachary nodded.

'He rearranges the shelves, thinks we don't

notice. He's overconfident, that one.'

'How does he get the stuff out of the shop?'

'His auntie does the cleaning. She's got pockets inside her skirt. I've told Mr Dawson, but he says we can't accuse Harry of pilfering when it's her that takes things out of the shop. We have to catch *him* in the act.'

'It wasn't like this in the old days, you know. The shop was a really happy place to work under Mr Blake. Those two shopmen are scared to open their mouths, so is the lad.'

'I'll tell Ralph Dawson you're on to it, then.'

'I don't understand why Harry does it. He has a good job, earns enough to live decently, because he's only himself to support. He certainly doesn't want for anything.'

'Some folk are like that. Worship money. Want more than their share. He's got his eye on your young lady, you know.'

'*My* young lady.'

Marshall grinned. 'A blind man could tell you two love one another. Why don't you wed her and get rid of Harry. Solve everyone's problems, that would.'

Why not indeed? Zachary thought as he let the other man out. Because it went against the grain to let Harry get away with stealing, that was why, and if they didn't prove he was cheating on his employer, it'd look bad to sack him. It was a small town and Harry would no doubt protest his innocence, putting them in the wrong.

If an experienced lawyer and his clerk thought they should tread carefully, that was the right way.

Pandora told Alice what had happened with the tea blending, feeling indignant all over again at the memory of Harry's petty, spiteful ways.

'The sooner we're rid of him, the better. Zachary will do a much better job of managing the shop.'

'Are you and Zachary courting?'

Pandora hesitated, then admitted, 'It's a secret, so don't tell anyone else, but we got married in Australia.'

Alice gaped at her for a moment, then smiled. 'How wonderful!'

'I fell in love with him very quickly. He's a lovely man, kind but strong.'

'Why are you hiding it?'

'We had to get married to get the last cabin on the ship. I wanted to marry him anyway, because I'd fallen in love with him by then. But he's worried about my money, so he hasn't — ' She blushed, 'I'm still only his wife in name. He says I need time to be sure, but Alice, I don't. I was sure within days of meeting him. And I know he loves me.'

'But people can be cruel about an unequal marriage, especially if there's trouble at the shop. Ralph is right. Something is definitely wrong. Dot hates going in there now for our provisions. And when I went in one day, that Prebble creature looked down his nose at me.'

'I can go for the shopping from now on. It'll be good to see what it's like to be a customer.'

'I'll ask Dot, but I think she'd rather continue

doing it herself. She prides herself on doing her work properly.'

'All right.' Pandora hesitated, then said, 'You're quite friendly with Mr Dawson and his sister, aren't you? You just called him by his first name.'

It was Alice's turn to blush.

Pandora smiled. 'I won't tease you. I like Mr Dawson and I hope things go well for you.'

'And for you too.'

★ ★ ★

When Zachary came to work the following morning, the shop lad was nowhere to be seen.

'Where's Joe?'

Harry gave him a triumphant smile. 'I sacked him this morning. Lazy little devil, he was. He left things dirty. I've already found a better lad, one who will work hard.'

Zachary said nothing but he knew this wasn't true. Joe had been a very hard worker. Unfortunately Zachary had no power to reinstate him. Not yet, anyway.

The atmosphere in the shop was leaden that day. Even Marshall, normally the most equable of men, was grim-faced, with a growling undertone to his voice when he spoke to Harry.

At dinner time, Zachary got out of the shop, picking up his free sandwiches and wrapping them in his handkerchief. He went to eat them in the nearby public gardens, sitting in a secluded corner. Afterwards, he walked briskly round the perimeter paths, relieved to be away from Harry, who hadn't stopped smirking and nagging today.

On his second circuit of the gardens he saw a lad he recognised walking into the alley where the side entrance to the emporium was — Harry's young cousin, another little weasel of a Prebble. He'd guess Ronnie was there for the job. The cleaner was Harry's aunt. How many other members of his family was the man intending to find jobs for?

Well, Zachary vowed, as soon as things were sorted out, Joe was going to get his job back. And afterwards the shop wasn't going to be filled with Prebbles. In the meantime, he'd slip Joe and his family some money and make sure they didn't starve.

Out of the corner of his eye, he saw another lad duck back behind a street corner as he turned down the side path of the gardens. When he was behind some bushes, he stopped to look back and saw the lad peering out from behind the corner, clearly watching him. There wasn't any doubt about it because there was no one else nearby.

No wonder Pandora said she'd felt as if someone was following her. Harry had a whole tribe of young cousins. Had he got them watching both Zachary and her? Why?

What was he up to? Where did he think this would lead?

★ ★ ★

Dot came back with some shopping that afternoon, her eyes fairly sparkling with indignation. She marched up the stairs and knocked on

402

the parlour door, finding Miss Blake sitting reading by the window and Alice writing a letter.

'Can I speak to you, please, miss? Well, both of you, actually.'

'Of course.' Pandora put her book down. 'You look angry. What's wrong?'

'That Harry Prebble has gone and sacked poor Joe.'

'The shop lad? What for?'

'Nothing. Joe's the only one in his family who's working and he'd *never* do anything to put his job at risk. He's a good little worker. I've watched him out of the window. He never slacks off, not even when he's alone in the yard. His family lives down the street from us. His Dad's not well and they rely on Joe's wages.'

Pandora had a sudden memory of the lad trying the tea and saying, 'Nicest cup of tea I've ever tasted', then worrying that Harry had overheard this remark. The two shopmen had not made any comment at all on the tea. Surely Harry wouldn't sack the boy because of that?

Anger rose in her. 'I'm going to see that Prebble creature and find out what's happened to Joe.'

'Shouldn't you leave that to Ralph and Zachary?' Alice asked.

'No, I shouldn't. I'm the owner of the shop. I can't bear to think of people I employ being treated so badly.'

When she went into the shop she found another lad packing goods in the rear, a dull-faced lad who didn't have the manners to stand up when she entered. She glared at him

403

and crossed to the half-open office door, rapping on it sharply.

Harry was sitting there, bent over some account books. When he saw her, he slid the top book under the other one and got to his feet. She tried not to show that she'd seen him hiding the book, but noted its colour and shape.

'Can I help you, Miss Blake?'

'You certainly can. Why did you sack Joe?'

He stared at her in surprise. 'That's my business. I manage your shop and I must do what's necessary in hard times like these.'

'*Tell me why you sacked Joe.*'

He drew himself up. 'Because he wasn't doing his work properly.'

'In what way?'

'He wasn't clearing up properly, wasn't working fast enough.'

'I've always found him polite and helpful, and this room has never looked anything but immaculately clean and tidy.'

Scorn dripped in Harry's words. 'My dear lady, you must allow me to know my job.'

'As I'm the owner, it is *you* who must allow me to oversee what you do and if I don't approve, then *you* are the one who must change your ways.'

Zachary, who had just come back from his dinner break, heard the conversation clearly. He turned to the lad and jerked his head. 'Go and help out in the shop, Ronnie.'

The lad smirked, looking so like Harry it made Zachary feel sick.

'I don't answer to you. I only have to do what

404

Ha — Mr Prebble says.'

Zachary lifted him by his shirt collar and seat of his trousers and propelled him out into the shop at a run, then shut the door. He went towards the office. To his amazement they didn't seem to have heard his altercation with the new shop lad.

'You will send for Joe at once and give him his job back,' she ordered.

Zachary suppressed a groan. Trust Pandora to rush headlong at this. She should have left it to him. If she didn't take care, they'd not be able to catch Harry out.

'There is no vacancy. I appointed a new lad this morning.'

'Who is he, the new lad?'

'I beg your pardon.'

'What is his name?'

'Ronnie.'

'Ronnie what?'

Zachary smiled. She'd noticed the resemblance too.

'Ronnie Prebble.'

'Another relative of yours. In other words, you sacked Joe so that a relative could have the job. Well, I'm not tolerating that sort of thing.'

Zachary thought it time to intervene. 'Sorry to interrupt, but you two can be heard from the shop.'

'Go away, Carr!' Harry said at once. 'And don't come into my office in future unless I invite you in.'

'Stay, Zachary.' Pandora said. 'Did you know Prebble had sacked that nice shop lad?'

'Yes.'

'Why didn't you tell me?'

Reluctantly Zachary decided he couldn't intervene, not if he was to keep working and watching here. 'It wasn't my job to tell you.'

Harry nodded, a tight smile on his face.

'Well, I want Joe brought back again.' She looked from one man to the other. 'It wasn't fair to sack him and put a relative in his place. What's more, I don't believe Joe did anything wrong.'

Zachary shook his head slightly to warn her.

Harry folded his arms. 'I'm sorry, but I can't do that.'

'Right. We'll see about that.' She marched out of the shop and strode down the main street, suddenly realising from other ladies' surprised glances that she was wearing neither hat nor gloves. Even the mill girls never went out without covering their heads with their shawls to proclaim their respectability. Well, she was too angry to go back for her hat. Let them stare.

She stormed into Mr Featherworth's rooms.

★ ★ ★

Ralph looked up and saw who it was through the open door of his office. Good heavens, Pandora Blake looked magnificent: colour high, eyes flashing. She really was a beautiful young woman. What had upset her? He got up and went out quickly.

'I want to see Mr Featherworth at once.'

'I think he's free. I'll just check.'

He hurried along the corridor, warned his employer that something was wrong, then ushered her in.

'Don't go away, Mr Dawson!' she said. 'This involves you too.'

She explained what had happened and it took all their powers of persuasion to prevent her from sacking Harry Prebble on the spot.

'I'll send some money to young Joe,' Ralph promised: 'And we'll give him his job back later.'

'But Prebble will think he's won. He'll think I have no control over my own shop,' she protested. 'It'll be humiliating.'

Ralph looked at her thoughtfully. 'That might serve our purpose very well. He's already scornful of others and far too confident about his own cleverness. Yes, I think this might be just the thing to make him do something rash.' He smiled ruefully at her. 'Please, Miss Blake, I know it's hard, but could you bear with us for a few more days?'

After a few rebellious moments, she sighed. 'I suppose I'll have to.'

'We'll catch him out for you,' Ralph said. 'I promise.'

'And the sooner the better,' Mr Featherworth said. 'This is all most upsetting.'

'I'll go home, then. Though how I shall face that nasty little man, I don't know.'

'Ignore him,' Mr Featherworth said soothingly. 'Don't go near the shop. Leave it to Zachary and Mr Dawson.'

'I'll call you a cab,' Ralph said. 'You really shouldn't walk through the streets in your indoor clothes, with no hat.'

She looked down ruefully at herself. 'I was so angry I didn't think about that. I doubt I'll ever make a fine lady.'

'I think you're a very fine lady already,' Ralph said. 'And one whose heart is in the right place.'

★ ★ ★

When Harry saw her come home in a cab and go straight up to the living quarters, he waited. She didn't come down again, didn't come into his shop.

As the day passed there were no messages from the lawyer, either.

By closing time he was jubilant, knew then that he was winning. Even Dawson could see how well he was doing and wasn't prepared to sack him or go against what he was doing.

He looked thoughtfully at Zachary, who was serving a customer, smiling and chatting to her. *You next*, he promised himself. *I'll take that smile off your stupid horse face, you long streak of nothing. And I'll get rid of you once and for all.*

21

There was a tap on the door later that evening and when Dot opened it, a lad gave her a note addressed to Miss Blake.

'Don't you want to wait for an answer?'

'He said there'd be no answer.'

She took the note upstairs, wondering who had sent it.

Alice was out at her cousins'. Pandora waited to open the note till the maid had gone, because she'd recognised Zachary's handwriting.

I need to see you. I'll come round to the back door shortly.
Zachary

She went running down the stairs to the kitchen. 'Zachary's coming round to see me, Dot. Can we open the side gate?'

'Mr Prebble has the keys to the padlock.'

'Surely we have some keys as well?'

'I don't think so. Mr Dawson took them all after they locked the mistress away. If he didn't give them back to you, he's still got them.'

'Oh, no!'

'Shall I go out the back and tell Zachary when he comes that we can't open the gate? He could come in the front way, after all.'

'No. He doesn't want to be seen.' At least

she'd get to speak to him even if it was through the wooden gate.

She went outside and waited till she heard the latch rattle. 'Zachary? Is that you?'

'Yes. Can you open the gate, Pandora love?'

'No, I can't. I've not got the key. Oh, Zachary, I'd have loved to chat to you.'

'I'll climb over the gate, then. Stand back.'

She stood back and in the light from the kitchen window, saw his head appear. He scrambled over the top of the gate, laughing as he landed beside her. She didn't wait for him to come to her, but flung herself into his arms. And this time he kissed her passionately, hungrily, as she'd dreamed of.

With a shaky laugh, he pulled back a little. 'Let's go inside.'

There was no sign of Dot as they walked through the kitchen, but as they climbed the stairs together Pandora heard someone bolt the outside kitchen door. She knew Dot was always very careful to do that.

In the parlour Zachary held her at arm's length, his eyes searching her face. What he saw there seemed to make him happy because he pulled her towards him, folding her into his arms as he said, 'I love you so much, Pandora. I can't hold back any longer. I don't want to lose you.'

'You won't.' She lifted her face for another kiss and lost herself in the bliss of it all.

When the kiss ended, he held her for a moment or two, then said quietly, 'Let's sit down. We need to talk.'

She led the way to the sofa, sitting with his

right arm round her shoulders, clasping his left hand tightly in hers.

'I was so sorry you had to be humiliated,' he said. 'When you didn't return and there was no message from Mr Featherworth, Harry was cock-a-hoop, never stopped sneering at me, kept boasting that the lawyer knew how to value a good manager and must have set you right about who was in charge.'

'He'll find out how wrong he is soon. But it is embarrassing and I shan't dare come into the shop again till it's all settled.'

'You're better staying away from him anyway.' Zachary hesitated, taking her hand and raising it to his lips for a moment. 'You were followed when you went to visit Bill's family and you're probably followed every time you go out. Harry's got a lot of cousins. One of them was following me earlier today.'

She stiffened. 'What if he followed you tonight?'

'I was very careful. I left our house by the back door and stopped a couple of times to make sure no one was following me.' He laughed. 'What can he accuse me of anyway? Climbing over your gate?'

'Who knows what that nasty little worm will do next?'

'Something rash, I hope. I need to catch him in the act of taking something or fiddling the accounts. If nothing happens, I'm going to ask Mr Dawson to let me into the shop at night and I'll go through every page of the account books. I know he's done that already, but I may be able

411

to spot something he'd miss.'

She suddenly remembered the account book that Prebble had hidden and told Zachary about it.

'There, that's something to search for. I'll definitely speak to Mr Dawson.'

After a few minutes, he broke off a kiss to say, 'I'd better go before I do something we'll both regret.'

'I'd not regret anything we did.'

'Pandora, my darling, when I make you mine, I want it to be perfect. I don't want to have to sneak out of the back door afterwards.'

When he'd gone, climbing over the gate again, she sat for a while, smiling at nothing, feeling warm and loved.

She didn't say anything to Alice about the purpose of Zachary's visit, but agreed to go with her friend the following morning to help out at a reading class held at the Methodist Chapel Hall for girls who were out of work. It'd give her something to do until this mess was settled and keep her out of the way of Prebble.

★ ★ ★

The following morning when Zachary went to work, Harry told him to go and serve in the shop. He was glad to get away from the other man's nasty remarks and sneers and always enjoyed looking after customers.

Just before nine o'clock he looked out of the window and saw Pandora leave the house with Alice. He smiled at the mere sight of her.

Soon afterwards Harry came out and said, 'I have to see Mr Dawson. You're in charge of the shop while I'm away, Carr.'

Half an hour later, Harry came back accompanied by two policemen. 'Can we speak to you for a moment, Carr?' He led the way through the shop without waiting for an answer.

Puzzled, Zachary handed over his customer to one of the others and followed them into the packing room.

'Did you climb over the side gate to the back yard last night at about nine o'clock, Mr Carr?' one policeman asked.

The little worm had had him followed even after work! 'Yes, I did.'

'May I ask why, sir?'

'It was private.' He wasn't having Pandora brought into this.

'Go and look at the back storeroom, Carr!' Harry ordered, looking as swollen with importance as a crowing cock.

He stared at the two of them in bafflement but did as they asked. The lock on the back door had been forced and the shelves in the other storeroom were missing some of the more expensive items. 'Have we had a break-in?'

'You know very well we have,' Harry snapped. 'Because *you* did it.'

'*I did not.* I didn't go into the shop at all last night.'

'The stolen goods have been found in your coalhouse,' the sergeant said.

'*What?* Well, I didn't put them there.'

'Zachary Carr, I arrest you for theft, breaking

413

and entering. I must ask you to accompany me to the police station.'

As he left the shop between the two policemen, Zachary looked round for Marshall, hoping the other would go for Mr Dawson, but saw no sign of him. The shopmen turned away from him, looking embarrassed, but the new lad grinned openly.

Not wanting to make a scene he walked along between the policemen. When they arrived at the station and he was formally charged, he asked them to contact Mr Featherworth and one of them laughed at him.

'What would a lawyer like that have to do with a common thief like you? Anyway, Mr Prebble has already assured us that Mr Featherworth is leaving this matter in his hands. He's suspected you were the thief because the goods only started vanishing after you got back. He reckons you must have overspent on your journey and be short of money.'

'That's not true! Mr Featherworth will — '

'Look, we found the goods at your home. It's an open and shut case, so you might as well save us all a lot of trouble and plead guilty. You'll be brought before the magistrate for a hearing later this morning, then committed for trial.'

'But if you fetch Mr Featherworth or Mr Dawson, his clerk, either of them can prove I'm innocent.'

They chuckled as they locked him up, ignoring his pleas to send for the lawyer's clerk.

★ ★ ★

414

Dot was dusting the hall and she watched out of the small side window in surprise as Mr Prebble arrived at the shop with two policemen. Wondering what was going on, she continued watching and to her dismay saw the policemen come out again a few minutes later with Zachary between them, looking like a prisoner. What had happened? She was sure he'd never do anything wrong.

She hesitated then decided she'd better go and tell Miss Blake about this.

When she tried to go out, however, a man stepped from the side alley and barred her way.

'Where are you going?'

'Shopping. Hey, what do you think you're doing? Let me past.'

'Mr Prebble thinks you should stay at home this morning.'

'I've got things to buy for my mistress.'

'Where's your basket, then?' He gave her a shove back into the hall and tried to follow her inside. She began to scream for help and got in a good kick to a very tender place before he realised how hard she was prepared to fight.

As he drew his fist back to thump her, the door banged fully open again and two other men pushed into the hall. More of Prebble's men! Despair filled her.

* * *

Marshall came up from the cellar where he'd been doing some tidying up for Prebble just as the policemen took Zachary away. He stood

415

staring in shock, not certain what to do about it.

Prebble came into the shop. 'Ah, Marshall, I need some more butter bringing up from the cellar.'

He went to get it, deciding to nip out and see Mr Dawson as soon as Prebble's back was turned.

It wasn't till he heard the cellar door bang shut behind him and a key turn in the lock that he realised he'd been tricked.

Growling in anger, he rushed up the narrow stone stairs to bang on the door. But it was very solid and he knew he couldn't kick it down from here.

He went to find some of the chopping and cutting tools, hoping to use them to break the lock, but they were missing.

Prebble had clearly prepared carefully for this.

Lighting a lamp and muttering under his breath, Marshall began to explore the cellar, but the window that led on to the light well beneath the pavement outside had bars across it.

As he looked out he saw Prebble walk across the grating — hard to mistake those boots with extra thick soles — heading into town.

There had to be a way to get out of here. There just had to be!

⋆ ⋆ ⋆

Pandora enjoyed helping at the reading class. The first people she saw were some girls she'd worked with in the mill. They gave her half-smiles but hesitated, as if uncertain whether to approach her, so she went across to them and they spent some time catching up on news.

'Congratulations on being left the shop!' one of them said. 'You won't go hungry ever again, you lucky thing.'

She smiled. 'The shop was left to me and my sisters, so I only own a quarter of it.'

'I'd be happy with a tenth,' one said.

'I know. I *am* lucky. How's your mother, Janet, and . . . ?'

No one stopped them chatting or snapped at them to get on with their work. The atmosphere in these classes was so different from those she'd once attended, run by the Vicar. For all his calling, that gentleman seemed to believe that poorer people were all stupid and lazy, and treated them accordingly.

She looked across the room at Mrs Rainey, the Minister's wife, who was smiling at the girls and treating them just as politely as if they were ladies. It was a peaceful and happy scene, with those attending making great efforts to correct and improve their reading.

★ ★ ★

For a moment all hung in the balance then the man who'd attacked Dot pushed past the two who'd followed him in, taking them by surprise and running off down the street.

One of the men followed him to the door then turned with a shrug. 'That's got rid of him, anyway. Wish it was as easy to get rid of that Harry Prebble. Are you all right, lass?'

417

She sagged against the wall for a moment in relief. 'Yes. I am now.'

'He didn't hurt you?'

'No.' She suddenly remembered what she'd been trying to do. 'I have to find my mistress. The police have taken Zachary away. I don't know what he's supposed to have done — well, he'd never do anything wrong — but she needs to know so she can help him.'

One of them frowned. 'I saw them go. I can't think now why Marshall hasn't come out to let us know what's going on. You'd think he'd be off at once to tell Mr Dawson, too.' He stood thinking for a minute, then said, 'You go with this lass, Gordon. I'll go into the shop and speak to Marshall.'

'All right, Daniel lad, but be careful. Prebble might have left, but his cousin went in after they took Zachary away and the shop lad's one of them, too.'

'Pete's just down the road.' Daniel put two fingers to his lips and whistled shrilly. Another man hurried towards them 'With two of us, I think we can hold our own. Marshall told me them two shopmen wouldn't say boo to a goose.'

With a sigh of relief that she'd not be on her own, Dot locked the front door behind her and hurried off down the street towards the Methodist Chapel Hall.

'I thought at first you were with that man who tried to stop me,' she told her companion.

'No, we're friends of Marshall Worth. We've been keeping an eye on things for him and Mr Dawson. I'd not give them Prebbles the time of day.'

418

When they arrived at the hall she saw Pandora across the room and ran to her, heedless of how everyone stared.

'They've taken Zachary away.'

'Who have?'

'The police. And one of Prebble's cousins tried to stop me coming after you.'

'Do you know why they took him?'

'No. But I came for you as soon as I could. Gordon here helped me get away.'

Once again Pandora ran through the streets without her hat or jacket. She couldn't imagine why the police had taken Zachary, but she could definitely guess who was behind it.

Whatever Mr Featherworth said, she was going to sack Harry Prebble — but not till she'd sorted out Zachary's problem. He'd never do anything against the law, she was quite certain of that.

She couldn't bear to think of him locked up, treated like a criminal.

★ ★ ★

As Daniel and his friend walked into the shop, one of the shopmen came towards them. 'Can I help you?'

'We need to see Marshall Worth. It's urgent.'

'He's busy.'

The door to the packing room opened and Harry's cousin came out, proving he'd been listening. 'Worth is working. I'm keeping an eye on things for Harry, who's had to go out. He won't want Marshall chatting to his friends in work time, though.'

'I told you, it's urgent.'

'Marshall can see you after he finishes work.'

Out of the corner of his eye, Daniel saw the shop lad smirking in the doorway to the room at the back, and was suddenly certain that something was going on here as well as at the police station.

He moved quickly forward, shoving Harry's cousin before him with a flat hand to the chest.

'What do you think you're — '

The shop lad rushed forward to help but Daniel's companion held him back, while the other two struggled. A woman customer let out a little shriek and rushed outside.

'Help us!' called the cousin.

The two shopmen hesitated. One backed away but the other said suddenly, 'They've locked Marshall in the cellar.'

'I'll see you're fired when Harry comes back!' the cousin yelled.

Daniel found it easy to twist his arm behind his back, because like most Prebbles, he wasn't a big man. 'Where's the cellar?'

'None of your business.'

The door leading from the shop into the packing room opened and he tensed, wondering if someone else had come to help Prebble. But it was the shopman who'd spoken out, the one who'd just been told he was fired.

'I'll show you where the cellar is.' He went across to a rack of keys, reached out then his hand stilled in mid-air. 'The key's not here.'

Daniel gave his captive a shake. 'Where is it?'

The smaller man just glared at him.

'Feel in his pockets while I hold him still.'

The shopman did so and in spite of the man's struggles, he managed to extract the key. He hurried along the narrow packing room and unlocked the cellar door.

Daniel said to his companion. 'You help keep an eye on these sods!' and started down the cellar steps, calling. 'Marshall lad, are you there?'

'Aye. What took you so long?'

Footsteps clattered towards him and Marshall ran up the steps two at a time. He saw the captive and stopped at the top, grinning.

'You'll be sorry,' Harry's cousin said. 'And you'll be too late to help Carr, anyway. He'll have been committed for trial now by the magistrate and they can't just let him out after that. He's been stealing from the shop and Harry's gone to give evidence.'

'I'd better let Mr Dawson know,' Marshall said. 'He'll soon sort it out. Keep them two Prebbles here, lads. I've a few bones to pick with them when I get back.'

He too ran off down the street.

★ ★ ★

Pandora arrived at the police station, followed by Dot, puffing badly now, and the man who'd helped Dot. She burst in and rushed across to the desk. 'Where's Zachary?'

The policeman stared at her. 'I beg your pardon, miss?'

'Two policemen took Zachary Carr away. I

421

need to see him. I can prove he's innocent.'

'They took him straight to the magistrate's house. Mr Thwaite is holding a hearing because it's an open and shut case.'

'Oh, no, it isn't!' She darted out of the police station and along the street, thankful Mr Thwaite lived close by.

When she knocked on the side door of his house, a maid opened it.

'I need to see Mr Thwaite. It's really urgent. I can prove the man they brought here is innocent. *Please*.'

'All right. His study is through here.' She knocked on the door. 'Another witness, sir. She says it's urgent.'

★   ★   ★

Pandora found herself in a large room at the rear of the house. The magistrate, a plump, red-faced gentleman noted for his bad temper, was sitting behind a huge desk while Zachary was standing in front of it.

'I can prove Zachary's innocent,' she said.

Harry, who was sitting at the side of the room, bobbed to his feet. 'This woman's his mistress, your worship! A woman of her sort will only tell lies.'

Zachary jerked round at this insult and the policeman took hold of his arm.

The magistrate scowled at her and Pandora was suddenly conscious of her windblown appearance.

'I'm sorry to be so untidy, sir, but I ran all the

way. And I'm not Zachary's mistress.' She wasn't given time to add that she was his wife, as Mr Thwaite pointed to a bench at the back.

'Sit down and only speak when spoken to,' the clerk whispered.

From across the room, Harry continued to glare at her, then turned back to the magistrate, opening his mouth to speak. But he too was gestured to keep silent.

Zachary looked across at Pandora, embarrassed at the predicament he was in.

The charge was read again and he was asked whether he was guilty or not guilty. He straightened up and answered in a clear voice, 'Not guilty, your worship.'

The clerk began to read out a summary of the evidence.

Part way through, the magistrate interrupted to ask, 'Do you deny that you climbed the gate into the yard behind the shop, Carr?'

'No, sir.'

'Why did you do that?'

He looked at Pandora, hesitating, and she stood up. 'He was coming to visit me, sir.'

The magistrate turned to stare at her. 'For what purpose?'

'We needed to talk.'

'A clandestine meeting, then. This won't reflect well on *your* evidence, young woman.'

She opened her mouth to protest, but the clerk made a shushing noise.

Harry smirked again.

The magistrate waved one hand. 'Continue with the evidence.'

If she didn't get a chance to say what had really happened, what her relationship to Zachary really was, how could she save him from being unjustly convicted? Should she shout it out? No, that might offend Mr Thwaite. Better wait and see if an opportunity presented itself to do it without upsetting him.

★ ★ ★

Marshall ran as fast as he could to Mr Featherworth's rooms. There he panted out a demand to see Mr Featherworth and Mr Dawson at once.

'They're with a client and can't be disturbed,' the junior clerk sitting in the front office said.

'It's urgent. They'll *want* to be disturbed.'

'I can't take it upon myself to do that.'

Marshall had had enough of delays, so strode along the corridor.

The clerk followed, bleating, 'Sir, you must come outside. You can't interr — .'

Annoyed, Marshall flung open the door of Mr Featherworth's room, muttering, 'Thank goodness' when he found the two men he was looking for. 'I'm very sorry to interrupt you, sirs, but something extremely urgent has come up and unless we can stop them, they're going to jail Mr Carr.'

That got their attention.

Ralph Dawson stood up at once. 'I'll go and hear what he has to say then come back if we need you, Mr Featherworth.' He turned to the client. 'I do apologise for this interruption, sir.'

In the corridor Marshall explained rapidly what had happened.

Ralph gaped at him for a moment, then went back to Mr Featherworth. 'We need you to come at once to the magistrate's house and stop Mr Thwaite committing Zachary for trial unjustly. You know how difficult it will be to sort things out quickly if they actually commit him for trial.'

Mr Featherworth stood up at once.

'I'll run ahead,' Ralph said, knowing his employer wasn't the sort of man to move quickly.

He arrived at the house and got the maid to show him into the magistrate's room. Just inside the door he stopped to bow his head and wait to be recognised, acting as if this was a court, because he knew Thwaite was a stickler for doing things properly.

'Well, what is it, Dawson?'

'Urgent new evidence, sir.'

'What evidence? Seems like an open and shut case to me.'

'Your honour, my employer, Mr Featherworth is following as fast as he can, but has asked me to run ahead and let you know he's coming, because it will save a lot of trouble in the long run if things are settled at this stage, as well as preventing an injustice.'

'Seems clear enough the fellow's guilty to me,' Mr Thwaite grumbled. 'Oh, very well. If Featherworth thinks he knows something, I'll wait till he gets here.'

Mr Featherworth arrived a couple of minutes later, face scarlet, panting audibly. He too waited by the door for permission to join them, then moved towards the front.

'Tell me what this new evidence is,' Thwaite said. 'I've already had the prisoner's mistress saying he didn't do it,' he pointed to Pandora, 'but she's hardly a reliable witness, now is she?'

Mr Featherworth stared at him in shock. 'Your worship, this young lady is not the prisoner's mistress but his wife.'

There was dead silence in the room, then Prebble exclaimed, 'You sneaky devil!'

'Silence!' roared the clerk.

Harry swung round, as if to leave.

'*Stay where you are!*' the magistrate bellowed. 'Where do you think you're going, fellow? You're the one who brought this case to our attention and you'll stay till I give you permission to leave.'

'They'll all stick together and tell lies. What's the use?' But Mr Thwaite looked so angry, Harry sat down again.

Speaking quietly now, Mr Featherworth said, 'As the husband of the owner of the shop, it isn't possible for Mr Carr to rob himself, nor would he need to break in.'

'You're sure they're married?' Mr Thwaite asked suspiciously.

'Certain, your honour. I've known for a while and have seen their marriage lines.'

'Then why are they not living together?'

'We were trying to find out who had been stealing from the shop, thefts which began while Mr Carr was still in Australia, I might add.'

The magistrate stared at Prebble. 'This is highly suspicious and if any evidence turns up to show *you* have been involved in planting false

426

evidence, then I shall be pleased to have *you* up before me.'

Mr Featherworth turned to Pandora. 'Tell Mr Thwaite what happened last night.'

'Zachary wanted to see me without anyone knowing, but we couldn't open the side gate because we didn't have a key, so he climbed over. He stayed for an hour or so, then left. I was with him the whole time, saw him climb back over the gate. I'd have heard if anyone else had climbed over, because the gate rattles loudly, so if anyone broke into the shop, they must have had a key to the back gate.'

She had spoken with her usual clarity and returned Mr Thwaite's stare with her chin up.

Mr Dawson cleared his throat and got a nod to speak. 'I can vouch for the fact that Mrs Carr hasn't a key to the side gate, your worship. I quite overlooked that when she moved in because no one uses that gate much. The shop people open the rear gate for deliveries.'

Mr Thwaite nodded slowly. 'I see. Case dismissed, then. Come and join me for luncheon, Featherworth. I want to hear more about what's going on with these young people. Our clerks can see to the details.'

Everyone stood up as the magistrate left the room and, with an apologetic smile at Pandora and Zachary, Mr Featherworth followed his old friend into the main house.

When the door had closed behind them, Ralph looked round. Prebble was missing. How had he managed to leave the court without anyone noticing?

As Pandora moved towards him, Zachary clasped her hands. 'I can't believe Harry got so far with this.'

'He didn't succeed, that's the main thing. And we'll have to tell people we're married now.' She beamed at the thought.

His face was still dark with anger. 'I'm not letting Harry get away with this. I'm going to follow him and punch him in the face.'

Ralph joined them, saying, 'You'll do no such thing, Zachary, much as he deserves it. And besides, we have various formalities to go through with the magistrate's clerk before you can go anywhere.'

When that was done, Zachary had calmed down. Ralph smiled at them, envying them their closeness. 'About time people knew you were married.'

'That's what I think,' Pandora said softly, still keeping hold of her husband's hand.

22

Ralph escorted the young couple outside. 'We'd better go to the shop first and find out what's happened there. I sent Marshall back to keep an eye on things but I doubt Prebble will have returned there.'

Pandora linked her arm in Zachary's as they walked along, smiling at him.

He slowed down to stare at her solemnly. 'You're absolutely sure?'

She shook his arm, pretending to be angry. 'How many times do I have to tell you? Yes, I'm sure I want to stay married to you. I've never been more sure of anything in my life.'

His beaming smile made him seem almost handsome, lighting up his bony face as it always did. 'You'll need to tell me you love me every day of our lives if you want me to go on believing that. And I'll promise to do the same to you.'

They stopped walking for a moment or two to look at one another, clasping hands, lost to the world. Then Mr Dawson, cleared his throat, gave them a warm smile and they all started moving again.

At the shop, they found Marshall serving a customer while the two shopmen were in the back room hovering over Daniel, who had a big bump on his forehead and was very pale.

'Prebble turned up. Took me by surprise.' He scowled. 'I didn't see him come in and the sod hit me over the head from behind.'

'He went into the office and came out with something stuffed down his jacket,' one of the shopmen said.

'You should have stopped him,' Zachary said. 'There were two of you.'

'And two of them,' the other said. 'Don't forget the shop lad. He's a Prebble too and he went off with Harry. Besides, I've never been any good at fighting.' He touched his wire-rimmed spectacles self-consciously. 'Too afraid of these getting broken.'

The shop bell tinkled and Zachary went to peer through the little window in the door to the shop. 'Go and serve our customer, but say nothing about what's happened. We'll sort everything out later.' He looked at Daniel. 'Are you all right or do we need to send for the doctor?'

'I'll be fine. It's nobbut a tap on the head. I went dizzy for a few minutes, but I can see straight again now.'

Mr Dawson went into the office and Zachary and Pandora followed him. 'Can you see anything out of place?' he asked.

Zachary stared round. 'Not at first glance.'

'I can,' she said. 'There was a blue book on the shelf there, behind the black one. I saw Harry hide it one day. Zachary and I were going to look for it after work.'

'And we'd better check the cash box,' Zachary said.

It was missing completely.

'Well, he must have taken it. I advise you to leave it to the police to catch him. Your main job

430

is to keep everything going smoothly at the shop.'
Mr Dawson took out his pocket watch and
checked the time against the clock on the wall,
clicking his tongue in annoyance. 'I'd better get
back to Mr Featherworth's rooms. He has an
appointment in five minutes' time, but he's
probably still at the magistrate's house. I'd better
send the office boy to remind him.' He moved to
the door. 'I think I can safely leave everything
here in your capable hands now, Zachary. I'll
send a message to the police about Prebble
coming here and stealing the money. I repeat,
leave it to them now.'

Pandora blocked his way. 'I want to make it
clear that from now on Zachary is to be the new
manager of the shop.'

Mr Dawson raised his eyebrows. 'Well, of
course. Who better?' He started to move away,
then paused again. 'Do you want me to make an
announcement about your marriage in the local
newspaper?'

'Yes, please.'

When they were alone, Zachary pulled her
into his arms for a quick kiss. 'Can I move in
with you tonight?'

'I insist on it. What about your mother and
sister?'

'We'll go and see them after work.'

'Will they be pleased, do you think?'

'I'm sure they will.'

'I hope they like me.'

'How could they not?'

They stared at one another a while longer,
then she sighed and stepped back from him. 'I'll

tell Dot what's happened, then I'm coming back to help in the shop. You're short-handed and if I only pack things for you, or tidy up, it'll be some help.' She raised her chin. 'I'll not be left out.'

He chuckled. 'I've realised that by now.'

★ ★ ★

She went back to find that Alice had come home, so quickly told her friend and Dot what had been going on.

'I knew you were married, miss, I mean Mrs Carr,' Dot said. 'I hear you talking to Mr Carr one day.'

'And you said nothing?'

She shrugged. 'It wasn't my business.'

'Well, I really value your loyalty and good sense and I hope you'll go on working for us.'

'Yes, please, miss — I mean, ma'am.'

When Dot had left, Pandora turned to Alice. 'You don't have to move out until you've found yourself a new job.'

'Thank you. But I can go to live with my cousins. You and Zachary don't need me here to play gooseberry.'

Pandora could feel herself blushing and couldn't deny that.

★ ★ ★

In the middle of the afternoon, one of the policemen came to Mr Featherworth's rooms.

'Did you arrest Prebble for the thefts?' Ralph asked.

432

'I'm afraid not. He wasn't at his home. We're searching for him now.'

'He may get away. He's a cunning fellow.'

'I don't think so, sir. We're keeping a watch on the railway station, as well as on the roads out of town. There are some advantages to being near the moors with only two or three ways to leave the area, unless he walks across the tops.' He smiled. 'No, Prebble will have to be pretty slippery to get past us, sir.'

Ralph wasn't as sure that they would catch him, but didn't pursue the point. 'I don't know what Zachary's going to say about this. He's very angry at Prebble.'

'I hope he'll not do anything foolish like getting into a fight with him.'

'I hope so too.' Ralph sighed. 'I'd better go and tell him how matters stand.'

As he was walking towards the shop, the door to the living quarters opened and he saw Alice come out, dressed in her outdoor clothes but looking worried. He hurried towards her. 'Are you all right?'

She smiled, but it was a strained smile. 'Yes, of course. It's good news that Zachary is taking over the shop, isn't it?'

'Yes.' He felt uncharacteristically shy. 'Um — what are you going to do now?'

Her smile slipped and the worried look returned. 'Go and stay with my cousins until I can find another job.'

The thought that she might move away from Outham gave Ralph the courage to say, 'No! You mustn't leave.'

She looked at him in surprise.

He took a deep breath. 'Alice, my dear, if I may call you that, if you don't object, that is — ' He faltered to a halt and then said it baldly because he couldn't think of any romantic words, wasn't that sort of man. 'Do you think you might like to marry me instead of finding a job?'

He held his breath, waiting for her response, sure she was going to turn him down, because he was a clerk and she was a lady. Instead he saw joy bloom on her face and heard her reply, 'Of course I'll marry you!'

'You will? I mean, I'm so glad. I'm a plain man and I'm not — not good at romantic words and — '

She took his hand. 'You don't need fancy words with me, Ralph. We've become such good friends, you and I. Yes, and your sister too. When we're married, Judith will still live with us, won't she?'

He nodded and grew daring enough to plant a kiss on her cheek. Drawing his head back for a few seconds he saw how gloriously she was smiling now, so took her in his arms and kissed her properly.

'Miss, I — '

He came back to an awareness of his surroundings to see Dot goggling at them and said simply, 'You may be the first to congratulate me, Dot. Miss Alice has just agreed to become my wife.'

★ ★ ★

As Hallie was walking to the corner shop, a woman cried out for help from the alley next to it. She turned into the entrance and before she could do anything, a man stepped out of the first doorway and grabbed her, muffling her cries with his hand.

A woman joined him, tying Hallie's hands tightly behind her.

Terrified, she struggled with all her might, but they were two to one and they'd taken her by surprise.

They stuffed a gag in her mouth, wrapped her whole body in a piece of musty cloth and began to carry her along. She tried to squirm and kick but someone clouted her on the head and the pain of that shut her up.

'Keep still or I'll knock you senseless.'

She didn't dare struggle any more. They laid her down and put a heavy weight on top of her so that she could hardly breathe. As they started to move, she guessed she was on a handcart, from the squeaking of a wheel and the way it bumped along the streets.

Where were they taking her? What did they want?

* * *

That evening Zachary and Pandora walked round to his mother's house to tell her the news. He called out as he went inside, 'I've brought a visitor, Mum.'

His mother looked up as they went into the kitchen. 'I thought you were Hallie coming back.'

435

'Isn't she here?'

'She went round to the corner shop half an hour ago and I can't think what's keeping her.' She looked beyond Zachary. Oh, I didn't see you at first, Miss Blake.'

Zachary hesitated. Should he go and look for Hallie? He saw his mother looking at Pandora as if puzzled. 'We have something to tell you, Mum. Some really good news. Pandora and I were married in Australia. Mr Featherworth asked us to keep it quiet because we were trying to catch Harry Prebble out. He's been stealing from the shop while I've been away. But now he's been found out, we've no reason to keep our marriage secret, so I've brought my wife to meet you properly.'

Pride rang in his voice and the look he gave Pandora spoke more than words ever could of his love for her.

By the time they'd all hugged each other and given more detailed explanations, Pandora felt completely at ease with his mother.

'Your son's a wonderful man,' she said to Mrs Carr. 'I'm so lucky to have found him.'

'I know.' Then Mrs Carr looked at the clock again. 'Could you just go and see what's happened to Hallie, son? It's not like her to take so long.'

* * *

It wasn't long before the cart stopped and the weight was removed from Hallie. The man lifted her up, slinging her over his shoulder so that her

436

head was hanging down, bumping helplessly against his back because her hands were still tied.

They went inside a building, she was sure of that, but he seemed to have to bend down to get inside. Then he went down some steps and his footsteps echoed as if it was an empty space. Was this a cellar?

There were voices, then one set of footsteps moved back up the steps.

Someone pulled the wrapping off her and dumped her roughly on a chair. As the person took the gag out of her mouth, she saw Harry Prebble standing in front of her and her stomach gave a lurch of fear.

'What are you going to do with her, Harry?' the woman asked, sounding nervous.

'Exchange her for some money, so that I can get away.'

'Shouldn't you just run for it? After all, you've got some savings. You can always start again.'

'I wouldn't have to start again if it wasn't for that damned Zachary Carr. He's going to pay for what he's done to me.' He turned to study Hallie and smiled slowly. 'Or rather, his sister is.'

The woman opened her mouth, not looking happy, but caught his eye and closed it again.

He fumbled in his pocket and held out a note. 'Get young Ossie to give this to Zachary. Tell Ossie to shove it into his hand and run off straight away. Then stay away for a while. I want to be alone with *her*.'

'Harry, please don't — '

'Do as you're told!'

The woman left them.

Hallie remembered how Harry had hurt her before and terror filled her as he turned to study her.

* * *

Zachary went out and was at the nearby corner shop in under two minutes.

The owner looked at him in surprise. 'I've not seen your sister at all today, Zachary. She's not been in since yesterday.'

As Zachary went out of the shop, a ragged lad thrust a note into his hand and tried to run off, but Zachary caught him by the collar. When the collar tore away in his hand, the urchin started running again but a man coming along the street caught him by the arm and swung him round, cuffing him when he tried to kick and scratch.

'What's this one done?' he asked Zachary. 'Picked your pocket?'

'No. Look, could you hold tight to him while I read this note?' Zachary scanned the two lines in shock, then read them again in disbelief.

Bring £100 to the old sheds behind Thorpe's Mill. Don't tell the police or you'll never see your sister alive again.

There was no signature, but he knew Harry's handwriting only too well. He turned to the lad and grabbed him by the arm, dragging him away from the bystander. '*Who gave you this note?*'

'A man. I don't know who he was.'

438

He looked at the lad, who was short with a weaselly face, a typical Prebble. 'I know who you are and I can guess who gave it you. If you don't tell me his name and where he is, I'll beat the information out of you.'

The lad looked up at him in terror, but still shook his head.

Zachary looked at the passer-by. 'They've captured my sister and want money to release her.'

'Never! Eh, if there's owt I can do to help, just you ask. I blame this Cotton Famine for such thievery. Folk are desperate. Not that that's any excuse.'

'Do you know Marshall Worth?'

'Aye. Used to work in the same mill as him. He lives in the next street to us. He was in the next street a minute or two ago.'

'Could you please fetch him to my mother's house and tell him to bring a couple of strong friends who're ready for a fight?' He gave the man the address and set off for his mother's house, dragging the still-silent lad with him, desperate to make sure she and Pandora were all right before he tried to find Hallie.

To his relief, they were both sitting in the kitchen. Pandora looked up and smiled at him, but her the smile faded when she saw his expression and how he was holding the lad captive.

He hated having to tell them such bad news.

By the time he'd finished and had again stopped the squirming lad from trying to make a break for it, heavy footsteps were pounding along the street towards their house.

'I'll answer the door,' Pandora said.

'You won't let them hurt our Hallie, will you, son?' his mother faltered.

'I'll do my best, Mum. My very best.'

* * *

'We've got to find him quickly before he hurts her,' Zachary said when he'd finished telling his tale again. 'Surely Harry won't have been stupid enough to take my sister to his home?'

'No. He's not stupid, I'll give him that. He'll have her hidden away somewhere else, I reckon,' Marshall replied.

'Could you go and ask around the streets, see if anyone noticed her being taken, or saw Harry?' Zachary asked. 'I'll have another go at shaking some information out of this one.' He indicated the lad.

'I live near here. I'll ask my kids to help, too.' One man slipped out.

'I'll go and visit a fellow I know down in the back slums,' Marshall said. 'You stay here, lad, then we can fetch you if you're needed.'

Zachary went over to the boy and shouted at him, but he wasn't the sort to beat a child, so in the end they shut him in the coal house without finding anything out.

After that Zachary paced to and fro while Pandora sat holding his mother's hand. Suddenly an idea struck him and he stopped dead. 'I wonder . . .'

'Wonder what?' she asked.

440

'If anyone's checking the back of Brewers Court.'

'I'm sure the police will have looked there,' Pandora said. 'It's the worst slum in town.'

'Well, there's a separate entrance at the back that goes down to an old cellar. I chased Harry and his cousin in there once when we were lads and he'd pinched my ball. You'd not know about that entrance if you hadn't been shown.'

'You won't — go on your own?' she asked.

'I'll find the other fellows on my way. They're searching in that area.'

'They said they'd come back here. Can't you wait for them?'

'No. I daren't.' He hesitated then came to grasp Pandora's hand for a moment. 'Will you stay with my mother?'

'Yes, of course.'

'Keep a rolling pin handy, Mum.'

As she went to get it out, he lowered his voice and whispered to his wife, 'He'll hurt Hallie to pay me back, I know he will.' Then he raised his voice again and said, 'Don't worry, Mum. I'm big enough to take care of myself.' With a quick kiss on her cheek, he left.

Pandora sat and worried, trying to reassure his mother and failing.

Ten minutes later Marshall came back to report that no one had seen Harry — or Hallie — and she stared at him in dismay. 'Zachary went out. He said he'd find you.'

'Well, he didn't. Where did he go?'

Quickly Pandora told him.

'I'll follow him.'

The waiting began again. After a few moments, Pandora could stand it no longer. 'Come on. We have to get help for them.'

'Zachary said to wait here.'

'Well, I'm not doing it. I'll go mad sitting here worrying. I'm going to fetch the police.'

'You do that, love. I'll wait here in case he comes back.'

'Get a neighbour in to sit with you, then.'

'I will.' Mrs Carr rapped on the wall three times. 'She'll come straight away. You get off.'

★ ★ ★

Prebble moved across to where Hallie sat helpless in the chair. He flicked her cheek so hard it stung. 'I might as well have a little fun to pass the time. It'll be a while before your brother gets the money for me, I'm sure.'

Her heart stuttered in her chest as his fingers trailed down her throat and stopped there. Suddenly he put his hand round it and squeezed, so that she couldn't breathe properly. When he let go, she gulped in air.

'Tsk, tsk! Did you have trouble breathing? You see what happens when you don't do as I wish.'

Then he grabbed the neck of her bodice and tore it down the front.

She couldn't help screaming in terror but he just laughed.

'You can scream all you like. No one will come to help you. They all do as I tell them round here.'

But the woman who'd been there before came

back into the room and leaned against the wall, arms folded.

'Go away, Nancy.'

'No. I want to watch how you do it with other women.'

He turned on her, fist raised and she pulled out a kitchen knife.

'Oh, no, Harry! I can look after myself, unlike this poor bitch here. I'm not stirring from your side till you get the money and after you give me my share, which you'd better do — ' she gestured with the knife, ' — I'm leaving town with you. She's seen us both now. I'm not going to be here when she tells the police who I am.'

He turned back to Hallie, stretched out his hand, then hesitated, scowling at Nancy again.

★　★　★

Zachary ran towards the slums and when he passed Daniel in the street, called out to him to follow and kept running. He ran past the narrow streets and alleys of the worst part of town, moving towards the reservoir at the back of the biggest mill.

Only when he got there did he slow down, looking round and gesturing to Daniel to move quietly now. Their caution paid off and they managed not to alert a man keeping watch behind a tumble-down shed.

'I'll get him,' Daniel whispered. 'Wait a minute then let him see you. I'll creep up and thump him from behind while he's looking at you.' He picked up a chunk of broken brick.

The man started to his feet at the sight of Zachary, but before he could call for help, Daniel thumped him and he crumpled to the ground.

Zachary moved forward. 'It's years since I was here but I know the entrance is round here somewhere.'

'You must be on the right track. Why would someone be keeping watch unless Harry is hiding nearby?'

'Ah!' Zachary said. 'This is it.' He bent nearly double to get into a low space that looked like the top of a former basement window, now not in use.

'I'd never have thought that was a doorway,' Daniel said.

'Shh!' Zachary pointed. 'Follow me.'

As quietly as they could, they went down some extremely narrow stone stairs.

Before they got to the bottom they heard Harry's voice. He was taunting Hallie, telling her how he was going to hurt her and her brother once he'd got the money.

'He'll be sorry he ever crossed me, that one will,' Harry gloated.

Just as he got to the bottom, Zachary's foot twisted on a small piece of broken brick and he nearly fell. He made enough noise to warn those inside the small cellar, so burst in quickly, to stop short at the sight of Harry holding a knife to Hallie's throat with one hand and holding her by the hair with the other.

'Stop where you are or I'll kill her!' he yelled.

Zachary froze, his eyes taking in Hallie's torn clothes and the terror on her face as the knife blade pricked against the soft skin of her throat.

'Get away from the door,' yelled Harry. 'Go on! Move round to that side.'

Zachary did as he was told, wondering desperately how to get his sister free of that knife. As he moved, Harry watched him and Daniel seized his chance to move forward, but a woman stepped out from the other side of the doorway and tripped him up.

As the two of them went down in a flurry of petticoats and kicking feet, Harry dragged Hallie to the doorway, yelling, 'I'll kill her if you don't stay back.'

'Well, I've got your friend, so let's do a swap,' Daniel panted, bleeding from a cut on the arm and struggling to hold the woman still.

'What do I care about her? You can do what you like with her. I've got your sister, Zachary, and if you want her to stay alive, you'll let us go.'

'The police are looking for you. You'll never get out of town.'

'I know this part of town better than they do. There are people who'll shelter me and see me safely on my way. She'll not be freed till I'm clear and you've coughed up the money. Now damned well stay back.'

Helpless, Zachary watched as Harry edged up the stairs, still holding the knife to Hallie's throat.

As they disappeared from view, Zachary moved quietly forward but yells from outside had him abandoning caution to leap up the stairs. He hesitated at the low doorway, groaning in relief.

Harry was on the ground, struggling against two men and Marshall was holding a weeping Hallie against him, murmuring, 'You're safe now, lass. You're safe.' He bent to pick up the knife and cut her bonds, still talking soothingly.

Daniel crawled out from the low opening, dragging the woman who'd been with Harry, cursing her as she tried to bite him.

Zachary moved to his sister and took her from Marshall, holding her closely against him as Marshall turned to help with the wriggling, screeching woman.

At that moment two policemen came running round the corner, with Pandora behind them.

She stopped at the sight of her husband, her face lighting up in relief, then came across to join him.

Zachary left Marshall and Daniel to explain to the policemen what had happened and pulled off his jacket, wrapping it round Hallie to hide her torn bodice.

He could hear Harry cursing and ranting, but he didn't care what they did to him now. He put one arm round his wife, the other round his still trembling sister.

'I don't think I've ever been as scared in my life,' he told them.

'You got to her in time?' Pandora asked.

He nodded. 'In time to prevent the worst. Shh, Hallie, love. You're all right now. I've got you safe.'

She gulped and tried to stop weeping, but couldn't.

Pandora found a handkerchief and passed it to

446

her, wishing she could do more to help.

One of the policemen came up to them. 'If you want to take the young ladies home, Mr Carr, we'll get your side of the story later. It's not good to take the law into your own hands, but in this case, I think your sister might have been in serious trouble if you hadn't got here so quickly.'

Slowly the three of them walked home, ignoring the stares of people they passed. Hallie gradually calmed down a bit, but she clung to both Zachary and Pandora as if they were her only comfort in a dangerous world.

They found the neighbour sitting with Mrs Carr, who first wept in relief, then pulled herself together and got everyone a hot drink. 'And after that, you'll all need a good wash.'

Pandora looked at the mirror and saw their reflections. She couldn't help smiling at the picture they presented. No wonder people had stared. Her face was still red from running through the streets — yet again — and her hair was streaming down her back. Hallie had torn clothing and equally untidy hair. Zachary's shirt was ripped and his face bruised. All three of them were covered in dust from the rubble in and around the hidden cellar.

'We look like three beggars,' she said.

★ ★ ★

An hour after they got back there was a knock on the door. Hallie stiffened and Pandora patted her hand as Zachary went to answer it.

They heard a short conversation then he came

447

back. 'They want me at the police station, to give my part of the story.' He looked at Hallie. 'You as well, if you're not too upset.'

She stood up. 'It'll be a pleasure to help put that horrible creature behind bars.'

'I always disliked him,' Zachary said. 'But even working closely with him, I never realised how bad he really was.'

'Dot's afraid of him,' Pandora said. 'I understand why now.' Then she stood up. 'We're all going to the police station together. I'm not letting you out of my sight again, Zachary Carr. You're coming too, aren't you, Mrs Carr?'

'I certainly am. I'm too old to run round town chasing people, but not too old to stand beside my daughter while she talks to the police.'

It was over an hour before they were able to leave the police station.

Zachary stopped just outside it. 'Just look at that. It's a beautiful evening.'

They all stood still for a few moments, taking in the blessed normality of it all. People were strolling down the main street, chatting and stopping occasionally to greet friends. A little boy was bowling his hoop. An old man was walking with his dog on a lead. A pretty young woman was smiling up at her escort, who seemed equally besotted with her.

'Yes, it is a lovely evening,' Pandora said quietly. 'This is what I wanted to return to Lancashire for. Let's walk your mother and sister home, Zachary love, then we'll go back to the shop.'

At the house door, Mrs Carr gave her a hug and a kiss. 'I'm glad my son's met you, lass.

Welcome to the family.'

Hallie gave her a big hug, too.

'You'll be all right?' Zachary asked her.

'I'll be fine now I know Harry Prebble's locked away.'

As they walked towards the shop, Pandora felt as if the world had settled into its rightful place around her. She was home, in Lancashire, with the man she loved.

When they reached the shop, they found it had closed early and the house door was locked. 'I've not got my keys.' Pandora smiled as she rapped on the door.

Dot came to open it, beaming at the sight of them. 'Thank goodness you're both safe. Daniel came round to tell me what had happened and then he stayed with me to make sure I was all right.'

'I think we're all a lot safer now,' Zachary said.

'They really have got that Harry Prebble locked up?'

'Yes. And I think he'll be in prison for a very long time. He's been stealing and frightening people. The woman he was with confessed everything because she was so angry at him for not caring if he left her behind.'

He stopped at the foot of the stairs. 'Is there anything to eat, Dot? I'm ravenous.'

This request, so typical of him, made Pandora smile. 'You'll find your new master's got a hearty appetite, Dot.'

The maid smiled. 'I'll fetch you something up at once, sir. I put a stew on and kept it simmering low.'

When she'd gone, Zachary put his arm round his wife's waist and they walked slowly up the stairs together.

'Welcome to your new home,' she said softly.

At the top he stopped, glancing down to make sure the door to the kitchen was closed. He pulled Pandora towards him and gave her a lingering kiss.

She nestled against him, then a sound down in the kitchen made them draw apart.

'We'll leave the rest for later,' he said with a smile. 'Now, show me round my new home, Pandora love. I've only ever seen the parlour before.'

When Dot brought up a heavy tray a few minutes later, she said, 'Oh, I forgot to tell you. Miss Blair has moved back to her cousins' until she marries Mr Dawson.'

She had their full attention now.

'She's going to marry Mr Dawson?' Pandora asked.

'Yes. It was lovely to see them both looking so happy. She deserves to be happy. She's a lovely lady.' Dot took out a handkerchief and blew her nose hard.

'I'm delighted for them.'

'Well, I'll leave you to start your meal, ma'am. I've got a pudding ready to serve when you ring the bell.'

Pandora watched with pleasure as Zachary cleared his plate and then ate two helpings of apple pie and cream.

He saw her smiling and chuckled. 'I've got my appetite back now those I love are safe.'

After Dot had cleared the table, however, Pandora felt unaccountably shy. She looked at her husband, wondering if he felt the same.

'Do you want to sit and chat for a while?' he asked.

She took her courage in both hands. 'No, let's go to bed. I love to lie in your arms. I've missed that so much.'

'I love to hold you.'

The room was filled with soft candlelight as they undressed and the bed was the most comfortable they'd ever shared.

All shyness fell away as they kissed, murmured and embraced one another, so that it seemed the most natural and wonderful thing in the world to make love at last.

She sighed with pleasure as she lay in his arms afterwards. 'Cassandra told me once that if I truly loved my husband, I'd enjoy loving his body as well as his mind.' She raised one hand to caress his face, idly tracing a line down it. 'She was right. Dearest Zachary, how much time we've wasted!'

'We'll not waste any more.' He kissed her again.

Epilogue

In October, Cassandra and Reece found a letter waiting for them when they went to church, because all mail for the district was delivered to the shop in whose barn the church service was held.

Her eyes lit up as she saw the handwriting. 'It's from Pandora. Look how nice and thick it is. I'll just have a peep at the first page before the service starts.'

She opened the envelope and found a short letter, then a sort of diary explaining in detail what had happened to Pandora and Zachary since she left the farm.

'She's sounds so happy!' Cassandra exclaimed. She scanned the letter quickly then reread it more slowly. 'I shan't worry about her half as much now she's safe in England. I really liked Zachary.'

Her baby daughter made her annoyance at being neglected known and Cassandra had to attend to her before she could do anything else.

She bent her head in prayer, but a tear slipped down her cheek. She was happy for Pandora, of course she was, but she missed her sister so much.

She felt a touch on her arm and turned her head sideways to see Maia looking at her anxiously. 'I'm all right,' she whispered. 'Just thinking of Pandora.'

Maia nodded and turned to look at Xanthe, who was staring out of the window. Cassandra followed her sister's gaze and sighed. Xanthe was getting very restless. Would she be the next to leave?

Shaking her head she banished those worries and cuddled her daughter close, feeling Reece's hand on her arm, knowing that all was as right with her world as it could be.

Tonight she'd read the whole diary aloud to her husband and Kevin, then she'd sleep by Reece's side. Tomorrow they'd have more than enough work to keep them busy.

She'd worry about the twins when she had to. For the moment, she'd enjoy her life and family.

CONTACT ANNA

Anna Jacobs is always delighted to hear from readers and can be contacted:

BY MAIL

PO Box 628
Mandurah
Western Australia 6210

If you'd like a reply, please enclose a self-addressed, business size envelope, stamped (from inside Australia) or an international reply coupon (from outside Australia)

VIA THE INTERNET

Anna has her own web domain, with details of her books, latest news and excerpts to read. Come and visit her site at
http://www.anajacobs.com

Anna can be contacted by email at
anna@annajacobs.com